No Turnin'
Back
A Novel by
Don Q

Dedication

This novel is dedicated to my beautiful grandma, Mrs. Clementine Council, and my uncle, Jeffery Autry.

We plan, but God's plan is better.

Acknowledgments

First and foremost, I would like to say, ALL PRAISES ARE DUE TO THE MOST HIGH, the creator of all that exists. Without his mercy, this journey would have been impossible. Nothing has shifted me into gear to succeed as much as the birth of my beautiful daughter, Sanaii. May Allah keep you safe, Ameen. I've never found a love like this before. May Allah guide you and keep you enveloped in his mercy forever, in this world as well as in the hereafter, Ameen. To Ms. Ventura, I want to take a second to acknowledge your love for our daughter and to express my gratitude for it. You are amongst the best mothers I've witnessed, and it's because of you and her beautiful sis, Mariah, that she will be worldly and amongst the elite, Insha'Allah.

I'm forever in debt to two of the most loyal women I have ever had the pleasure of meeting. Mom, I love you and my sis to no end. Thanks for allowing me no passes along my walk. I learned many lessons the hard way, but the most important part is, I learned!

To Hollywood Razz (Queen's finest). I thank Allah for you. In life, you encounter people often, but the bottom line is they are either a blessing or a lesson. You were a blessing. Thanks for teaching me the rules of writing; we're here now! To your beautiful wife, Chelle, genuine love, Gal. (lol) Thanks for your assistance.

To my sista in faith, Maryam, Wallahi, I have never met a woman like you. Most are dazzled by the unimportant superficial glitz of this world, where you, no matter the amount of zeros on the end of the deal, you remain steadfast and encourage others to do the same. Such reminders are a

NEED as we tread these vicious waters. I couldn't express my gratitude more. THANK YOU!

To my brother, Travis, and my brother Steph, as young teens we ran hard, we ran recklessly, and the end result, they tried to set out of our favor. My BROS, never despair the mercy of Allah! I got the pen now; watch how I change the script. I LOVE Y'ALL, my day one niggaz!

This game we call LIFE is very Tricky, so when you are blessed with one genuine person you are leading the pack, two good fellas etc... I think its a blatant blessing from Allah. SPECIAL S/O to my BRO, Maserati Styles. Me and this brother literally been rocking as friends, as brothers since young boyz. So to look up in our adult years and to identify the greatness in you simply amazes me. YOU ARE that deal, MY NIGGA lets WIN!

And SECONDLY, I smile at this brotha, my NIGGA NUMBERS a.k.a RICH PORTER.... This brotha keep me reaching, He inspires many through creative entrepreneur mind. I Salute you big bro, I'm geared up.. LETS GO!

To ALL ENTREPRENEURS, I encourage you to keep dreaming and strive hard. It's not easy; however, it isn't impossible! FREE ENTERPRISE! The American way, benefit from this mentality. GOD only changes the condition of a people who first strive to change the condition of themselves!

FINAL SCORE, My brotha, TITO... special s/o to you, my bro. We've alwayz seen vividly, each other's vi$ion. From day one, you've been a hunite with me. I appreciate you extending your rolodex with no agenda attached. WE got NOW, next may NEVER come.

To my big bro, International Illa, my guy never changed on me. From teens to adulthood, same guy alwayz! Salute you, my guy, (BREADWINNER)!

My U$FH Family... Sheesh! Where do I begin, lol. My Youngens are da truth, reminds me of when it was my turn.... JOFFIE JOE, CHATO, TWIZZY FLEE, 1st TEAM, PREME,PLAY BOI, SINCERE, and the 2 Lyrical assassins, K

FLAG & The Golden Boy... DAY NIZZY! All I'm going to say is... Only one that can hold you back is YOU. #FACT!

To my ENVIOUS SOCIETY fam, LIGHTY, what up, FLY, you got it, boi! Don't let up on these niggaz! Tim McQueen, we at da round table, so you know I know! Mastermind salute.

LASTLY, TO MY KOMRAD FAMILY... NOTHING comes before this family but God, & ALWAYS want for your brother what you want for yourself. UNITED we'll forever stand, DIVIDED we'll NEVER prosper. This is the peak of the iceberg. Now the biggest challenges lie beneath the surface. Stay focused, we shall WIN!

Finally, I would like to give the biggest and warmest S/O to my beautiful editor, THE QUEEN, Ms. TINA NANCE. **A note to the world.** If you are a writer, more importantly, if you are SERIOUS About your craft and you are seeking PROFESSIONAL EDITING services for unmatched reasonable prices, I advise you to contact Ms. Nance at www.perfectproseediting.com.

She's dope, honest, and a likeable person to say the least. Before she ever knew my name, barely heard my voice, and never seen my face, the love she extended was like that of friends bonding for YEARS! I named her QUEEN because she runs such a tight ship. I can run on forever literally, but we gonna get to it! Tina, YOU'RE the equivalent of a sister reeking the smell of love. I appreciate you beyond the expression of words, but at the very least, I would like to say thank you. Thank you for believing in me, for being a genuine person. NEVER change, Allah will alwayz look after you (God willing) PEACE!

A NOTE TO OUR YOUTH

We live in a time where excuses are unacceptable, and anything is literally possible. Our president is a man of color, which is a living testament of what prayer, hard work, and resilience can lead to. Remain ambitious, and stop at the cause of nothing! Nothing beats hard work. Never misplace that FACT!

In conclusion, acknowledgments are the most difficult because there're so many individuals to mention, unfortunately not enough space to list them. So, if I didn't mention you, it doesn't mean my love isn't there for you. I genuinely appreciate my Tru few, more importantly, the FANS! Without your fuel and inspiration, I would have BEEEEEN BURNED OUT. It's a tiring and vigorous road one must travel in order to achieve, but I openly confess, IT'S SO WORTH IT!

Now take this Ride with me through the minds of QURON, NURI, YOUNG-ONE, GHOST, STEEL, SCAR, TAY, KIYAH, & BRI!

NYS thruway, 87 North, EXIT 17 NEWBURGH NY. Once you enter into these barren pages, I can promise you ONE THING... NO TURNIN' BACK!

Chapter 1

June 2000

"All I need is one mic, one beat," Nuri chanted, bobbing hard to the baseline on Nas' smash hit, "One Mic."

"Nor', fuck that music right now, bro! Get focused, we gotta make sure this shit ends tonight."

"You know I get hyped off this shit! Nas smashed this one." Nuri continued, disregarding his brother's concern.

Quron whipped the raggedy crackhead rented car around the corner and came to an abrupt stop on Grand Street. The gurgling engine hiccupped, causing the old, dented Buick to convulse. Nuri cocked the slide back on his 9mm, easing one into the chamber.

Quron clicked the hammer on his.38 special and stepped out. "You ready?"

"Let's do it." Nuri answered, high stepping behind his brother as they navigated quietly through the graveyard. "I 'ont even see son."

Nuri slouched next to a rigid tombstone, peering in the distance. The police precinct and the hood's infamous hole in the wall, Pops Paradise, next door were surprisingly empty. Sunday had to be the reason.

Quron could see a few fiends snooping around Gidney Avenue basketball courts. More than likely, they were scheming on one of the local drug dealers' package. Other than that, the scene was dead. "It's better like that." Quron took a quick glance at his two-way pager. "We got like ten minutes before those pigs make their rounds. Let's go."

Nuri stayed low to the uneven grassy terrain, shuffling quickly through the maze of tombstones. Quron, on his heels, reached the opening on Liberty Street across from the precinct and kneeled to catch his breath. The air was crisp, easily filling their lungs.

"Stay low," Quron panted, latching onto the back of Nuri's belt and pulling him down to a duck stance. "Somebody's definitely in there." He pointed to the lights on in the apartment windows above the precinct.

"This nigga, Casper, gotta be the slickest muthafucka in America. Sell all the drugs in the world, and got the nerve to rest right on top of the police. Ain't that some shit?" Nuri asked in disbelief.

"He did that shit to keep the wolves at bay. But I don't give a fuck who he live on top of, ain't enough law enforcement in this world to keep me off his ass."

Quron looked up and down the street for oncoming cars. A taxicab cruised by. No other vehicles were in sight. He and Nuri quickly shot across the street into the hallway attached to the precinct. The dimly lit staircase cast shadows around the gloomy setting, making it seem more closed in. They trampled up the stairs with one thing on their minds. MURDER.

"Nur' we ain't got much time." Quron reminded, checking his two-way for the second time. "So don't waste none."

Nuri spun around and cocked his leg, ready to mule kick the door off its hinges. Before he could act, the door flew open.

"Casper, where the fuck yo—"

"Shut the fuck up."

Quron smacked the young lady flush in the mouth with his pistol, while clutching a handful of her blouse. He shoved his revolver aggressively down her throat, muffling her words. She gagged. Pure fear traced her pretty features. The girl had never seen these young boys before, but she knew instantly that they meant business.

"Where the fuck is Casper?" Quron shouted, saliva falling from his mouth.

The girl stumbled as Quron backed her into the apartment. She was noticeably shaking, clearly petrified. Before she could answer, another set of feet hurried up the steps. Quron spun toward the door and yoked her around her neck with the quickness. His long barrel nudged her temple as he waited with a death stare for a body to appear at the door.

As soon as Casper showed his face, Nuri crept from the shadows and gun butted him. "Ahhhh!" Casper yelled, and reached for his 9mm on his hip. As soon as his hand brushed the cold metal, another paralyzing blow from Nuri painfully vibrated through his body.

"You stupid muthafucka," Nuri spat.

Casper dropped to his knees, blood oozing out of his dome. His equilibrium was impaired.

"Oh my God, please don't kill my husband!" The young lady was frantic, trembling in Quron's arms as her hand extended toward Casper.

"Shut your mouth. He shoulda thought about that before."

Quron threw her hard against the wall. The impact rattled the radiator and split the sheet rock. Tears glistened on her cheeks, as she lay still. Quron instantly moved toward Casper and kicked him flush in his forehead. The force from the blow caused his body to rise. Blood leaked like a faucet from the gash beneath his hairline.

Their eyes met. "I told you not to fuck wit' me and mine!"

The resonance of three shots in quick succession filled the room, as three hollow points spun from the revolver, sending an intense fire through Casper's chest. He gasped, inhaling deeply, cherishing the breath that he knew was his last. His body stiffened. Everything suddenly began to move in slow motion. He peered up, gazing in Quron's direction, but clearly looking straight through him. It was as if Casper had seen the light of the hereafter slowly closing in on him. In his final seconds, his life flashed like clips from a highlight reel, right before his eyes. A smear of a smile traced Casper's lips as the memories of his wife and kids played before him.

Nuri looked on in silence. There was nothing to talk about; they had been diplomatic, yet still violated. He took aim as he stood behind, hovering over. An agonizing scream from the young boy standing in the doorway pierced Casper's ears. Without sympathy, Nuri squeezed the trigger. Two loud claps rang throughout the building, echoing in the distance. Brain fragments mixed with pieces of skull scattered across the floor.

The pretty young lady had regained consciousness. She could not believe what she had just witnessed. Her cheeks inflated, mouth filled with vomit. Her body went numb, and huge knots of anxiety formed in her throat, preventing her breathing. Insanity was gripping her mind, but the despair in her son's eyes begged her to hold on.

The howling outcry of their son could have awakened the city. "DADDYYYYYY!"

"No!" Beads of perspiration covered his face. Expressions of internal pain wreaked havoc on his features. He shook violently as his demons took advantage. "No," he tossed, "no," he turned. "Get off meeeeeeeee!"

"Yo Ron, wake up. Yo Ron!" Nuri yelled at the top of his lungs.

Clank clank clank clank "C.O., crack cell three thirty-seven."

Nuri cupped his hands around his mouth and yelled down the tier. "It's not rec time Redford, still a few minutes." Nuri sucked his teeth and put his face as close to the metal bars as possible, without touching. "Yo Ronnn!"

"Wha, wha, what..." Quron snapped up on his elbows, mouth ajar, breath humming, and chest quickly rising and falling as he gasped for air. His vision was blurred. Panic lingered in his expression. His head whipped to the right, then left, trying to digest his surroundings. His eyes roamed ahead, settling on the fuzzy outline of someone standing in front of his cell. They thinned to narrow slits, and then closed. He squeezed tightly, rubbed them, and then opened wide. A soft grin surfaced. "Alhamdulillah," Quron whispered. "Top of the mornin' baby bro', how you?"

"Top of the mornin'. I can't complain, just bein' easy, ya know." Quron unraveled the state sheets from his torso and stood up. "Pardon me."

He took two steps, and was at the back of his cell, hovering over the ceramic toilet bowl. His rock hard dick slid through the boxer slit, and urine flowed from his swollen head as a loud, disgusting fart leaked out of his butt.

"C'mon man, wit' ya stankin' ass." Nuri shook his head and pushed back from the gate.

"Better out than in." Quron cheesed.

"So what has you up so early? Sweepin' floors at that." He pointed to the push broom Nuri leaned on and chuckled. He grabbed the Colgate, his toothbrush, dressed the bristles, and then held down the button operating the sink right next to the toilet.

"I mean, you've only been drilling me with the cliché, 'the early bird gets the worm,' all my life." Nuri grinned.

Quron rinsed his mouth, wet his face-rag, and faced his brother. "Don't run that B.S. game on me, you ain't been taking heed, so why now?" A long pause settled while he wiped the snot from the corner of his eyes. "Just like I thought, what's really good with you?"

"That's what I'm wondering about chu. You still buggin' in ya sleep." Nuri flipped the script.

"Tsss, you don't know the half." Quron threw a t-shirt on, slid on his state green pants and pulled a green and tan kufi over his ears. "I really don't understand it. Not glorifying our past, but we put major work in back then. I got past it though, by makin' peace with Allah, so I feel cleansed, but this body on this case here…" He stood, and then he flopped right back down on the twin sized paper-thin mattress. "It won't let me live. Casper the friendly Ghost, ah-ight. One thing for sure, he is definitely livin' up to his name. These nightmares have haunted me for the last decade, damn near. That same scene, I hit 'em in his chest, you put two in his head, then the cry of the little boy. Only in the dream, the lil dude is holding a burner to my head. It's crazy."

"You'll be ah-ight once you hit the town. Bri's pussy gon' wipe ya memory clean of all this nonsense." Nuri smiled. "If not, just go see a head doctor, they got some crazy man meds for that ass."

They both burst out laughing.

"On the Recccccc!"

The cell gates popped open from the front of the tier where the police bubble was, to the end of the tier, for morning recreation. Some convicts rushed out so they could be first for whatever they did out in the yard. Others fell back and rested. Standing on H-gallery, Nuri looked around. Keenly aware of his hostile environment, making sure it was safe while waiting for his bro.

Quron stepped out. They embraced and proceeded down the narrow tier. "Yo, I was reading last night, and I came across an ill quote that made me think of you. It was so deep, it just stuck to me." They reached the staircase on the third floor and walked down, looking at each other.

"Word, let me hear it." Nuri was curious. His brother always came across some deep stuff, and he always had a unique way of explaining it, an easy way to understand it. It was his gift. "Ah-ight listen…We are family, and the loyalty of the family must come before everything and everyone. We must protect each other, and we must be bonded to each other. For if we honor that commitment, we will never be vanquished. But if we falter in our loyalty, we will be condemned." Silence ensued.

The paragraph of loose words marinated between the two brothers as they strolled. "All we got is us, bro. I swear, 'til the casket drop." Nuri voiced, sincere about every word that left his mouth.

"Absolutely. Take it for what it's worth."

Silence rejoined the two as they kept it moving toward the yard. "Water is free in this bitch, and these rotten ass niggas still runnin' round here smellin' sour and shit."

"Tell me 'bout it. Neither of my neighbors bathe religiously. They both smell like a box of top, an' mold mixed." Quron chuckled.

"On another note," Nuri said and sighed. "Now that I'm three months away from the bricks, the load hasn't eased up an inch. Keepin' it a hunite, the end of the bid seems like the slowest and most stressful part of this stretch. Anxiety is settlin' in now, ' cause all things real, we left the streets as babies... teenagers, big bro. Now, we goin' back out there as grown ass men. I don't even know where to start, or what to expect, once I touch. I never had a 9 to 5 a day in my life, and hustlin' drugs ain't my forte. That was ya thing."

Nuri dropped his head then draped his arm over Quron's shoulder as they turned the corner and started for the yard. His tone dropped to a disappointed murmur. "I can't even consider my major anymore, but that ratchet is all I know. If I put ma gangsta down again, them rat bastards out there gon' make sure I get natural life without the chance of parole. I can't go out like that, Ron. But I can't starve either. So I don't know exactly what we gon' do out there, but whatever it is, it has to work. If not, ma back will be against the wall, an' I won't have a choice but to bring hell on earth."

Nuri and his older brother, Quron, were born and raised in the poverty-stricken city of Newburgh. They shared the same father, but came from different wombs. Ironically, it was hard to tell, because their bond was tighter than a virgin's treasure. The ten-year bid they caught for a body turned out to be a blessing in disguise. Truth be told, the route they were traveling was a short cut straight to hell, or the next worse thing, life in the joint without a chance of parole.

Things had changed for the better over the years. Books like *48 Laws of Power, Think and Grow Rich, The Art of War, Webster's Dictionary and the Holy Qur'an* sculpted Quron's character, while they only molded and added charisma to Nuri's cunning ways. Not to mention, the proper nutrition, required hours of rest, and years of banging in the weight pit had chiseled their physiques to perfection. Quron had grown from a frail 5'9 160 lbs., to six feet even, carrying 210 pounds of solid muscle. His skin, now tatted, was toned a pretty bronze under the intense summer sun. His Indian and black heritage enhanced his features. He had matured into a handsome young man.

Nuri, on the other hand, reflected the crack era in which he was born. His skin complexion was cocoa butter fine. He had grown a few inches too, now 5'9", cut like a razor, 185 pounds, with a mean swagger. Over their 10-year stretch, they had split and done hard time in some of the most dangerous maximum-security prisons in New York State. Clinton seemed like a lifetime away from the hood, so despair was always lurking up there. Coxsackie housed adolescents that didn't give a fuck about anything. Comstock rang the red dot alarm so much, that it became known as Gladiator school. Attica resembled an attic; dark, gloomy, with racist crackers doing anything in their means to assure you had a taste of hell. In that bitch, life and death held equal meaning. Whatever happened, happened.

At the end of the day, God's plan had proven to be greater. The brothers were brought back together, to finish how they had started... together.

Quron absorbed each word Nuri spoke. An awkward feeling settled deep in the pit of his stomach. He knew that Nuri was as serious as a heart attack. For as far back as he could remember, he had always been the breadwinner and mentor for his family. Now that they were adults, that responsibility remained. Quron gave his brother a sympathetic glance, hoping the worst was not in store for them.

Before he could utter a word, the voice of two red neck correctional officers severed his chain of thought. "Come the fuck on, boys, before I lock this gate an' send y'all black asses back to your cells!"

Quron calmly looked to his right, and then left, then turned slightly to see whom the C.O. was talking to. When he turned back to face them, Nuri had already charged forward like a raging bull. At that moment, Quron knew he had less than a split second to react and prevent his brother from committing suicide. There wasn't a doubt in his mind that the officers would pull the emergency pin connected to their walkie-talkie and beat both of them to a pulp.

In a flash, Quron jumped on Nuri's back, wrestling him to the floor. "Get the fuck off me, Ron. Who the fuck these cowards think they talkin' to like our names don't demand respect?"

"Calm down, bro!" Quron growled in a vicious whisper through gritted teeth. "We only a gate away from the town, and I'll be damned if you let these white boys mess that up. What's on ya mind? You crazy?" Quron raised his gaze, settling on the devious grin that adorned the pig's face. It hurt him to his heart, but he knew he had to swallow this one. Still lying on Nuri's back, he continued. "I'ma let you go. Don't. Do. Nothin'. Stupid."

In one swift motion, they were on their feet, dusting off their gear, and staring into the eyes of the oppressors. Quron could feel the tension regenerating, and he couldn't afford for things to get ugly. There was too much at stake. "Listen C.O., short, cut an' dry. You accomplished what you set out to do, and I know that neither of us wants this situation to boil over. So let's avoid it while we still can." Quron held a cocky stance. His whole demeanor was intimidating. "I'd hate for innocent people to get hurt behind your personal feelings."

"So what is that, Redford, a threat?" The corrections officer's nose flared as he looked menacingly at the two black men.

"Realists call things how they see it, so you can construe it however you want."

The officer would never admit it aloud, but he knew Quron was right. Quron was strong as hell within the Muslim community, and just as respected outside of his religious ties, which were not a secret to the administration. Any harm done to him or his brother, would cause an up-roar throughout the prison, instantly placing the welfare of all civilians in jeopardy.

"Redford, this one is on me. If there is a next time..." The pig turned beet red as he shook his head from side to side, emphasizing his point. "You won't be so lucky."

"I appreciate it." Quron smiled mockingly, sarcasm saturating his expression. "As long as the respect remains mutual, there won't be a next time. But if you ever disrespect me or my brother again, I promise that you won't be so lucky."

Quron spun on the bulky guard, not entertaining a response. Nuri followed. The thick electrically operated gate was already open. They stepped through and entered the E and F yard.

Chapter 2

The yard was one big square, enclosed by two brick walls, and two walls of gated windows that were attached to different housing units. Metal benches were welded into thick slabs of deeply rooted concrete. Each slab was strategically placed in front of every TV in the yard. A row of pay phones was lined up, separated by a thin wooden partition. The partitions provided little to no privacy for whoever was using them. A remote shower area had been built out of cinderblock that extended from the ground to waist level, with measly copper pipes holding affixed showerheads. Weight courts were strategically situated around the basketball court. Make no mistake about it, what appeared to be an area designated for recreational purposes, often flipped into a dangerous war zone. The whole lay out was segregated. Each court was the territory of a separate group. Muslims, Dominicans, rat-hunters, white boys, Rastas, five percenters, the Bloods, and even those that were neutral stuck together when the intense atmosphere thickened.

The environment could be very hostile at times. Fortunately, during this morning module, the atmosphere was settled. Even with programs up and running, the yard was still packed. Disciplinary tickets would be written and given to those who had skipped their program. They didn't care much. The cause was worth it. Nationalities varied. Their differences were as prominent as the various cultures that extended across the earth from east to west. It was obvious that the sacrifices made by convicts in 1971 had gone unnoticed. It was a shame, because prisoners had lost their lives during the Attica riot, to ensure that prison would take on a new meaning. Because of their sacrifice, new programs were implemented, and a chance to benefit from the misfortune of being incarcerated was born. Decades later, the same conditions that the revolutionists of that time fought to vanquish, had resurfaced. God knows they were turning in their graves.

Greetings of all sorts filled the air as Nuri and Quron stepped onto the neutral court. A few from every group was present. Those that were pumping iron and pulling their own weight on the pull up bar finished their set and joined the rest. Quron smiled at the sight of all his brothers, and then placed his foot on a flat bench. For years, this had been the best part of his day. "Assalamu Alaikum, wha gwaan, peace, what's poppin', may God bless you, and any other greeting of peace that means well." The whole group shared a hearty laugh.

Quron raised his hands and patted the air so they would settle down. "Wow." Quron gazed firmly at the men standing before him. A deep sigh penetrated the morning air, and a smile surfaced before he began. "For some time now, we've been gathering in the morning to discuss life. Everything from personal family issues, the nature of our crimes, to ways we gon' chase this paypa upon getting outta here. I have nothing but love for many of y'all. A lot of us been in the trenches for years together, bonding together as brothers around the state. Brotherly bonds formed under these circumstances, behind enemy lines, can't be comparable to anything."

From their expressions, Quron's words marinating on their minds was almost visible. He held onto the silence until he was certain his connection was made. All those in attendance stood with different postures, providing their undivided attention. "For those that don't know, my number has finally played, and I'm ' bout to get reacquainted with society. Many of you have molded me with jewels that have helped shape me into a balanced young man. For that alone, I'm thankful, and I leave my spirit with you. I encourage y'all to keep hope alive, and always stand for whatever it is that you believe in. If y'all wanna stay in touch, Ty-Real and Grimy got my info, so holla at me any time." The words began to settle in his throat as he spoke. "I didn't want to just disappear without seeing y'all. I love all you brothas, and I hope one day we all get to feel this wonderful feeling. In the meantime, before this becomes your truth, the most important thing is to remain focused. May Allah reward us and make it easy. Ameen."

Quron started from his right side, giving everyone dap, gradually making his way through the crowd before reaching his boys, Grimy and Ty-Real.

"Yeah, baby." Ty-Real smiled and gave Quron a pound.

"I know right." Quron sighed.

"So what's next for you?" Grimy asked, while Nuri and Ty-Real stood close by. Grimy was a frail dude, dark skinned with coarse hair and a tight edge-up. He, Quron, Ty-Real, and Nuri were all tight, and it showed whenever they got together.

"I can't call it. One day at a time."

"You know whatchu gotta do." Ty-Real's raspy voice reminded him.

"Without a question." As much as he wanted to stay and chat, there were more pressing things on his mind. "Y'all already know what it is. I ain't gon' leave y'all stranded. Not that type of brotha, wouldn't be able to live with myself. As soon as the wheels start turning for me, I'ma do all I can to help y'all beat the odds. Do what y'all do, and watch over my hot-headed brother." They all laughed as Quron rubbed his palm in circles on top of Nuri's head. "Don't let 'im get in no nonsense." Quron stated clearly with a raised brow.

"We got 'im." They giggled.

"Ah-ight." Quron smiled. "Be easy." Quron embraced them firmly then stepped off.

Each stride was acknowledged by various stares. Outsiders looked on with pure jealousy, while some were genuinely happy that another brother had survived the struggle. There were some inmates that would have sold their souls to be in Quron's shoes. Truth be told, many convicts in maximum-security prisons would never see the outside world again.

Tears of pain and sympathy gathered along the lids of his eyes. Quron thought of his mentors who he was leaving behind. It all hurt deeply, but his time had come. Everything he had studied, all that he had learned along his travels, was now summoned. It all had to surface; the time had come for it all to be used.

He continued his stride. The good brother is what he would always be remembered as.

Chapter 3

A couple of days passed, and the moment of truth finally came. The month was June, the sky an ocean blue, and the air was fresh. No body odor mixed with cigarette smoke, no asshole police, and no state greens. In the Green Haven facility parking lot, Quron stood with the little property he had kept, peering up, admiring the beautiful birds swooping under the fluffy, white clouds. In one motion, he kneeled to the ground and ran his fingers over the scaly surface, finally accepting that what he was experiencing wasn't a dream, but rather a reality; his reality. A gracious smile traced his lips as he rose back up into a more relaxed stance. His sharp senses caused him to shift toward the purr of an approaching vehicle. The car rolled slowly. The features of the driver seemed familiar. Quron's mind strolled down memory lane, trying to put a name with the strange face. *Who is this?* He looked on with an inquisitive stare.

The car suddenly stopped. The Q45 Infiniti was still pretty, and the cream paint job looked just as new as it did eight and a half years ago. Quron shook his head in disbelief. The young lady's identity was no longer a mystery. The sight of her really changed his mood from enthusiasm to crap in a matter of seconds. Betrayal was one of those things that Quron never took lightly. Malai and Quron were a couple before he caught his bid. They were in love and their relationship was grand. They were young at the time, but they were very much in harmony with each other. Quron was a serious player in the underworld's drug trade. Money was never an issue. As a token of his love, he kept Malai dipped in the finest threads, her hair in the best styles, and her feet in the flyest shoes money could buy.

Malai was bad to the bone. She was a pretty girl, mixed breed, half black and half Caucasian. Her mother was of the original people. Her father... please, straight coward. He abandoned his responsibility before he even knew the gender of his child. It was all good though, once Quron came into the picture, things smoothed out. They shared a similar struggle. With her pops M.I.A., and his dad strung out on crack, having each other seem to be all that mattered. Unfortunately, Quron had miscalculated. Two years into his stretch, visits from Malai started to slack. Prior to that, corresponding via mail had taken a back seat too. Ironically, her gradual distance never aroused suspicion in Quron's mind. Empathy was amongst his better characteristics, and at the time, she was still coming through to some extent.

The days started to come and go, with no signs of Malai. Naturally, Quron started to worry about the welfare of his boo. He began to stress hard. The unknown was killing him. But even then, foul play of the woman he loved with all of him never crossed his mind. After some time had elapsed, the day had come for his wounds to grow deeper. One of his friends came through on a parole violation and told him he had recently seen Malai cruising through the hood in the same Q45 Infiniti that he had bought three years ago. At that point, it was impossible for him to deny the facts that were obvious to a blind man in a pitch-black room. Just like that, Malai had bailed on him. Quron was sick, literally sick. His heart felt like it was in a vice grip, being squeezed by one of the strongest men in the world. He began to lose weight from not having an appetite and vomiting back up whatever he had eaten. His grooming slacked a little as well. The affects were vicious, yet human.

Quron didn't have much of a choice, but to accept Malai's decision, but he damn sure didn't respect it. She could have had a little class about how she went about it, he felt. And no, he didn't feel like Malai should have stopped living because he had slipped and fell. However, at the very least, he did expect her to be his friend. He needed her to be a true supporter while he endured the hardest years of his life. The opposite was given. The mantra, time heals all wounds, is true, including Quron's. He eventually learned to cope with it, and he vowed that face value would never hold any value in his life for as long as he lived. Snakes came with high heels, miniskirts, same blood, short, tall, all forms.

Malai's heels, steadily clicking against the concrete, snapped Quron from his zone. *This broad must really got me twisted, she don't know how bad I wanna spit in her face. Trifling ass.* His menacing stare caused her toned legs to lose life. She stumbled, nearly falling before regaining her composure. *Look at you, all scared. I ain't gon' do nothin' to you.* Quron chuckled to himself as he looked on. He hadn't seen Malai in years, and he couldn't front like her sudden appearance didn't catch him off guard, because it did. An explanation of any kind, he didn't want. Nothing she could say would justify the fact that she had vanished without a trace. The more Quron thought of what she did, the angrier he became. But instead of giving her the satisfaction of seeing him still scorned from her disloyalty, he concealed his rage.

Malai stood within arm's reach of the man she had deserted for reasons she only knew. It had taken all the rationale in the world to bring her to this point. Deep down inside, she knew it was something she had to do. Silence crowded the air. Quron gave her a once over, noting the praise worthy changes in her physique, but his expression remained stale. Even though she wore wide face Gucci shades, Quron's gaze seem to penetrate through, making her feel uneasy.

"Quron," she sighed pitifully, knowing that she had to go for broke. "I know I played myself like a real bird bitch. You probably hate me." Her words lingered with no interruption. Malai's voice started to crack, and tears gathered in her eyes. "I swear, I'm sorry. God knows that I love you to death. But Q, I love me more. This jail stuff was starting to drive me crazy. Then my parents were on my back. Too much pressure from sources I eventually realized didn't matter. But we were young, I was vulnerable, and without you, I felt lost. All of a sudden, women from everywhere started coming out the sky, and to make it worse, these bitches were claiming you. That's some straight bullshit and you know it. How was I supposed to feel? I was LOYAL to you, 100%, so how was I supposed to handle shit like that as a teenager? It messed me up. It clouded my judgment and made me lose hope in anything good that I ever associated with love. It fucked me up, can't you understand that? You fuckin' left me out here all alone with these savage beasts that only gave a fuck about my beauty, my flesh." Tears were pouring as she stepped closer. Her internal anger was obvious.

She placed a hand on his shoulder and removed her shades while looking Quron in his eyes. "I never ever stopped loving you. And you might think I got some nerve even showing my face on your out date, but I had to." Tears continued rolling. "I just pray that you will find forgiveness in your heart. You know I can be LOYAL. I want us to start over. Try to find love again. I don't want to know the truth of the past. I'm not gonna ask you. I just want to start us over. It took a lot, but I've realized, babe, I realized you are the best thing that ever happened to me and I'll do whatever in my reach to make it right. Please, let's make it work."

She held her contact with saddened eyes, trying to read Quron's expressionless face. She hoped her words struck the special place in his heart that once belonged to her. Unsure if she wanted a response or not, a forced smile covered the traces of confusion that lurked. Stalling for time, her arms spread open.

Quron hesitated before falling into them. Little did she know, the hug wasn't for her satisfaction, it was for his own perverted reasons. It had been ten long years since he had been able to touch a woman unsupervised. As he held Malai around the small of her back, their past sexual escapades raced to the forefront of his mind and he couldn't help but smile. He had to calm himself, because his dick recognized her scent and stiffened a little. Malai's pussy was always the bomb, taste like cotton candy, snug as a glove, and warm like heated oil.

Quron blinked a few times and their moments of passion faded. He did not want to see her facial expression once his words settled in. He still had love for her, even though their relationship had reached a point of no return. He embraced her waist as his words caressed her earlobe. He wanted her to hear him clearly and respect his position.

"Malai, let's not play games, or pretend like things are all good, 'cause it ain't. But umm, I'm not gonna dwell on the past, because it'll only bring foul thoughts, and I'm not wit' it. I just did ten years in prison, so to be out here free, makes me the happiest man in the world right now. Not you or nobody else is gonna mess that up. You need to know that I'm far too mature to be holding grudges. So honestly, I do forgive you, but me forgivin' you don't mean that the facts don't remain. I'm not even gon' waste your time, shorty. Our flame died the second you left me for dead. I could do you filthy 'cause you vulnerable right now. But nah, I'ma let chu live. I'm not one of them dudes. I'd much rather let my home girl, karma, get you. Just remember one thing. Life goes on. Do what you been doin'. I appreciate the life lesson."

The sound of a horn came right on time. Quron knew it was the taxi he had called before leaving the facility. No one in society, other than Momma love, knew his out date, so it was a wonder how Malai found out. Quron's hands fell from her waist, but she remained draped around his neck. She whimpered lightly, sniffling as they stood in silence. Reluctantly, she freed him. It was then that Quron saw the years of abuse and suffering she had endured during his absence.

"Please don't do this to us. Quron, I am sooo sorry." Her tears ran in succession. She extended her arms, desperately pleading.

Quron had never seen her like this. A part of him wanted to console her and assure that everything would he ok, but his pride and principles that govern his life would not give in to the sucker shit. It was very clear that hustlers, gangsters, pimps, and whoever else that had the ability to spit game had sensed her vulnerability once Quron left. They wasted no time capitalizing off her weakness. She had been dragged through the mud, and the scars from such brutal treatment bruised her soul.

Malai's sobs grew louder and her breaths deeper. Quron showed no sympathy. He gathered his belongings and got in the cab.

"Where to?" The Mexican driver asked.

"Any bank in Newburgh."

As the cab pulled away from the curb, Quron turned and glanced through the rear window one last time. He shook his head. Malai dropped to her knees as anxiety gripped her lungs. All Quron could hear was her wailing, and the sight of her crumpled, crying hysterically.

Chapter 4

It felt strange, cruising through the streets that he once knew so well. Everything seemed so different from the images preserved in Quron's mind. The potholes that used to spread throughout the inner city streets were now filled with smooth blacktop. Most of the abandoned buildings that once sheltered the homeless and infected rodents were now renovated, remodeled, and homes for low income families. *It's gon' take a while to get used to this,* Quron mused. After cashing his institutional check and paying the cab driver, he relaxed in the back seat, naturally high.

They cruised through block after block at a moderate speed. Quron admired all of the monumental moves that the mayor and other council members had made in the city during his absence. Before he knew it, the cab was creeping up to his final destination. Quron searched for a familiar face. Names he knew he wouldn't remember, but faces he wouldn't ever forget. Home sweet home. The cab stopped and Quron got out. He looked up and down the strip and exhaled a sigh of relief. Damn, finally, he was here. The place where it all started; Lander Street. The heart of the hood, where natural born hustlers were bred. Many hoods were established around this street, and guns blazing for the love of money, power and respect was the norm.

Through his peripheral, Quron caught a young kid walking in his direction. The young thug observed Quron's presence, immediately taking in his stocky build. *This big nigga can't be no fiend, fuck he want ova here?* Shorty slowed his pace, but kept stepping with a change of motive. Initially, he thought he was going to make a quick dollar, but now his curiosity craved to know who the fuck was this new face.

"What's good, homeboy? You lookin' fo' somebody?" The youngster wasted no time. He was courageous, eager to learn about Quron. He crossed his arms and stood waiting for a response from the stranger.

Gradually, the young goons started to file in behind him. "I ain't never seen you 'round here before. Strangers aren't liked around these parts, ya dig?" A sly smirk traced his lips.

Quron set his property down on the concrete sidewalk, then looked around mockingly as if the young thug wasn't talking to him.

"Stop fuckin' wit' me like you don't know who I'm talkin' to!"

Quron braced himself and squared up with the youngster. He already had the drop, and the kid had no idea. Their eyes locked and Quron instantly forgave the young punk. He was a stupid ass kid that didn't know any better. Misguided, probably left to fend for himself out in the heartless streets. Quron knew he couldn't convince himself to punish him. He recognized that familiar look beaming out of the young man's eyes. That same look was once his. He too was young, ignorant, figuring it out. The young thug's features looked familiar, but Quron couldn't put a finger on who he was. Quron was almost certain he had to have known the young man's parents. The city was small. If you were in the same age group, more than likely, you attended the same schools. That made him feel even worse; a grown man out there styling on a kid. What was he thinking? *Damn, he doesn't know any better.*

"Listen young man," Quron reasoned.

"Hold up, homeboy, my name ain't young man or none of that. It's Ghost, so don't call me nothin' else, you heard?"

Quron sighed again, this time to let out the steam that was clogging his chest. This young nigga was straight up ignorant. He had already been pardoned, but he was still pushing. Years ago, he would have been sentenced to death, regardless of his age or ignorance.

"Yo, listen, muthafu—" Quron's tone raised to a notch short of a growl. He caught the obscene words slipping from his lips and silenced himself to gain a little more control. He was certainly approaching that point of no return.

Simultaneously, Ghost's goons reached for their waists, awaiting the signal to lay Quron's ass down. Quron wasn't moved. He didn't flinch, not so much as a blink. "I don't know who y'all think y'all dealing with, but I promise you, I ain't him." Quron's demeanor was cool, but his stare was menacing. "I'm easy, young brotha. Don't get it twisted like I'm new to these streets and won't put my thug shit back on in a blink if need be." He paused and inhaled deeply, knowing he really did not want any parts of the streets.

"But please, let's not take it there. I'm not with hurting my own kind. If anything, I need to hip y'all lil niggaz on how to touch some real bread. Before any of y'all even thought about selling crack, I was running these streets. Yeah, you looking at me all cock eyed, but this real talk." He laughed. "Look up an' down the block, and imagine it being zero below and you being out here wit' a pocket fulla crack, but not a fiend in sight. Just you, ya team, and a fully loaded Glock, pacing up and down the block, and stopping anybody who looked like they smoke crack." The young men looked on attentively, while the old head gave them the game.

"Those were hard times, li'l homies, but we persevered and got through. The result of all the work we put in, is this gold mine that y'all holding down. How y'all think Lander Street got the name, "Crack Alley?" We responsible for that. I ain't glorifying my past, 'cause ma past is these streets and these streets ain't about nothing. These streets don't love nobody. Not you, not me, not nobody! Don't die for this nonsense. Never judge a book by its cover. I could've been a connect, ready to give you a hunite bricks, then what?" Quron questioned with a smile.

"Or I could have been the police. You think it would be wise to make the police mad? You young brothas these days gotta be more sharp and calculated with your decisions while out in these streets. Y'all was ready to throw it all away, 'cause a new face stepped foot on ya block. That's insane!" He yelled to emphasize his point. "I know y'all getting money, so why throw it all away for no reason? See what I mean?" Quron shook his head. "There's a major difference. The sooner y'all understand that, the tighter ya game will be. If y'all plan to last out here, being thinkers is the only way. The second I let my emotions supersede my intelligence, was the second prison became my home. Take heed, or don't." He shrugged carelessly. "It'll only benefit or hurt you. Oh yeah, make sure y'all do ya homework on Born. A nigga all the way authentic. Peace!"

Quron retrieved his property, spun, and walked up the steps to his childhood home. Ghost's team gradually filed out and resumed doing what they do, once they saw that their boy, Ghost really didn't have much of an issue. But Ghost himself stayed put. He stood, admiring the back of the brother who turned out to be an O.G. A smile formed and a sudden warmth settled within his heart. Until this point, for as far back as he could remember, no one had ever even attempted to show concern for him or the lifestyle that he was living. He really appreciated the old timer and his wisdom.

Chapter 5

Quron walked through the front door, not a bit surprised by all the faces that were present. The commotion grew as people started to recognize the man who had parted from them when he was just a teen. All in attendance were family. Sadly, but true, hardly any of them had made as much as an attempt to contribute comfort throughout the course of his incarceration. To add salt to injury, many of his family resided right there in Newburgh, approximately thirty minutes away from the facilities where he did most of his time. Quron's feelings were indifferent, upon seeing their phony asses.

Ms. Johnson obviously couldn't hold water, because in spite of what her son wanted, she had told everybody and their momma that her baby boy was finally coming home. She was a trip. It was all love, though. At the end of the day, Ms. Johnson and her daughter, Quron's sister, Amil, had held him down, earning their keep. Amil, had grown to be such a star. She was a beautiful girl, with smooth brown skin, small feet, long brown hair, and a feminine swag with brains to match. Quron felt proud that she made it and had not fallen victim to the streets during his absence. He knew that she had survived only because of the tools he had equipped her with when they were young. His method had paid off.

Hours had drifted away and the gathering had finally concluded. This was the down time that Quron had craved over the years, sitting in the living room with the three women that shared his heart; Ms. Johnson, Amil, and his boo, Bri. Bri was a pretty young lady who resembled a typical southern girl. She stood average height for a woman, very curvy and well mannered. Initially, Quron was on some bullshit, still stuck on Malai, and he preferred more exotic looking women. Bri just didn't fit the bill. As time went on, Bri's morals and intellect started to overshadow the superficial things that he desired. Before he knew it, the friend that he had seen in her had evolved into an attraction that was far more intimate. They had attended elementary school together. Even back then, the couple seemed to have a natural attraction to each other.

Upon completing the sixth grade, the most drastic thing happened. Bri's mom was offered a gig that benefited her situation, so she packed up and moved. They shared some noteworthy moments on the occasions that she visited, but it was clear that they were no more than friends. At least, that's what he thought.

Quron sat on the couch across from his woman, replaying the day that she reappeared in his life. He was still in prison, locked in his cell, stressing. Mail call had come. Quron had begun to pray the Asr prayer when the officer appeared at his gate. Not disturbing him, the officer placed the envelope on his cell gate flap. Quron was so in tune with Allah through prayer that he hadn't noticed. He slowly rose from his hands and knees, brushed his hand over his beard, and exhaled gently. He felt rejuvenated, hopeful. It was then that he realized an envelope was on his flap. Bri's name had him excited and anxious to see what his homegirl was talking about. He cracked the seal, unfolded the letter and began to read.

Dear Quron

I know this letter may have caught you off guard. Sorry for the surprise. To be frank, for some reason you've dominated my thoughts, lol. I figured writing you would help me clear my head. As I write, I'm discovering that it'll take more than a pen and pad to satisfy this need that I have to see you, smell you, and touch you. I heard you gotcha weight up too. (I'm smilin'). I understand that this may not be a good time for you. The grapevine told me about your girl breakin' out, that shit's wack. But as foul as it may sound, I'm glad she did. I feel like it's finally my time with you. My love for you has always been real, and I know you know that. I've always wanted you; just never had the courage to pursue you. There's so much that needs to be said so I'll be in town on Monday to say it. Look forward to seeing your face, see you then.

Always True: ya homie lova friend,

Bri

Ms. Johnson's voice snapped him out of deep thought. He looked at Bri and smiled. "So how does it feel to be home, baby?"

"Momma, it feels sooo much better than bein' locked up," They all giggled lightly. "Since we havin' welcome home parties, what does Quron's angels have planned?"

Ms. Johnson waved her hand at her son, noting his sarcasm. "Boy, please." She chuckled. "You my son, and I'll do whatever I want when it comes to you. But since you asked, I know it's been a while since you and Miss Bri spent some real quality time together. So, me and your sister decided to go over your aunt's house for tonight."

"Nope, nope, nope! Don't front, Ma, you know I had to convince you to let my big brotha have his space." Amil started laughing. "You know you was hatin'." Amil blew her mother up.

"Whateveeeer," Ms. Johnson rolled her eyes, smacked her teeth, and did the snake with her neck before bursting out laughing too. "Dang, you got a big mouth, Amil. Come your behind on, girl." Ms. Johnson stopped at the door and turned suddenly. "Oh yeah, I almost forgot, Young-One, Young-Man, Young-Child or whatever that boy name is, called. What y'all call'im again? I know what his momma named him and it wasn't young nothin'." Her face was wrinkled like she ate something sour. Quron couldn't help but enjoy his mother's youthful soul. Very little in regard to her had changed.

"Ma, it don't matter. After all these years, and you still ain't got it right, today ain't gonna be no different."

"I guess you're right, but anyway, he said to call him whenever you find the time. I left his number on top of the dresser. Love you baby, see y'all later."

Amil waved at her brother and Bri before closing the door behind her.

Chapter 6

The eye exchange between Ms. Johnson and Bri had not gone unnoticed. If nothing else, prison had definitely taught Quron to read body language and pay close attention to everything. He wasn't sure what their exchanges meant, or if it was about anything at all, but he would definitely inquire when the time is right. That shit could wait. The only thing on his mind was pussy, pussy, and more pussy. A decade in captivity will do it. Quron felt like he wanted to recreate the same ecstatic feeling that enveloped him the very first time he and Bri had ever made love. The setting had to be perfect.

The couple met in the center of the floor and hugged. Bri's sniffles broke their silence. "Don't cry, sweetie. It's all good now, I'm home." Quron kissed the tear that rolled down her face. While clutching her soft hand, he gestured with his head.

Bri led the way toward the spiral staircase that twirled round and round until it reached the second level where Quron's room was. It had been years since he had stepped foot on the other side of his door. Although he had rented a few other places before his bid, none held sentimental value like this. There was no place like home. Bri opened the bedroom door and they stepped in. Surprisingly, to Quron's recollection, mostly everything was just like he left it, with the exception of there being new linen on his bed, and the room was recently cleaned. It still held a stale smell though, and judging by Bri's expression, she was disturbed by the lifeless odor.

Sensing her discomfort, Quron walked over to the dresser, grabbed one of the three vanilla scented candles, placed it in the candleholder on his fondue set, then lit it.

Gradually, the built up tension lingering in the air began to fade, replaced with a relaxing feeling that was nothing less than therapeutic. "Damn." Quron exhaled, then spread out across his queen-size bed, enjoying the slight sensation from the satin sheets caressing his skin.

Bri escaped to the bathroom and started the water in the tub, filling it with various Victoria Secret products while undressing at the same time. While Bri was preparing for the night she had longed for, Quron was still in the position that he had grown to appreciate over the years. His back on the mattress, eyes to the ceiling, and his mind fixed on wherever he could find peace. After a few minutes, his eyes scanned the room and it dawned on him that he felt absolutely no connection to the materialistic things that he had acquired from the game. The clothes, the jewelry, the 60-inch TV, the five thousand dollar bedroom set, and anything else that he had gained didn't mean a thing to him.

His chain of thought was broken when his peripheral caught Bri stepping back in the room. He never realized she'd left. He rose up and a satisfied grin decorated his lips. She stood in front of him butt naked, with her hands on her hips, wearing a devilish grin. "Look at you, ma. All this I been missin'?" He smiled and brushed his hand over her plump ass as she did a 180 spin, teasingly.

"Yep." Bri sashayed to the Sony stereo system and pressed a button. No one even used CD players anymore, but it was there, and the two lovebirds anticipated the mood that the player would set. The CD that rotated in the disc player spilled into the surround sound speakers, expressing a classic hit, "Always and Forever," by the Heat Wave.

"Girl, what you know 'bout this?" Quron laughed, dick harder than a brick.

"Enough to know this that lovemaking music."

"Talk that talk, girl."

They laughed.

A person would think that the young couple was outdated, according to their choice of music, but according to their souls, they were right on time. Before they knew it, an hour had slipped away. More hits like "In the Rain" by the Dramatics and "Natural High" by Blood Stone enhanced their euphoric state.

Quron pulled Bri to him and delivered soft, passionate kisses on the sexual parts of her body that can only be seen when nude. In one motion, he rose from her ankles and swooped her up in his arms. He nudged the bathroom door, entered, and eased Bri down into the lukewarm bath water.

"You ah-ight?"

Bri nodded and watched attentively as her man peeled from his garments.

The combination of Quron's massive chest, chiseled stomach, and bulging shoulders drove her crazy. Quron eased down beside his boo in the round tub and immediately started foreplay. He was thirsty to get some of that pussy. They kissed lustfully, groped each other and nibbled on each other's ears. Bri traced Quron's six-pack all the way down to his manhood.

"Shhh." The touch alone caused her to clinch her teeth, tilt her head back, and shudder. Scented, floating candles danced around the two while Quron remained adamant in succeeding.

He slowly raised Bri out of the water, gripping her fat ass. Her pussy was neatly trimmed, just as he liked it. It had been years since his last hands on experience with a woman, but that didn't alter his memory on how he meticulously earned their hearts, entered their mind, and connected with their souls. Leaning Bri back on the edge of the tub while pulling her thighs forward, he placed her in a vulnerable position. She threw her hand back and braced herself on the sink while looking down.

Quron stiffened his tongue and penetrated her tight, horny pussy. "Oww." Her feminine moans stroked his ego as he twisted, turned and swiped his thick tongue all over her meaty vagina. Slowly, his focus became her long clit. Bri's eyes rolled, and her hand balled into a fist. It felt so damn good. Quron smiled inwardly and continued to flick his tongue back and forth.

Bri shook violently. "Ahh." Her grip began to weaken as ecstasy took over.

Quron rested his elbows on the edge of the tub and held her in his arms, not missing a beat. He sensed her desire to cum. Two fingers slid into her heated womb, curved in an upward position.

"Please babe, ahhh." She whined, speeding up the circular motion in her hips.

The electrical waves rolling through her spongy G-spot combined with the ecstatic feeling bouncing off the nerves in her clit compelled Bri to succumb. With one loud outcry, the sweet juices that begged to be released from her fat pussy were set free. Rich, white cream flowed freely down Quron's index and middle fingers, coating his knuckles and moistening his tongue. Bri's body was numb before she became limp. She slid back down into the cool water; her eyes were shut as she heaved like she had run a marathon. The night was far from over, though. It had really just begun in Quron's mind. He stepped out of the water first. After a while, the water became more chilled and Bri followed.

He wrapped her in an Egyptian cotton bathrobe and watched her strut back into the bedroom. Obediently, Quron followed like a dog trailing its master. Bri looked behind her and noticed her knight in armor standing with both hands on his waist, dripping wet, dying to get his nuts out the sand.

She smiled. "You looking like you like what you see." A light snicker followed. "It's yours daddy, take whatchu want."

Quron was so used to taking orders that it didn't immediately register that it was ok to take control. He stood dazed. Bri's body was crazy, much better than any memory he could recall. Her countless hours in the gym had really paid off. She was well proportioned, 36-28-40. She bent at the waist, spreading the top half of her body across the bed while her feet remained planted on the floor.

Bri winced and grew excited when she felt her pussy expand, contract, adjust, then relax. Quron stroked forcefully in a steady rhythm, zoning to her greedy pussy, slurping and farting. "Uhh daddy, please fuck this pussy, don't stop. I love this dick."

Quron tightened his ass cheeks and started digging harder, faster, harder, and faster.

"Oh God! Fuck me daddy, fuck me harder! Right there, bang it right there, that's my spot, that's my spot, yeaaah! Yeaaah!"

Just when she was about to explode, Quron pulled his big, slimy dick out of her pussy and eased his swollen head into her asshole. He wrapped his arm around her waist, using his fingers to finish her off. Bri let out a painful scream, but made no attempt to stop the pleasurable pounding. On cue, the CD switched to Donnell Jones' "Where I Wanna Be" and Quron continued punishing her rectum with no regard, as if it was a virgin pussy.

Bri suppressed the pain and marinated in the newfound pleasure she was experiencing. Although she did not know what had brought forth this new desire of her man wanting anal, she was just happy to be introduced to this unique type of sensation. Quron's grip tightened on Bri's waist as he humped more violently, totally forgetting he was literally digging off in her ass.

"Ma, I'm 'bout to cum! Ahh, I'm 'bout to cum!" Bri worked her ass muscles as best she could, taking all ten inches. "Ahhh, Ahhh."

Within seconds, she felt his dick swell. It hurt so badly, but she took it like a champ. In one motion, Bri freed herself from the vigorous pounding, spun, squatted and took as much of him as her throat would allow. She gagged. Quron was so big, he had both length and girth and Bri was loving every part of it. Spit mixed with pre-cum produced as she rammed him down her throat, causing herself to gag continuously, yet she never stopped.

Two slurps later, Quron buckled. His toes curled underneath his foot, and thick, creamy nut flew out of his head like an erupting volcano. All of a sudden, he felt dizzy. He stumbled, and then crashed on the bed. Staring down at Bri wiping his soft dick clean with her mouth, he couldn't help but wonder where, and even more importantly, when she learned how to perform like a professional porn star. Looking deep into her eyes for an answer, he found none; only love lingered in her gaze, and a desire to please her man.

Bri walked into the bathroom, rinsed her mouth, then returned and cuddled in her man's arms. There was no need for words. Just like the night began, their love session had also ended. Whispers of Donell Jones still echoed off the pale walls, and the two lovebirds lay intertwined, trading deep, passionate, kisses of affection.

Chapter 7

Early the next morning, Quron rose from the arms of his beautiful queen with the intention of offering the morning Fajr prayer. This was a daily routine to fulfill his religious obligation. For some reason, he didn't feel that same enthusiasm that he normally felt when it was time for him to bond with his lord. As he made his way to the bathroom, it suddenly dawned on him and it became quite clear why he was feeling down. Instantly, he felt like crap. He had committed two grave sins that were forbidden in Islam, and now the evil deeds were weighing heavy on his conscience. He knew that there would come a time when he would have to stand face to face with society and its temptation. Honestly, until this point, he really felt he had the discipline to make it through. But instead, he had been driven by his lower desire.

Sex with Bri, in Islam, was a no-no without first being married. Curiosity had gotten the best of him. He was curious to feel what it was like to be with a woman again, instead of beating his dick to bust a nut. True indeed, Quron was a Muslim, but a perfect human being he was not. While in the joint for so many years, he was compelled to explore the only avenue to women, "Paper Hoes" as some called them. Porn mags like Buttman, Nasty, Black Video and other publications praised butt fucking, the pleasure from it was visual, and monogamous relationships seem not to exist.

After jumping in the shower, performing Ghusul to purify himself, he still felt that he needed some spiritual nourishment. Without hesitation, he walked over to the dresser, retrieved his Holy Qur'an and flipped it open. As soon as he began to read, all he could say was, "Wow."

He paused. "Allah, what are you try'na tell me?" As soon as Quron looked in the book, the first verse his eyes settled on read. *And whatever of misfortune befalls you, it is because of what your hands have earned. And Allah pardons much.*

After pondering on the holy verse, he knew there was no two ways about this one-way street. The verse made it clear that you will reap what you sow, no matter what. Feeling a little better, he offered prayer, then grabbed the phone number his mother left. Looking to his left, he noticed Bri was still knocked out, lightly snoring. Quron chuckled, knowing he'd represented well last night.

He picked up the phone and dialed the number. Three rings later, a whisper like voice answered. "Hello."

"Hello, may I speak to Young-One?"

"Who's callin'?"

"Quron."

"Ma dude, what's good, homie?" All of a sudden, the sleepy voice was vibrant.

"Who's this?" Quron's face scrunched up as he stepped into the bathroom to smother his tone.

"It's the nigga you called lookin' for."

"What up, Young, why you playin'?" Quron laughed.

"It's six in the mornin', I ain't know it was you. I been chasin' paypa all night, and I ain't really try'na holla at nobody right now, I'm tired as fuck." Young-One chuckled. "Anything for my boy tho', so shout it out. What chu doin' up so early?"

"I guess it has become routine for me over the years."

"I know you gotcha dick out the dirt. Mad bitches hollerin' about a nigga. I told'em they gotta put their own foot work in, 'cause Bri my home girl and I'ma respect y'all bond."

"I heard that, my morally inclined brotha."

Quron's sarcasm caused the friends to share a laugh. It had been a while since they enjoyed a conversation. It felt good to have each other back. After a few minutes passed, there was a yawn before the lingering silence was broken.

"So, what's really the issue? I know you didn't call me just to say what up at six in da mornin'. What's on ya mind?"

"Nothin' major, Momma love told me you called and left your number with a message for me to holla, so I'm returnin' your call."

"Since that's the case, give me a few hours and I'ma come scoop you. Tell my girl, Bri, don't trip. I'ma only borrow you for a hot minute."

"Ah-ight Young, I'll see you when you come through." Quron chuckled. Young-One was still crazy.

"Luv."

"Peace."

Four hours had passed, and the piercing sound of a car horn rudely interrupted the conversation Quron and Bri were having. The couple tried to ignore the chaos of the outside and continue their vibe, but not before the phone began to ring.

Bri sucked her teeth, peered at the phone, then shifted her gaze to her man. Quron knew what she was thinking, and he couldn't blame her for thinking it. She was being selfish, and reluctant to let anyone get a millisecond of his time. Making his way to the jack, he suddenly stopped, turned around and headed back toward his seat. Bri rolled her eyes when the voice rang from the answering machine.

"Yo Born, I know you ain't sleep. It's Young, pick up the phone."

"I'm comin'." was all Quron said before he hung up the phone and proceeded out the door.

"Where you going?" Bri started to pout.

"I don't know, but I'll be back soon." The simplest explanation was best, because Quron could see it all in her face that she wanted to argue.

He kissed her lips and brushed past. He felt her eyes burning a hole in his back and he kind of felt bad, but he figured she would get over it. Outside, Young-One was lamping; his Beamer was official. Triple black with chrome rims. He was stunting hard, smiling from ear to ear when he saw his dude. Judging from the vibrating concrete, he had a mean system hidden in the trunk. The sun had the studs in his ears twinkling like crazy. One thing for sure, the game seemed to be treating him very well.

"You gon' stand out here all day or what? C'mon nigga lets ride." Quron walked over to his man wearing a Colgate smile and they embraced. It was a heartfelt moment.

"Ma dude."

They let go of each other and hopped in. The destination was unknown to Quron, but it felt good to be riding in style. This is how he envisioned it, but not by the same means as his man took to get it. Make no mistake about it; he still loved the glitter of the drug game, it was just those moral boundaries that must be crossed in order to succeed, that made the streets not an option.

Quron zoned out to the deep lyrics pumping through the system. The way niggas on each block were shouting them out made him feel like he was that nigga again. They cruised slowly, honked the horn repeatedly, and waved like they were on a float with political figures participating in a parade.

"I see you got yaself a fan club." Quron giggled.

"Everybody loves a winner." Young-One looked over at his man, wearing a smile.

"I know that's right."

The quick tour of the town was appreciated, but it had ended too soon. The Beamer swerved into a parking space and

Young-One turned the engine off. "We're here. This thang is crazy, right?"

"Word." Quron looked around admiringly, absorbing the sights. "I read in the newspaper what the developers had planned for the river front, but I couldn't see all this. I remember when we used to stand right there and throw rocks in the Hudson." He pointed to where they played as kids and took in just how much had changed.

"Yeah, alotta shit changed over the years. You ain't no different." Young-One said jokingly, but Quron knew that some truth usually lurked behind the lines of a joke.

Quron chuckled softly. "Ain't nothin' wrong with change, Mr. Sarcastic. I'm still that same dude, I'm just not wit' the B.S. no more."

Young-One gave him a funny look, then turned back forward.

"What's good wit'chu though? The streets takin' care of a brotha, huh?" Quron smiled, reaching over and flicking the studs in his ear.

"I mean, I've been fortunate enough to avoid the system, but I haven't stacked paypa like I was s'pose to. It's like I lack the strict discipline needed. On top of that, I don't trust these fake ass niggas as far as I can throw 'em. That is a problem in itself. Not trustin' a muthafucka has kept me limited to a certain level of success out here, 'cause I can't take over the world, dolo. So what was I to do?" He shrugged. "After you and Nuri got caught up, I mingled wit' a few dudes, but y'all irreplaceable. I swear no bullshit. I made do wit' what I had."

Quron peered forward, silently digesting Young-One's words.

Young-One cut his eyes to the side and saw that he held his boy's attention, so he went for the kill. "Basically, that's part of why I wanted to holla at you. I know you jus' touched the town, and you'll probably feel like I'm dead ass wrong for comin' at you like this, but I need you homie. I want you to become my partner. Before you say anything, you should know that I ain't insulting you, askin' you to work for me. Nah, in fact I'm not askin' you to get ya hands dirty at all."

Quron looked over, his brow wrinkled. "So what exactly are you asking me?"

"I jus' want you to oversee the operations. You know, make sure shit function right. You've always been sharp, and even more important than that, I can trust you. Nur' will be home soon, so I figured with you as the overseer, me puttin' in that groundwork, and Nuri's muscle, we can't lose, sky's the limit. All we need is a year. Whatever we clear in a year, we retire wit'. I don't care if its ten dollars, a year is the dead line."

There was no question about the seriousness of Young-One's proposition. Quron knew it was sweet, and he'd be lying if he said he wasn't tempted. But at the end of the day, his intentions were legal, pure from his old sinister ways, while Young-One was still stuck with that underworld by any means mentality. The game was a fork in the road for these two.

Quron sighed. "Young, you know you my dude and I got crazy love for you, but I can't accept your offer." Shaking his head, Quron continued. "I'm headed in another direction, and there's way too many other ways to get dough. I got a lot of ideas that really have the potential to be very profitable if they are carried out and perfected. What we can do is combine whatever paypa you are willing to put up, with what I have in mind, and make it happen like that. You'll be a partner, and we'll learn the dos and don'ts as we go. It's a risk. I mean all investments are. But the bigger the risk, the bigger the profit or loss, dependin' on how you look at it. Whatever the outcome, at least you'll be free and alive to learn and capitalize off your mistakes. Getting money is easy; it's keepin' it that requires brains. So the least you can do is think it over and get back at me." Quron gave his man a pound and gripped his palm tight.

Young-One had never been exposed to this side of his boy. He did the bid with him, but it was done from a distance. He supplied money, clothes, some footwear, flicks, etc. But the transition in Quron's thought process, he had not witnessed. Young was mad as fuck that he had been turned down. He had been planning this moment for some time. It was his ace in the hole when all else had failed. Truth is, the superficial glitz hyped Young-One's street cred. In reality, though, the streets were sour and the inconsistencies in the quality of his coke had made his come up much further away than he had planned. He was livid, but in the same breath, he accepted the balance that his boy had in his life.

A half smile traced Young-One's face, and then faded just as quickly. He sighed. "I respect it. No promises, but we'll see how it goes.

"Kool, that's wassup." Quron smiled.

Chapter 8

The next day, Quron found himself in Beacon, New York, waiting to climb aboard the Metro-North. He had convinced Bri that he could handle himself, and he preferred to travel alone. She understood where he was coming from. He clearly just wanted some him time. The train arrived on schedule. He got on, but was indecisive about where he wanted to get off. He narrowed it down to two stops, either Marble Hill in the Bronx or 125th Street in Harlem. The ride seemed to take forever. Maybe that was because everywhere he looked, white men clad in suits, wearing dark shades, clutching a briefcase were posted everywhere. He assumed their presence was the result of the terrorist activity going on in the country. They didn't leave much to the imagination. Law enforcement was plastered across their faces.

Although Quron had convinced Bri to fall back, he still knew what the streets entailed. Being out of the loop for a decade hadn't made him naïve. In so many ways, he still processed shit in his brain like a street nigga. He never overlooked the possible hazards that could easily come his way. The game as he knew it was a cycle that never changed; the players just added more menacing things to the rules for the next generation of players to implement once the last breed dies off or gets life in the pen. Bearing that in mind, Quron snatched up his li'l man, Steel, to come along. Steel wasn't too far behind Quron in age, and Quron loved him genuinely. He had taken him under his wing years ago, when he was running the streets. Ever since then, Steel had remained loyal. He was a quiet dude, often misunderstood because of his mild demeanor and his stuttering speech. But when shit got funky, son transformed into a psychotic beast, and not even the devil himself wanted drama.

125th was thick as always. The street and sidewalk alike was flooded with people. The two comrades strolled through, taking in the scene. Quron made it his business to mingle and make favorable impressions on as many folks as possible. He understood the significance of networking. Everything was a stepping stone. No one ever went from crawling to running, without walking in between. That was his logic. The Apollo Theater was holding an event of some sort. Bootleggers were all up and down the strip, hustling any and everything you could think of. The SUVs, V8s, and V6s shooting through were impressive.

Quron instantly had a flashback to the days when he, Young-One, Nuri and Steel used to breeze through to see the Harlem broads, cop some coke uptown, and make a few statements with their attire and whips. "It's funny how life flips around." Quron mumbled in a whispered tone.

After window-shopping in Dr. Jays and a couple other stores, Quron decided to go uptown to see if he could get into something before heading back upstate. "Steel, you wit' goin' uptown?"

"I'm... I'm wit'chu. It's ya da... day." Steel smiled.

Quron and Steel ran over to the cab that was yielding at the red light. He tapped on the window.

The driver looked up and waved them in. "Where to?"

"Umm... you can drop me off on the corner of 145th and Broadway."

The driver merged with traffic and proceeded to the requested destination.

Uptown had not changed much. The liquor store was still in place, clothing shops on the strip were there also, but ran by different owners. Copeland's, Quron's favorite soul food establishment was gone, He smiled at the memories as he walked into B.J's.

A female employee wasted no time in trying to assure Quron's comfort. She must have known a little about business, because the first rule of business is that first impressions are what one is judged by, and it seemed that she was executing that rule to perfection.

"Hello, how may I help you today?" The young lady had a confident approach, which was a good thing. She was smooth, feminine, and professional, not forceful or rude. Her appearance was that of a young lady who took pride in taking good care of herself. Cute face, petite frame, long hair, and nice attire.

"I'm basically looking for somethin' simple that I could run around in." Quron responded.

She smiled. "What type of footwear do you have in mind? Just give me an idea and I'll do what I can to help."

"Just keep it plain, but fly," He laughed at his own wit. "A pair of white on white Air Force Ones will do. I wear a size nine and a half. I need all the help I can get. I know my swag is outdated." They all laughed in agreement.

"Okay, just give me a few minutes and I'll be right back with your selection."

"Ah-ight." He watched her ripe backside sway from right to left in a rhythmical motion. He shook his head and suppressed his lust. He allowed his attention to be stolen by the many activities that were taking place outside the storefront, but nothing in particular.

Lost in thought, the pearl white S500 that slowly came to a stop brought all of his senses back to the present. "That Benz is fire." Quron spoke aloud to himself.

"Excuse me?" The cute employee interrupted.

"Oh nothin'. You caught me thinking out loud, pardon me," Quron admitted, embarrassed. "I didn't notice you had come back."

"I didn't mean to startle you. I noticed something had captured your attention." The pretty worker said while making a head gesture, indicating that she was speaking about the white Mercedes that had pulled up outside.

"It's a small thing, don't worry about it. On anotha note, I appreciate you helpin' me out. I intend to come through more often in the near future. What's your name?" Quron asked with a smile.

"I'm sorry, that was rude of me. All this time and I haven't introduced myself."

"Don't trip. The same is true for me."

"My name is Peaches."

"And mine is Quron. It was nice meeting you. Take it easy, I'll see you around insha'llah." Quron smiled and pulled out a knot of big face bills. He peeled off two crisp hundred dollar bills and handed them to Peaches.

Her eyes lit up as she said a few words that expressed her gratitude.

Quron waved it off, as if the deed was a small thing, and made his way toward the door. His view was much bigger and his blessings came in abundance from Allah always. You only get as much as you give. Quron learned that lesson a long time ago.

Chapter 9

Back up north, the streets of Newburgh were flooded. Thugs, ratchet lil divas, big time dealers, police, and everyday corner hustlers populated the inner city blocks. It seemed strange, because the strip hadn't been that thick in a while. The feeling was good and it flowed freely through everyone on Newburgh's rough barren streets. Young-One was loving his position. He knew that the recent release of his childhood friend from prison was the reason for the hopeful expressions that he had seen on everyone's face. Quron was young when he got knocked and sent off to prison. Nevertheless, he was a good dude and everyone knew that when he ate, so did everyone around him.

His timing was perfect. The streets were much different now. Gangs and senseless violence had the hood in a frenzy. The dealers weren't really hustlers anymore; they just sold drugs. They didn't have the fortitude, nor the mental capacity to really take the game to the next level. They spent the little money that they were getting, faster than it came. For the most part, everybody was starving, which always resulted in an increase in violent crimes.

A short female with a tight ponytail, wearing slippers called Young-One to the broken down porch that she was sitting on. Young-One put his finger up. After he finished his conversation with the female that he was talking to, he strolled over to the porch to see what the young lady was so impatient to tell him.

"Heyyyy, Young-One. What's good, baby? You look happy today, what's the occasion?"

"Ain't nothin', Fee, just coolin'. Loving my position in life at the moment, feel me?"

"Uh-huh, it must be nice. What you need to do is take some time out for yourself. You know, get away, relax, and let a sistah take care of your sexy ass. We both know these streets will survive without you. A sistah could use a tune up right about now." She chuckled seductively and batted her eyes, letting her lustful intentions linger with no shade.

Young-One giggled while shaking his head. "I swear, I knew you were up to no good." Smiling from ear to ear, he pointed out jokingly, "You should know by now that I see through all your bullshit. One thing for sure tho, I respect your persistence like a muthafucka. You never, ever, eva, give up. Keep up the good work. You'll be surprised how far it'll get you."

No the fuck this nigga didn't. Funny ass niggaz be so stuck on they self. Arrogant fucker act like his shit don't stink. Fee twisted up her face and sucked her teeth in disgust. "Whatever, nigga. My pasis-pa-pa or whatever you said, hasn't gotten me very far with your black ass. I've been try'na get that chocolate dick ever since high school. But you be frontin' like you scared of this fat ass." Fee did a half spin and smacked herself extra hard.

Young-One looked on, lustful thoughts causing the blood to rush with urgency to his penis. Fee was undeniably cute, with the banging video vixen body. Her shape was a mean hourglass figure. Any man in their right mind would have loved to marinate in Fee's bundle of love. But even with those attributes in her favor, in Young-One's eyes, she had no class and her mouth was like the district news. A nut just wasn't worth all the extra drama that he knew would come along with her.

"You know what they say though, Fee. As long as you are alive, there's still hope."

Young-One found humor in his own sarcasm.

Fee shook her head. The expression on her face said it all. *This bastard here, he swear he the shit. Don't even know why I bother.* She stepped off the porch, feeling like her effort was useless. She walked up the street, not giving Young-One the satisfaction of seeing her disappointment.

Aggravated and upset, in mid-stride, she turned around and shouted, "Nigga you got some shit wit' you, but trust, I'ma catch you slippin'. Mark my words, I'ma catch you slipping." Fee held a sly smile, but there was a hint of seriousness that went unnoticed.

"I hear that hot shit." He laughed. "I need my dreads twisted later, you got me?"

Lawd, this boy done lost his damn mind. Shit on me like he do, and think I'ma look out. Fee rolled her eyes. "Maybe, you know what they say, as long as you are alive there's still hope." Fee's sarcasm tickled her insides. It took everything within to prevent her from bursting out laughing.

Young-One's facial expression was priceless. "You better stop playin' fuckin' games wit' me. Do I look like these young niggas that you be runnin' around here fuckin'?"

Helllll No! These young niggaz ballin', giving up that doe, busting they guns, and putting that dick down like grown ass men. Yo ass, on the other hand, acts just like a bitch, all arrogant and souped up. Fuck outta here nigga. Fee's thoughts unraveled quickly, but not a single word left her mouth. She just giggled and kept her cool. She actually enjoyed his obvious frustration. It felt good to finally get under his skin.

"Touchy nigga, I see you don't like when the shoe is on the other foot. More than likely, I'm gon' be at the crib all day like I usually am. Come holla at me. Deuces, playboy." Fee threw up the peace sign and stepped off.

The sway in her hips was hypnotizing. Each step a little harder, causing her round butt to jiggle for a little longer. As she continued to walk on clouds, her smile widened. She knew that he was looking; he had to be. Her own private thoughts of Young-One's sexy chocolate ass crept in. Fee shuddered, and then blushed as she felt her pussy contract. All her warm juices dripped, moistening her panties. She shook her head. *Damn, I really got it bad.*

Damn that Benz is crazy. I wonder who pushin' that, Quron stood silently in front B.J.'s sneaker spot uptown. Just as the thought settled in, the driver's door opened and a 5-foot three Pocahontas look alike stepped out of the luxurious car. She was so beautiful, with so much swagger; she could have easily been a supermodel if she was taller. With each step that she took, the concrete seem to soften and massage the beautiful feet that stood upon it. The picture was perfected when she came into full view, revealing her hourglass figure.

"Damn," was all Quron could muster.

Steel, on the other hand, felt no emotions. To him, she was just another pretty face.

The gorgeous woman must have felt Quron's gaze burning through her back, because suddenly she turned, as if someone had informed her of her new fan. Boldly, she locked eyes with him.

Quron noticed that his cover had been blown. He felt a little embarrassed about being caught staring, but he continued holding his ground, not blinking or shifting his gaze. He couldn't seem to shake his eye candy.

The gorgeous woman was impressed, and attracted to his thorough stance. To show her attraction, she broke eye contact and gave a sensual smile, knowing that if her pursuer was smooth and really interested, he would act on her discreet invitation. Not missing a beat, her steps were steady. Without looking back, she kept it moving toward the store across the street from where Quron was standing. Before she pulled back on the door handle, she turned around one last time before disappearing into the interior of the store.

Quron peeped game, but shook it off and accepted it for nothing more than what it was. He took out the cellular phone that Young-One had given him as a part of his care package, and dialed the only number that he had memorized due to his consistent calling while in prison. On the first ring, a feminine voice answered.

"Hello."

"May peace be upon you. What's good, my love?"

"Awww, your voice has always moistened my panties and brightened my day all at once, babe," the sweet voice said as the woman smiled. "I'm fine, but I'll be even better when I get up with you."

"Music to my ears. How could I not love a woman like you?"

"You so nasty."

"Whaaaaaat?" Quron laughed. "I didn't even say nothin', ma."

"Ummm hmm, boy you crazy. You know I know you better than anybody."

"Yeah! Crazy for being crazy in love with you."

"I know." Bri responded arrogantly while laughing.

"Ma, it's mad loud in the background. Where you at right now?"

"Right now, I'm in the city getting my hair done by these Africans on 125th street."

"That's wassup, 'cause I'm uptown on Broadway, shoppin' a little and enjoyin' the scenery. But you know I can't wait to see my baby." Quron could feel her blushing through the phone.

"Well, I should be done in about ten minutes, so wait for me and I'll come pick you up. I need to feel your presence." Bri let out a soft moan and giggled.

"That sounds like a plan. I'll be in Mickey D's on the corner of Broadway and 145th St. Beep the horn or call me when you get here."

"Okay."

"I love you."

"I love you too, daddy."

"Peace."

"Peace."

Quron hung up the phone and attended to his growling stomach. After handling his business, he positioned himself to see outside of the glass window while patiently waiting for Bri. After a few minutes, his ride pulled up and his hip started to vibrate. Without answering the incoming call, he stood from the wooden table and made his way through the exit.

Quron was Muslim, so he didn't believe in accidents or coincidence. The beautiful woman that he had encountered earlier from a distance was making her way back to the Benz that he assumed was hers. She hadn't noticed him, but he definitely spotted her. Her walk was so sexy. Her bowlegs, along with her feminine bounce, made him shake his head in lust and admiration. Guilt flowed through his veins because he knew that his heart belonged to the beautiful queen that was waiting. She did the bid, she came during his lowest point in his life, and for that, she was entitled to wear the crown of his queen. But even with that being so, his penis still reacted to another woman. It was the nature of a man to be attracted to the opposite sex. A natural attraction he just could not control.

A local city transportation bus slowly passed, temporarily blocking his view. He looked on, while keeping his pace steady. Once his view became clear, he caught the taillights of the pearl white Benz slowly mixing with traffic. Just like that, she was gone. Quron opened the door to the Acura TL and he was greeted with a question.

"Babe, what you lookin' at?"

Completely caught off guard, he stuttered. "Nothin... nothin' really. I'm just observing my surroundings. So much has changed in Harlem over the years. By the way, ma, while we were on the phone, I meant to tell you that I brought Steel along for the ride. It slipped my mind before I had the chance to tell you." Quron said, immediately changing the subject.

The evil look that Bri gave him left no need for words. Bri stared off into her own world and couldn't help but wonder if all her years of sacrifice were even worth it. Although she understood and respected the code of the streets, in the same breath, she knew that people, places, and things would ultimately decide her man's fate. This reality brought tears to her eyes because she was almost certain that dealings with people like Steel would bring death or a very long time in the penitentiary. Neither of the two burdens could she bear. She wasn't built for those types of obstacles anymore.

"What happened now, ma? Why are you cryin'?"

Bri wanted to express her rage so badly, not caring how it came out. She wanted her words to be harsh. She felt like Quron needed to hurt at that moment, because she too was hurting. But instead of going that route, she decided that it was best to use diplomacy. Diplomacy always brought forth a better outcome when it came to dealing with Quron. She paused for a few seconds and arranged her thoughts within. She knew that she couldn't let what she was feeling ride. That would have been counterproductive for her and her sanity. She had to get her point across, but she did not want to offend Steel during the process of doing so. Bri didn't really like him, for her own private reasons. But at the end of the day, she did respect him, because for as long as she had known him, he had always been loyal to Quron. She finally got her approach together and responded, trying to control her voice tone.

"What happened, what happened? Are you freaking serious? What happened is the question you should be asking yourself. You are so selfish and self-centered. You haven't been home for a week and you are already jeopardizing your freedom and our union."

Quron was lost. He couldn't pin point the reason she was bugging.

"You are so full of it. Everything you said while you were locked up is going out the window. Quron, God knows that what I am saying is true, and I love you with all my heart, but please hear me out when I say this. I cannot, I repeat, I cannot go through the years of suffering again. I love you, but I ain't built for that shit. The harassment, perverted ass police flirting, always trying to get my cooch, the women officers feeling me up on the low, all the inhumane nonsense, Quron. I just can't do it, I just can't."

Bri wore her emotions on her face. Not from sweat, but from the pain that was oozing out of her eyelids. It was painful to see her like that, especially when the pain was caused by him. He grabbed her hand and squeezed tightly as she continued to drive.

"Ma, you know that the last thing I wanna do is bring confusion or any type of pain into your life. I don't have a response to what you said, because there is nothing to say, right is right. But I don't ever want you to question my love for you. My love for you has always been unconditional. Without you, life would have been much more complex. This is why it is extremely important for you to understand that for every strong man, along his side is a stronger woman. Where I'm weak, you are strong, that's why I need you by my side. Please stop crying. You gotta stop stressing and believe in my judgment. You were loyal to me when I went away, and I made you promises. I don't know about other people, but my promises aren't made to be broken, and I promise that I will never leave you again. Bri, look at me."

She complied.

"I promise."

The sincerity in his voice melted her. This was the side of him that she had fallen in love with. It was the reassurance that she needed, and it placed her in a zone of comfort. The discussion ended with a passionate kiss, easing the moment with the legendary sound of Marvin Gaye's "Sexual Healing." Now that the tension had passed, the two lovebirds' mental state was together, but apart in so many ways.

They merged onto the George Washington Bridge in silence. Bri was happy because she felt that her nightmare was over. Quron, on the other hand, rode in the passenger seat with thoughts crowding his mind pertaining to the promise that he had made to his babe just moments ago. To an extent, he meant every word that had come out of his mouth. However, in the back of his mind, the fact remained that he would rather spill his blood in the streets before being confined to the environment of prison again. The thought of leaving his only true love stranded in the cold world really tugged at his soul. The temptation, along with the evil spirits, were really getting to him. This game of life isn't made easy. His eyelids became heavy, and sleep slowly over took his physical.

Quron awakened from his deep sleep. The classic album, *Reasonable Doubt* by Jay-Z was thumping through Bri's speakers. He seem to be well rested, at least that is what Bri thought until she gave him a good look and noticed the large drops of sweat covering his face. Damp stains from perspiring so much were seeping through his shirt, and immediately Bri became concerned.

"Are you okay, honey?"

Quron looked around as if he had forgotten where he was before responding. "Yeah, I'm ah-ight, ma."

The truth of the matter was that he was not in good spirits. He had awakened from the bang of a .44 magnum, along with the excruciating pain caused by the two bullets that blew baseball-sized holes through his frame. When he woke up, he thought that his life on earth had ended and the life after death had begun. Actually, it was his worst nightmare that was about to begin. He became bothered, because he couldn't accurately interpret the dream or gain a sense of direction from it. He had recently come home, and he was not involved in anything that could possibly bring him or his family hurt, harm, or danger. Growing up in the streets, along with the wisdom he had learned in Islam about dreams taught him not to overlook things like this, so he didn't. Intuition made him certain that his life was about to change. For better or for worse, remained unknown. What he did know, is that no matter what, he had to maintain. He had to hold on, hoping for the best, preparing for whatever came his way.

———————

Three months had gone by since Quron's release. Getting reacquainted with society was not as difficult as he thought it would be. His family's support helped a lot. In such little time, he had managed to secure a job at a company where he could practice some of the vocational skills that he had acquired while incarcerated. He maintained a low profile, rarely mixing with his old crowd. Young-One came through every now and then, but for the most part, they were pretty much doing their own thing and living their lives. Quron was an ill dude, he never perceived himself as being better than the brothers who had chosen to stay in the game. How could he, when they all were men that came from the same soil of poverty, the same soil of desperation? Over time, he had realized that people change, him included. They don't desire the same things that they once did.

Unfortunately, this was not true for the majority of his peers. Many of them were stagnated. After sitting back and analyzing the situation in depth, he realized that there was very little that he could do for them. Before his incarceration, he and many of his peers were joined at the hip. Newburgh's demographic was set up in a unique way, where everyone pretty much in some way had to interact with one another.

But it was rarely harmonic; drama was like the Wild Wild West. There was only one high school, and two junior highs mixed in with many individual blocks that were getting a lot of illegal money. If you were popular, it was easy to connect with the city as a whole.

Quron was well liked and moved like he owned the city. It killed him to see his people in the state that they were in, but it had come down to either them or his freedom. Instantly, he realized that most of his peers had not experienced anything similar to his trials, and because of that, he knew he had to love them from afar. Taking this into consideration, Quron didn't see a reason why he should put forth an effort to get back in the mix. Lots had changed. He accepted the fact that they had outgrown each other, and continued to live accordingly.

Chapter 10

"Redford!" A corrections officer yelled from the front of the tier. It was approximately nine o'clock in the morning and Nuri's turn had finally come. He no longer had a debt to pay to society. He could not believe it.

"Yo, C.O., I'm comin' right now. Let me holla at my man first." Nuri answered back as he walked toward his friend's cell. As he passed, other inmates that were serving hard time showed him a lot of love. They shared words of wisdom and encouraged him to make it happen out in society.

"Yo, N.O., hold ya head out there, son!" a fellow convict screamed out from the second tier.

"Fight the temptations... they are promised to come." Another brother yelled.

Now, standing directly in front of Grimy and Ty-Real's cell, the three comrades exchanged stares, not knowing exactly what to say. Ty-Real was serving life for murder, and the joy he felt was the closest he would experience to freedom. He cleared his throat before he began to speak. The real thing was much harder than what he had anticipated.

"I guess this is it, homie. We've prepared ourselves as best we could for this moment. I ain't gon' front, all the preparation that me and the fellas called ourselves doin' went right down the drain. The reality of you actually leaving, bro, is a lot harder for me to swallow. I'm happy as hell that you are finally getting your second chance. You know how it is though, it's much deeper than a bond of friendship, we family. I'ma let you know now. I'm gon' reach out every now and then, 'cause I know you gon' be doin' you, and I ain't try'na stop ya flow."

A soft chuckle escaped as a cover up of his true emotions. "Just keep it true, and be strong. Don't fuck up. From buildin' wit' you, I already know that you know your position, now all you gotta do is perfect your role. I'ma leave you with this, lil homie... always remember this experience. This was your struggle, this was ya war. You won, bro. Don't... Fuck... Up. As long as you remember this, you'll stay sharp and alive. It's a whole new world out there. You'll win. I love you, my nigga, hold it down."

"Redford!" The corrections officer yelled for the second time in an impatient voice.

Nuri's face twisted as he turned toward the officer and yelled in a hostile manner, "Hold the fuck up, I told you I'm comin'!"

The officer immediately shouted back. "Oh, you wanna act a fool because you're going home today, huh? You piece of shit! Well guess what, your buddies aren't going anywhere. They'll still be here, and I'm gonna make sure they pay for your smart ass mouth."

"Whatever, you racist cracka, suck a dick!" Nuri carried on. He knew his comrades could hold their own, and he figured that regardless of what he said to the officer, the police would still be the police. So why not tell the officer something that he had on his mind for so long now?

"Grimy, why you laughin' homie?" Nuri asked while smiling.

"Nah, these pigs are comical, but nigga you are hilarious." Grimy said as he continued to laugh, and at the same time, gasping for air. He finally caught his breath and there wasn't a hint of humor in his voice when he began. "Seriously though, all jokes aside, shit is real, N.O., point blank period. This is my second bid, so I know the crazy feelin' you are feelin' right now. I also know how easy it is for a weak minded nigga to go back out there and get caught up. The bitches, the money, the game, all are realistic temptations that you gonna face. The key word is weak minded. Homie, you ain't a weak nigga. Don't allow the temptations to make you into one. Trust me, lil brah, shit ain't as easy as you may think. I don't want you to go out there thinking shit sweet, cause it ain't. I love you like you my own, you know that. Your brother, Quron, he a special type of nigga. That man heart is gold, always wanting good for the next man. You his lil brother, so it's mandatory that he wants for you what he wants for himself. Let him guide you, but at the end of the day, you know you gotta stand on your own two. When shit gets thick, you know how to survive. Out in the world, only the wise survive. Prayer is real. Pray to be amongst those that will survive. Give me some love, and go rep the right way." He smiled.

Grimy and Ty-Real put their hands out through the double bunk cell bars. Nuri gave both of his friends brotherly hugs. After moments of silence, they broke their embrace, looked at each other, and placed their right fist over their hearts and pledged allegiance to the flag of blood, struggle, and true brotherhood.

"I'ma holla!" Nuri shouted in a loud enthusiastic voice as he walked off the tier, passing the heated officer sitting inside the police bubble.

The escort officer climbed the staircase two steps at a time, nearly crashing into Nuri, who was hurrying down the steps. Both Nuri and the officer were startled from the sudden appearance of the other. After a brief stare down, the officer realized that Nuri was the face he had been looking for.

He calmed down before he addressed Nuri as they walked down the hallway toward the front of Green Haven Correction Facility. "Redford, you are acting like you don't wanna leave," The officer laughed before continuing. "You might as well stay, because you'll probably be back before we get a chance to realize you were released."

Nuri looked at him like he was mentally ill or had really lost his damn mind. "You really got me fucked up. I ain't the average dude, runnin' around here like a chicken wit' his head cut off. You must be out of your fuckin' mind if you think I'm gon' ever live anotha day behind these walls. Believe me when I tell you that I'm the illest nigga you'll ever be around. You should be payin' homage instead of talkin' that bullshit. I'll die in the streets before I come back. Just for the record, death is the only thing I was promised when I was born, and I'll embrace it like a true 'G' muthafucka, so spare me all the extra psychological bullshit and let me go about my business."

The escort officer was stunned. He didn't know how to respond to Nuri's hostility. That was not his first time saying something like that to a convict that was scheduled for release. But it was the very first time he had ever witnessed an outburst like the one Nuri demonstrated. Sadly, what the escort officer expressed is not farfetched. Too often, prison doors revolve, recycling a large percentage of men who had previously been incarcerated. With this fact standing, the officer really did not see any harm in stating the obvious. With a bewildered and offended look on his face, the officer addressed the elderly woman that was working behind the office desk.

"Mrs. White, can you help this young man by gathering his personal property and filing any necessary paperwork that is required for an inmate who is being discharged?"

"Sure." The elderly clerk answered.

Fifteen minutes later, the elderly clerk reappeared from the back office. Nuri accepted his property, signed a few forms, and walked through the red doors that read EXIT in big white letters. He didn't say a single word to the officer or the elderly woman; freedom was the only thing on his mind.

The month of September brought a cool autumn breeze. This season was Nuri's favorite. He loved to style in all the designer wear, and it seemed that in the world of fashion, the clothing racks were most impressive during this time of the year.

Nuri stood outside of the forty-foot high stone wall, holding his photo albums and mail in one hand, with his New

York clothing that was sent out by his brother draped over his shoulder. Across the parking lot stood Quron, leaning against Bri's Acura, playing 50 Cent's "Many Men." He didn't want to spoil his brother's moment, so he looked on with patience, loving the fact that finally after a decade, they were both free.

Nuri bent over and placed all of his personal items on the sidewalk. To the casual observer, it appeared that he was in a trance, but in his mind, he was just feeling really good about what life had to offer at that moment. He inhaled a deep breath, blew a kiss in the air, and thought about what he had told the corrections officer earlier, *I would die before I come back here.* The thought played repeatedly in his mind. He looked around and realized that his big bro, Quron, had been watching him from a distance the entire time.

"What up, my nigga!" He shouted with enthusiasm while walking toward his brother.

"Ain't nothin', baby boy, just praising Allah for letting us finally be here. It's our time, daddy. We prayed for this chance. This is the opportunity we dreamed of having." Quron paused, and then looked his younger brother directly in his eyes. The excitement left his voice as he spoke with seriousness. "Now that we are here, what are we goin' to do?"

Nuri heard the question that his brother asked him, but he didn't like the way it sounded. To him, it sounded like a question asked out of desperation, and that really bothered him. Nuri hugged his brother and held him tight. "I don't know, homie, we'll put it down some way. You know how we give it up. I'm really not worried."

"Honestly, I ain't really worried either. This little gig I got is makin' ends meet, but you know how it go. A nigga is used to a certain way of living. Its gon' take some time to get used to this new way. It's going to take some time to get my bread up too, but when my bread get right, I wanna get into the real estate game, stocks, charities, etc. If we could get a few buildings in run down condition, it'll be easier to buy under the market value. Once we get 'em in that condition, we good.

That's a guaranteed profit once we fix them up. The only thing that's stoppin' me now is the startup money. It's gon' take a little longer than I planned, but what Imma do? Anyway, let's blow this joint. We'll finish this conversation later after you do whatever it is that you have planned."

Nuri sat slumped in the passenger seat of the car. The banging new song by rap star, Drake was now screaming through the speakers. The only words Nuri seem to hang onto were the lyrics, *started from the bottom now we here.* He could tell that his brother was frustrated and had reluctantly accepted the life that he was currently living. Something about Quron's demeanor told him that he was struggling with keeping the balance. Only three short months had passed, and stress had already managed to find its way into Quron's life. He clearly did not carry it well. His shoes were not as fresh as he normally preferred, his shirt was wrinkled, and his pants looked like they badly needed an iron, and that wasn't his style.

By the time they reached Newburgh Beacon Bridge, Nuri had already made up his mind. He judged by his brother, and decided that a normal life as a civilian was not for him. You only live once. Nuri was determined to live it to the fullest. He would live by the gun, and if necessary, would die by the same fate. His only obstacle was to somehow convince his brother to ride with him. From the years of being with him while in prison and witnessing Quron's transition, Nuri knew that it would not be an easy thing to do, but he was determined to win his support one way or another.

Pulling up on Lander St. behind a parked Honda Civic, the engine to Bri's car died.

"Yo, I'ma come snatch you up around ten, so go get some sleep."

Nuri gave his brother a pound and decided to accept his advice. He stepped out of the car and then leaned down. "Don't be late, nigga."

Quron smiled, and then answered back. "I'ma do you a favor and come early, 'cause Momma and them is gon' talk you to death. Don't feel bad, they got me first."

"Thanks for the heads up, home boy, but I got this. You just be on time. One."

Nuri shut the door and proceeded up the brownstone steps. Quron threw his fist up to the young hustler that was sitting on a milk crate across the street, before speeding off toward Broadway.

It was fifteen minutes after ten, and Quron had not pulled up yet. Nuri sat on the steps of the brownstone taking in the nightlife. The breeze was steady and the sidewalk traffic was heavy. It reminded him of old times, the good old days when the Southside was like 125th street. Nuri looked at all the baby faces and wondered who their parents were. Drug transactions were happening everywhere, in alleyways, behind parked cars, on the side of abandoned buildings, and in any other secluded area that the hustlers could blend into.

A platinum colored brand new Lexus GS crept through the scene. The driver, from what Nuri could see, was a very dark skinned brother with a banana shaped scar running down the left side of his face. He appeared to be heavy set and caked up. The majority of the street dealers hurried to the passenger side window once the GS came to a complete stop. The overhead night-light provided a visual of their activity. The passenger seat was reclined, so Nuri couldn't really discern the features of the second rider. He could only see the passenger's do-rag and the quick movement of his hands, collecting money in exchange for what appeared to be white chunks of rock, tightly wrapped in clear sandwich bags.

These cats must be supplyin' these little niggas. Nuri just sat and observed from across the street. He couldn't believe how reckless they were. They actually conducted business like it was legal. They were loose, moving without a care in the world. Things really had changed since Nuri was last home. "They must think shit is sweet." Nuri said to himself.

After a while, Nuri became restless and figured it would be best to cash in for the remainder of the night. As he rose to make his way back into the house, a white 760 BMW sped down the one-way street, flickering the high beams, obviously trying to attract someone's attention. Off impulse, Nuri turned toward the approaching car. The whip screeched to a halt. Immediately, Nuri recognized the driver and made his way down the brick steps.

"What up my nigga, you ready or what?" Young-One shouted, sounding happy and excited.

"Playboy, you know I'm ready."

Young-One hopped out of his Beamer and challenged Nuri's memory by greeting him with their childhood handshake. Surprisingly, Nuri tossed it up with no problem. The longtime friends gave each other a hug before jumping back into the BMW and quickly driving off. The little homies that populated the area watched from their posted positions, wondering who was the new face that received all the love from Young-One. They felt that whoever he was, he wasn't a threat to them, so the cautious thoughts faded just as quickly as they surfaced.

"I didn't think y'all was comin'." Nuri said seriously.

"Fuckin' with your brother, we almost didn't make it. Bri got that nigga on lock." Young-One mentioned with a dead serious face before bursting out laughing.

"Whatever, nigga. You know I'ma don, I run this." Quron responded with a smile.

The 760 rode smoothly under the city lights. Nuri stretched out in the back seat, enjoying the night scenery. He did not know where they were taking him, and he really didn't care. All he knew was wherever they were taking him would be ten times better than where he slept the night before.

After a while, Nuri's curiosity started influencing him to inquire about where they were headed. Just as he decided to start the questioning, the BMW made a swift turn into a nearly full parking lot. They made a few rounds before finally finding a parking space. On their way to the front entrance, they laughed and reminisced about old memories that were now a part of their history.

Inside the club was a chill atmosphere that automatically freed the mind from any stress or worry. The three friends felt mixed emotions once they entered the spot. It was beautiful. Whoever did the interior decorating knew exactly how to make the customers feel like they were celebrities, even if they weren't. Most of the time, money was not a problem. Drug dealers from all over the upstate region escaped to the Island for hours of entertainment. The walls held up beautiful portraits of professional porn stars. The exotic dancers that controlled the floor were drop dead gorgeous. Flavors were many. Black, White, Latino, Asian, Jamaican, Indian. You name it; they were there.

The tables in the club were made of marble, purposely set up to ensure a good view of the hardcore porn DVD that was in heavy rotation on the 70-inch plasma screen. Off to the left of the stage was a secluded room, hidden behind two thick silk drapes and a three hundred pound bodyguard that made sure everything ran smoothly. Above the stage, extending from the high ceilings was a beautiful fancy script, illuminated by multi-colored neon lights that read, Welcome to Player's Island.

The exotic dancers were making it their business to assure that the two new faces noticed them. Young-One was a regular at the Island. He had even established a rapport with some of the women that worked there. From time to time, he would have sexual relations with a few of them, but it was never misconstrued as anything more than a fun escapade. Those that knew him liked him a lot, mostly for his charm and his ability to convince whichever girl that he was conversing with that his concern was truly genuine. Not many people took as much interest. In that line of work, dancers were perceived to be inhuman, so his kind words of encouragement made him special.

Nuri led the pack to their seats, moving as if he owned the spot. In reality, he was just eager to get as close to the dancers on stage as he possibly could. His swagger was crazy. His fitting Tru Religion jeans over lapped the beige construction Tims that he wore. A brown Gucci belt secured his waist and a cashmere polo, knitted the same color as his boots, clung perfectly to his well-defined frame. The team eventually settled for some soft cushioned stools that were a foot away from the stage. The DJ was doing his thing on the turntables. He played every type of R&B and Hip-Hop from the east coast to the west coast. The actual song that he spun depended on the dancer that was announced to appear on the stage.

Two bad dancers were working the sliding poles with experience. Both of the gorgeous women were nude, leaving absolutely nothing to the imagination. Nuri, Quron, and Young-One looked on with lust blinding their vision. Young-One grabbed a few stacks of ones off the table, snapped the paper bank wrap, and made it rain dollar bills. The club went crazy. Fat butts and tits flocked all around them. Enough was enough. Nuri's dick was hard like a rock. Hormones raging, he turned toward Young-One.

"Yo, what up with these broads? They teasing dudes or are they wit' whatever?"

"Don't stress nothin', I gotchu homie. Ya boy got this spot on smash. I spend crazy bread in this joint. You know how we do." Young-One bragged as he made hand gestures, getting the attention of three young dancers who were huddled in a corner. They didn't know exactly who he was talking to, but they had all seen his gesture.

One of the girls pointed a finger to herself, but became disappointed when Young-One shook his head no. Another one of the strippers pointed to herself and received the same result as the first. The last amongst the three looked around and noticed that her and her girls were the only ones in the vicinity, and she was the only one left. She smiled and began to strut toward the three men that sought her attention. Looking at them, all she saw was dollar signs. *Oh, I know these niggas got bread, especially fuckin' with Young-One.* She thought.

"Damn, Ron, shorty is proper." Nuri stated.

"She ah-ight." Quron responded, hardly impressed.

Even though Quron showed little interest in the young dancer, she really was a beautiful female. Her hair dangled a little past her earlobe, cut in a style that complimented her cute face. Her breasts were bare and perky, and bounced a little as she walked. The G-string that she sported could hardly be seen from behind, because her fat cheeks took pride in hiding it. Her brown sugar colored legs were long, and her French pedicured toes relaxed in a pair of all white Gucci stilettos as they rested in front of Young-One.

He moved close and began to whisper in her ear. Judging by her change in demeanor, Quron and Nuri could see that whatever game Young-One was spitting was definitely working.

Back in the corner, the two other dancers remained huddled up, admiring Quron and Nuri as their friend kicked it with Young-One. They were very anxious to learn about the two handsome men that accompanied him.

"Them two niggas are fine, girl. The one with the beige knitted is too light for me though, but the other one could get it," The two women shared a laugh. "I dig his whole style. He got little feet too, but he look like he got a big dick. Look at that bulge in his sweats. That's my word, that nigga don't gotta pay a dime to hit this. Passion better put us on." Ice Cream stated between laughs.

"Girl, you know she peoples, she got us. Matter fact, she's heading toward VIP with the one you wasn't really feeling as we speak. That's my bitch, she don't waste no time. She about her paper." She smiled, feeling her girl, Passion. "I guess that leaves me with Young-One sexy ass. For some reason, he look different today. I think it's that red button up that he's wearing, and he's killing them Louie sneakers. Hope he know he special, because I don't even like dark skinned men, but that nigga there is fine as hell. I'll make an exception for him any day."

"Damn, Secret." The young woman giggled. "You dun spoke him up, now his horny ass is coming over here." They turned toward his direction, smiling as if they weren't just talking about him. "You know he want some pussy, horny ass. I need that bank though. All the bitches talk 'bout that tricking ass nigga. I'll have him spending his whole stash on this snatch." Ice Cream said arrogantly while pointing to her neatly shaved vagina.

"Bitch you crazy," Secret said jokingly. "Of course that nigga want some pussy. We prancing around here showing our goods, show me a nigga in here that don't want no pussy. And while you at it, you show me one bitch up in here that don't wanna give it to his fine ass." She giggled. "I definitely got time for a quickie, my set is at one. But you on the other hand, you better stop fronting. You see his fine ass friend over there waiting for you. Better go handle your business and throw some of that pussy at him." They both laughed. "I'ma be over there with Young-One, I'll see you later." Secret pointed to a secluded area behind one of the plasma TVs, indicating where she planned to be.

Ice Cream shook her head and watched her friend sway off, smiling and giggling at whatever Young-One was saying to her. She briefly entertained the thought of approaching Quron, but quickly decided against it. Her pride would not allow her to. Instead, she retreated to the costume room and prepared for her performance.

Quron sat alone, splitting his gaze between the stacks of ones in front of him, and the beautiful women that surrounded him. Their choice of occupation was degrading in a sense, but he respected their reasoning. Not all of the girls liked what they did to earn money. Some of them had valid reasons for their actions. Some danced to pay college tuitions, others danced to make ends meet in their single parent homes, and some just viewed the skill as a quick means of supporting themselves. *Can't knock the hustle.* Quron thought, as he focused on the performer that was being introduced.

"All y'all ballers out there, share some of that green with my girl, the one and only, Miss Seductive!"

The DJ gave the upcoming dancer a formal introduction, but the response from the crowd was abnormal. Quron had heard dancers being introduced all night, but none of the previous acts received recognition like this dancer. It seemed like all the hustlers in attendance made their way to the stage. Everything seemed to have stopped. Quron started to feel uncomfortable from the crowd that was closing in around him. Once the smoke cleared from the stage, and Miss Seductive appeared, he understood exactly why the crowd had reacted with such enthusiasm.

She was beautiful, to say the least. Over her face, she wore a half transparent veil that only exposed her slanted cat like eyes. Her hair was long and straightened. Gold bracelets dangled from her small wrist as she worked her hips in a sexual circular motion. Her moves resembled that of a Hawaiian dancer. There were no words to go along with her heavenly rhythm, just a beautiful instrumental. Quron was forced into a state of relaxation as he absorbed every move of the beautiful dancer. She kept smiling in his direction, but he didn't think those smiles were personally for him. There were too many men in the same vicinity to personalize her gesture. The instrumental that guided her hips, slowly faded and her performance followed. She gathered the pillow of bills that were tossed by the generous hustlers, took off her veil, and disappeared behind the stage curtains.

Quron thought his eyes were playing tricks. He didn't think he saw what his mind told him he had seen. As he rose from the stool to find Nuri and Young-One, the same 5 foot 3-

inch dime that was putting on a show moments ago on the stage swayed his way. Only this time, her costume did not include the veil. His eyes now agreed with his mind. The beautiful woman that pulled up in the pearl white Benz three months ago while he was in Harlem, was now standing within two feet of his reach. Her manicured fingers were extended, expecting a formal introduction.

Quron embraced her soft touch and smiled to help ease the awkwardness. Butterflies were forming quickly inside his stomach.

"I can't help but to think that you and I have already met." Quron said, pretending to be absentminded about their brief encounter on 145th St.

"I'm sorry, but I don't think that we have. Names, I might forget, but faces are something that I've been trained to remember, and yours does not come across as one that I've previously seen." Miss Seductive said, enjoying the role-playing.

"Anyway, as you see, everyone around here knows me as Miss Seductive. But my name is India, and yours is?"

Still clutching her little hand, Quron replied. "Mine is Quron. I'm sure many people compliment you on your beauty. I can't help but to think the same thing. And I can't seem to control this question that keeps ping ponging around in my head." His grin widened."

"Sooo, ask." Her expression was priceless. They both shared a brief laugh.

"Ok, since it's like that, what is a gorgeous woman like you doing in a place like this? I mean, I acknowledge the fact that not everyone in here like what they do to make a living, and it's not my intention to offend you or disrespect you in any way. But to keep it a hunnit, I personally feel like a lady that's as bad as you belongs in Hollywood making big moves or something. If you don't mind sharing, what's your story?"

"Aren't we nosey? My story is *my* story, and it is on a need to know basis."

Quron chuckled and held up both his hands. "Don't shoot, ma. I'm just making conversation."

Quron was really feeling India's vibe. She was gorgeous and intellectually inclined. The pair continued to converse about a variety of topics, not once coming onto each other sexually. If it wasn't for his girl, Bri, he probably would have tried his hand. Fortunately, Bri was the love of his life. How she rode with him while he was incarcerated was the primary thing that reassured him that he could not take on a more serious approach. He was loyal. Bri was the one.

The club scene was still popping. The DJ was spinning hit records, and the dancers were enjoying the attention from the hustlers. They were in a zone, intoxicated by all of the ass and pussy that floated around freely. Nuri was still missing in action, caught up between orgasms, while Secret took pride in entertaining Young-One.

Not everyone in attendance was having that same intimate fun. Laying low in the back of the club, were two men who were both dressed in dark colored clothing. Their presence didn't arouse suspicion. They seemed to be enjoying the fun activities that occurred in a strip club, just like everyone else. However, their presence was business related. They had thrown bills at the dancers all night, but now they were focused. They patiently waited for an opportunity to surface. Timing was everything.

Meanwhile, across the club, India and Quron were carrying on like old friends. "So India, what are you, anyway?" Quron asked.

India laughed. "Silly, what do you mean, 'what am I'? I'm human, just like you." India giggled at her own sarcasm, knowing exactly what he meant.

"Very funny, ha ha ha. You know what I mean. What's your nationality?" As soon as the words left his mouth, his mind began to roam. *This girl has a great personality. I wish we could be cool without becoming intimate. But I ain't even gonna front to myself. Being around her on the regular without touchin' that thang is torture; I ain't built for those games.*

"I'm a mixed breed. My mother is Indian and my father is Columbian."

Quron's eyes traveled quickly over India's short frame, and then he smiled at the sight of his approaching comrade. Young-One put up two thumbs, showing his approval. Quron shifted his attention back to India. Physically, he was present, but mentally, his thoughts continued to roam. He could not believe how fate had operated. It was bugging him out. He believed that everything happens for a reason. He just couldn't figure out the reason behind him and India coming across each other months ago, and eventually reconnecting in a strip club of all places.

The sound of his name brought him back to the present.

"Are you listening to me?" India asked with a giggle.

"Of course I am." Quron lied, peering over her shoulder. The dramatic change in Young-One's facial expression had piqued his interest. His eyes had turned cold and his pace quickened.

India became irritated by the fact that she was no longer receiving Quron's undivided attention.

Quron couldn't make out what Young-One was screaming. It wasn't until he saw him back out his nickel-plated Beretta that danger registered in his mind. Wasting not a second, Quron quickly spun around, just in time to see two men parting the crowd with their guns drawn. One of the armed men was tall and slim, while the other stood average height with a medium build. Both were packing large calibers and moving swiftly.

"Oh shit!" Quron yelled as he pulled India and ducked low to the ground. He tried to use his speed to escape the vulnerable position that he was in, but as he turned to run, the roar from the .357 magnum took over his plans. An unbearable burning sensation settled in his body.

The loud sound from the Smith &Wesson startled Nuri. He shook as if he had been hit with the bullets. Nuri slid out of Passion's fat, warm, pussy and stumbled to pull up his pants. He recognized that sound anywhere, and it bothered him that he didn't know what was going on, or where his brothers were. All he could think about was Quron and Young-One. Left with no choice, he cautiously crept through the drapes. As soon as he stepped through, five more shots rang out in rapid succession. The first thing Nuri saw was his comrade, Young-One, rise up from the side of the stage and let loose.

"FUCK!" He knew it was on. His heart pounded from the unknown. *Where's Quron?*

The scene was hectic. Strippers were everywhere, running around naked, screaming, and fearing for their lives. Nuri's heartbeat sped up even more when his brother's face didn't appear in the crowd. At that moment, he cursed himself for not being strapped. Even though he had just come home, he knew that the rules of the game could not be compromised. He had underestimated the possibility of retaliation for their sins of the past. Now he was feeling helpless, and between a rock and a hard place, living with regrets.

Quron staggered to the back of the club. India stood by his side, acting as his crutch, and doing her best to support the nearly dead weight that draped over her body. Nuri spotted them and instantly recognized his brother's bloody sweats. He took off running in Quron's direction, not even pausing when a bullet grazed his ear.

"Ahh fuck!" Nuri shouted, grabbing the side of his face.

The graze hardly affected him. His adrenaline was rushing and he kept his stride, feeling like his brother's life depended on him. Finally reaching India, he noticed that she was feeble and crying hysterically.

"Please help me, please help!" India cried out in desperation.

"Stop crying and help us get the fuck outta here. You work here, right? Where's another exit?" Nuri demanded.

"It's right over there." India pointed to the doors that were next to the speakers.

"You got a car?"

"Yeah, it's right outside of that door." India answered.

"Go get it and keep it running. Open the back door and sit in the passenger seat. I'm driving."

India wanted to object, but his blank expression made her obediently comply.

"N.O., don't let me die like this, don't let me die, bro'." Quron whispered.

Holding his brother in his arms against a wall, rocking back and forth, Nuri felt scared for the first time in a long time. He didn't know where his brother was hit, but he knew that he had to hurry, because Quron was drenched in his own blood.

The confusion and the screams remained in the background, but the gunshots had stopped. Nuri turned and saw Young-One rushing to his side. The sight of his comrade fighting death hurt like hell.

With tears in his eyes, Young-One spoke. "What the fuck, homie... nah, not my nigga."

Quron lay in Nuri's arms, almost unconscious.

"Help me snatch him up, and let's get him to a hospital. The coast is clear, right?" Nuri asked.

"We good, I banged out with them niggas until they got the fuck outta here." Young-One responded with tears running from his eyes. Guilt flowed through his whole body. "Come on, big homie, work with me."

It took all of Quron's energy to cooperate with Nuri and Young-One.

The white Benz was running and ready. India had done exactly what she was told to do. Quickly, they piled in the Benz. India sat in the back seat, catering to Quron. He was sprawled out across her lap. Blood was everywhere; clots seeped from his mouth. She kept him awake with jokes and encouraging words.

Young-One hopped in his Beamer and trailed them.

"Hurry papi, we are losing him." Tears were now rushing down India's face nonstop.

Quron's head was elevated in India's lap. Things seemed to be moving in slow motion as he flashed in and out of consciousness. The sound of screeching tires filled the air. That was the last thing Quron heard before total darkness overcame him.

Chapter 11

A small puddle of water formed on the glass nightstand from the tears that constantly fell from Bri's eyes. At 2:30 in the morning, the ringing phone had disturbed her sleep. The gut feeling that she had, told her that she would not like the news that she was about to receive. She tried to convince herself otherwise while staring at the digital clock, wondering who would be calling at that time of night. After the fifth or sixth ring, she reluctantly picked up the cordless phone. She inhaled deeply, exhaled slowly, before she decided to speak.

"Hello." She answered in a tired voice that was filled with anxiety. The caller's words stumbled over each other, making it extremely difficult for her to understand what they were saying. All she knew was that the caller was a male and he was eager to convey a message.

"Hold up, please calm down so I can understand what you are saying."

The caller took a deep breath. "My fault Bri, this is Young-One."

"Young-One, I thought I told you not to call my house, especially not at this time of the night!" Bri interrupted.

"Yeah I know, but I ain't have no choice. I'm callin' to tell you that Quron was shot."

A loud thud vibrated through the phone as it came in contact with the thick carpet. Bri's sobs could be heard through the phone's receiver. Young-One felt that he had messed up his responsibility to keep everyone safe. Now, his right hand man was in the operating room, in a battle for his life. He really felt that he had let his boy down. He knew that it was a rough time for them all, but he really needed Bri to pull herself together because her role was very important.

With this in mind, he patiently waited, hoping she would pick up the phone from the floor sooner than later.

After a few long minutes of silence, Bri decided to pick up the phone with the intent to find out more about Quron's condition and his whereabouts.

"Young-One, are you still there?" Bri asked, still sniffling.

"Yeah, I'm here. Listen, Bri, we need you right now. We dropped Ron off at St. Luke's Hospital a little while ago. The only thing is, Nuri had to breeze and I had to disappear before the questioning started. No one is there to look after him. You gotta hurry up and get down there. The jakes gonna be there real soon with a list of questions, and you gotta hold it down. Tell'em that y'all was strollin' through the hood and a car drove by, and then all of a sudden, you heard loud gunshots. The next thing you knew, Quron was on the ground bleedin' and shakin'. Call me when they leave and let me know what's what. If they keep try'na pressure you to tell them more, just tell 'em that that's all you know, ah-ight?"

"Yeah, I got you."

"Just take it easy, everything is gonna be ah-ight." Young-One assured before ending their conversation.

Bri hung up the phone and rushed to gather her things. She left her new apartment in shambles. After Quron came home from prison, she moved into an apartment that was near the high school, Newburgh Free Academy. Everything was good for them until this point. All she could think of was the promise that Quron made when they were on their way back from Harlem. Now, within a blink of the eye, it seemed like her biggest fear was on the verge of becoming a reality. She cried for the whole ride to the hospital, feeling like her life was over.

"Tay, you ain't gonna believe this shit that I'm about to tell you. That call that I just got was about the hit. Them fuckin dudes missed the target. They said some nigga that she was talking to played captain save a hoe. They even think the lame ass nigga took a few slugs for the bitch. I hope the stupid ass nigga end up in the obituary section if he got hit. That will teach him to mind his business."

"So why didn't they off both of them?" Tay asked as if it was a no brainer. She was pacing back and forth, trying to understand what had gone wrong in their plot.

"They said they ain't really have a chance because some other kid backed out and started dumpin' at them. They think them dudes was together, now ain't that some shit? Just talkin' about it is making me heated. Matter fact, pass me that blunt of Branson and see if we got any more of that Rosé. If not, there's some Henny in the fridge."

"Scar, that's crazy. Shorty got like nine lives for real." Tay said, while pouring two shots of Henny. She sat at the bar overlooking Mount St. Mary's college campus. Chadwick Gardens was a housing complex across the street from the college. Certain apartments within the complex provided a clear view of the campus. Tay was glad that she and Scar were able to secure one of those particular apartments. She often found peace on the balcony. Watching the young men and women on campus made her wonder where she went wrong. Her mind always painted a picture of Trey as an answer to her question.

Trey was Scar's only brother and Tay's only lover before he was murdered five years ago. That was the turning point in her life. Trey was the only dude that she had ever been with. The only man she had ever loved besides her father. Before Trey, she found herself to be only sexually attracted to women. Through his persistence, he gradually earned her heart. After his death, she felt no other man could replace her Trey. So instead of trying to meet someone like him, which in her mind was slim to none, she chose to revert to her first love, women.

Trey's death left a big void in his brother, Scar's drug organization. Trust was the issue. Trey was the overseer of everything. When Trey died, Scar didn't have anyone that was qualified for a position that entailed so much. None of his runners had proven their loyalty to the point that it wasn't questionable, but Tay on the other hand, had proven that she was loyal. On many occasions, Tay had unknowingly been put to the test while Trey was alive. She had passed every single time, and that was impressive to Scar. That's what influenced him to put her under his wing. It started out slow, and he had to school her to some of the rules of the game, but not many. Tay was a natural, and over time, he had molded her into the chameleon that everyone had grown to know.

After moments of deep thought, Tay got up and walked around the bar. She stood in front of the sliding glass doors that led to the balcony. With her back turned toward Scar, she inhaled the thick smoke of haze.

"I just can't seem to understand this shit. Things are not makin' sense. Now Niggas pop up out of nowhere and take a slug for a bitch. Ain't no pussy I fuck that good," Tay said, enjoying the hard laugh from her high. She passed the blunt and sat down. "On some real shit though, I don't know who them niggas are, but we definitely gotta find out. I ain't gon' wait around for them to get the drop on us. If they a threat, then we gonna set the tone, straight like that. There is no other way around it."

Scar stood from his seated position and started pacing back and forth, as he expressed himself. "Yeah, I see ya point. If one of them boys was gettin' busy like they said, then them boys can definitely be a potential problem. I'ma holla at a few of my people and see what info they can come up wit'. In the meantime, let's stick to the script. Right now, we got like two bricks left. We gonna cook one and leave the other one raw. The game don't stop, as long as our money right. Fuck everything else, we ready for war. So fuck it, don't get all stressed. Whatever happens, happens. Ya hear me?"

Quron laid on his back, squinting from the irritation caused by the fluorescent lights of the hospital room. No one knew that he had awakened. It had been two days since the shooting incident initially transpired. The emergency surgery that he had undergone was a success. One of the.357 slugs that entered his back ruptured a kidney, damaging it beyond repair, which ultimately led to its removal. The second bullet traveled straight through his thigh, damaging some ligaments in that area. His limbs had only showed life once since the anesthesia wore off, and that was briefly. Since then, he had remained unconscious. Although his family never voiced aloud what they were feeling or thinking, it had become obvious through their actions that they felt death was closer than it should have been.

After blinking a few more times, Quron's eyes adjusted to the lights and his vision gradually became clear. Not recognizing his surroundings, he made an attempt to move, but instantly reconsidered because of the deep soreness that he felt. Tubes flowed from every orifice in his body. The agonizing pain forced a weak grunt that grasped Bri and Nuri's attention.

"Oh God, my baby is awake," Bri clasped her hands around her mouth and nose as her eyes filled with tears. "Thank you Lord, thank you so much!" Bri shouted.

Nuri calmly walked over to his brother's bedside. For the past two days, he and Bri had occupied their time with old memories from their childhood. Nuri had always liked Bri more than the other females that had traveled in and out of his brother's life. She had made it obvious that she had Quron's best interest at heart long before they ever entertained the thought of being an item. That alone separated her from all of the others.

Nuri looked down at his brother and a smile formed across his face. Anyone who knew him could tell that his facial expression was forced. The drama at hand began to clutter his thoughts. It was weighing heavily on his mind. There were way too many questions without one single answer. He knew that he could not prepare for a situation that he knew nothing about. His only connect was his comrades, Young-One and Steel, and he hoped that they would produce some beneficial information from their contacts on the streets.

Nuri made a sincere effort to hide his worry and frustration, but his brother saw straight through the mask that he was wearing. Quron wished to inquire about the situation, because his brother's facial expression showed that something was bothering him. When he tried to speak, he was cut off.

"Bro, don't worry yourself. Everything is good, just get your rest and get well soon." Nuri said then looked at Bri and asked her to make a quick run to the McDonalds that was on Broadway.

"No problem, just text me your order." She kissed Quron before leaving the room. Visiting hours were almost over, so Bri made a mental note to hurry.

Five minutes later, three huge men entered the hospital room unannounced. Nuri immediately hopped out of his chair with his black colt.45 tightly gripped in his palm. Clicking from each gun present echoed within the hospital room. Two of the three Hispanic men were just as quick to draw. The sound of metal colliding with the tiled floor lingered in the air.

"UGHH," Quron grimaced. Out of fear, Quron had used all of his strength to turn his bed over.

Nuri took a quick glance at his brother lying on the floor in pain, but his focus was on the strangers who had pistols aimed at him. At first, Nuri hadn't noticed India standing in the middle of the three men. It wasn't until she stepped forward that he recognized her face as the girl who had helped him in the club. Her presence made him feel a little better, but things still did not make sense, and he definitely was not putting down his hammer until he had an explanation.

One of the men stood on India's side with both of his hands up in the air, showing that he was not strapped. Nuri's facial expression remained stale. He was not impressed by his effort to gain his trust. Keeping his hands high where Nuri could see them, he started to speak in a Spanish dialect.

"Mi amigo, nosotros estamos aqui por problema, pero estamos aqui por la paz."

"Yo no entiendo muthafucka." Nuri responded.

"I'm sorry." The gentleman bowed slightly. "I did not know that you do not understand my language. What I initially said was, my friend, we are not here to cause problems, but we are here for peace. These two men are my bodyguards and this beautiful young lady, is my sister." He pointed at India before shifting his gaze toward his men. "Tito and Flaco, it's cool, put your guns away." Nodding, he shifted his focus back to Nuri. "I am aware of the incident that happened the other night. It's obvious that you are aware of what took place as well. My name is Pedro." He extended his hand, only to be met by air. Not offended by Nuri's disrespect, he continued, "I'm here to show my respect and appreciation to the man who risked his life to save my sister's life."

Nuri kept his grip tight on the.45 automatic. He wore a distraught expression on his face, not wanting to believe what Pedro had just said. He took a second glance at his brother, not believing that he had actually risked his life for a woman that he didn't know. He knew that he would definitely ask about this when the time was right.

Seeing that his humble approach was not getting the positive response that he had hoped for, Pedro started to become very frustrated. "Come on, my friend. I've placed all of my cards on the table and I have ordered my men to put away their weapons, just to prove that my intentions are pure. Look how you react, you react by keeping a big black gun pointing in my face. That's not how you treat a friend." Pedro's smile was mischievous.

"I know about the murder that earned y'all ten years in prison. I know that you just came home from prison. I know that you and your brother are stand up people, and I know that prior to your arrest, you two pretty much controlled these streets. So let's forget about the past ten minutes, and let's have a sit down like civilized people. As you see, I did my homework and I find it a pleasure to be amongst you men. Just relax and allow me to reward you and your brother for what he has done. That's the only reason that I'm here, and you are making this extremely hard."

Nuri looked at Pedro for a minute longer, contemplating. *Who the fuck is this nigga?* So uneasy and desperate to know who this stranger was, Nuri reluctantly tucked his .45 inside his waistline. He did not like the fact that he had never seen Pedro a day in his life, but he seemed to know so much factual information about him and his brother. That alone told Nuri that he was connected. To whom, he had no clue, but it had become his mission to find out.

"Ah-ight, Pedro, you've earned my ear. Now talk about it. We don't need no introduction, you already seem to know who I am. Visiting hours are almost up, so let's make this short and to the point, if you don't mind." Nuri said, while helping Quron off the floor. He grimaced in agonizing pain.

Oh my God. India sat amongst the men with thoughts of her own. Most of the information that her brother revealed about Quron and Nuri was new to her. Their situation just added to the burden of guilt that hovered over her head. She felt that it was her responsibility to add some clarity to the situation. In her eyes, Quron deserved to know that he was not the intended target. It was fate that placed him at the wrong place during the wrong time. Although Pedro knew the reason behind all of the chaos, he would never volunteer such information out of fear of retaliation from Quron and Nuri against his baby sister. India was fully aware of this, but she felt deeply in debt. Staring at Quron from where she sat, she had made a conscious decision. She had to use caution, but she made a vow to clear her tab with the brothers once the right opportunity presented itself.

"Okay, my friend, since we are pressed for time, I'm going to make this short and simple." Pedro smiled. "Inside the briefcase, there are three kilos of pure cocaine." Pedro cut his sentence short and asked Tito and Flaco to watch the room door to assure that no one would join them unexpectedly. Once they complied, he popped open the briefcase to add emphasis to what he was about to say.

"This, my friend, is yours, free of charge. You placed your lives on the line to save a loved one of mine. The second you did that was the moment we became family. Please don't feel like you have to accept this gift of appreciation, because you don't. I understand that you recently came home and you may not want in on this lifestyle anymore, which is fine. But if you choose not to accept, I can arrange to show my appreciation in another way. Here's my card. This number is a direct phone line to me. Don't hesitate to give me a call." He extended his hand, card resting between his index and middle finger. This time, Nuri didn't hesitate to accept. "Oh, one more thing, like I said... we are like family, which means we can have a lot of fun together. You are welcome in my home on Long Island and you are welcome in my household in Columbia, but my friend, with all due respect my sister over there," he pointed to India, "no matter what, she is never available. She's always off limits. Please don't ever cross that line. Not now, not ever, tu comprende? Gentlemen, it was nice meeting you two, don't be strangers. I would take it personal if you chose to be. Hope to hear from you soon."

Pedro stood up from his chair and Nuri did the same. The two met in the middle of the room to shake hands like men. Nuri knew that there was no turning back. Pedro looked Nuri in the eyes and recognized the familiar features of death. It didn't intimidate him; it only made him respect him more. With nothing more to say, Pedro gave Quron a friendly nod and made his exit through the door. Tito led and Flaco followed, while India stayed close by her brother's side in between.

Moments later, Bri came rushing into the room. She was breathing hard, and appeared to have been rushing to get back.

"Who were those people that just left this room? And what is that terrible smell?" Bri inquired with a sour facial expression. The aroma of the cocaine was loud and disturbing. Bri's senses had picked up on the foreign smell immediately.

Nuri quickly picked up the briefcase and placed his free hand on her shoulder.

"Ah sis, don't worry about it, they are some old friends. They heard about what happened, so they stopped by to make sure we were ah-ight. It's getting late, give my brother some love and let's get outta here. Tomorrow is another day."

Quron was feeble, very faint, and Nuri knew that. He felt bad in a sense. He knew that Quron wanted nothing of that life, but he still made a decision that would greatly affect his family. Nuri had found his way in. He needed money, and the opportunity he was waiting for had surfaced. Bri kissed Quron with passion, while Nuri couldn't even look his older brother in his eyes. Nuri patted his thigh, kissed his forehead then left.

Only Quron and his thoughts remained. The drapes on the big hospital windows were left ajar. Being fourteen stories in the air had its benefits. The height provided a beautiful view of the clear night sky. The moon was full and its radiant light soothed Quron and helped organize the many thoughts that raced through his mind. It was written.

The devil was winning the war. No matter how hard he tried, he could not escape. The game had chosen him. With his hands placed comfortably by his side, he stared up at the full moon. He couldn't help but wonder what his future had in store. He had heard everything that Pedro said, and he wished so badly that he had been able to participate in the details of discussion, but he couldn't. What was done had already become the past.

Damn you, lil bro. You know I'm not gonna leave you hanging. Looking at the moon, his thoughts continued to travel. So much was at stake. He feared where this would take him. But no matter what, thick or thin, they stuck together. *You've caused more damage than good with this one, lil brother. More stress. Hope you know what you're doing.*

He felt his back hitting the wall with nowhere to go. Stuck between his loyalty to Allah and his loyalty to his little brother, his head was spinning. His eyes closed, and his mind finally found ease. He knew that he was in for a major challenge, and preparation was a must for him and his team if they intended to take over. The game only offered two things, all or nothing. Only one was he willing to accept. Quron let out a loud sigh. "Damn you, Nuri."

Chapter 12

Scar and Tay were making their daily rounds, collecting some of the money that was owed, and distributing the product that was purchased. Some of the hustlers around the neighborhood didn't care much for Scar. He had a foul mouth and he had developed a bad habit of not showing respect to those that were under him. It never dawned on him that the dealers he disrespected were the same individuals that held the key to his freedom.

Scar maintained the upper hand because he was the most consistent in the business. His flow of cocaine was constant, and the quality was always above average. When the city got hot, and transporting drugs from the boroughs to Newburgh became too risky, Scar still held it down. People speculated and assumed that he was purchasing his coke from Newport News, Virginia, because that's where he was originally from. But speculations are all it was, because no one really knew. In the past, attempts had been made on his life, but somehow they had been unsuccessful. Scar would always keep his cool. His retaliation was smooth, and on each occasion, he would make his move quietly.

He wasn't the type to talk about what he was going to do. Out of the blue, there would be a well thought out reaction that always seemed to leave the victim's family in mourning. Just like his business, people could only speculate and assume that it was he behind the acts of violence. Real bad boys moved in silence.

Scar's platinum colored GS drove smoothly across William Street's pavement. He had been thinking of ways to find out about the guys that had intervened during the night of the hit. He became very angry when no one out of his crew seemed to have any helpful information about what had happened. While he continued to drive and consider ways to get some feedback, Tay leaned back in the passenger seat with her Air Max's propped up on the dashboard. The combination of the strong purple haze, and Mary J. Blige had her in a zone of her own. Her green eyes hid behind a pair of Fendi shades.

Over the years, getting high had become her way of escaping her reality. She was not happy with how her life had turned out so far. In the beginning, it was all good because she was still mourning over Trey's death and wanted so badly to do anything that she thought Trey would have wanted her to do. As she matured and became more in tune with herself, the excitement of the game had faded and she had outgrown those feelings. The routine of a drug dealer had long ago started to bore her. In her eyes, it appeared that the lifestyle was repetitious and came without a challenge. She really loved Scar dearly, and she would ride with him without a question, but it was her younger sister that kept her in the game. If it weren't for their complicated situation, she would have left the game a long time ago. Their mother had overdosed on heroin when they were young children, and their father had encountered a horrible death when he got smashed by tractor-trailer while on his way to work.

That chain of events left the state of New York with no choice but to get involved. Tay and her younger sister, Kiyah, moved around from group home to group home. Finally, Tay got fed up and decided to go AWOL with the intentions of securing a better future for her and her baby sister. Now, ten years later, Kiyah was expected to be released from the system, hoping to reunite with her only sibling to live like a family. Tay knew that she only had one year to get her life in order, and she could feel the pressure.

Kiyah didn't know that Tay was doing the immoral things that she was doing just to afford her an extravagant lifestyle. Tay was twenty-five and her sister was seventeen, but their age difference didn't matter; Tay had the utmost respect for Kiyah. When the time came, she was determined to bow out gracefully and retire from the lifestyle of the streets. She hoped Scar would understand and send her along with his blessings. Her sister was her priority and she felt that he had to understand, but if he didn't, she was prepared to face whatever consequences came her way.

Scar pulled over and put on the hazard lights. He hopped out of his Lexus and ran into the store that was on the corner of William and Renwick Street. When he came back out and got into his ride, Tay lowered the music with the system's remote. Sitting up in her chair, she turned toward Scar. "You know what, while you was in the store, I was out here thinking to myself. I'm like, damn, why are we out here running around asking these dudes for information about what happened at the strip club, when we could go straight to the source ourselves? Somebody at the Island has to know somethin'. All we have to do is find out who that somebody is. Once we do that, it's a wrap. Money talks and bullshit walks, you feel me? Simple."

Scar looked at the wad of money that was in Tay's hand and smiled. He extended his hand and gave her a pound. "Baby, you the brains to this shit, and I'm the muscle. Without you, I don't know what I would do. I knew shit wouldn't stay in the dark forever, I guess it's gonna be a good day after all."

Scar adjusted his seat and put the gear in drive. He turned his head toward Tay and winked his eye before he sped off. He felt like he would finally get some answers to what had started out as a mystery.

––––––––––

It was a regular night out for the dancers in Player's Island; the lights were dim and the major players in attendance showed a lot of love toward the strippers that were hustling. They had to pay to play.

Tay and Scar decided to settle down at an empty table that was positioned next to the room that held private sessions. They were enjoying the feel of the club, and the marijuana that they had smoked a half hour prior only added to their good mood. There were a variety of dancers to choose from that night. The number of men that were present could not compare. The club's planner anticipated a big turnout, but the sudden change in the weather had caused a setback.

Scar and Tay weren't very popular at the Island. Normally, they preferred to party out of town, and had always considered the Island to be too local for them. Now that they were there having a good time, they looked forward to returning in the near future. Their faces weren't familiar to most of the girls around the club, but Scar's iced out medallion and Tay's princess cut earrings and diamond front teeth painted a clear picture that money wasn't a thing.

A beautiful dancer exited the VIP room with an expression of disgust on her face. A short man who resembled an older Bow Wow, but with bad skin, followed behind her, smiling. Tay looked at Scar, waiting for him to make a comment about the couple. She knew it was only a matter of time before he did. Surprisingly, Scar remained silent. He smiled at Tay, letting her know that he knew exactly what she was thinking.

Tay smiled back and shook her head. They knew each other like a book. Their inside joke was cut short when another stripper strutted past and almost bumped into their table. She was light skinned with a body that was preserved through healthy eating and constant exercise. Her ass was so fat, hips were wide, and her waist was small enough to make her lower body a main attraction. The older woman's breasts sagged a little from aging, but overall, she was built in all the right places. Tay laughed at her attempt to grasp their attention.

Scar peeped her game and decided to play along. Before the beautiful woman could get out of his reach, he leaned forward and grabbed her arm. She turned around with a surprised look on her face and played into her role.

"What's happenin' miss, how you doin'?" Scar asked, now holding her hand.

"I'm fine." The older woman responded with a slight southern accent.

Scar pulled her closer and she sat down on his lap. Her soft skin and her naked body instantly aroused him. But the sweet aroma that seeped through her pores really made him fantasize about what he would do to her if the opportunity presented itself. He gently kissed her earlobe and whispered, "If you don't have plans, shawty, I would like to see you later on after you get off of work."

The woman looked at Scar, trying to read his motives.

Scar giggled. "You ain't gotta look at me all cross eyed." He chuckled again. "I know this pay ya bills, but don't stress no bread, 'cause I gotchu. Shit, we got plenty of that." Scar chuckled. "If nothin' else, I respect the game. A nigga ain't lookin' fo' no hand out, all I'm lookin fo' is a good time, ya heard me?" Scar paused, lowered his thick lips to her neck and gently kissed her. "Is that too much to ask fo'?"

The cute woman looked Scar in his face; she couldn't stop blushing. She felt good to see that she had enough sway in her hips to attract a younger man.

"No, that's not too much to ask for." she responded.

"I didn't think so. Take this number and hit me up later." Scar told her while writing his info down. She took the napkin and studied it for a few seconds, making sure that his information was logged into her brain before she got back to work.

"Handsome, I'll be looking forward to seeing you later on tonight, so you should expect my call. I'm sure you'll know when it's me." She said in a seductive voice, while giggling.

"Fo' sho'." Scar replied with a satisfied grin on his face. She placed a soft kiss on his cheek and stood to her feet. In business, time is money, and it was obvious that she was not going to compromise any more of her time. She waved goodbye and switched away, making sure that her round ass sent its own message.

Got Damn. Scar shook his head.

"Yo Tay, what up?" Scar shouted with a sudden boost of energy.

"You know me. I'm always on top of my game. While you was over there puttin' your thing down, I was over here watchin' ol' girl that was tryin' to get away from duke earlier. From what I'm seein', she cool with a lot of these playas up in here. I can tell by the way she moves that she is about her business. I'ma go holla at her in a minute and see if she gonna come fuck with us.

Tay slid off and made her way over to the bar. The dancer that Tay was expecting to talk to was engaged in a conversation with another stripper. That made no difference to Tay. If anything, it only made the situation better, because what one did not know, the other one had to at least have an idea about. She kept her confidence and walked up to the two beautiful young ladies. She interrupted the feminine conversation that both of the ladies seemed to be enjoying. The facial expression that they wore showed that they didn't appreciate her bothering them.

"Pardon me, ladies," Tay smiled. "I don't mean to be rude, but I've been watching all the girls around here, and I can honestly say that you stand out the most." Tay reached into her front pocket and pulled out a knot of hundred dollar bills. Their eyes lit up as their moods changed and they suddenly became interested in what Tay had to say.

"I just want to buy a few minutes of your time, if you don't mind." Tay explained to both women, but was more so directing her offer toward the dancer that she initially planned to speak with. The two dancers looked at the stack of hundreds, then at each other, and mumbled something that must have been an inside joke. They made small talk with their eyes, giggled and followed Tay as she walked back toward the table that her and Scar shared. Once the girls sat down and became comfortable, Tay showered them with compliments through harmless conversation. She and Scar patiently waited for the right opportunity to surface before they started questioning.

After about an hour or so, the two beautiful girls were really feeling their company. Scar and Tay had increased their bankrolls by $300 apiece and they weren't spreading their legs or sucking any dick to earn it. To them, that was the best part about the whole situation. It was getting late, and the club had started settling down. The strippers that did their thing on the side after hours had already established whom they were creeping with, while everyone else sat around, enjoying the closing show.

Tay looked at her diamond-flooded watch and realized that the night was ending. She gave Scar a look that was filled with words and he knew what time it was. His moods operated like a light switch. He quickly turned off the mood to party and became very serious as Tay started her pursuit.

"Chocolate, I was hollering at one of my mans, and he told me that shit popped off up in here a few days ago. What was that about?"

"To be honest with you, Tay, I really don't know the facts about how that went down. I wasn't working that night, I only picked up bits and pieces from the girly gossip that be floating around here." Chocolate paused as if she was caught up in her thoughts, then all of a sudden, it dawned on her and she turned toward Passion and asked innocently, "Passion, weren't you working the other night when that shit went down in here?"

"When what shit went down?" Scar interrupted, acting like he did not have a clue about what was going on.

"Some crazy shit. These dudes came up in here shooting at Young-One and these two other niggas that was with him."

Scar and Tay exchanged surprised looks as Passion continued to fill them in.

"Them two dudes that was with him I never seen before. Young-One holla'd at me and told me that one of them had just came home from prison, I think his name is Nuri, but other than that I don't know what that shit was over. All I know is when those fools started shooting I got the hell out of dodge. Bullets ain't got nobody's name on them, and I be damn if I get shot or killed over some bullshit. One of my girlfriends said somebody was shot that night, I just thank God that it wasn't me. But anyway, let's move on, 'cause just thinking about that nonsense put a sour taste in my mouth. I hate that negative shit, word." She sucked her teeth and rolled her eyes.

Passion's frustration was easily noticed. They got what they came for anyway, so it was all good. Before everyone could reset the mode to a positive vibe, the dim lights of the club brightened and the music tone lowered as the DJ spoke into the microphone.

"Ladies and gentlemen, tonight was a beautiful night. We appreciate the support. Y'all travel safely and make sure y'all come back next week!"

The DJ kept the volume of the music low as individuals made their exit from the club. Some of the dancers accompanied the hustlers and their entourage, while the majority of the girls stayed behind to get themselves together. Tay, Scar, Passion, and Chocolate all stood to their feet, one after the other. Tay and Scar were cool with the fact that the club was closing. Everything had gone according to plan. Tay had her back turned toward Scar as she stood face to face with Chocolate. Chocolate disliked the fact that their night had come to an end, and she felt the need to express her appreciation.

"Tay, I don't know if you know it or not, but me and my girl, Passion, had a really good time with you and your boy tonight. Y'all cool peoples for real. Hopefully, we can get up with each other in the near future. It ain't gotta be about no money shit, neither. We gonna just chill and have a good time."

Tay turned around and saw Passion giggling as she escorted Scar to the door. Scar wasn't the most handsome individual that a woman could lay eyes on, but his charm was undeniable and it always worked in his favor. Tay wrapped her arm around Chocolate's waist and followed her boy's lead.

"Don't stress it, shorty. It was our pleasure to take some pressure off you and your girl tonight. A good conversation every now and then is healthy for the mind. We definitely gonna link up tho. My homie and me enjoyed y'all company as well. Can't lose when everybody had fun, feel me? I gotta get goin', though. You be easy, and take care of yourself." Tay ran her hand through her hair and kissed her lips. "I know where to find you. That's my word, I'ma holla."

Tay slid her small hand down from Chocolate's waist and placed it on her smooth apple bottom. Her mission was complete. Once she captivated Chocolate's mind, getting what she wanted was an easy task. Tay was beautiful, with many street smarts, and she took full advantage of those blessings every chance she got. Not too many people knew that she was born a female, because her true identity was hidden underneath her manly personality and the extra baggy clothes that she wore regularly. She was known to put in work, so her ability to get violent was hardly ever questioned.

Tay pulled Chocolate close and gave her a reassuring hug. She broke their embrace, smiled, then walked calmly out of the club's doors.

Chapter 13

Quron was released from St. Luke's Hospital the day after the unexpected visit from Pedro. He couldn't really move around the way he wanted to, so he maintained a low profile at Bri's apartment. Roe Street was in the shadows of a quiet street on the outskirts of the hood. He did not feel that his life was in danger, as long as his whereabouts remained low key. The reality of not knowing who shot him tugged at his soul daily. He planned to utilize Pedro's resources to get some answers. The only thing that prevented him from requesting such a favor was his pride. He did not want to come across as an individual who always had his hand extended. Pedro would be his last resort.

On his free time, he sat at Bri's desk making calls and brainstorming while Young-One and Nuri hit the streets. The three comrades had agreed to split the product evenly. Due to the fact that Quron was injured, Young-One had taken on the responsibility of getting rid of his portion of the drugs. The cocaine was pure, just like Pedro said. They added cut to each kilo, turning each one into one and a half, giving them all an extra five hundred grams of cocaine. Things were definitely starting to look up for the team. Steel stayed by Quron's side whenever he decided to step out. Nuri told Quron to be easy and fall back, but he had become tired of being lax, especially when he felt that he could be active and contribute to the empire that he was looking forward to building.

While Bri lay asleep in the master bedroom, exhausted from a day's work at the office, Quron, Nuri, Steel, and Young-One sat comfortably on the leather sofas in the living room. On top of the coffee table were stacks of money piled up on top of each other, forming a small mountain. Quron waved his hand at Young-One, indicating that he did not want the bottle of 'Moe' that he was trying to pass him. He switched the channel to BET, raised the volume a little, and began to speak.

"What feedback are you getting from the streets about the product?"

"You see all that bread? They lovin' this shit. It's crazy 'cause we cut it, and they still comin' through nonstop, so imagine if we would have left it how it was, shit would have been gone!" Young-One responded to Quron's question with obvious enthusiasm.

"Playboy, you have a point. But we are in this game for one reason, and one reason only. That reason is to make money, just in case you forgot." Quron chuckled sarcastically. "If we can step on the product and still maintain the quality of the coke, then why not do so? This is only temporary for me. I'm not making this into a career. As soon as I reach my quota, I'm out, 'cause none of this nonsense lasts forever. I've accepted my fate and I'ma play my position in the team. When I'm gone, there ain't no coming back. Where I'm trying to go, the game can't take me, so stack your bread and prepare for whatever is ahead." Quron explained as he stared at the stacks on the table.

Everyone was enjoying the music coming out of the TV speakers. They listened to Quron speak his piece before adding on.

"You right bro, this game don't promise longevity, but fuck it, we dealing with reality. I'ma ride wit' you and support whatever it is that you choose to do, whenever the time comes. But right now, we all need to stay focused on this operation, 'cause shit ain't sweet. Yeah, we held shit down in the past, and niggas know what caliber of dudes we are, but a lot of our memory on that level has faded to black. There's a whole different breed of thugs out here that don't give a fuck about you, me, or what we stand for. I don't mean no disrespect by this, but I can tell that those years behind bars has you a little shaken up, which is normal, but bro, you know the rules to the game, and they can't be compromised. We gotta be wise and we gotta play for keeps. There is no other way around it. You already got hit. That won't happen again under my watch. And when word get back bout the fuckers that did it, I don't think I gotta share my thoughts on that. Them niggas graves being dug as we speak.

"Let's focus on this business at hand, and whenever that time comes for us to leave the game, we will make the transition accordingly. But until then, we living for today, and tomorrow don't exist until we get there, ya dig." Nuri finished saying what he had to say and leaned back on the couch cushions. He looked at his brother, expecting him to respond, but Quron said nothing.

Instead, he leaned forward and grabbed one of the stacks that was tightly wrapped in rubber bands. The smell of dirty money always gave him a rush. He inhaled the aroma of the streets before placing the stack back with the others. He turned toward Young-One. "How much money is that all together?"

Young-One slightly tilted his head toward the ceiling, wearing an expression that showed he was thinking about the question before actually answering. "Before we came over here, me and Nuri counted damn near a hundred and thirty thousand. We gave six hundred to shorty that owns the apartment that we used, that left us with a hundred and twenty-nine on the dot, and we still got half a brick left."

"So, what you sold it for like thirty dollars a gram?"

"Nah, they went for like $900 an ounce, so that's like thirty-two and a half per gram."

"What other hustlers selling their ounces for?"

"Like a stack, some niggas eleven hunite. Prices high like a muthafucka."

"Oh boy, we about to smash the market. I spoke to Pedro earlier, and he said that he hopes we liked our gifts. He also said to give him a call soon, and he would make it worth our while. I'ma holla at son tomorrow and see what he talkin' bout. If he got three bricks to give away for free, then he has to have a hundred more that he is willing to give away for a little to nothing. I'ma try to get 'em for like ten apiece. If he bite, it's a wrap; we got the city. A lot of dudes gonna be upset. We definitely gotta get our guns right, 'cause when everything hit the fan, there won't be no room for talking. Gun talk will be the only means of communication, squeeze first and ask questions last."

"I'm already prepared, Ron, 'cause I know what it is. Niggas seen me spinnin' the hood wit' Young, and automatically started puttin' two and two together. Remember Fat-Roc from back in the day?"

Quron looked at Nuri and shook his head no.

"Homie, you gotta remember son. He went to North High with us. He got expelled and the authorities sent him to D.F.Y when our gym teacher searched his book bag and found that chrome.380."

"Ah-ight, I remember son now."

"From what I'm hearing, after he came back from that juvenile bid, he never looked back. He got from Dubois and First Street all the way down to Dubois and Broadway on smash. You know all that up there is a gold mine. Everybody out there is scrambling for him. I personally don't give a fuck about him, but son do get busy, and apparently, he is strong. So all I'm sayin' is, when we decide to touch his territory, we gotta come correct. He already asked Young was you gettin' back in the game. Young told him no, but you already know where that question stemmed from. I ain't gonna say he scared, but niggas is definitely on point. We gotta be low and move with perfection whenever we strike—"

Young-One interrupted before Nuri could finish. "Yeah, Ron, Nuri right, dudes are conscious of you being back on the streets. Fat-Roc ain't the only one that asked about you. But like Nuri said, I don't think it's out of fear. I think the questions are more so out of nosiness, they try'na figure out how you thinkin'." Young-One stated with a slur.

"Young, don't even stress it. let them think whatever they wanna think, keep feeding them what they wanna hear. Check it, I gave it some thought, and I'm thinking this how we gonna do it. Everybody know us for selling weight around the hood. Being that we are going to have the purest coke out here, we gonna flip the game by going back to how we started." Quron looked at Nuri and Young-One, shaking his head up and down while he continued to share the game plan. "That's right my brothas... grindin', pitchin' hand to hand on the blocks. It would be far more profitable if we could maintain quick flips, and it would be safer for all of us. If we happen to get caught up, then what's the worst case scenario, a sealed indictment or a buy and bust? With the new drug laws in effect, we'll be good, the courts will have mercy on us, and we will see the streets again.

"On the other hand, if we fall into an investigation and one of these niggas out here turn state while copping bricks from us, we finished. Taking over is the only major task at hand. Niggas ain't gonna just submit and lay down, we know that. The streets is a lot of dude's bread and meat. Anytime you try to come between that, it's gonna be some bloodshed, so we gotta stay on top of our gun game. No games, no exceptions, no pardons, understand?" Their silence confirmed that they knew exactly what Quron meant. "The head is the strongest part of the body. Without it, the body dies. If we gonna put the town under our wing, then that's what must be done. We gotta find the street governors and make it happen, I'm sure ya'll get the point."

Young-One stood up and saluted Quron as he staggered toward the door. Nuri decided to follow.

"Ah-ight bro, I'ma holla. No more needs to be said. We already know what must be done. Get at me whenever you make that move. Give Pedro my regards, and stay away from his sister. I seen how you was looking at shorty. We don't need that drama. I see the seriousness in his eyes when he spoke about her. There's more to that bitch than we know, I'm telling you."

Smiling, Quron stared at his brother. "Why she gotta be a bitch though, bro?"

"Oh nigga, you feeling that chick, huh?" Nuri smiled. "And yeah, that reminds me... since when do we risk our lives and start taking bullets for strangers, a broad at that, my nigga? Have you lost your damn mind?"

Quron giggled with a confused look on his face. "I know it may have appeared that way, but that's the furthest thing from the truth, believe it or not. It was actually a spontaneous reaction. Once I seen them guns blazing, I grabbed the nearest thing to me with the intention of using whoever it was as a shield. It just so happened to be India, and I just so happened to still get hit. In a weird type of way, I guess it was meant. What can I say? I unwillingly took one for the team. I'm alive, and we are on top of our game. At the end of the day, I could live with that."

Nuri held the entrance door open and laughed sarcastically. "Yeah, yeah, yeah, I guess you could save that story for somebody that's try'na hear it. I'ma put my helmet on to protect myself from getting beat in the head."

The two brothers shared a laugh while carrying on.

"Nah bro, I'm serious. That's how that thing went down."

"Ah-ight, whatever. I'ma holla though. Me and Young-One got some pussy lined up across town in the heights, so be safe and keep Steel by your side. You know he gonna always hold you down. Make sure you put that money up. I love you my nigga, one."

Nuri closed the door behind him and descended the stairs with the intention of joining Young-One.

Quron sat quietly on the edge of the sofa. The smile that was apparent seconds ago disappeared. His thoughts began to drift toward more serious issues. He thought of the lives he would take, thought of prison, thought of Allah, then sighed aloud. With his palms upward facing the ceiling, he took in a deep breath, and in a humble tone, he began to pray.

"Oh Allah, I come to you seeking your forgiveness during these trying times. I am slowly, but surely, deviating from your righteous path. Please have mercy on me, my brother, and those whom I love. Help me maintain the balance as I walk amongst the shadows of death, and show me the way back into your correct way. Indeed, you are most merciful, thank you my heavenly father, Ameen."

A cherry red stretch Chrysler 300 pulled up to the entrance gates of Pedro's estate in Queens. Quron relaxed patiently as he enjoyed the smooth jazz that was playing through the customized audio system. The luxury transportation was courtesy of Pedro. Quron had spoken with Pedro earlier that morning, and Pedro had assured him that he would see to it that he traveled safely. He wasn't surprised when he received the call informing him that his ride was outside of his house on Lander Street.

There were a variety of entertaining things inside to choose from. With the Ps3 and X-box at his disposal, the choice seemed easy, however, his mind and body was consumed by the classical jazz and R&B that filled the air. With no one near to keep him company, Quron's gaze settled on the scenery outside. Then his eyes closed and his plan continued to circulate in his mind.

An hour and fifteen minutes later, Quron's eyes fluttered open from his nap. He yawned. "Musta been tired. Don t even remember dozing off." he said. He looked around and realized that they had arrived. Running his hand over his face, a sudden boost of energy shot through him.

He looked forward to the business meeting that he had scheduled with Pedro. The chauffeur spoke briefly into the intercom. Seconds later, the electronically operated gate slid from one side to the other, inviting the stretch Chrysler into

Pedro's privacy. The driver navigated through the wooded area until an open space appeared suddenly. Pedro stood dressed in casual clothing, expecting his guest's arrival. Standing on his shoulders was a beautiful parrot, just staring at his company. The limo stopped, and the doors opened shortly after.

"Mi amigo, how are you? I hope you enjoyed the ride!" Pedro shouted in an excited voice, showing his genuine concern.

"Under the circumstances, I can't complain. I definitely appreciate the ride down here. It gave me some time to really organize my thoughts." Quron admitted with a smile as he shook Pedro's hand for the first time.

"I see that you know a little something about fashion, huh?" Pedro stepped back and acknowledged Quron's fine attire.

"I guess you could say that." Quron replied modestly then chuckled lightly.

Quron was dipped, and definitely dressed for the occasion. It was the first impression, and he wanted to make sure that he got his point across. To him, life was similar to the game of chess; you had to stay ten steps ahead in order to dominate your opponent on the board. Everyone had ulterior motives, and everyone had a position to play. In his eyes, he was just playing his position.

Quron's broad shoulders complimented the Armani long sleeve that he sported.

His hair was braided neatly. The light tinted Gucci frames gave him the Hip-Hop executive look, and the Armani loafers fit comfortably on his feet. Every time the autumn breeze picked up, the cool air penetrated the good quality material of his Armani slacks, but he didn't mind. He was just pleased to be in Pedro's presence.

"Well, my friend, let's not stand out here any longer. I have the whole day planned out for you. First, we enjoy ourselves, then we talk business, entiende? Now c'mon and accompany me into my home," Pedro stated as he made a forward hand motion, indicating that he wanted Quron to follow him.

Complying with Pedro's gesture, Quron retrieved his miniature sized Louis Vuitton duffle bag and accompanied Pedro as they entered the large doors of his mansion.

"Wow. Pedro, your place is really nice." Quron said while stepping through the mansion's main doors. He was impressed by what he saw. The landscape outside was very clean and beautiful, but it was nothing compared to the interior of Pedro's home. Quron felt like he was walking through a magazine shoot for the Robb Report or DuPont Registry. The double-stair foyer provided scenic views of Mother Nature through a huge customized wall of two-story windows. From the twenty-foot ceiling hung a huge diamond shaped chandelier that gave off a beautiful reflection of light during the day when the sun was at its peak, and that was just the beginning.

"Yeah, this is my palace. I built it from the ground up, approximately three years ago. It's practically new. Every so often, I like to treat myself. It doesn't make any sense to have so much money then hesitate to spend some of it. In this lifestyle, anything can happen at any time, so it's only fair for us to enjoy the fruits of our labor while we still can. If anything does happen, we won't be marinating in misery. We'll be somewhat content." He paused. "Sheesh, and when we die, you can't take a penny. All the money in this world, and no matter who you are, we all die broke." He shrugged, looked at Quron and chuckled. "Essentially that's what it is."

Quron and Pedro continued to walk and talk. He was really enjoying the tour through the mansion. He looked on with admiration, and stored some of the wise words of wisdom that Pedro shared with him. Quron was nobody's fool. He knew that the past chain of events had earned him favor in the Martinez family, but something about Pedro's vibe that made him feel like their bond was unique, genuine.

The two acquaintances continued to engage in casual conversation while enjoying the amenities throughout the house. Pedro entered a room that was designed for entertaining purposes only. There was a dance pole extending from the ceiling, running down into a small platform that was connected to the wall in the corner. In the center of the wooden floor sat a built-in heated Jacuzzi, which was occupied by two gorgeous Latino women who seemed to be having a great time pampering each other. Pedro patted Quron on his shoulder and laughed at the expression that spread across his face.

"So, you like what you see, my friend?"

Quron couldn't believe he had allowed his lust to be so easily noticed. He giggled.

"Do you remember my friend, Tito? He was one of the guys that came with me to visit you while you were in the hospital. By the way, I meant to apologize for all of that chaos. It was not my intention to cause any more confusion. I understand that it's done and over with, but I never addressed it, so I wanted to clear any possible misunderstandings so there wouldn't be any hard feelings."

Quron acknowledged Pedro's words with a head nod.

Pedro turned toward a waiting Tito. "Tito, toma su boisa y lo coloca dentro de Ia banera."

Tito reached for the Louis Vuitton bag that was in Quron's hand.

Quron looked at Pedro.

"My friend, don't feel uncomfortable or disrespected. I spoke to him in Spanish because his English is not that good. He knows just enough to get by, but he prefers to be addressed in Spanish. It's okay, you can hand him your bag."

Reluctantly, he did what Pedro asked of him. Tito exited the room and Pedro continued to speak.

"You and I must build a bond of trust. I understand that everything is happening at such a fast pace, and I could only imagine that you have experienced some form of betrayal in your past. We all have, but papa, I'm not one of those lowlifes. I like your style, and I feel like you have a lot of potential. I let you into my intimacy for that very reason. I plan to help you reach your peak, but first you gotta help me help you. Good people aren't made like they were made once upon a time. That's why whenever they do surface in your life, you embrace them and cherish them because you never know when or if another one will surface again, comprende?"

Quron sat down on one of the two beach loungers that were welded into the floor.

"These two women are the cream of the crop. They are beyond beautiful, si?"

Quron smiled and nodded. "They are here for you, my friend. Choose which one you would like for your personal entertainment."

"With all due respect, Pedro, I appreciate your offer, but I can't accept. These women are gorgeous and very attractive, but to be honest with you, my mind is on something else right now."

Pedro hesitantly stood up from his seat and walked over to the two gorgeous women. He kneeled down and spoke to them in a soft tone. Seconds later, he held both of their hands as they exited the bubbling Jacuzzi. They were average height, exotic, with shapely bodies. Their petite frames dripped a trail of water as they walked with a seductive sway toward the door. One of the beautiful women was clad in a pink G-string, while the other wore the bottom half of an orange bikini set. Their breasts were firm and golden brown from the weekly use of a tanning bed. Standing at the exit door, Pedro kissed both of the young women on their cheeks before lightly patting their smooth behinds. They kissed him back simultaneously, giggled, then walked out of the large room to settle down somewhere else.

Pedro secured the door then turned around and walked back toward Quron with his arms spread apart as if he was about to embrace him. He smiled as he began to address his guest. "So, my friend, I see that you were planning to come here and get straight to the point." Pedro sat in his beach chair and leaned forward. "I personally don't feel like there is anything wrong with that. I just assumed that some sexual attention from two beautiful women would help you loosen up. I like to have fun as much any man does," Pedro said with a hearty chuckle. "But I understand your current state of mind. Since business is obviously on your mind, let us discuss the specifics of our business. How can I help you?"

Quron swung his legs over the side of the beach chair as he sat up to face Pedro. He took off his Gucci frames and placed them on the small granite table that sat between them. Both men were now sitting erect, offering their undivided attention to each other.

"That product that you gave us was pure, just like you said. I did my homework, and I know I could become the primary distributor. It's just a question of whether or not you are willing to back my operation 100%."

Pedro dropped his gaze to the wooden floor, contemplating where he should go from here.

"My friend, let's say I decide to support what you are trying to do. What, in return, could you promise me that'll make me feel that it's worth my time?"

Quron shook his head. "Financially, there probably isn't much that I could offer that would make you get excited. I mean, look around, what can I possibly give you that you don't already have? You have it all, and my little money is peanuts."

Pedro didn't know it, but Quron was lost for words. Pedro's question had caught him off guard, and he struggled to gather what he thought would be the correct thing to say. He took a deep breath and clasped his hands together, looking Pedro directly in his eyes.

"Pedro, I'ma be all the way honest with you. All I can offer is my loyalty, and I can promise you that it would be death before I bring dishonor upon this family. The morals and principles that govern my life are priceless, but are worth more than anything in this world. My word is worth more than your time and your support, no disrespect." Quron held up his hand and sighed. "I can only hope that you feel the same."

Pedro's expression remained stale. He studied the bronze toned man sitting before him; a moreno at that. But there was something about Quron. His aura was different, much different than Pedro's typical encounter. Not arrogant, yet confidence reeked. Humble, but held the eyes of a murderer. Most importantly, an earner. An earner who cherished loyalty over any dollar amount. Pedro read this all. His expression loosened. He extended his diamond studded ringed fingers. Quron held onto his serious facial expression meeting Pedro's hand with a firm grip.

"My friend, your word is all you can give to a man that has everything. I respect you and I respect your ambition. Your honesty has earned you my support. Nothing more. I don't need your money, I'm well off. You saved my sister, I don't feel in debt, but I am forever grateful. My resources say you check out. I'm gonna supply you with whatever you want. Of course, that's as long as you can move the product. All I ask is a small fee... never betray me. Always stand by your word. I'll make sure the cocaine reaches you. All you have to do is secure a drop off location. The sooner you give me a street name, address, or location, the quicker we will be in business."

Quron and Pedro stood one after the other. Quron wanted to bust out in smiles, but he maintained his subtle demeanor. He felt like a burden had been lifted off his shoulders. He had successfully connected the first dot, but he knew that the good feeling he was experiencing was only temporary. The final destination was a long way away, and his mission had just begun. It had been a decade since he dabbled in anything illegal. Just his luck, his introduction back into the illegal lifestyle was grander than before.

The pair exited the entertainment room and made their way down the lengthy hallway. Hours had gone by since Quron first arrived. The sun was slowly fading behind the hills. The two acquaintances, who were gradually becoming friends, stood at the mansion's main doors saying their goodbyes.

"Pedro, I appreciate your hospitality. You have really shown my family and me a lot of love. I guess you were right, good people don't come as often as they should. But I recognize and I'm definitely gonna hold it down, trust that."

Pedro shook Quron's hand and gave him a brotherly hug.

"My friend, one hand washes the other and both hands wash the face. Everyone gets one chance. Never forget that. There's only one, though, and it's not the opportunity that is the deciding factor of your life. It's what you do with that one opportunity, that will change your life forever. Don't be foolish, be wise and be safe. Give my regards to your brother, I'll see you soon."

With that said, Quron opened the huge wooden door. The Chrysler limo was parked in the wishbone shaped driveway in the same position that he had left it. Pedro escorted him down the stairs. Half way down the driveway, Quron stopped and turned toward Pedro.

"Ah man, I was so caught up in thought, I almost forgot to discuss my numbers with you! Inside of that bag is $129,000."

Pedro waved him off. "No, no, no. We are family. Your money is no good here..." Quron cut in. "But I can't conduct business like that, Pedro. With all due respect, I don't wanna ever put myself between a rock and a hard place. If I keep a clean tab with you, a problem could never arise between you and me on a business level. At this point, I don't know how much I can handle, so instead of frontin' me somthin' on consignment, just give me a fair price, that's all I ask. But in the future, if things change, then so will my decision."

They continued to walk and talk as they approached the awaiting limousine. "I understand your reasoning. Since you insist, what do you have in mind?"

"The number that I have in my head is ten. If you can give me each kilo for ten thousand that would be a beautiful thing."

"Ten thousand!" Pedro's quickly pinned Quron with a questioning stare. "Are you serious? Cocaine is very expensive these days. However, I believe in you. If that is what you want, then that is what I'll give you. So you want thirteen kilos for what's inside of that duffle bag, am I correct?" *This young fella reminds me of Rico when he was younger. He has style and he's a thinker,* Pedro thought.

"Yeah, that's the deal I'm looking for." Quron responded.

"Alright, then that's a deal."

With nothing more to say, Quron found comfort in the back of the stretch Chrysler while Pedro walked to the driver's door and addressed the chauffeur. "Charles, you are free to go. After you drop him off, check back in the morning. The remainder of the night is yours. Just do me a favor and make sure he makes it home safely."

Charles nodded his head and Pedro walked off.

Quron relaxed in the back seat with his window down, inhaling the cool breeze, while taking in the beautiful night scenery. The Chrysler paused as the gates slowly moved from one side to the other.

India's white Mercedes pulled up on the other side of the gate as she waited to enter her brother's estate. The two acquaintances locked eyes as both cars pulled off. India waved and Quron smiled as they parted ways, heading into separate directions.

Chapter 14

Some loved the late October weather, while other people disliked the signs that a cold winter is near. The leaves that had fallen from the trees decorated the poverty-stricken neighborhood, hiding the struggle of the community underneath a wave of beautiful colors.

It was Friday morning and the commotion was up and rolling outside of Quron's home on Lander Street. The loud noise might have frightened a typical family, but this was the norm for Quron. The traffic, the noise, and the transactions were all normal activity throughout the hood.

Earlier that morning, while Quron was asleep at Bri's house, his cell vibrated. He was grumpy and upset at the anonymous caller's timing, until he answered the phone, and was told that he had to make a run.

Bri wasn't feeling the way Quron had been acting lately; his demeanor was gradually changing. She hoped that his transition had nothing to do with another female. The thought alone was heart breaking. It was phone calls like the one that Quron was on, which made her consider the possibility of there being another woman.

Bri lay on her flat stomach, pretending to be asleep as Quron eased out of the bed, while speaking softly into the phone. The conversation was too brief for her to pick up on. Bri laid motionless, thinking of a way to counteract what she perceived to be bad karma.

The sound of her closing door echoed throughout the apartment. She sighed, wishing she had an answer to the many questions that ran through her mind.

The message was brief and the caller spoke straight to the point. He stated that there was a U-Haul truck in the small parking lot next to the furniture rental business on Chambers Street. He read off the license plate number and hung up. That was more than enough information for Quron. Luckily, Chambers Street was right on the next block.

Pedro had contacted him few days prior, and his voice gave off the impression that he was a little frustrated that Quron had not secured a safe drop off location as he had asked him to. Quron had no idea that their shipment would be delivered to him. He thought about it and felt funny. After replaying the event in his mind, he calmed down. *As long as it's safe,* Quron thought. Irresponsible was the very last impression that he wanted to make, so he made a mental note to whip things in order immediately.

The block was nearly deserted when Quron stepped out. His heart beat inside his chest like a drum, and beads of sweat drizzled down his chest. Within, there was panic, but his breathing was steady paced. The sun had begun to illuminate the sapphire sky, and the dope fiends had started their mission in search of their morning fix. The small parking lot was cluttered with different vehicles. The U-Haul truck stood out, being the only one.

Quron entered and moved quickly as he sifted through merchandise that was neatly packaged inside cardboard boxes. He didn't have the slightest idea where his product was stashed. Intuition was all that he had to go on. The next box that he chose was slightly heavier than the others. He cracked the seal on the box and lifted the wooden statues that were secured by Styrofoam. Looking deeper than a glance, he saw a familiar glossy white substance peaking from underneath a wool cloth. Snatching the cloth off, Quron stood face to face with the product. The feeling was awkward; it had been so long.

The jitters had faded, and that rush that he once knew so well began to flow through him. Each kilo was stacked neatly in fours, one on top of the other, tightly compressed, with no odor coming through its seal.

The moment of appreciation was over, and his state of mind switched to business. Currently, he was in a danger zone. He had to transport thirteen kilos of pure cocaine from one destination to another. The biggest problem was transporting the drugs. Where the drugs were stashed, to where they had to go was located in the center of a well-known drug area. The local police was always on the prowl, hoping to catch a drug dealer slipping. With this in mind, Quron fixed himself up and made sure that his appearance was presentable. He was extremely cautious as he slid out of the U-Haul truck and made his way toward his basement apartment on Lander St. It was officially day now, and the hustlers had started their daily routine as the morning birds chirped in unison.

The yellow school buses held up traffic while Quron kept his pace steady, blending in with the morning activities. Without raising any suspicion, Quron branched off and found safety in the seclusion of his home.

Young-One and Quron hadn't spoken much while they worked. Their thoughts placed them in separate worlds of their own. The two carried out their skills as chemists, chopping and bagging two out of the thirteen kilos that lay scattered on top of the table. The quality of the cocaine was so pure, they added cut that stretched the quantity. On a scale of one to ten, the quality remained outstanding. Samples were given and people were nearly collapsing. The keys that they transformed from coke to crack, they kept pure.

Young-One stood in front of the electrically operated stove. The pot of water that sat on the metal eye was noticeably heating toward a boiling point. Young-One poured baking soda into the thick open faced Pyrex pot. The digital scale in front of Quron flashed 500g. Young-One smiled and poured the contents into the same pot as the baking soda, before placing the pot into the heated water. He dropped a few tablespoons of the heated water onto the product and the cocaine and baking soda began to bubble, forming into one substance. The two powdery substances broke down from a solid into a white liquid as it settled. Quron walked over to the stove and observed the cooking coke.

"It's been a long time since I baked a cake. I gotta get back into the swing of things." Quron said to Young-One as he held the pot underneath the cold water.

There was a light thumping sound. Their focus shifted to the tiled floor, considering that something could have possibly fallen from the table. They heard the same tapping sound again, only this time, they were sure it came from the door.

Young-One snatched the Desert eagle that sat on the table and cocked it back. Quron moved to open the door. They moved in silence. Young-One was prepared for whatever. He had a clear view of the front and back door. All it took was the wrong move from either door and he would empty every shell that rested inside his clip. He had never been to jail, and he was determined not to go now. Jail just was not an option.

He held on tightly to the large caliber. In his mind, he wondered if the police were really waiting on the opposite side of the door. Although he had not personally been a victim in a raid, he had been a bystander that had witnessed many of them. Never had the police knocked politely and patiently waited to enter into their targeted spot; it wouldn't be any different now. *Wish these faggot ass niggas would try to stick us.* Young-One's grip tightened.

Quron peeped through the peephole. A sigh of relief escaped. He recognized the person standing on the opposite side of the door. Surprised, he suppressed his smile as he looked back toward Young-One.

"It's cool, homie, it's India. I'm gonna step out here for a minute and see what's good with her, so do you, I'll be right back."

A smirk crept across Young-Ones face too. He placed his hammer in his waistline and shook his head as he went back to focusing on the cocaine. Quron opened the door and stepped through the crack before closing the door behind him.

India's expression was sour. She had driven over an hour to see him and he had the nerve not to invite her into his home. India didn't say a word; she turned around and walked back up the small flight of stairs that lead to the sidewalk.

"Yo, India, what up?" Quron asked in a humble tone as he followed her up the steps. She kept it moving toward her Benz, not acknowledging a single word that came out of his mouth. Confusion shot through Quron's mind. He reached out and softly gripped her waist.

"India, you don't hear me talking to you?"

India turned around and looked into his eyes. "Yeah, I hear you talking to me, but you are being very rude, so I'm acting the same way you actin'." She rolled her eyes and placed her hands on her curvaceous hips while anticipating his response.

"Rude! India you can't be serious... Ohhhhh! I see what this is about. You upset because I didn't invite you into my raggedy ass apartment." Quron mentioned as he smiled, trying to make a joke out of the situation.

"Girl, you know I got mad respect for you. I can't let you in my little hole in the wall. That would be disrespectful, especially after seeing your brother's crib." Quron chuckled, hoping to break the tension. "Besides, you need to stop trippin'. You know you're my shero. You really saved my life, remember?"

India couldn't hold back her smile.

Quron noticed her expression and seized the opportunity to make amends. He wrapped his arm around her and pulled her close, knowing he had the upper hand. "Look at your cute face all twisted up, you need to stop actin' like that."

"I ain't acting like nothin', you the one acting funny. I traveled all the way from the city just to see you, and you got the nerve not to invite me into your crib." She flipped her hand.

"Nah, it ain't even like dat. I told you why I didn't invite you in, but since it's bothering you, I'm gonna take you out just to make up for it, aight?"

"Oh really?" India said, looking surprised.

"Yes, really." Quron shot back sarcastically.

"Soooooooo, you're telling me that you are taking me out, or are you asking me if you can take me out?"

Quron laughed, enjoying how India took his words and flipped them to her advantage.

"It ain't funny." India said, liking Quron's humor.

"It really isn't. It's a shame that you are treating me like this. What, you want me to beg?"

India smiled.

Shaking his head, Quron giggled. "Nope, don't get no ideas. Since you insist though, I'm asking, will you allow me to take you out tonight?"

"That's the gentleman that I know. Sure, we can go out. What time is good for you?"

"Eight o'clock is cool."

"Well, I guess it's a date. I'll come pick you up from here, 'cause you still aren't in any condition to drive, so be ready."

As Quron walked India to her car, a group of thugs looked on with admiration. India was so bad. Some of them ignored his presence; they hissed and made attempts to gain India's attention with gestures, all to no avail. Quron was hot, but he overlooked their attempts. India was not his girl. The nerve of the younger generation blew his mind, though. That reality made him think about something his brother had said. Nuri's statement could not have been truer. The new breed that governed the streets couldn't have cared less about him or what he stood for. They only respect violence.

India hopped in her five. "Later, handsome," she said as she drove off.

Quron just stood, watching India's taillights disappear into the night. He looked around and felt offended. His unstable physical condition made him keep his composure. He had to swallow that one. He felt his consciousness slipping. Islam was drifting further and further away from his heart. The grit of the streets was overtaking him and there was nothing that he could do. His sigh was loud as frustration lingered. India occupied his thoughts, but Pedro's warning was ringing inside his head much louder.

After Quron and Young-One finished handling their business from earlier that day, they were exhausted. It had taken them all day to bag up one kilo. The crack that Young-One brought back with his cooking skills looked marvelous. It was smooth, with a pearly white shine. They had the product spread out on paper bags so that the bags could absorb all of the extra water. Drying the product was the only way for them to get an accurate reading on how much the drugs weighed. Once they got that information, it was back to the table to chop, bag, and prepare for distribution.

Young-One had fallen asleep, and Quron decided to wait on his mother's porch until India came to pick him up. He tried calling Nuri because he had not heard from him all day. All he got was his voicemail. He thought nothing of it and figured he would be patient and try to call him back later.

The Friday night scene was crazy. It seemed that everybody and their mother was hanging out on the street corners and on the broken down porches of the apartment buildings that populated the area. It was kind of early, but Quron could tell that everyone was looking forward to having a fun night out. Even with the cool breeze that swept through the streets, the heavy aroma of angel dust and marijuana lingered in the air. Quron sat there leaning against the railing while observing the activities that transpired on the block. Customers were coming nonstop. Quron didn't know if that was the normal flow of things, or if it was the result of it being check day. Either way it didn't matter, he knew he wanted in.

The sound of his name caused him to sit up from his relaxed position and look to identify who was seeking his attention. The block was so packed, he didn't immediately see who was trying to chop it up. He knew whoever it was had to have known him for a long time because they addressed him by his old street name. He looked to his right and spotted the young thug that was crossing the street, coming toward him. He recognized the kid and started walking down the stairs.

"What's poppin' Ghost, how you?" Quron asked as he gave him a pound.

"Ain't nothin', I'm maintainin' doin' what I do. What up wit you though, I haven't seen you in a while."

"Yeah, I just been low. Out of sight, out of mind. But I see you still out here on your grind." Quron stated.

"Unfortunately, this is my only way to provide for me and mine right now. Ever since my pops got killed, shit has been hectic. I'm the breadwinner, so you know how that go."

Quron sighed while listening to Ghost. He knew from his personal experience what Ghost was going through. In so many ways, their childhood stories were the same. The only difference was that he had already lived through that stage in his life and Ghost was currently living it. Although Quron's father had not literally died, he was so caught up in the world of drugs that it seemed like he was dead.

Quron understood the burden of responsibility that Ghost was forced to take on. He looked him in the eyes and offered some words of wisdom that he hoped would help him get through the wild lifestyle of the streets.

"Lil homie, you can believe that I know what you're going through. When I was a shorty, I was in the same position as you. What I'm about to tell you, I unfortunately had to learn the hard way. I didn't have nobody to school me, not 'cause I was a foul nigga, but because the older homies that had love for me didn't know themselves, so how could they put me on? I got love for you and I would hate to see you get swallowed up in these streets. The streets don't breed no success stories, shit is definitely real. Regardless of the situation, we are men, and we have no choice but to live with the decisions that we make... I'm not sayin' stop doin' you, by all means get ya paypa. But know and understand that this shit that we see every day ain't livin', there's much more to life. You can't allow your situation to be an excuse for you to fail. Your mind is your strongest weapon. Whatever you want to do, just put your mind to it and do it. That's the only way you're gonna secure a better life. Nobody ain't gonna give you nothin' in this world, you gotta go out and get it.

"It might sound fucked up, but that's just how it is. So from me to you, stack ya paypa and make some goals. You don't have to be rich just to think like a rich nigga. Nothin' lasts forever, including this game, so be smart and stay sucka free. Women are always a part of a hustlaz dream, but they are often the reason for a nigga's downfall. Don't stress'em, they'll alwayz be here. You ain't gonna lose ya broad chasing paypa, but you'll definitely loose ya paypa chasin' behind these women, feel me?"

Quron looked up and spotted headlights coming toward him. As the lights got closer, he noticed that it was India's Benz cruising down the one-way street.

"Yo Ghost, it was good kickin' it with you lil homie, but this my ride right here, so I gotta breeze. I'ma see you, though. Stay focused," he said, pointing at Ghost. "Remember what I said, real nigga talk, always. MOB."

"Ah-ight, Born, I'ma holla."

Quron extended his hand and gave Ghost another pound. As he walked around the front of India's car, he looked back and shouted, "Ghost, I told you Born is the past. Quron is the present and the future, you feel me?"

"Yeah! I feel you, Quron." Ghost giggled making his sarcasm obvious. Quron and Ghost looked at each other and shared a laugh.

Ghost turned and walked down the block and Quron found comfort inside the Mercedes with India as she pulled off and made her way toward the restaurant that she had in mind.

"What's good, love, you seem to have something on your mind, is everything okay?" Quron asked basing his question on her body language and her distraught facial expression.

"Yeah, I'm alright. I'm just a little nervous because I haven't been on a date for years."

Quron looked at India and twisted up his face. "Years!" *This chick must take me for a fool. Sucka written all over my face, huh?*

"I know you probably think that I am lying, but I'm really not." India let out an aggravated sigh, making it clear that she did not wish to talk about it.

Quron got the message and decided to let the topic go. If it was meant for him to know, then it would come to the light sooner than later. He reclined in the seat and his mind settled on thoughts of Ghost. He liked the young kid. Ghost reminded him a lot of himself when he was younger. Ghost was a wild boy with a swagger that his peers really admired. He had a certain aura that gave him an edge, and people respected that about him. All he lacked was a mentor that would mold him and give him the knowledge and guidance that all good leaders had at one point or another.

Quron wanted to contribute to the young man's growth, but he knew that a big responsibility that came along with accepting another member into the family. In the family, everyone is responsible for the actions of each other. With that in mind, he knew that he had to base his decisions on what would be best for Young-One, Nuri, Steel, and himself. At that point, he did not know what was best, so he decided to play it by ear and see how life would play out.

India's soft voice broke his trance and brought his mind back to the present. "Okay, we are here."

Quron got out and made his way to the driver's side of the car. India was halfway out the car before he appeared to assist her. She looked up, smiled, and grabbed his extended forearm. She seemed to be more relaxed than before, and Quron felt good about that. He noticed that they weren't very far from the hood. The riverfront was beautiful and he was pleased that India chose to take him to the waterfront. He had seen it in the Times Herald Record, and once in person when Young-One brought him through, but the night-lights gave the whole scene a different look.

The parking lot reflected the type of people who entertained themselves there. The flock of Bentleys, Jaguars and Range Rovers made it obvious that they were not the typical hoodlums. The full moon's radiant light bounced off of the Hudson Rover's calm water, setting a romantic vibe. India and Quron stood side by side while patiently waiting to be ushered to a table. Quron was surprised when the receptionist announced India's last name. She had made reservations and he was genuinely impressed.

The waitress made small talk with India as she escorted them to their table. Quron followed behind the pair and admired India's beauty. She looked stunning in her turquoise Versace garments. Her well-shaped body was provoking, but Quron managed to control his lust. Her closed toe Christian Louboutin stilettos added to her sex appeal and made it extremely difficult for him to view her as a friend. In his mind, he cursed himself because he knew from the very first time they met, that friendly ties with India could be a potential problem because of his attraction to her. It seemed like the more he dealt with her, the more he started to feel for her on a more intimate level. After thinking about his options, he always concluded that there was a bigger picture, and he knew that if he pursued India and disregarded what Pedro told him, things would get ugly.

He sat on the opposite side of the small, decorated table and looked on as India's lips moved. The words that came out of her mouth were not acknowledged. Quron was caught up in his own thoughts, feeling the pressure to make a crucial decision before it was too late.

"Quron, why are you shaking your head? Is there something wrong?" India questioned with a concerned look on her face.

"Don't mind me, everything is cool. I just have a lot on my mind."

India looked at Quron and noticed the confusion he spoke of. She continued eating her garden salad and Quron sat attentively with a mouth full of his delicious seafood dish. Couples and friends that were sitting at the surrounding tables engaged in friendly conversation, laughing, allowing the fine wines and the soft liquors to captivate the moment. The vibe at India's table was not as pleasant. Not even the beautiful view of the Hudson could ease the tension that was slowly building. The longer she sat in the company of Quron, the more she felt the need to clear her conscience. She vowed to herself that she would do the right thing once the right opportunity came, and she would not go back on her word, despite the potential harm that her truth could bring. She sipped the grape colored liquid from her wine glass and extended her small delicate hand toward him. His masculine touch reassured her decision. India looked into his eyes, inhaled deeply, and began to share one of her most personal secrets.

"Quron." She pronounced in a low tone, still feeling a little scared of how he would react once he knew the truth.

"I have something that I need to tell you. But first, I would like to apologize, because it was not my intention to get you caught up in the middle of my drama." India's voice started cracking and her eyes watered as teardrops slowly descended her cheeks.

"Calm down, India, what are you talking about, and what drama did you get me caught up in? I don't have no drama." Quron said feeling confused, but now seeking to get to the bottom of India's claim.

"Just hear me out and give me a chance to explain. Like five, almost six years ago, I had heard about how it be goin' down up here in this upstate area. I talked to my brothers and they let me come up here for the summer. One of my cousins used to live in Poughkeepsie. We were young and naive back then, and all we used to do was party. You know how it is when a new face comes around. All the niggas wanted some of this. Me and my cousin was lovin' the attention. Niggas was spendin' their money and we was just living. Not sayin' we needed their money, 'cause we didn't. My brothers made sure we didn't want for nothing. It was just the thrill that came with taking advantage of them, that kept us interested.

"So one night, me and my cousin was out and about, and everybody was talking about going to this club. Supposedly, some big time drug dealer was throwing the party, and all the ballas was supposed to be there. To make a long story short, we ended up going out that night. When we came through, bitches was hatin'. All the niggas was lookin', thirsty as fuck. I know that I'm pretty, but my cousin, Trinity, is a dime for real. She had on some pink and white Air Max with a white mini skirt. Her cute halter-top exposed her 36DD's, but it was her all white Christian Dior shades that brought her whole outfit out. We were young, stuntin' hard. We didn't want to mix with the crowd too much, so we found a spot in the corner and settled down.

"Of course, dudes was tryin' to holla but we weren't payin' them no mind. We were doin' us, and all of a sudden, the DJ gave these two dudes a shout out. I looked up to see who he was talkin' about, and I spot this fine ass chocolate dude coming through the crowd with another dark skinned brotha and a female. They had money written all over them. Their jewelry was flooded with diamonds, and it seemed like all the niggas and chicks was worshiping them like they were Gods.

The female was tagging along, playing her position, but I could tell that she wasn't feelin' all the attention that the fine brotha was getting. Common sense told me that she was his girl. She was a real attractive girl, and none of the cats that was there tried to scoop her up. Come to fmd out, I was right. Shorty's name was Tayasia. Like I said, I seen them when they first came in, but I'm not with no groupie shit at all, so I acted like they weren't there and kept doin' me.

"Too bad they didn't feel the same way, 'cause once they spotted me and Trinity, the pursuit was on. They sent bottle after bottle to our table with these little cards that had messages written on them. At first I didn't think anything of it, but after the third bottle of Moet, I'm not gonna front to you, he started to gain my interest. I think it was his creative approach that attracted me to him, to be honest. All the messages were written like a poem, and at the bottom, it would say 'look up'. When I would look up, he'd be sitting on the bar stool looking at me, smiling. He was a thug that lived on the edge. His girl was standing right in front of him and he was still tryin' to get at me. In a weird way, I'm a little embarrassed to admit, but that turned me on.

"The last card that he sent me said, Bring this bottle of Moet outside and enjoy the rest of the night with me. After we eat breakfast at the diner, I'll take you home, no strings attached! Sincerely, Trey.

"I was a little skeptical at first because of his girl, but I figured she couldn't have meant that much to him if he was tryin' to get at me while she was on the scene. So I gathered my things and walked outside. When I got out there, he was already out there sittin' in his Range Rover with all the windows rolled down playin' R. Kelly's *Twelve Play* album. I liked it, but at the same time, I didn't like it 'cause it seem like he knew that I was gonna accept his offer, and I didn't want him to think that I was one of those bird head bitches. Once I got into his truck, it was all good. He had a good sense of humor. Cool would be an understatement. He was really that chill. I was giggling the whole time. He told me that we had to make a stop before he headed to the diner. I was already a little tipsy from the champagne that I drank back at the club, so I didn't say nothin'. I enjoyed the ride and went with the flow.

"He pulled into a gas station, handed me a fifty dollar bill and asked me to go inside and pay for the gas while he stayed outside and pumped it. On my way out of his car, this motherfucker had the nerve to touch my ass. As soon as he touched me, it was like a natural reaction, 'cause I turned around and smacked the shit out of him. He looked so surprised. I could tell that he wasn't expecting that, but I couldn't have cared less. I rolled my eyes and kept it movin', heated at the fact that this nigga just bobbed his head to the smooth R&B, acting like nothin' ever happened. I guess he could tell that I was still tight behind that stunt he pulled. He lowered the music and apologized for touching me like that. Then he handed me a small plastic cup that was filled with champagne and said that our toast was to the start of our new beginning..." India's voice mellowed to a whisper.

"Drinking from that cup was the worst thing I could have done. First, my vision got blurry, then my ears started ringing, and everything sounded slow. That was the last thing that I remembered."

India paused, and tears started rolling down her face. The ugly memory that she was currently reliving hurt her so much, but she felt that she had to finish explaining her story because Quron deserved to know. Quron picked up the napkin from off of the table and wiped her tears. The thought of him actually caring caused her to slightly smile.

"When I woke up, Trey had me pent down to the bed, ramming himself inside of me. I cried and begged him to stop, but he ignored my cries. I was still a virgin until that point. The pain that shot through my body was overwhelming. I struggled and fought for as long as I could, but after a while, my body went limp, and the next thing I knew, the bright rays from the sun was peeking through the broken window shades. I tried to move, but my body ached from the beating that I took. One of my eyes was hurting and the other one was swollen shut. I almost threw up because of the rank smell that lingered inside of the apartment. The bedroom that I was in was filthy. A ripped up couch with springs protruding through its cushions and a dirty mattress was the only furniture in there. Trey was nowhere in sight. I felt so disrespected. Blood was everywhere. All I could do was cry, hoping that my tears would soothe the pain that I was feeling."

"India," Quron interrupted before she could continue. "I see how difficult it is for you to talk about this. I can see the pain all over your face. If you don't want to talk about it anymore, I'll understand. I would rather be in the dark and not know about the situation, than to see you suffer from reliving this nightmare."

India didn't respond to Quron's sympathy. She looked him in the eyes, tightened her grip around his hand, and continued releasing the pain that was bottled up inside of her.

"Once I got myself together and made it out of the building, I found a pay phone and called Trinity. I had no idea where I was, all I knew is I was standing by a graveyard that was across the street from a Laundromat and the corner street signs read Liberty Street and South Street. That was the only information I had, and that's what I told her. She knew something was terribly wrong because my breathing was uneven and my sobs were loud. I heard the fear in her voice. I tried to control my emotions, but the event kept replaying in my head and my tears would not stop flowing. Trinity stayed on the phone with me until she arrived. I knew that I looked really bad because Trinity started crying as soon as she saw me. It was a real painful experience for me. I wanted to hide it because I knew that my brothers would flip once they found out.

"My aunt wasn't trying to hear it. Once she saw my face, she called my brothers immediately and told them what little she knew. They were up here within the next hour. I had never seen my brother, Rico, so upset. Pedro had to calm him down because he was losing it. I had no choice but to tell them everything that I remembered. They blamed my aunt because she was responsible for me. I tried to stick up for her, but they totally ignored what I had to say. I gathered my things and we headed back to Queens. The ride home seemed like forever. No one said anything. The only sound was the sounds of fast moving cars passing us. I was so scared. I didn't know what to do. Once we got home, my brothers had our family doctor come through. He gave me a thorough check up, and thank God, everything was okay, other than a few cuts and bruises.

It was hard for my family and me, but we did everything and anything that would help us get past the incident. Months had gone by and I was undergoing psychiatric treatment, gradually trying to regain my peace of mind and the regular lifestyle that I once had. One night, I was sitting in my living room studying for one of my college exams and a special news flash aired on the Channel Nine ten o'clock news. Something told me to pay attention to the television, so I put my books down and watched the news. A black male in his early twenties had been brutally murdered in the dangerous streets of Newburgh, New York. The motive behind the young man's death was unknown by local authorities. Innocent bystanders told the local police that a Latino man, appearing to be in his early thirties walked up to the young man and blew his brains out in broad daylight. The victim was identified as Treyman Harris and the description of the gunman resembled my brother Rico. They posted a picture of Rico and said that he was wanted for questioning.

"Ever since then, my life has been in shambles. They never got the chance to question Rico. Once he heard that authorities were looking for him, he fled the states and went back to my country. Pedro and me are close, but Rico was my heart. I was so hurt. I could have gone with him, but he knew that his life would never be the same again. He said that traveling with him would be dangerous for me and he did not want me to ruin the rest of my life. Pedro took responsibility of watching over me, and ever since then, it has been him and me. I'm almost sure that those men that came into the strip club shooting that night were sent by Scar. Scar is Trey's older brother and he has a big reputation out here in Newburgh.

"I was attending LIU at the time and I came out of class, ready to hop in my car and go home, but I noticed a piece of paper underneath my windshield wiper. I opened the folded up paper and read the note. It was a message from Scar telling me that he remembered my face from the nightclub and he knew that I was responsible for his brother's death. He promised me that he was gonna be responsible for my death. That shit scared the hell out of me because it was obvious that he had someone watching my every move. I guess he just wanted me to suffer from the fear of not knowing when he would come for me. The crazy shit is, I never asked Rico to do what he did, but since he's my brother, I have to constantly watch over my shoulder hoping that God will spare my life for another day."

Quron wore a blank expression on his face. India's secret had caught him off guard. He tried his best not to interrupt or give his input, because he really did not know what to say. He could tell that this was something that she needed to talk about, but was not able to do so because she did not feel comfortable with confiding in anyone.

"Why didn't you tell me sooner?" Quron asked in a calm voice after thinking things through.

"Honestly, I didn't know how to tell you. I was thinking how could I tell this man that he almost died because of me, a total stranger? I didn't know what to do, especially after hearing my brother say that you had already done time for murder."

"So why the sudden change of heart now?"

"I haven't had a change of heart. I never said that I wasn't going to tell you. From the time I laid eyes on you in that hospital bed, I vowed that I would tell you the truth one day. It was only a matter of time before I did. I could never forget you. You risked your life for me, and I will always feel indebted to you for that."

India's confession touched him. What she said made a lot of sense. He thought about it and understood why she had chosen to be cautious. He pictured himself in her shoes and knew he would have gone about it in a similar way. What touched him the most was her sacrifice; she had taken a chance of endangering herself just to make sure that he was aware of the truth. That took a lot of heart. She shared one of her deepest secrets and he knew that she didn't have to do that, but she did, and that was what mattered.

Quron looked up and sympathized with her. Women of lslam are honored, cherished and protected. All he could think about was the women in his life that he held inside his heart. His temper began to flare. He felt like it had become his duty to assure her safety while she was with him. It became clear why Pedro had firmly made it known that India was off limits. Pedro didn't trust anyone and he had found out the reason why.

"Are you mad at me?" India asked in a depressed tone of voice. Her eyes were still puffy and bloodshot red from crying so much.

"Not at all... what's done is done. I mean, by no means do I want you to think that I took those bullets for you. That just isn't the case. But I am sorry that you experienced those horrible things. Real talk, it crushes me that niggas stoop so low. What's important is you are safe and I am still alive and breathing. India, my wounds are physical, and if I take good care of them, over the course of time they will heal. What that creep did to you won't ever leave your mind and that scar that he left on your soul will always be there. I can't imagine the effect that this has on you mentally and emotionally, so don't worry about it, I'm good."

India massaged Quron's hand and smiled as she let out a sigh of relief. She didn't think that he would be so understanding about her situation. For the first time in years, she felt emotionally connected to a man that was not a relative. Within, it felt so good, but she knew that she could not ever voice how she was feeling aloud. Even if Quron felt the same about her, she knew that Pedro would never understand, and that meant trouble for Quron. She would rather live unhappily, than to jeopardize the life of someone she cared for.

India picked up the leather bill book and paid for the bill that the waitress brought over to their table. She knew that Quron would have handled the bill, but she wanted to show her appreciation. Quron rose to his feet and walked beside her as they made their way toward the exit. The cold night breeze caused India's hair to dance. She shivered and Quron wrapped his arm around her small frame. She pressed a button on her key chain, causing the engine to come alive as the doors opened simultaneously. Quron activated his cellular phone and five missed messages flashed across the screen. He ignored them and relaxed as India drove off.

Quron's mind was cluttered with thoughts that all seemed to revolve around Scar. It was a complicated situation, and he needed some time alone. He wanted to have a clear mind when he decided how he would handle this situation. The main thing that bothered him was the fact that he didn't know much about Scar, other than what India had told him. He could have been looking at this dude every day and not know it. That really bothered him.

Minutes later, India drove slowly down Lander Street and made a right turn onto 31st Street. She parked approximately a block away from Quron's apartment. He looked at her, but said nothing. He figured she had stopped short of his house for a reason, and whatever the reason was, it was fine with him.

"I had a really good time with you tonight, it may not seem like it because I was crying most of the time but that's where the respect came from. I really needed to get that off my chest, and you made it easy for me to do. My past has made me cold and bitter toward men in general. It has been very hard for me to trust people, but it is a different feeling that I get whenever I'm anywhere near you. I don't know what it is, but it's strange! I feel very comfortable and safe when I'm around you. I didn't think that I would ever feel like this again. I guess God's plans really are greater than ours."

Quron smiled. India's words made him feel good. For him to hear India express how he contributed to her life really made him feel like he was doing the right thing.

"Tonight will definitely be a night for me to remember as well. I had a nice time. You have the type of personality that anyone would like and I really love that about you. You have my number. Don't be afraid to use it whenever you feel the need to do so. Now give ya boy a hug and be safe out here on these streets."

Quron paused and contemplated whether he should carry out what he had in mind. He figured it would only help the situation. He reached down and lifted his pant leg that draped over his Timberland boot. When he sat back up in his seat, a pearl handled .22 was gripped tightly in his hand.

"You know something about this? You ever shot a gun before?" India didn't respond to his question, she wore a timid expression and shook her head no.

"So I guess givin' you this won't do you any good, huh? It wouldn't hurt for you to have it though. I want you to accept this as a gift from me to you. It would be wise for you to learn how to use it. You never know when it might come in handy."

As if it was planned, they both leaned forward with their arms apart, looking to embrace. Before they could realize what they were doing, it was too late; their moist lips were pressed together.

Suddenly, Quron pulled away. India looked confused and Quron felt embarrassed.

"I'm sorry India I didn't mean to dis—"

"Shhh," India placed her French manicured fingernail on Quron's lips. "Apologizing really isn't necessary, you haven't done anything wrong. Whatever is meant to be, will certainly be. Thanks for respecting me. I had a wonderful night. it has been succcccccch a long time." A soft giggle escaped. "I won't ever forget this."

Quron kissed her hand and stepped out of the car.

India waved goodbye as she slowly disappeared into the night. Quron turned the corner, keeping a steady pace as he made his way to his building. He looked at his watch and realized that it was the first day of November. He had been a free man for five months, and now found himself up to his neck in the game. That fast life had spun out of control. All the discipline he thought he possessed had been put to the test and he had failed. DAMN.

In his mind, he questioned his motives. He honestly wondered if he really was in the drug game to raise enough capital to pursue his dreams, or if he was simply in the game because of his infatuation with the glamorous lifestyle of the streets. He had so much to think about in what felt like so little time. He opened the front door to his basement apartment and entered into its darkness. The solitude was something he very much needed.

Chapter 15

Beep, Beep, Beeep! Tay pressed down on the car horn repeatedly.

A young female with beautiful features looked out of the screen door. "I'm coming right now, Tay, hold on!" She yelled before disappearing back into the large single family home that sat on the corner.

Tay smiled upon seeing her face. Her mind drifted as she reminisced about the memories that her and the teenage girl had accumulated over the years. The sound of her car door slamming snapped her out of her daydream. She immediately reached over and hugged the pretty young lady like she had not seen her in a very long time. Many people did not have the opportunity to see this side of Tay. It was almost like she had transformed into a totally different person.

"Kiyah, what's up, sis? I've missed you!" Tay shared, not holding back the affection that she had for her younger sister.

"I'm chillin', just tired of living like this. It was cool when I was younger, and I appreciate everything Mrs. Robinson has done for me, but I'm about to be eighteen and this group home stuff is not what's up." Kiyah sighed heavily, emphasizing how uncomfortable she was with her current living condition.

Tay listened to her sister as she turned onto the highway. She felt bad, even helpless.

"Ki, I know you are going through it, but please work with me. I never lied to you before have I?"

"No," Kiyah answered in a low tone.

"So you should believe me when I say we are going to be together soon, just like old times. I spoke to your social worker and she told me that the system cannot hold you after you tum eighteen. You have to be a little more patient and let me do what I have to, so everything will be straight when you come home."

Kiyah looked out the window as they passed by the trees and the rocky slopes that served as landmarks along the highway. Tay knew it was Kiyah's way of showing that she accepted what she was told. Tay loved that about Kiyah. She never talked back, not even if she disagreed. She would just find a way to accept and deal with it. Tay didn't want their day to be spoiled, so she pushed the iPod change button and switched the subject.

"So what's up Ki, why haven't you called me? One of these lil boys takin' up all your time now?" Tay smiled as she looked back and forth from the road to her sister.

Surprisingly, Tay's question caused Kiyah to blush. Her cheeks turned red and her mood lightened. "How'd you know?"

"Oh my God! You have a boyfriend?" Tay shouted, surprised that her question might actually be her sister's truth.

"Yeah, something like that." Kiyah answered.

"Girl, I can't believe you didn't tell me, let ya sister know the deal." Tay said happily, excited about Kiyah's experience with a boy.

Kiyah didn't hesitate to comply with her sister's request. She placed her hands on the dashboard, bowed her head, and started wiggling like a happy child in a toy store.

Tay watched Kiyah practice her acting skills and erupted in laughter.

"Tay, he is fine. Everything about this nigga is fly. The way he walks, the way he talks, the way he dresses, umm." The two sisters busted out laughing. "Where'd you meet him?"

"School."

"Word! So you dun bagged a school boy with a lil swagger, huh? What's his name?"

"Why? You don't know him."

"Girl, how do you know who I know? I might know his mama, now what's his name?" Tay asked again while smiling.

"His name is Lamar Strings."

Tay remained silent. Her eyebrow's came together as she slightly frowned. Kiyah knew that she didn't know him; she patiently waited for her to finish searching through her memory bank before admitting it.

"You're right, I don't know him." Tay giggled and Kiyah joined in with a chuckle of her own.

"See, I told you."

"So when do you plan on bringin' him around so that I can meet him?"

"I don't know yet. I'll probably bring him around when we get situated." Kiyah answered with an uncertain expression.

"Girl, whatchu mean you don't know? You don't want ya lil boyfriend to meet ya big sis?" Tay asked in a playful way.

"Nah crazy, by the time ya'll meet you're not gonna have much to tell him about yourself. I talk about you all the time."

Tay smiled. "Ah-ight, I'ma let you do you, but I'ma tell you this..." Tay's voice trailed off, and then suddenly her thoughts continued. "Your lil boyfriend better act like he know who his girl is. Cause if he hurt you in any way, all I'ma say is he'll have a personal relationship with God way sooner than he ever expected."

Kiyah looked at her and noticed how serious she was. There was no smirk, smile, or chuckle. Tay's gaze had turned cold and silence briefly filled the air.

"I know, Tay. I know," were the only word's that Kiyah could think of.

She had heard what her sister said and her facial expression told her that she was serious. Kiyah didn't understand exactly what she meant by it, but she had a good idea. Kiyah wasn't stupid. She had heard rumors about a dude named Tay, and she knew that it was her sister that they were talking about all along. But she refused to believe everything. The person who they described did not fit the sweet, loving, sister that she had grown up under and admired. The person who they described had the characteristics of a monster. Kiyah could not accept that. The large sums of money, the shopping sprees, the jewelry, and the luxury cars were impossible for Kiyah to overlook. Tay's material gain told her that her sister was involved in some type of illegal activity. Which activities and to what extent she didn't know, but she was sure that Tay was involved in something.

Tay looked at the digital clock that was installed inside the wood grain dashboard and realized that 45 minutes had gone by. She got off at the next exit and drove a little further down the road before turning into a nearly full parking lot. She cruised slowly up and down the lanes before she realized that a parking space had become available. With one quick twist of her wrist, the brand new Infiniti G37 coupe was secured between two cars. Tay turned the engine off and placed her hand on Kiyah's chest, indicating that she wanted her to wait a second before she got out of the car.

"Ki," Tay said softly. "Listen, I know at times I might seem to be a little overprotective when it comes to you, but that's only because I love you. I really wouldn't be able to function if something bad was to happen to you. That's why I make it my business to keep you safe and away from all the bullshit. I don't mean to be like that, but I can't help it. You are my only connection to Mommy and Daddy. We are all we got, Ki, you shouldn't ever forget that."

Tay's gaze shifted to the cars that passed by. She didn't want Kiyah to see the light tears that rolled out of her eyelids. The memory of her parents always caused her to become emotional. She discreetly wiped her face and dug into her front pocket to retrieve the knot of money that she had for the day's shopping spree. Tay's effort to hide her emotions had not gone unnoticed, as she had planned. Kiyah noticed the wet streak on her cheek. She felt bad for causing her sister to cry. Kiyah knew that Tay meant no harm. They loved each other unconditionally, and nothing or no one could ever change that. Tay was the only mother that Kiyah had ever known.

Over the years, Kiyah had always kept her personal life to herself. She did not allow herself to open up while in the group homes because she had seen how the other girls acted upon learning about each other's situation. At first, they would act like a true friend, but once they found out about your situation they would tease and make fun of you. Kiyah didn't want to feel that pain, so she stayed to herself and bonded with her sister. Whenever she wanted to talk, Tay was there to listen, whenever she wanted to learn, Tay was there to teach, and whenever she did not understand something, Tay was there to explain. Tay was her everything and she wouldn't do anything to hurt her.

Kiyah leaned across the armrest and kissed her sister on the cheek. "I know that you don't mean any harm. I really do understand, and I love you just as much as you love me. Let's go, we aren't gonna spend our whole day in this car. I read about the sales in the Palisades mall and you know how I get when it comes to stores and sales."

Kiyah laughed and grabbed the knot of money off of Tay's lap, trying to lighten her mood before she got out of the car. Tay smiled and followed Kiyah's lead.

"Hurry up, Tay. I see this bracelet that I wanted to buy you the last time we were here!" Kiyah shouted with enthusiasm. "Taking forever, I'm tryna spend this paypa."

Tay quickened her pace as they rushed to get into the mall. Kiyah had a way of making her feel like the most important person in the world. Kiyah had a good heart. She was always thinking of others, and on this beautiful day, it was no different. She had intended to utilize some of the money that she had taken from Tay to buy her a gift. Although it was Tay's hard earned money that the gift was going to be purchased with, Tay thought nothing of it. At the end of the day, it was the thought that really counted. Tay cherished the thought of having close ties with someone who loved her more than anything else. As long as she had Kiyah by her side, nothing else mattered.

———————

Rihanna's latest banger lingered inside the plush interior of Tay's coupe. RiRi's record was on fire throughout the nation. Tay was zonin' out to the "Diamonds" tune. The song sort of brought out her feminine side, a side that she often felt like she had lost contact with. She found herself at times wondering what her life would be like if she decided to revert back to her nature as a female. The unknown frightened her and she discarded the thought without considering it, every time.

French Montana's voice came through the speakers of her cell phone for the second time. Panicking, she pulled over and started searching through her car thoroughly. She finally looked inside her Armani Exchange shopping bag. Laying on the surface of her clothes was her iPhone 5. She scooped it up quickly.

"Hello," Tay answered almost out of breath. Her chest pumped up and deflated quickly. She made a mental note to get back into her cardiovascular exercises. All the drug money she was getting was making her comfortable and lazy,

"What up Tay, where you at?" Scar asked with a sense of urgency in his voice.

"I'm drivin' down Vaness Street. I just dropped Kiyah off. Why, what up?"

"I've been lookin' for you all day, where you been?"

"You know I spend time with Kiyah on the weekends!"

~ 144 ~

"Oh copy. My fault, baby girl, I forgot. But umm, I'm comin' up City Terrace right now. Park on the corner of City Terrace and Vaness, I need to holla at chu."

"Ah-ight." Tay managed to say before her phone went dead.

Seconds later, a tan Dodge Charger made a sharp turn off Broadway and shot up City Terrace with lightning speed. The autumn leaves lifted out of the road and twisted in circles like a whirlpool as the Charger came to a halt.

Tay pulled up simultaneously and parked in an empty space that was near the corner. As she got out and secured her car, Scar was rolling slowly toward her. Tay hopped in and Scar peeled off, leaving a cloud of smoke.

"So what's the emergency, Scar?"

"Damn, who said it's an emergency?" Scar asked, wearing a mischievous grin.

"Nigga, don't act like you don't know what it is. We been around each other for too many years. I know when somethin' is botherin' you."

Scar glanced at Tay and felt genuinely impressed with how good her skills at reading people had become. Scar made a right turn onto 1st Street and headed down the hill toward his destination.

"You strapped?" Scar asked.

"All day, every day. Why, what up?" Tay asked again, becoming irritated with Scar's silent treatment.

"I really don't have time to explain. I just need you to hold me down."

Before Tay could ask any more questions, Scar pulled in front of a convenience store on 1st. and Lander St., and calmly got out. Crack alley, the Dark Side, the barrio for real, and Tay was oblivious to what was going on. Scar was her boy though, and she trusted his judgment. She unzipped her Komrad jacket and checked the twin glocks that rested inside the holsters that were underneath her armpits. Moments later, she opened the passenger door and followed Scar's lead as he made his way over to the group of thugs that were standing on the corner. Lander Street was packed like always. Tay looked around and hoped that the crowd of people was not a bad sign.

"Peoples, pardon me," Scar interrupted with a slight southern drawl attached to his words. "Anybody out here know a kid by the name of Nuri?"

As soon as Tay heard the name, Nuri, she was no longer oblivious to what was going on. Tay figured the drama that happened at the club must have been weighing down on Scar's conscience, so he wanted to clear any misunderstandings by addressing the issue.

No sooner than the words left Scar's mouth and entered the air, a brown skinned, frail looking kid with dread locks turned his back to the small group that he was engaged in conversation with and looked directly at Scar.

"Wh... wh... wh... wh... why? Who... who wanna know?" The frail kid stuttered as he struggled to ask his question.

"Yo name Nuri?" Scar asked, keeping his anger suppressed underneath the smirk that formed on his face. He felt that it was bad enough that he had convinced himself to come into a potential enemy territory to talk and make amends for something that he had done. Now his humiliation grew deeper as he was questioned by a lil dude that was clearly not on his level, or so he thought.

"Nah, he ain't Nuri." Quron said as he stepped out of the corner store to confront the unfamiliar face.

"You Nuri?" Scar asked, keeping his conversation short and simple until he found who he was looking for.

"Not at all, but I'm his other half." Quron was now standing within arm's reach of this stranger. He felt no fear though. He was standing on the corner of a strip that he had help build years ago. He wished a muthafucka would come out of pocket while in his hood. The outcome would not be pretty.

When Quron walked toward Scar, Scar noticed his slight limp and immediately put two and two together. Quron was the brother that had accidentally gotten shot. Things were turning out better than he planned. He had asked for Nuri because that was the only name that Passion had given them other than Young-One. Now, he was actually speaking to the individual that he really wanted to speak with.

"What's poppin' potna? My handle is Scar, and from what I understand, you and yo brother got caught in a situation a way's back. Brah, I ain't come down here fo' no drama, ya dig. I came down here to man up and apologize for what happened. It wasn't meant for you and your people to get caught up in that situation, you understand?" Scar's smirk turned into a wide spread smile.

Quron's insides were boiling. He maintained his subtle look, but his mind was racing in different directions. Scar's presence had caught him off guard, but he was always prepared to hold his own.

"So let me get this straight," Quron spoke with no signs of anger in his voice. "You the kid behind that shooting at the club?"

Scar knew the question that Quron asked was a rhetorical question. To answer the question would only add insult to injury, and place himself in a more vulnerable position. Through his peripheral, he could see the frail kid standing on an angle with his right hand tucked inside his army jacket. He was no stranger to this tactic, which is why Tay was leaning against a nearby parked car, watching everything that went down.

"I'ma pull yo' coat to somethin' that you probably don't know. I feel like it's only fair to put you up on game, ya dig. Dat lil bitch, India, is bad news. I mean real bad news!" Scar paused so his words could sink in. "Whoever befriended her, befriends these 45 slugs I got for her ass. On everything I love, no nigga don't want no part in what she got comin'. Dawgz, I don't know you from a hole in a wall. I advise you to stay away from shawty, ya dig. I'll hate fo' shit to get ugly cause of her, so please, do me dat fava. What I got against her is personal, and you ain't got nothin' to do with that."

Quron looked into Scar's eyes. Neither blinked. Quron's prolonged silence told Scar what he needed to know. Scar extended his hand and Quron gripped it with a manly, firm grip.

"No man but me makes decisions for me, and a man that fears God don't fear nothing." Quron said seriously. "And all that other B.S. you talking bout don't mean much to me either, homeboy. Muthafucka, you should've thought about that when you sent them niggas up in da spot clappin'!"

"Oh word, ah-ight potna'," Scar said as he made his way back to his Charger. "Say no more, I'ma see you!"

"Yo, fu... fu... fuck that nigga, Ron! He ain't bui... bui... built to be makin' no muth... muthafuckin' threats! I'll lay that nigga down ri... right now!" The skinny, brown skinned, dread said with hostility in his voice and rage written all over his face.

Scar and Tay hopped in the Dodge Charger. The frail kid pulled out his gray and black 40 caliber, but Quron grabbed his arm firmly. The two comrades locked eyes and the scrawny kid knew that he had allowed his emotions to supersede his intelligence.

"Yo, Steel, be easy and play your cards. Don't let them niggas pull you out of character! You know you can't win while dealin' wit' emotions. If shit has to happen, then it's gonna happen! It won't happen on their time, though. It'll happen when we want it to happen!"

Quron freed Steel's arm from his grip. He looked up and noticed Scar's Charger cruising by. The passenger and Quron's eyes met. Tay placed one of her glocks against the window, winked her eye, and blew him a kiss. Quron grabbed his dick through his pants and smiled. He felt no anxiety until he turned toward the corner. Sitting at the stop sign was India. Scar's threats kept replaying inside his head. He looked down Lander Street in the direction that Scar had driven and there in the middle of the road, sat the Charger with its brake lights on. That confirmed what Quron had already known. Scar had spotted India's Benz. It was on.

Quron pulled out his Hi-Point 9mm and moved as fast as he could through the crowd, trying to get to India. A loud screeching sound filled the air as Scar peeled off. He made a sharp left turn into the parking lot that was in the back of Newburgh's DMV. Quron realized that time was something that he did not have a lot of. He hopped in India's Benz and demanded her to drive. She noticed his gun, and the fear that overtook her body caused her to cry instantly. Quron lowered his tone, but continued to shout orders.

India finally complied and sped down 1st street. Scar was awaiting their arrival on the corner of the one-way street. India's headlights highlighted Scar's cynical smile. Quron forcefully pushed India's head down as the sound from Scar's Tec-9 rang loudly through the streets. Quron slumped low in the seat as the bullets tore through the hood of the car, shattering the front windshield off impact. India screamed out in horror, not knowing if she would live to see the next day.

The wheels inside of Quron's head were rapidly turning. He needed a plan, and he needed it fast. He knew that if he stayed inside the car, he was a dead man. He needed to buy a few seconds so he could escape and take the attention off of India's car. He stayed low and pointed his Hi-Point over the dashboard in Scar's direction. He pulled the trigger, causing three hollow point bullets to eject from his cartridge. The sound of sirens was loud and seemed to be getting louder by the second. Memories of prison popped into his mind, but they were quickly removed when the roar from a larger caliber came from behind Tay's whip. Quron turned slightly and saw Steel running full speed toward Scar's Dodge with his.40cal erect and sparking.

Tay got out of the car and crept to the tail end of the Dodge. In one swift motion, she had spun off the trunk, with both glocks raised. She pulled each trigger as fast as her fingers would allow her to. Steel was caught off guard by Tay's sudden appearance, but it was too late to turn back now. Bullets flew past his head and body, but none penetrated his skin.

"They comin' down da hill, Tay, let's go!" Scar screamed out at the top of his lungs.

The trail of police cars were now in his view. Without hesitating, he put the Charger in drive. The wheels turned and turned, kicking up thick gray smoke before screeching off. Tay was halfway in the car when her small body jerked from the car's sudden force. Scar quickly reached for Tay's belt buckle as she was falling.

Tay reached out in desperation, trying to latch onto anything that would prevent her fall, but there was nothing. Just when she lost hope, Scar grabbed a handful of her clothes and used all his might to pull her petite body into safety.

India did not hesitate this time, when Quron commanded her to pull off. Pieces of glass broke off what was left of the windshield as they sped down 1st Street. She reached the stop sign on the corner of 1st and Chambers and shot through, just missing the tail of a passing police car.

Quron looked back, and what he saw sent guilt through his veins. Three police cars and six officers were standing and kneeling with their guns drawn. In the middle of the semi-circle stood his comrade, Steel. His hands were placed comfortably behind his head and his .40cal lay on the cold slab of concrete with smoke coming from its heated barrel. He watched Quron disappear into the night.

"Damn!" He smashed his fist into the dashboard. A deep exhale followed.

India sat unfazed. She remained in a blur, silent, trapped as she navigated through the city.

Chapter 16

"Damn!" Quron screamed out of frustration. It just wasn't his day. The argument he had earlier that morning with Bri was the first sign that a terrible day was ahead. Lately, he had noticed how Bri's demeanor had changed. He didn't beef about it because he knew that her mood swings were the result of him coming up short on his end. The streets were occupying a lot more of his time, and she was feeling neglected. Playing the field was the only way for him to take over the streets. His presence was needed. When he wasn't handling business, he was at Bri's apartment resting, or running around spending quality time with India. He understood where Bri was coming from, but he had to do what he had to do. The end would justify the means.

Throughout the day, his problems only got worse. The war between himself and Scar was in full motion, which meant his street family was in danger and they didn't know it. Quron could only hope that word reached his people before Scar did. He attempted to call Nuri and Young-One, but neither of them answered their phones.

The unknown was really wrecking his nerves. It had been a few days since he had last spoken with Nuri. He found himself reluctantly thinking the worse. The biggest problem of them all was his close friend, Steel's, arrest. Steel was loyal to the end and he had saved his life, but this time his ride or die mentality had cost him his freedom, and Quron felt responsible.

With his head buried in his hands and his body slouched forward, Quron sat on the sofa thinking about the recent chain of events. The custom designed couch was turned on a slanted angle in the middle of the spacious living room, facing the huge TV screen that displayed a gorgeous Latino woman speaking seductively in her Spanish dialect. Quron raised his head and extended his hand toward the large remote control that reminded him of a hand held game system. He was interrupted when India came and flopped down on the fluffy pillow beside him. She looked in his eyes and smiled gently.

"Asking you what's wrong or how are you would be silly questions, so I'm not gonna ask you that. I just wanted to express how much I appreciate everything that you are doing for me. No matter what, I am here for you, and I will always be here for you." A brief silence came over the large living area. "Not even my brother could change that."

India did not wait to see how Quron would react to her comment, she was afraid that his reaction would be what she expected. Her slender arms wrapped around his neck and she held him tightly in her arms. There were many occasions when a hug from someone that she cared for was all she needed. She hoped that her genuine concern was enough to free his mind from the drama that surrounded his life.

After a few seconds of silence, India released her hold and moved over a little, leaving a space between them. Quron looked at her, and he could not blame himself for wondering if India was really worth jeopardizing his life, along with everything else that was at stake. His job was to oversee the family's drug operation, assuring profits, and assuring everyone's safety. He questioned if his decisions lately were making him do the exact opposite.

Quron continued to stare deep into India's eyes. It was there that he found comfort. India was innocent, she was the victim, and she could not change the fact that Scar wanted her life as a compensation for his brother, Trey's life.

"I appreciate the reassurance," Quron said in a low tone with saddened eyes. "This shit has me goin' crazy. I've been tryin' to contact my brother for the past couple of days. This isn't like him, he knows how I get." Quron let out an aggravated sigh. "This nigga better be ah-ight... I swear by Allah he better be ah-ight."

India stood from the soft pillows that made up the couch. She placed her car keys and her cell phone on the glass coffee table that sat in front of her.

"Would you like something to drink?" India asked as she walked toward the kitchen.

"Nah, I'm good."

"Quron, you shouldn't be stressin'. I'm sure that your brother is somewhere enjoying himself. You know he just came home, more than likely, he's somewhere doin' him. Makin' up for lost time. If something bad would have happened, you would have known by now, don't you think?"

Quron sat quietly, thinking about what India said. "Yeah, I guess you're right."

"What time is it?" India asked.

Quron took a quick glance.

"It's almost eight o'clock."

"Okay, it's still early."

"India, I don't know what your plans are, but I gotta get back to the hood. I need to see what's up wit' Steel. I know they ain't gonna let him go tonight, but tomorrow morning he'll be in city court and they'll arraign him. I have to make sure he gets a bail."

"Is there anything I can do to help?"

Quron sat attentively and thought about India's question. Before she offered to help, he hadn't thought of a role that India could play that would actually contribute to the solution. After a few moments of brainstorming, he came up with a simple role that would get him the information he needed regarding Steel, without personally being present.

"Well, now that I think about it, there is something that you can do to help. You can be my eyes and ears."

"What do you mean by that?" India asked, a bit confused.

"What I mean by that is, I'ma need you to appear in court tomorrow morning to see what's goin' on. A lawyer by the name of Thomas Williamsberg will be there to represent Steel. He'll tell you everything you need to know."

"Okay, but how will he know that I am there for Steel?"

"He'll know because I'm gonna tell him. I'll be there with you, I'm just not going inside. I'll be in the rental layin' low."

"No problem, I see you have it all figured out. Give me a few minutes to freshen up before we head out, maybe I could wash off some of this bad luck."

Quron nodded his head and India proceeded through one of the many doors in the beautiful mansion. Quron leaned back on the soft cushions of the sofa and made himself comfortable. His muscular arm rested on the rounded armrest as he pressed down on the large remote control. After skimming through the channels, he came across one of his all-time favorite movies, *Scar Face*. This movie was every drug dealer's favorite. It gave hope to the lowest man on the totem pole. While involved in the drug trade, if you worked hard enough, you could rise and become a kingpin. This message is what inspired people, and at one point in Quron's life, he was no different. He secretly admired Al Capone's ambition and determination. Although the movie in itself was fiction, within the script, there were many jewels for those that looked past the fictitious part of the movie and took heed.

Quron looked around and allowed his mind to become consumed by the thought of living an extravagant lifestyle. The interior to the beautiful estate was breathtaking, and what he saw was exactly how he wanted to live. The marble floor, the plush carpeting that was creatively positioned on certain parts of the floor, the ceiling to floor framed paintings, the expensive furniture, and everything else that he was exposed to, sent a feeling of motivation through his relaxed body.

"Ahhh!" water filled Quron's eyes as he yawned. The day's events had taken a toll on him. Being negative required a lot of energy. He was happy to hear a set of slippers clicking against the marble floor behind him. A few more minutes alone on India's couch, and he would have fallen asleep.

Quron turned toward the direction of the clicking sound and froze. India was strutting seductively toward him, clad in a beautiful silk robe. The color pink enhanced her Indian features and the drops of water that moistened her caramel skin helped the fine threads cling to every curve of her well-defined body. Her shiny black hair dangled loosely as she rubbed the cotton mini towel through it.

Quron was caught in the moment as he absorbed India's intoxicating beauty. Lust was blinding his vision, and blood had filled his penis. Neither of them heard the front door open or close, so Pedro's sudden appearance took both of them by surprise. The beautiful woman that accompanied Pedro wore a clueless expression. Everyone seemed to have stopped moving. The voices of the characters on the television were the only voices heard. The moment was so awkward. Quron knew the scene appeared to be something that it really was not. He really dreaded the thought of Pedro feeling violated or disrespected, especially since he hadn't violated. It was an awkward situation, but Quron knew that he could not blame Pedro if he did feel such a way. Being the man that he was, he reasoned that he would have probably felt the same way if he had walked into his home and found his sister in a robe with a man stretched out on the couch. Them not being engaged in sexual activities was not the issue, sexual tension was in the air and that painted its own picture.

Quron was surprised when Pedro showed no signs of disappointment or anger. If he was bothered, he concealed his rage very well.

Pedro smiled politely and walked calmly toward him. "My friend, how are you? It's good to see you. I started to think that something had gone wrong."

Pedro reached India and greeted her with a genuine hug and kiss on her cheek.

"Not at all, things are running rather smoothly." Quron said as he forced a smile. It wasn't his style to lie or beat around the bush. He wanted to inform Pedro about the drama that he had, but he didn't want Pedro's respect to come from what he was doing for India. He wasn't protecting India for that reason. When he first got shot, it wasn't his intention to risk his life for India. It happened accidentally, but once he became informed about the facts of her situation, he held no regret.

Quron believed in doing what was right. He struggled with decisions on a daily basis, and he had fallen back into the lifestyle of the streets. But at the end of the day, he was a Muslim, and he hadn't aborted all of the pure beliefs that Islam had instilled in him. He accepted the responsibility of holding India down, as a deed from his heart. Pedro would respect him because he was a thoroughbred, and not for any other reason. That's how Quron saw it, so he said nothing of the incident he faced.

"So how long were you planning to stay? I am about to have my chef cook dinner. He makes a delicious pork roast with potatoes and gravy. I would love to have you as my guest." Pedro spoke with a touch of enthusiasm.

Quron was flattered by Pedro's offer, but pork was not a part of his diet. More importantly, the issues that he had to deal with back at home were his number one priority. "I respectfully have to decline this time. I was just about to leave, but India wanted to freshen up before she drove me home. I appreciate the offer, though."

Pedro's joyful expression turned into a slight smirk. Quron couldn't read if that was his way of telling him that he was not buying his story. There wasn't anything that Quron could do, the truth was the truth, and if Pedro chose not to believe him, then so be it.

Quron knew that it was time for him to leave because he started to feel uncomfortable. He didn't want to say something that he did not mean or would later regret. He stood from the couch and looked toward India. Before he could say a word, Pedro presented an offer that Quron could not deny. It would have been blatant disrespect if he did, and he did not want to give that impression.

"Since my beautiful sister isn't quite ready, Charles is on the road, and you are ready to leave, I'll put my dinner off until I return, and drive you home myself." Pedro smiled and studied Quron's expression.

Quron showed no signs of disagreement; he looked toward Pedro, smiled, and made his way toward the door. "Not a problem, I appreciate that."

On their way out the door, Quron said a few departing remarks to India and waved at the beautiful woman that accompanied Pedro. India looked on, entertaining her own thoughts as the large mahogany door closed behind the man that she'd grown emotionally attached to. She wondered what would be the topic of discussion during their long ride up north. She hoped and silently prayed that Pedro wouldn't bring harm to Quron, but she knew that if he had made up his mind, Quron was already dead. By the time she would find out it, would be too late for her to cry and beg for his life. These thoughts brought her pain and stress. India walked quietly to her master bedroom, hoping to find peace.

Meanwhile, outside of the customized mansion, Quron patiently waited for Pedro to return from his five-car garage. It wasn't long before Pedro pulled up and Quron hopped into the new Bentley GT. The leather was extremely soft, and the black piping coordinated with the light tan seats. They pulled out of the gated estate, and before he knew it, Pedro was passing signs that read the miles between their location and Newburgh. The ride home was fast and smooth. Quron was surprised and relieved that Pedro hadn't said anything in regards to him and India. He did not inquire about his reason for being at his home while he was not present, nor did he say anything that would make Quron feel like he was questioning his loyalty. Pedro had only spoken about the contradictions within the political views in the world. As if he knew of

Quron's strife, he reassured him that he was available if he ever needed him, but not once did he insinuate that foul play had taken place between him and his sister.

Now, an hour later, the golden colored coupe cruised through Newburgh's barren streets. The 200k machine captured the attention of anyone who spotted the luxurious car. Moments later, they rolled to a complete stop in front of Quron's Lander Street residence.

"I hope to hear from you soon, my friend."

"You will," Quron assured as he stepped out of the car. "Once again, I appreciate the lift. Thanks." Quron shut the door and moved toward his building.

Pedro smiled and slowly pulled off.

Quron ascended his mother's stairs one after the other. The feeling of someone watching him overcame his body and caused him to turn around. The feeling was too strong to ignore. He scanned his surroundings nervously, and became at ease when he saw nothing that aroused his suspicion or appeared to be out of the ordinary. He reached inside his coat pocket, grabbed his phone, and scrolled through its memory until he came across Young-One's name and number. After a few rings and still no answer, Quron decided to hang up. He pulled his house keys out and turned toward his mother's front door. Protruding out of the door crevice was a neatly folded piece of paper.

Quron unfolded the sheet of paper and read the note.

Hey boo, I just wanted to apologize for beefing with you this morning. I was angry, but I am more concerned, and scared to lose you again. I'm not stupid, I know what you are doing out there in them streets, and yes, I am very disappointed that you allowed yourself to get caught up after all these years. But the fact still remains that you are my man, and for that reason alone, I'm gonna support you and hold you down. I'm just asking you to be true to me like I am to you. If you decide to come to the house tonight and I'm not there, it's because me and the girls are at Tonya's house having a few drinks. I hope to see you soon, be safe and know that I am loving you always.

Your Baby,

Bri

Quron folded the note back up and walked into his mother's home, smiling. The hug and kind words that India gave him earlier helped out a lot, but Bri's warm words were like a breath of fresh air. He knew he liked India a little more than he should, but he could not deny the fact that Bri held the key to his heart.

"Snake, you seen that?" asked the brown skinned skinny kid who sat in one of the parked cars across the street from Quron's home. His hair was short and kinky, and his mischievous smile revealed a chipped tooth that had rotted over the course of time.

"Yeah, I seen duke. He was lookin' around like he knew somebody was watchin' 'em," Snake answered before snorting some of the powdery substance that was spread along the crease of the dollar bill. Snake stood about 5 feet, 5 inches from the ground. His skin complexion resembled midnight and he was built like a bull. His big, full lips attracted women, and his wide nose enhanced his African features. Snake was a big dreamer as a child, and he had a great mind to carry out and achieve whatever his mind conceived. The lack of support in his household made the task to succeed much harder than it should have been. During these hopeless moments, the wicked streets of Virginia embraced him and showed him something that he hadn't felt in a long time. True love was hard to come by, so when his cousin, Scar, Trey, and his best friend, Trife, showed him love, he became a soldier of the streets and never looked back.

Trife and Snake had been friends since elementary school. They connected because they could identify with each other's struggle. They were the only boy siblings and both of their households were destroyed by the crack epidemic. Trife's mother was strung out on drugs, but most of his pain and ruthless thoughts came when he thought of his only sister. She had given up on life after experiencing abusive relationships, and had decided to follow her mother's lead. Whenever Trife saw her, he would console her and shower her with gifts. He never gave her money, because he knew that she would only purchase drugs with it. It hurt him, but that was his way of preserving her life for another day. There were times when Trife expressed his agony through tears and deep discussion with his sister. She would even agree to go into a rehab so that she could get her life together. But on each occasion, her mind was never set and she couldn't complete the cycle. The craving from her crack addiction was too strong, and the result was relapse.

Because of Snake and Trife's destructive childhood, they vowed to never distribute drugs to their own people. Instead, they found ease in robbery, extortion, and murder. When Scar paid them $20,000 a piece to handle some business, they didn't hesitate to catch the next plane to New York. They had arrived at Stewart Airport a few hours earlier and they were already on their job waiting for the right time to strike.

"You ready, fam?" Snake looked at Trife and asked.

Trife pulled out his Tec-22 and checked the chamber before placing it back inside his deep coat pocket. "Yeah, I'm ready." Trife answered in his high-pitched voice.

"Ah-ight, lets breeze. I'll come back tomorrow and pick up the car. I don't wanna put these dudes on point."

Trife agreed and got out of the darkly tinted '97 Honda. They looked at the house that Quron walked into one last time before walking in the opposite direction of the crowd that was gathered in front of the tenement buildings along the block.

"Get off me, boy. You huggin' me like you miss me or somethin'," Bri said playfully, pushing her lover away while showing her Colgate smile. "You only on me because you want some." Bri sucked her teeth and waited for him to respond.

"You better stop playin' and get over here. You know I always miss this pussy. It's hard for me to stay away from my boo." They laughed.

Bri blushed and the couple tickled each other as they fell on the bed, laughing and playing. Bri loved these childish games. It seemed like no matter what stress or rough times they were experiencing, when they were together, there were no worries.

After wiping the tears that had formed from laughter, Bri stood to her feet and walked with a seductive sway toward the hotel door and made sure that it was secured by the inside lock. She was dressed quite provocatively.

Her beautiful long hair was swooped up into a neat bun, exposing her neck and the elegant diamonds that twinkled whenever light hit them. The full-length mink that Quron bought, fit her snugly. The blood red colored fur outlined her voluptuous body, but none of her classy attire indicated that she was naked underneath.

Upon securing the door, Bri did her best impersonation of a professional ballerina as she spun around, wearing a devilish smile. Slowly, she unfastened one button at a time, allowing her full, round breasts to dangle. Using her moist tongue, she outlined her soft lips and strutted confidently back toward the man that she had grown to care for over the years.

The hotel room was average. The outside was clean, and resembled a two-story town house. Upon entering, there was a kitchen, a living area, and a flight of stairs. Up the stairs and to the right sat a regular full sized bed that was closed in by a half wall that overlooked the living room below. Constant change in their love life was the main key to keeping their fire alive. She made the necessary arrangements, knowing that her boo would thank her later for doing so.

The lights in the hotel were dim, and provided a relaxing atmosphere for the lovebirds. Bri kept her stride slow and steady, until she stood teasingly in front of the dresser. She dug into her mink pocket and pulled out an R&B CD that she had brought in from her car. She inserted the disk, and a nice mixture of instruments played through the speakers. The feeling from a warm hand sliding rhythmically between the slit in her plump cheeks took her by surprise, instantly sending chills and goose bumps up and down her spine. She turned with a smile to face her partner and placed soft kisses on his cheek, nose, eyelids, then mouth as their moist tongues danced passionately to the rhythm of Lyfe Jennings' *Phoenix* album.

Bri slid back on the wooden dresser into a sitting position with her smooth legs spread slightly apart. Her cute feet hung inches from the floor.

"Boo, umm-you-act-umm-like-um-you-don't-want-this-pus-pussy." Bri moaned as she spoke between kisses.

In one motion, he slid his tongue out of her mouth and descended with finesse. He licked slowly and skillfully on her shaved vagina. The pleasure from the oral sex caused her eyes to close and her head to lean as she lifted her shapely legs and placed her wiggling toes on his defined shoulders simultaneously.

"Oh my God, please don't stop eatin' my pussy, please pa, please don't stop." Murmured words escaped as her eyes rolled from the pure ecstasy that she was feeling. After minutes of overwhelming pleasure, she could not hold back any longer. Her body shook violently and a thick cream oozed from the interior of her fat vagina.

Usually, Bri took pride in making the love of her life beg for the pussy after cumming in his mouth, but today was different. Earlier, she was stressed and on the verge of having a nervous breakdown because of the cruel words that Quron had used during their argument. But now, she was feeling herself, loving every second of the special treatment that she was receiving. *Maybe we should argue more often.* She reached down and interrupted the fiery sensation that seized her silky insides. She pulled on his ears gently and pulled his dreads as he placed a trail of kisses around her navel, up her stomach, and on each nipple.

"Umm baby," slipped out of her mouth as he sucked forcefully on her erect nipple. "Please let me feel you inside of me, oh yes daddy, I need to feel you inside of me." Bri begged, barely able to control herself. She felt the walls to her vagina contract and she knew that it was on.

The small size of her baby's penis didn't bother her. At first, it was an issue because of what she had been exposed to in her past relationships. Once she gave him a chance, to her surprise, she could hardly tell the difference. To his advantage, he definitely knew how to work the middle.

He moved his hips with experience and she grinded back. "Fuck me harder, fuck me harder." Her round ass slid off the edge of the wooden dresser and her firm legs formed a V in the air, as he pumped his uncircumcised dick in and out of her warm vagina.

"This how you want it, bitch?" Her lover shouted as he quickened his pace. "Answer me when I'm fuckin' talkin' to you!"

"Yeah daddy, talk dirty to me. Talk that shit, daddy, uww!"

The couple drifted into separate zones as they role played. Bri's eyes closed as she felt her orgasm closing in. She latched onto his chiseled back and started bucking wildly.

"Is it good, ma? Is this fuckin' good enough?" He asked through gritted teeth.

"Yes daddy, yes!"

"Say my name, bitch!"

"Ahh, I love you. Hit it right there, don't stop!"

"I said, say my name!"

"That's my spot, daddy. Ahh, I'm cumin', I'm cumin', please don't stop, go faster. Please don't stop, uww I'm cumin'. Quron I love you, oh Quron!!!" Bri dug her pretty nails into his back and buried her perspiring face into his flat chest as the wave of orgasms ripped through every inch of her body. Breathing irregularly Bri raised her head and settled on the piercing eyes that stared menacingly down at her. She smiled at her lover's facial expression, becoming more aroused as he continued to role-play.

"You smilin' like I'm a fuckin' joke. I'm not playin'." He spat aggressively with rage in his voice. He grabbed Bri underneath her armpits and pulled out of her womb.

Bri was confused as she looked on, not knowing what she had done wrong. After realizing that he was seriously angry, she stood to her feet and moved toward her man as he gathered his clothes and started to dress. She extended her hand to touch him, but he smacked her small fingers and grabbed her wrist with force.

"I told you that I ain't playin', this ain't no fuckin' game. You dun lost yo' mind!"

"What is your problem?" Bri asked. "Five minutes ago, everything was good. Now, all of a sudden after you got ya nut off, you wanna start buggin', actin' all stupid like I did something to you!" Bri was enraged now. She did not appreciate how her so-called man was treating her.

"You should be ashamed of yourself. It's sad that you really don't have a fuckin' clue, do you?" he asked while shaking his head in disbelief.

"What are you talking about?" Bri shouted, obviously frustrated.

"What I'm talkin' 'bout is you callin' out the next nigga name while we fuckin'." He paused and looked deep into her eyes. "How you gon' call me Quron? I can't believe you, Bri, I really can't believe you. While we fucking tho, really Bri?"

Bri stood in silence, at a loss for words. She felt embarrassed and humiliated. She could not believe that she had slipped like that. Her lover stood motionless with a hurt expression on his face. He waited for her to justify why she was with him, but had obviously been thinking about the next man. Bri could not gather the appropriate words that would emphasize how truly sorry she was. Instead of digging herself into a deeper hole, she decided to remain quiet.

"So you aren't gonna say anything? You gonna just sit there with the puppy look and expect me to feel sorry for you? Well guess what, it's not gonna happen. I'm the victim here, and I be damned if I allow you to flip the guilt on me!" The handsome brother said. As bad as he wanted to get disrespectful, he could not bring himself to do it. He wanted to appear to be angrier than what he really was, but it was hard.

He had a huge soft spot in his heart for Bri, and it was working against him. He never understood exactly why this was so. He didn't even recall when this level of emotion had developed, but it had. He had plenty of gorgeous women that were willing to submit to whatever he wanted or needed them to do. On many occasions when Bri occupied his thoughts, he pondered on the love that he had for her and wondered why it ran so deep. He never could pinpoint the specific reason. There were so many little things that she did that stood out and placed her into a category separate from the other women that he'd known. In his heart, he never wanted to lose Bri. Just the thought alone aroused ill feelings.

When they first started seeing each other, there was nothing intimate about their connection. They had been friends for quite a while. During the cold and lonely nights that Bri craved attention, she reached out and used the opportunity to express herself, hoping to receive some beneficial input about her situation from a man's point of view. Over the course of time, their innocent phone conversations evolved into hours of meaningful discussions. They spoke about the ties that she had established with Quron, and just like a real woman, she never denied the unconditional love that she possessed for him. It was the pressure of being out in society, and Quron being in prison, that pushed her into this vulnerable state. Now years had passed, and genuine feelings had formed, which led to the love triangle that she found herself caught up in.

Still feeling embarrassed, but not wanting to lose the man that stood in front of her, Bri gently touched his hand and started to massage it.

I didn't say it on purpose. I'm sorry and I really hope that you can find it in your heart to forgive me." She tightened her grasp on his hand adding emphasis to her words. "We've been through so much over the years and you have done nothing but stayed true to our bond. You have supported me through it all. I cannot begin to show how grateful I am to have someone like you by my side." She dropped her head out of guilt. "I've grown to appreciate and love you." Bri paused and released a drawn out sigh. "But I would be lying to you if I told you that I'm not in love with Quron too."

He looked at Bri and found that he could not resist her any longer. Her confession to still be in love with Quron didn't matter. He wanted her in his arms and he wanted her now. He stopped dressing and wrapped her in his arms. Her honesty was one of the many things that he loved about her. He kissed her on her forehead and lifted her chin until their eyes settled on each other.

"I love you, boo."

"I love you more." Young-One responded before kissing her long and passionately.

The secret lovers wasted no more time expressing themselves with words. Making love was a better remedy to their problems. Young-One allowed Bri to undress him piece by piece, as they fondled and nibbled on each other. Young-

One's Tru Religion jeans dropped to the floor and Bri kneeled. She pushed the skin back on the head of his penis and tasted every inch of him. She moved up and down his shaft with perfection. Spit oozed from her mouth as she gave him sloppy head.

Young-One placed his hand on the back of her head and humped her mouth as if it was her pussy. So much had transpired in one day, but neither of them had an idea of what had taken place. They were so caught up in each other that nothing outside of what they shared mattered. They were playing a dangerous game, but none of Bri's foul actions raised enough fear in her heart to make her reconsider. Still on her knees, the warm saliva coated Young-One's fully erect dick. Her slurps grew louder as she became even more aroused by the bomb head that she was giving. The thoughts that flashed through her mind brought forth comfort and good feelings. Pleasing her boo was all that mattered.

Chapter 17

Early the next morning, Bri was sound asleep. She looked so innocent and peaceful. Her nude body lay motionless on top of the pillows and linen. Something wet, thick, and slimy skillfully glided across her smooth skin, arousing her hormones, causing her to awaken. She discreetly eased up on both elbows and looked toward her pelvic area, where the continuous tingling emanated from. She smiled as Young-One slowly licked and kissed her flat stomach.

"Stop, silly, that tickles." Bri giggled.

"Bout time, I thought you wouldn't ever wake up." Young-One said jokingly, and then positioned himself so he could kiss her.

"Get outta here, boy. You all in my face and I just woke up, morning breath an' all." Bri stated with humor after turning her face away from Young-One's lips.

"I ain't tryna' hear that, give me a kiss, girl," Young-One chuckled. "I don't care if ya breath stink or not, I still want my suga'."

Young-One's comment earned a smile. Bri knew he was serious as a heart attack. He had really grown to love her for who she really was, and not for the superficial things that most men lust for in a woman. It was the very small things like this that she loved, but at the same time, it made the decision she knew she would eventually have to make, more difficult. She often pondered on the love that she and Quron shared. She even entertained the possibility of their bond being a childhood thing. The solution to her dilemma never became clear, but she hoped and prayed that she would be able to sort out her mixed emotions before it was too late.

Realizing that Young-One wouldn't stop trying to get a kiss until he was successful, Bri reluctantly submitted and gave him a quick peck on his moist lips. Young-One loosened his hold around her small waist, and Bri seized the opportunity to free herself. She quickly jumped out of bed and ran into the bathroom. Young-One sat on the bed laughing and shaking his head as Bri freshened up.

The remainder of the morning moved on relatively fast. The couple enjoyed a well-balanced breakfast of grits, pink salmon, and a cheese omelet with freshly squeezed orange juice as a beverage. With a full belly, they could hardly relax and allow their food to digest. Their physical infatuation with one each other led to excessive touching and continuous lovemaking until fatigue overtook their bodies. After sharing the water from a steaming hot shower, the secret lovers reluctantly decided to leave the privacy of the hotel that held their moments of passion.

They gathered their personal items and prepared to leave. Frustration settled when Bri couldn't find her overnight bag. In the midst of searching, it dawned on her that she had somehow managed to forget her bag, along with a fresh change of clothing. So excited and aroused with the thought of spending quality time with Young-One, a plan to cover up her tracks had slipped her mind.

The frustration that she initially felt when she had begun searching had turned to fear. She came to the hotel wearing a mink with nothing underneath. She knew she couldn't take a chance and drive home like that. Just her luck, Quron would be at her apartment when she arrived.

Young-One noticed her hesitant motions and her dismayed expression told him that she was bothered.

"What's wrong, boo? Why you lookin' like that?" he inquired.

"I'm just mad 'cause I forgot my overnight bag, and now I don't have any clothes."

"Last night when I put my coat in ya trunk, I saw a small duffle bag. Ain't nothin' in there?" Young-One questioned.

"Oh yeah, thanks so much sweetie," Bri remembered, relieved as she gave Young-One a hug. "I forgot all about my gym bag." She quickly made her way to the car, retrieved the bag, and got dressed. It helped, but not much. Her hair was a mess, and to make matters worse, the stretch pants and t-shirt inside her bag was clothing that she wore only while cleaning her home, and Quron was aware of that.

Inside the car, they joked and made sarcastic comments about their behavior during their love sessions. As they continued to drive, the conversation faded and silence eased into the air. Young-One reclined in the passenger seat and closed his eyes. It seemed like the closer they got to the city of Newburgh, the faster Bri's heart beat. Small drops of perspiration formed on her forehead and inside her palms. It suddenly dawned on her how big of a risk she was actually taking, and her anxiety showed.

Young-One was a popular person in the hood, and a lot of people knew her as well. Newburgh was a small town where everyone knew each other. If anyone spotted them together, there wasn't a doubt in Bri's mind that they would mention it to Quron, and that's what she feared. She knew that she was not ready to face any questions pertaining to her and Young-One. One slip up could arouse suspicion, and she definitely didn't want that.

The Acura turned off the Newburgh Beacon Bridge, and minutes later, Bri was passing by Newburgh Free Academy North Campus. Her composure began to slip. All she could think of was getting caught, and how Quron would react if he found out that she was having an affair with his best friend. The consequences that unraveled in her mind were horrifying.

The car rolled to a halt at a traffic light and she tried to use the brief pause to calm down, regain control over her emotions, and develop an optimistic mind state. It was to no avail. The light turned green and she was just as nervous as she had been before. Noticeably shaking, she applied pressure to the gas pedal and accepted the fact that she was not mentally or emotionally built for the risk that she was taking. Without hesitation, she clicked on the right turn signal and pulled over across the street from Downing Park.

Young-One opened his eyes, realizing that they had come to a sudden stop. He thought they had reached his honey comb hide out, but when he looked around and recognized the Robinson Avenue scenery, his gaze shifted toward Bri. She gazed out of the driver's side window. She didn't have the courage to tolerate Young-One's stare without breaking down. She felt bad. She didn't want to come across as a person perpetrating a fraud about how she felt for him. Their reality was still a complicated situation, and she felt that it was in their best interest for her to take control, utilize her mind, and temporarily suppress the sincere emotions that she harbored inside of her heart.

Young-One shook his head in disbelief and forced a smile to cover up the disappointment that he was feeling. Without words, he dug into his pocket and retrieved the haze rolled blunt from that morning. With his free hand, he grabbed the lighter off the dashboard. The high flame touched the tip of the Vanilla Dutch Master, and he inhaled slowly, causing the moist scented leaf to ignite in flame. The potent marijuana tickled the back of his throat like a bird's feather gliding back and forth across skin. He formed his lips like he was going to blow a whistle, and out came a stream of smoke. His eyes lowered and became chinky. His breathing settled and he reclaimed his relaxed demeanor. The passenger door to the Acura opened and he calmly stepped out. Before closing the door, he stooped down so that his eyes could be fixed on Bri.

She respectfully gave him the attention that he sought, hoping that he would respect, and more importantly, understand her position.

"I ain't gon' flip on you, so you can stop lookin' at me like that." He smiled. "I know you in a fucked up position, in fact, we both are. Sometimes you don't know how bad I wish I could change the way I feel about you." Young-One pulled slowly on the blunt and exhaled just as slow. Shaking his head, he continued. "I don't know why, but I can't. I understand ya struggle, only hope our situation gets greater later, 'cause eventually, shit gon' hit the fan. Really, I'm at a point where I don't give a fuck. It's sad, but it's the truth. I'm tired of creeping, tired of tiptoeing around. I'ma keep gettin' this money, but if things come ta light, fuck it, whateva happen happens. I'ma see you around though, be safe, ah-ight."

Young-One shut the door, crossed the street and walked nonchalantly through the park.

Business on the block was much slower than it had been in the past couple of months. It was not the first of the month, nor was it the fifteenth of the month. The slow movement on the block had all of the hustlers on edge. They had gotten used to their packages moving at lightning speed. The actual day of the month had not been a factor since Quron, Nuri, Young-One, and Steel hit the streets with the pure coke that Pedro supplied.

Usually, business was booming and everyone was happy because they were eating. The majority of the addicts throughout the small city had stopped buying drugs from the other areas that sold them. Lander St. had quickly converted into crack alley and had become the primary block to cop work from. Although it wasn't true, the word on the streets was every hustler on the strip had the same coke, and had unified under one umbrella.

When Quron heard about the circulating rumor, he smiled. He actually liked the concept of there being one block with one product. He knew that it would be very profitable for him and his partners. Seven blocks made up Lander St., and to have control of them all, equaled millions. It was definitely an idea that demanded deeper thought, but at the time, it was something that was too far out of his reach, with his mind and energy focused on Scar.

The autumn season was slowly fading and the cold, brisk air confirmed that winter was not far away. Lifeless trees hovered over Newburgh's lifeless streets. Their flake, and spear shaped leaves had turned colors, fallen to the ground, and had been taken away by the strong, gusty winds that swept through the city. Their bare branches quivered from the chill, and left the scene looking plain. The dark gray clouds that cluttered the sky made it appear to be later than the clock reflected. Quron didn't allow the slow production or the bleak setting to bother him. He was just happy to be on the block, in the presence of his crew. Scar hadn't gotten to them after all.

Not much was happening on this gloomy afternoon. It was obvious that the weather had an effect on almost everybody. The vibe seemed depressed.

Quron was sitting on a brick porch near the corner, dressed fly for the fall weather. He sat quietly, observing his surroundings looking out for police or anything else that appeared suspect.

The coldness from the bricks seeped through his Ralph Lauren jeans, causing him discomfort. He stood from his sitting position, walked down the stairs, and moved to join his boys.

"What up, Young. How you?" Quron asked. "Damn boy, since you cut your dreads, you look like a representative from corporate America." He smiled.

"True story, Ron. Young, killin' them wit' that wool pea coat and those Armani frames," Nuri added.

"We gotta take a trip to Yale or one of them other spots and bag a few of them bad, innocent, soon to be lawyer broads. Put you on the front line or somethin', nah-mean. Run some game by shorty and see what it really is. Once you get her thinkin', we got her. I'ma be ya side man, and hold you down, look at her wit' the dead serious face and ask her, aren't you the female that sit behind us in criminal justice class? By the time she realizes we runnin' game, it's a wrap. She'll be lovin' you and I'ma have one of her girls on smash, ya dig!" Nuri laughed.

"Oh word, genius? So what we gon' do when shorty tell you she don't have a criminal justice class?" Young-One asked with a smile.

"What chu think I'm gon' do? I'm gon' apologize and move on to the next chick!"

Young-One, Steel and Quron listened and started dying laughing. Nuri's split personalities were incredible. He was a cool brother that loved to joke and be silly most of the time. But in the blink of an eye, if provoked, he would transform into a cold-blooded murderer and not think twice about it. His ability to control the two personalities made him unpredictable to outsiders, but a valuable asset to his crew.

Quron regained his composure and rose from the bent over position that Nuri's humor had caused him to curl into. He held his stomach and chuckled some more.

"Ya'll two together is a trip. Them females will have ya'll twisted," Quron smiled. "I was tryin' to contact both of ya'll yesterday." He turned to face his brother. "And Nuri, I've been tryin' to reach you for the past few days. Young, who is shorty that got you turnin' off ya phone? Nigga, you don't ever turn ya phone off. If home girl pussy good enough to make you do that, then I want in. You know how we do. Everything is open game except for wifey, so stop holdin' out, ol sucka for love ass nigga." Quron said with sarcasm, and the crew fell out.

"Never dat, daddy! You know these hoes don't mean shit to me. Real talk though, yesterday I was at the crib all day, restin'. After days of runnin' around, a nigga body start shuttin' down. Gotta fall back sometime and recuperate, ya dig. Too much eatin', fuckin', suckin', and all that typa shit, feel me!" Young-One lied.

While Young-One spoke, Quron took note of his left eye twitching. Normally this wouldn't have been an issue, but

Quron was offended because his man was lying to his face for no reason at all, or so he thought. He knew he was lying because as kids, they had gotten so many butt whippings because of his twitching eye. Young-One's mother always said that was her way to determine if he was telling the truth or not. Over the years, Quron had found her accusation to be true. Now it was manifesting itself again.

"Young, I know you ain't sittin' here lyin' in my face," Quron said, not overlooking the sign. "Bro, you know you can't lie to me. That eye always gives you up."

"Lyin for what? Brah, we grown men, what I gotta lie about? Especially to you, you my bro!" Young-One spit, defending himself.

"Nah Ron, I know the... the homie ain't caught up in... in no pussy like dat," Steel interjected, still finding humor in the situation.

"I'm serious, Steel!" Quron retorted, obviously bothered.

"Aww, how cute," Nuri cut in. "Young, look at big bro' getting' all over protective cause he couldn't contact us." Nuri opened his hand and shrugged. "Ain't our fault you locked down by one woman, but lovin' the next chick." Nuri, Young-One, and Steel laughed.

"Uwwwwww"

"Do I have clown written all over my fuckin' face? 'Cause it seems like whatever I say is bein' taken as a joke! Shit isn't a game! Ya'll making jokes like it's a game, but y'all didn't know that this clown nigga, Scar, tried to gun me down yesterday. While ya'll was M.I.A., disconnected from the world, I was out here gunnin' it out!"

Quron's words cut through Nuri's heart like a sword. His mood visibly changed.

Young-One suppressed the ill feelings that he felt and became very attentive. His concern even took him by surprise.

"Real talk, if it wasn't for our boy, Steel, I probably wouldn't be standin' here right now." Quron explained.

"What chu mean Scar tried to gun you down? Why you just tellin' me this?" Drops of spit fell loosely from Nuri's mouth as his voice rose. "We spoke this mornin' and you told me everything was everything. You said nothing of this shit." Nuri angrily stated, not pleased with his brother's choice to withhold such serious information.

"I didn't mention it because I know how you are for one, and two, I don't like talkin' about anything over the phone! You know that!"

"Yeah ah-ight, whatever you say! So what happened?" Nuri demanded.

Quron explained in detail what had transpired the day before between him and Scar. Whatever slipped his mind, Steel added, until everything was out and made sense.

"What! These bitch ass niggaz!" Nuri was furious. He spoke aggressively through gritted teeth. He wanted to take immediate action.

Quron wouldn't allow his emotions to dictate his decisions. Nuri looked at his brother, wearing a disgusted expression, and shook his head. He never understood how his brother could practice patience during a time like this. He couldn't help but to think that Quron's humble approach would someday bring about their demise. The thought of this really bothered him.

Young-One leaned against a parked car and absorbed what was said. Ironically, he felt that he had to ride for the cause. He knew he was living foul, but none of that negated the fact he and Quron had experienced a lot together, from smoking their first blunt, to getting their first piece of pussy, to selling their first brick together. Those were unique events that only best friends and brothers experience, which is why he couldn't understand how he had allowed himself to get so caught up with Bri, his right hand man's wifey. The ill part of it all was that he was so blinded by his love for her, he was willing to do whatever it took to make her his lady. He stood silently in a zone, weighing his options, but not once did he contemplate backing out of the situation.

"Damn, Steel, you got knocked? What happened when they took you to the precinct?" Young-One asked, genuinely concerned about his comrade.

"Them... them jakes is crazy. You... you... you know they was try... tryin' to convince me to... to talk. Usin' the good cop, bad... bad cop tac... tactics," Steel explained. "But you know I'm to... to... toooo thorough and too clever for their... their games. They said they... they knew I wasn't alone 'cause, 'cause they found too many differ... different shell casings. I told the fat pig that was... was in my face, 'since you know every, every goddamn thing, why the fuck you... you tryna get... get in for... for... mation outta me for. That crack... cracker turned beet red and curse... cursed me the fuck out." Steel laughed.

"You went to city court this mornin' right?"

"Yeah."

"So what the judge say at arraignment?"

"Basically, all they... they did was charge me wit'... wit' reckless endangerment and poss... possession of a weap... weapon in the first degree. I got a grand jury court... court date for... for next month. That's when they gon', gon' decide if they want to... to indict me or not, if... if they do I'ma... I'ma have to fight them until they... they talkin' what I wan'... wanna hear, ya... ya... ya dig."

"Don't even stress that shit, homie," Nuri cut in reassuringly. "We family, and I give you my word that we gon' do everything in our power to get you off, ya heard!"

Steel gave him a pound, then hugged him. "I know, fam, you ain't have to say... say that. We been down for each other fo... fo' for forever and I know how we... we do. Ron already got me a... an official lawyer. Son sharp wit'...wit' his shit. Ron put up the... the ten thousand dollar bail that they... that they gave me too. So I ain't worried, I'm... I'm good. They can eat a... a dick."

"Pardon me, Steel. Not to cut you off, but somethin' you said made me think of somethin' that I've been meanin' to ask," Quron said, then turned toward Young-One. "What up wit' our product? How many bricks we have left?"

Caught off guard, Young-One took a second before the question registered.

"Oh, I umm, went to the stash house this mornin' after I left shorty, I mean the crib, and did a quick inventory. Unless one of ya'll went up there and snatched somethin', I only counted four bricks." His mind flashed back to the blissful moments of passion that he shared with Bri the night before and a pleasant smile formed.

Quron's gazed shifted from one comrade to the next. He wore a confused expression on his face. Slowly, the look faded and a boisterous grin appeared. "Damn Young, I wasn't expecting you to say nothin' like that," Quron shook his head unbelievingly. "We broke down nine keys between the four of us in a matter of months on one block. That's crazy!" He smiled. "What's even crazier is we haven't moved on any other dude's territory yet." He looked around in admiration. "We produced all this bread from one block. Hard work and determination always pushes us through.

A brief silence replaced the enthusiasm. Quron gathered his thoughts and posed a question. "Y'all gave Young all the bread like we agreed, right?"

Nuri and Steel both nodded, indicating that they had done what they had agreed to do.

"Ah-ight, Alhamdulillah. So that means it should be like six..." He tilted his head and calculated the numbers in his mind. "Like six hundred and forty-eight Gs inside the safe, right?" Quron asked, directing his question to Young-One.

"Yup, that's exactly what I counted. I see you still swift when it comes to countin' that guap." Young-One said and laughed.

"No question, gotta stay sharp wit' that." Quron chuckled and gave his man a pound. They were all excited. "Do me a favor, Young. Split all that bread up evenly and give it to the brothas. Between the four of us, we should all get like a hundred and sixty-two Gs a piece. But umm, instead of giving us that, I just thought about somethin'." He made hand gestures as he spoke. "Take out a hundred-thousand of the whole amount, and then divide the rest. That should give us a hundred and thirty-seven thousand a piece, which is still money. I'm gon' use that hunite that I told you to set aside to make a move wit' and get some more coke. Don't stress that, that's money in da bank. As for that other thing, as soon as those last four go, we gon' split up that bread too. Despite the drama, things are lookin' up. We killin' 'em 'cause we got the best coke that these streets seen in a long time. We getting' back so much more on the cook up than what we puttin' in the pot, we can afford to make our dimes and twenties bigger than our competition. Right now, we bringin' back $2000 off every ounce sold. Majority of the cats out here got our product."

His last statement caught a nerve. The fellas looked at him with strange expressions. When they came up with how they planned to distribute their product, selling weight to the other hustlers was frowned upon. With this in mind, they didn't understand how the other dealers had the same product if none of them was supplying them.

"Nah man," Quron chuckled. "Why ya'll lookin' at me all cock eyed? The reason why I said most of these dudes got our product is 'cause I sold a few of them my packs as wholesale. They think they gettin' over, but at the end of the day, our profit margin is still out of this world. How? let me answer my own question. 'Cause our dimes is still bein' bought for $10 no matter how you look at it. In a sense, it's like we movin' weight, but in essence, we profit way more than a dude who pushin' his product in weight. It is what it is. We savin' dudes mad time, they don't gotta bag up no work or none of that. All they doin' is coppin' our dimes and flippin' 'em for twenty."

He opened the bottled water that Nuri had brought him earlier and took a swig. He could tell that what he'd shared was on their minds. "We can't lose, we just gotta stay focused and hustle hard for a little longer." He embraced each of his comrades. The feeling was almost strange. He hadn't felt so good in a long time. Finally, he felt like he was making progress in the streets. Slowly, but surely, his financial goal was materializing into reality.

The sound of a horn startled Quron. He turned toward the rented vehicle and noticed his little man, exiting the car along with two other men who appeared to be a lot younger than he was. One of the young men sported a loose fitting sweat suit with a matching hat and a pair of Air Max running shoes. The other was dressed in a pair of denim designer jeans that hung off his waist, exposing his Polo boxers. A black hoodie draped over his medium built frame. Neither of them had facial hair, and they had similar features.

"What up, y'all!" Ghost shouted, acknowledging everyone on the block.

"What's good, Ghost?" A crowd of hustlers responded almost simultaneously.

"Same shit, y'all know how it go." Ghost explained as he walked with a cool sway toward Quron and the rest of the crew. They greeted him with love. The team had found themselves interacting with Ghost on the regular, lately. Their constant run ins were not planned. Ghost was just a likeable youngster who controlled a certain level of the street circuit. He had a smooth swagger with a big reputation, and was he known to put in work on dudes who didn't respect his hustle. Nuri, Steel, and Young-One dug his style and took a liking to him almost immediately after Quron introduced them.

After a while of kicking it, Ghost asked Quron to accompany him across the street to await the food that he had ordered over the phone from the Fish-n-Chips. They excused themselves and walked across the street where Ghost's rental car was parked. Ghost looked around. He felt a bad vibe. The feeling came over him when he first pulled up on the strip. He tried to brush it off, but now the same feeling overcame him again. Intuition told him that something was definitely out of place. Still observing his surroundings, he couldn't put his finger on what it was that had obviously slipped past him.

Quron noticed the sudden change in his expression. "What up lil homie, what happened?" he inquired.

Ghost started to speak on what he was feeling, but decided against sharing. He didn't want Quron to think he was paranoid.

"Ain't nothin', just thinkin'. What up wit' you though, ol' timer? Everything good?" Ghost asked, flipping the question. Ol' timer was a nickname that he had made up for Quron. Ghost always said that Quron's mind made him seem like an old man who had traveled around the world once and seen everything within it twice. Quron burst out laughing when Ghost first broke it down to him, but it was true. Every time they got together, Quron made it his business to share words of wisdom. Ghost didn't care to hear his experience based views at first, but gradually he started taking heed, and his game escalated to the next level. His results were far better than what they had been previously. This aroused a new perception and a level of admiration had developed.

"All is well, why'd you ask? What's on ya mind?"

Ghost pondered the question and hesitated with his response. He knew his position. More importantly, he knew that no matter what, he had to play his position. True, they had grown tighter since they had initially met, but he was not certain if they had reached a level where they had the green light to inquire about each other's personal business. He looked Quron in his chinky eyes. Fuck it, he'd rather get in his business than fall back and allow something bad to happen to him.

"Ain't nothin' major. I was just askin' 'cause I heard about the shootout that you had wit' Scar and Tay." Ghost paused and gave Quron an opportunity to check him. When he didn't say anything, Ghost continued sharing his concern.

"I don't mean to get in your business, it's just that..." Ghost became silent and gathered his thoughts. "When shit got back to me, somethin' inside made me feel obligated to extend my hand. To let you know that I'm here for you, and if need be, I'll put work in on them niggas. I know you just came home from doin' a stretch behind murderin' one of these clown ass dudes. It'll do me more harm than good if you get caught up. Real talk, you the closest thing I ever had to a role model, and I'd hate to lose you over some sucka shit. Ain't nothin' in the world worth doin' life for..."

Quron was surprised, but nevertheless genuinely flattered by Ghost's feelings. Ghost continued sharing his thoughts, but they had fallen on deaf ears. Quron's mind had drifted. A part of him wanted to put Ghost to the test to see if he really walked what he talked. The compassionate side of him wouldn't allow him to do so. He cared too much about the young fella. The possible scenarios that could bring Ghost harm while trying to get at Scar, repeatedly flashed through his mind. He knew he wouldn't be able to live with himself if Ghost were to suffer on his behalf. He couldn't bear such a burden on his conscience.

"O.T., what you think about that?" Ghost asked, breaking Quron out of his trance. He anticipated a response. When none came, he looked at Quron and noticed his far away expression. "Aww man, you aint payin' me no attention. You over there zonin'." Ghost chuckled.

"Pardon me, lil bro', no disrespect intended. I'm not gon' lie, you got me over here twisted," Quron admitted. "Nah baby boy, you don't gotta look like that. I was just caught off guard by how you feel. I never expected you to share that side. Being able to express yourself without feelin' like you are less than a man is gangsta, but most dudes don't see it like that, ya dig. A lot of you younger brothas have a hard time expressing ya selves, so to see you do it really shows me that you are slowly comin' out of that immature stage. Real is real, though. I would be lyin' if I said I don't appreciate the love, 'cause I do. But on an even realer level, the better side of me won't let me put you on the line for me. I got a lot of love for you, and along those same lines, I really respect ya mother." Quron took a breath.

"Ron, you know my mother?"

Quron smiled. "No, not personally. What I do know is she is the person that brought you into this world. I respect her 'cause I have a mother too. We crazy close, and I know how much pain she'll feel if somebody called her and said I was gunned down by one of these lame niggaz out here. She'd be twisted, just like anybody else's mother, includin' yours. Lil homie, she already lost ya father to these streets... I ain't gon' be the reason why she lose you." Quron said, shaking his head. "Let me ask you somethin' though, Ghost. You made it obvious that you know the repercussions from takin' a life, so why would you be willin' to sacrifice yourself like that?"

A smile spread across Ghost's face and he raised his lanky arm and pointed toward the young men that had exited the car with him earlier. They were posted on the corner, diagonal from where Quron and Ghost were settled, and across the street from Nuri, Steel, and Young-One. They looked innocent, but skilled in their trade as they huddled next to a parked vehicle, serving the crack addicts that walked up to them.

"I'm far from a fool," Ghost stated as a matter of fact. "Like you said, I know what comes wit' catchin' a body. But I understand the rules of the game. Sometimes a nigga is better off dead than he is alive. O.T., you told me a while ago that it ain't so much about what you do, it's about how you do whatever it is that you do. That's one jewel that stuck wit' me ever since. But umm, don't let their baby faces fool you. Those set of twins gets busy, trust me when I say that..."

"Ayy there Ghost. I ain't know you was out here standin' in this cold. Yo' food is in here waitin' fo' you, chile. It's gon' get cold if you don't hurr' up, ya hear?" The elderly woman said in a deep southern drawl from behind the screen door.

"Ah-ight Mrs. James, I'll be right there." Ghost assured.

Mrs. James nodded and went back into her place of business.

"Yo Ghost, I think that fiend over by the pay phone is pointin' at you."

Ghost looked in the direction that Quron pointed and noticed a male addict gesturing with his hand to come over. The fiend had on a filthy goose that appeared to be a few sizes bigger than what he actually wore. His dread locks were long, thick, and dirty. His shoes were mismatched, and he looked as if he smelled like garbage.

"You know this nigga, Ron?" Ghost asked in a stern voice.

"Nah, I never seen duke." Quron admitted.

From across the street, the crack head looked on impatiently as Quron and Ghost spoke. He was fidgety and seemed like the thought of getting high excited him so much that he couldn't stop himself from twitching and moving.

Ghost brushed his hand across his waist and cocked the hammer to his gun. Caution signs flashedin his mind. It wasn't a coincidence that he nor Quron knew the fiend. On top of that, the majority of the crack fiends that came through to cop knew not to approach Ghost, because he didn't deal hand to hand. All of his customers called him before coming to buy. Ghost looked up and down the block, searching for an unmarked police car that he felt was near. He didn't see any. His curiosity was eating him up and he made a decision that he knew was not best for him.

"Yo what up, everything good?" Quron asked upon noticing Ghost's bothered look.

"Yeah, I'ma see what up wit' duke. I'll be right back."

Ghost pushed off the rental car that he was leaning on and started walking with caution toward the fiending crack head.

Mrs. James peeped through the window shades. She eyed Ghost walking away and knocked hard on the restaurant's fiberglass windows.

Ghost stopped in his tracks and turned around.

Mrs. James had her hands on her wide, sagging hips, shouting at him. He stood for a second in the center of the road looking back and forth from Mrs. James to the fiend and decided to go pay for his food.

Looking over his shoulder, he shouted, "Yo twin, go see what up wit' homeboy over by the pay phone, ya heard. I'll be right back!"

Ghost turned around and made his way toward Mrs. James' Fish-n-Chips. One of the twins did as he was told. Quron leaned with his back against the car, deep in thought. He couldn't seem to shake off the fact the Young-One had lied. He didn't comment on it, but he'd taken note of Young-One slipping up when he mentioned where he had been before going to the stash house earlier that morning.

This nigga is lyin' over basically nothin'. Over a female. If you don't want us to know who ya chick is, then just say that. Don't be lyin' to dudes. Quron's thoughts continued to run. *Ron, you gotta tighten up all loose ends. If Young would lie over nothin', imagine what'll happen on a more serious note. You only as strong as your weakest link, stop slippin'! Fam' or foe, if they violate, they get dealt wit' period.*

In the streets, not even some of the smartest survive, and Quron knew this, so he had to be that much smarter. As he continued to discipline himself, across the street from where he stood, twin was handling his business.

"What's good, pop? What you need?" Twin asked, not aware of Ghost's suspicion. The fiend was still twitching and appeared to be even more excited that he was finally going to get his hit.

"What you got, rude boy? Dime, nick, twenty?" The addict asked in a desperate, distorted accent.

"I got dimes, dread. How many you want?"

"Me got fifty-dalla. Dis me lass money so make sure me get a play, ya hear."

"No question. I got chu, dread." Twin looked up and down the one-way street to make sure that there weren't any patrolling police around. In one motion, he slid his hand into his boxers and retrieved the package of crack that was secured between his butt cheeks.

"Yo, hold me down." Twin shouted as he blocked the view by turning his body so that the pay phone and the run down tenement building could shield his transaction.

Moments later, Twin turned around with the drugs in his hand. He looked up, and his gaze settled directly upon the dread's threatening eyes. Immediately, Twin knew that he was in dangerous position, but it was too late.

The dread grabbed a handful of Twin's clothing and pulled with force. Twin was in total shock and couldn't find the words to cry for help. Swiftly, with repeated motion, Scar stabbed deep into Twin's chubby body. Muffled grunts were the only sound that escaped Twin's mouth.

Scar left the 6-inch blade deep in his flesh. Time was of the essence. No one had witnessed what transpired. Scar quickly stepped in the road and moved with skill toward his main target.

Quron was still leaning against the car, patiently waiting for Ghost while entertaining his troublesome thoughts. He didn't realize that death was coming closer and closer with every step that Scar took.

Ghost said goodbye to Mrs. James and stepped out of the restaurant with a Styrofoam container in his hand. He was smiling, and appeared to be relieved from the tension that he'd felt earlier. His presence broke Quron's trance, just in time for him to see Twin's punctured body slide off the payphone and smash hard onto the cold concrete.

"Oh shit!" Quron yelled as he instantly ran toward Twin.

Before he could get into a full stride, he used all of his might to stop his forward progress. His strong legs swept out from under him and he hit the ground hard. He lay helplessly on the gravel. His heart thumping hard and fast as he awaited death.

Scar stood a few feet away with his cannon pointed directly at him. "Tawk dat tawk now, playboy!" Scar shouted aggressively. He took his wig off and threw it to the ground. "Shit ain't, unnnt—"

The heavy impact from Ghost's.45 knocked him off balance, sending him stumbling backwards.

Quron wasted no time. He scrambled to his feet and dove behind Ghost's rental car for cover.

The gunplay instantly created chaos and put the crew in survival mode. Just when the situation seemed to be under control and Quron thought that they had Scar outnumbered, four masked men emerged from the depths of the alley way.

Trife immediately opened fire, sending a wave of bullets aimlessly toward whoever stood in his peripheral. The remaining three men spread throughout the populated street and sent bullets raining through the streets. Tay was amongst the armed men. She slouched low behind a parked vehicle, peeping around its bumper every few seconds. Things were not going according to plan. They were supposed to utilize Scar's distraction to their advantage, and ambush Quron from another angle. The element of surprise usually worked in their favor, which is why Scar designed the set up like this. This time was different. Everyone was on point and strapped, with the exception of Steel.

Steel had just been released from the city's precinct that morning, and he hadn't given any thought to picking up his heat, especially after his arrest for illegally possessing a weapon. Actually, he did not plan to be outside for long. But when India picked him up, she relayed the message that Quron wanted to see him. Now he found himself sprinting, on a mission not to be gunned down.

From where Snake was positioned behind the tall, wooden telephone pole, he could see Nuri quickly closing in. "Shit!" Snake shouted while aiming his pistol at Nuri.

Nuri was moving so fast, using the cars, garbage cans, trees, and houses as a shield, that it made it too difficult for Snake to get a clear shot.

Snake wanted to run full speed toward him, letting loose his twin Berettas, but to do so, he had to place himself in a vulnerable position. A dumb sacrifice that he was not willing to make.

The sound from Nuri's shoes shuffling against the ground put the masked gunman on point. He spun around with his smoking Mac-11 firmly gripped, but it was too late. Nuri's Desert Eagle barked like a raging dog, and five.44 slugs smashed violently into his flesh. The momentum of the slugs knocked him off his feet. A fiery sensation raced through his abdominal area, ripping muscle, breaking bones, melting arteries, and killing him instantly.

Breathing hard, Nuri stood over the corpse. He looked down at the lifeless body with no shame and pumped his last two slugs into his head. "Hold that, muthafucka." Nuri hog spit on the dead thug, picked up his Mac-11, and stepped over the thick brain fragments that leaked from his skull.

Young-One had Quron locked in his view, and the most foul thoughts settled in his mind. He looked around nervously, and the same thought influenced him again. Here's your opportunity. *Fuck y'all childhood ties. He has somethin' you want. He ain't the man, off that nigga.* Young-One's face wrinkled. He crouched low and hustled in Quron's direction.

His grip was firmly wrapped around the butt of his .357 Desert Eagle. Sweat quickly formed in his palm. Just when he was about to act, Nuri suddenly appeared and they reached Quron's side simultaneously.

Damn! I'm buggin', Young-One thought as he stood curled over, with his hands resting on his knees. *I was really about to off my man. Maybe I should fall back from homegirl.* He considered for the first time ever.

"What happened, Young?" Nuri asked.

"I'm good, ain't nothin'." He quickly responded.

"Yo, where's Steel?" Nuri inquired while bent over trying to catch his breath.

"Last time I saw him was when these nigga's came out that alley way clappin'." Young-One quickly answered.

"Fuck! We gotta find Steel!" Quron shouted.

Nuri ejected his clip, checked his ammunition, and inserted the magazine back into his hammer. "I'm running low on bullets."

"Me too," Young-One added.

"We gotta get outta here," Quron reluctantly admitted.

"These dudes had the drop. It's a fact that the whole police force gon' flood the strip in a minute. Split up and make a move, we'll meet up later."

They nodded and slid out from behind the abandoned building. Tay and Scar saw them creeping and riddled the cars and brick walls with bullets. Nuri, Quron, and Young-One sent rapid fire back at them. The flying bullets created an opportunity to retreat, and they did just that. They stuck to the plan and headed in opposite directions, away from the hectic crime scene.

Trife and Snake hopped in a dark colored SUV and sped off toward Scar and Tay. Running down the street, Scar realized that the two men that ran in front of him were not a part of his team. With no hesitation, while in full stride, he raised the barrel of his.38 Smith & Wesson and pulled the trigger until the cylinder emptied.

The impact from the hollow point slugs caused Twin to hurl forward. Ghost and Twin's bodies tangled and launched face first over the three-foot high iron fence. Ghost's face smashed into the cold, hardened ground, and Twin's stocky body came down hard on top of him. Blood was all over Ghost's face. The pain that he felt was excruciating. Twin was twisted in an awkward position, lying motionless on top of Ghost. He was unconscious, with a very low pulse. Life was slipping away from him and there wasn't anything that Ghost could do to help his friend.

With all of his might, he managed to push Twin's dead weight off him. He stood to his feet with his gun tightly gripped. Staggering through the yard, he struggled to get a hold of his senses. Blood gushed from his head wound, drizzling into his eyes and affecting his vision. Ghost looked around nervously, fearing that harm was still near. Everything appeared in a blur. The last thing he saw was the taillights of Snake's SUV fading away. He used his hand to apply pressure to his injured head and staggered through an alleyway to what he hoped would be safety. He looked back, stood still, contemplating his decision. He pulled out his phone, dialed 911, and reluctantly left Twin's riddled body laid out in the yard.

"Holy shit, Fish. Look at this mess we have on our hands." Detective DeJesus Garcia said to his partner, Michael Fisher as they stepped out of the lightly tinted Impala and walked through the crowd of people that had gathered around the crime scene.

Detective DeJesus was well known throughout the streets of Newburgh, the same streets that he ran as a young boy, growing up. For this same reason, he had every intention to change venue to another precinct, so that he could be efficient without any conflicts of interest. When the opportunity for him to transfer came, ironically, he declined. After months of thinking about his situation, he figured that there wasn't a better way to give back to his community than to police the streets where he had grown up. As a regular patrolling officer, he was very passive. It was seldom to see him make an arrest. In most cases, it was childhood friends who were living above the law. He had lost many friends because of his job title. But at the end of the day, he had a family to feed.

Now, years later, he could see that his hard work had paid off. With a beautiful wife, house, a luxury car, and children, DeJesus found very little to complain about. His 5'7", 170lb frame reflected good health, and his urban attire along with his 5 o'clock shadow preserved his youth. His best friend and partner, Fisher, was just as smooth, but built differently. His skin complexion was like melted chocolate, rich but smooth. He stood an intimidating 6 foot 3 inches, and carried 240lbs of muscle. His bald-head got waxed weekly, his thick eye brows arched, and his face clean except for the neatly trimmed goatee that brought out his dark, full lips.

Obviously bothered by the continuous violence that they were exposed to daily, neither detective spoke a word as they took note of what was going on. Yellow tape had been set up around the perimeter of the crime scene.

Detective Fisher, also known as Fish, ducked under the yellow tape while his partner, Garcia, walked through the opening in the fence.

Detective Fisher stood erect, and the first thing that his eyes settled on sent pain through his veins. A young African-American woman who appeared to be in her mid-thirties was an emotional wreck. She used a nearby tree for support as she hovered over a body that was covered with a white sheet, crying hysterically. Detective Fisher's mind drifted as he looked on helplessly. The day when he lost the person that meant the world to him replayed slowly in his mind. He had just graduated from the academy, and everything was going well until he received the nerve-wrecking phone call.

"Hello."

"Yes, may I speak with Officer Fisher please?" The caller asked in a low moderate tone.

"This is he. May I ask who's calling?"

"Yeah, umm, this is Officer Jesus Garcia."

"Oh, what's up, Garcia? I didn't mean to be rude, but it is three in the morning and I know you didn't call just to say hello, so please get to the point." Silence came over the phone followed by a deep breath.

"Since you insist, I have some terrible news for you, Mr. Fisher. I am calling from St. Luke's Hospital and I was asked to call you and inquire about your relation if any with a young kid by the name of Robert Fisher. Do you know anyone by that name?"

"Oh my God, yes. What has happened to Robbie?" Officer Fisher shouted as his heart began to race.

"Is he of any kin?"

"He's my youngest brother." Fisher confirmed, fearing the news that would follow.

"Well, I am truly sorry to be the carrier of bad news, but you should get up here as soon as possible. We found your brother's body marinating in his own blood in an alleyway on Beukard Avenue. He was brutally beaten. One of our colleagues found his wallet. A picture of you, along with his school identification card was found. That's what connected us to you."

"Thanks for calling, Jesus. Where is he now?"

"Currently, he's undergoing surgery. You should hurry up here, he really needs you."

Officer Fisher hung up the phone, immediately gathered his things and ran to the hospital. He arrived within minutes, *and just as Garcia said, his younger brother, Robert, was in surgery. A doctor brought him up to speed on what was going on with his brother.*

Robert was suffering from broken bones, bruised ribs, a fractured skull, and internal bleeding. There wasn't much that Michael could do, except be patient and pray that God would spare his brother's life. A few days later, Robert went into a deep coma, and died shortly after.

"Yo Fish, you alright? Fish, snap out of it." Detective Garcia said, snapping his fingers.

Fisher looked his partner in his eyes and smiled a sad smile. "So what are we workin' with, Jesus?" Fisher calmly asked.

"We are about to find out right now," Detective Jesus assured as they walked toward the young uniformed officer that appeared to be on top of the facts. "Excuse me Officer..."

"Officer Kelly, sir. How may I help you?"

"Right, Officer Kelly." Jesus smiled.

The young officer removed his latex gloves and extended his hand toward the detectives.

"Nice to meet you, Officer Kelly. My name is Detective Garcia, but most people call me Jesus because of the justice that I bring to these streets. To my right is my partner, Detective Fisher. You might've heard other officers around the precinct refer to him as Fish, but that's just a nickname that he earned from his unique strategies in capturing some of the most dangerous criminals that ever walked these streets. Anyway, what happened here today? What's our situation?"

"As it stands, we have three people shot and one person severely stabbed. Two of the three who were gunned down, died instantly. The other two victims survived."

"Really, so where are the victims that survived?" Detective Jesus asked with a raised brow.

""The paramedics rushed them to the emergency room. Both men lost a lot of blood and needed immediate medical attention."

"What about the two that didn't pull through?" Fisher inquired.

"The masked man over there is hard to identify because of the large bullet holes in his face. The bullets really destroyed his facial bone structure. No identification was found."

"What about the other corpse? Who is the woman screaming and crying over there?"

"Well sir, it's a sad story. From the information that I've gathered, the other victim is her fourteen year old daughter. It was told to me that the teenage girl was on her way to the store when the shooting started. It looks like she got caught in the cross fire."

Detective Fisher slapped his forehead with the palm of his hand, repeatedly. "I can't believe this shit, Jesus. A fourteen year old child! This is unbelievable. When these ignorant idiots run around here like mad men, killing themselves, it is a thought out decision that they've made. But when innocent people, especially children, fall victim to their foolishness, it becomes a major problem. I take it personal. Why? Because these are the same type of monsters that murdered my youngest brother!"

Detective Jesus saw that his partner was enraged, so he placed his hand on his shoulder to reassure him that things would be okay. "Calm down, buddy. In due time, we'll get to the bottom of this. We always do, don't we?"

Detective Fisher inhaled a deep breath and exhaled slowly, trying to regain control over his emotions. After a few moments, he calmed down. He stood in silence, patiently waiting for his partner to finish giving directions to Officer Kelly. Jesus summed up his instructions and Detective Fisher added his input.

"Officer Kelly, make sure those two victims that survived are not discharged from the hospital until Jesus and I question them first, understand?"

"Yes sir."

"Good."

"Is there anything else, detective?"

"In fact, there is. What evidence do we have so far, and how many witnesses are willing to cooperate?"

"Well, there weren't any weapons found on the scene or on the victims. As for witnesses, we have none. No one seems to have seen anything, and if they did, they aren't willing to talk about it."

"So basically, all we have is a bunch of empty shell casings with two bodies and a lot of questions with no answers."

"Yup." Officer Kelly confirmed.

Detective Fisher shook his head and walked off.

"Well, it's a start," Jesus stated with a grin. "Don't mind my partner, Officer Kelly. He's just goin' through a lot right now. He doesn't like to see innocent people get hurt. Whenever he does see it, he reacts the same way every time. Don't take it personal, you are doing a great job. I have to get going. It was good meeting you. Make sure you run fingerprints on each casing that you find. If anything comes up, don't hesitate to call me. Here's my card, both me and my partner's number is on there. Keep up the good work." Detective Jesus shook Officer Kelly's hand and walked back to his Impala.

Chapter 18

Bzzz! Bzzz! Bzzz! Quron looked at the name and number that flashed on his phone screen.

"Hello."

"Yeah Ghost, I told you don't even stress that. Whatchu sayin' is deep though... No question, I dig where you comin' from, and you are 100% right. I agree wit' you, homie. You definitely gotta keep it true wit' dudes that keep it the same way wit' you... Oh word, we gon' talk as soon as you get here... You outside now? Ah-ight cool. Give me a few minutes and I'll be out there, one."

Quron ended his phone conversation with Ghost. He sat for a minute, then stood from the unmade bed and calmly walked into the bathroom. Steam from the hot shower filled the secluded space. He slowly eased open the maroon plastic shower curtain and observed Bri's voluptuous body. The water sprinkled onto her face, descended her smooth skin and trickled down the drain. Bri was unaware of his presence. Her eyes were closed and her body rocked back and forth as the R&B artist, The Weekend's lyrics spilled from her vocals. Quron stood admiringly in silence. He loved Bri dearly and looked forward to the day when she would share his last name. He extended his hand, intending to touch her smooth skin. Coincidentally, she opened her eyes and jumped.

"You scared the mess out of me. How long have you been standing here?" Bri clutched her chest, wearing a frightened facial expression. Soap covered half of her naked body and her hand was over her heart. After she realized that her peeping Tom was no one other than her boo, she calmed down and regained composure.

"My fault, sweetie. I didn't mean to scare you. I just came in here to let you know that I was steppin' out for a minute. I seen you was in a zone, so I decided to wait. I didn't want to interrupt your moment." Quron smiled.

"Aw daddy, you are so sweet. You are such a gentleman," Bri turned off the shower and stepped out of the bathtub onto the fluffy floor mat. "Well, I guess I'll see you later. By the way, I had a wonderful time last night. It reminded me of our early days. A lot of things that we used to do, for some unknown reason, we don't do anymore. I think that is the main reason why we've been at each other's throats lately. We'll work on it, though. Your mother and I are going out to the stores today. She is such a sweetheart. I'ma let you go though. I'll see you later and be safe, okay."

"Yeah, ah-ight. Tell my mom's I love her. I'ma see you later, Insha'llah. Now that I got my license, I can drive, so I'm gonna scoop you later and take you out. We definitely have to stop this arguin' shit and get our old thing back. So be ready, love you."

"Love you too." Bri wrapped the plush towel around her body and gave Quron a hug. The couple shared a passionate moment as they kissed long and deep. Moments later, the pair said their departing remarks and went their separate ways.

Quron stepped out of the apartment. Routinely, he looked to his left then right before securing Bri's place. Quron had always been a leery type of guy. This is what he believed kept him alive. In his eyes, there wasn't anything wrong with being cautious. In the game, a player never knew when death was near, so as a player you always had to be on point.

With a steady pace, he descended the steps one at a time and walked toward Ghost's car. The two friends greeted each other with firm handshakes and kind words. Seeming anxious, Ghost quickly shifted the gear into drive and drove toward their destination.

"What up playboy, how you?"

"Same song, O.T. I know it's been a coupla weeks since that shit popped off, but I'm still try'na get my mind together from that. It really ain't about the actual trauma of this war poppin' off. I been puttin' in work all my life, shootin' it out wit' niggas who violated." Ghost paused and then continued, with pain reflected in his voice. "But never have any of my close comrades suffered repercussions like this. I got love for a lot of dudes in these streets, but those twins, Dex and Ja, is my heart. True story, I'm fucked up 'cause they fucked up. I can't even function on this little drug money that I'm gettin'. That's my word though, Ron, when I get my head back together and hit these streets, it's over. I'm goin' hard and I ain't playin' wit' it no more. Fuck all these niggas, word. If they ain't wit' me then they against me. Only thing I'm missin' right now is a thorough connect wit' some bangin' coke. I'm goin' to the city tomorrow and I ain't comin' back 'til I plug in wit' somebody, somewhere."

Ghost stopped at a stop sign, looked right then left, and made a right turn onto Dubois St. He had finally shared what had been on his mind for the past week or so, and it felt like a burden had been lifted from his shoulders. Moments later, he turned into the hospital's parking garage and parked his new rental car in an available parking space. Quron got out of the car. Ghost turned the ignition off and followed.

"Baby bro', I listened to everything that you said during our ride over here. I might be wrong, but I assume that what you said wasn't somethin' that just popped into your head when you started drivin'. You probably had those thoughts bottled up inside, waitin' to release them, hopin' to get some feedback about what's goin' on wit' you. Well if what I'm sayin' is true, I feel fucked up 'cause I can't help you with this one. You'll learn as you continue to grow as a man, that some things that we go through as people, only life itself can define and help us understand. You are human like everyone else, and you are only feelin' the pain that is felt when someone close has been inflicted with hard times. That isn't abnormal, so don't feel outta pocket for being affected by conditions of people who you love. Allah's will, the two homies will recover in due time. Believe it or not, your recovery is the key. A team is only as strong as the weakest link. Think about it, that's real. Take it for what it's worth, and make sure all your pieces to the puzzle are in place. Scar will get his in due time. I have somethin' in motion right now as we speak, and he don't even know it. Some people play checkers while other people play chess. I just so happen to be one of the people that think chess, and dudes can't fuck wit' me." Quron patted Ghost's shoulder reassuringly. "Just go with the flow, everything will fall in place."

Ghost turned toward his man and smiled as they walked up to the entrance doors of the local hospital. The automatic doors slid open and they proceeded toward an elevator that was located down a lengthy hallway. A short, dark skinned security guard who wore glasses and held a flash light stopped them. He informed them that before visiting someone, they had to first check in at the front desk and they would then receive visiting passes. Quron thanked the security guard for his assistance and then complied with the hospital's visiting procedure.

The female that worked at the front desk in the hospital was beautiful. She wore the same security uniform as her colleague. Blue slacks that hugged her wide hips perfectly and a lighter blue button up shirt that came with a clamp on tie. Her blond hair dangled in big curls that bounced whenever she moved her head. Her soft white skin laid smoothly across her facial bone structure and her ocean blue eyes made a person feel welcome.

Quron and Ghost provided the information that the young woman needed. She processed them and they walked in silence toward the elevator. Both comrades acknowledged how beautiful the Caucasian woman was, but they were so focused on the drama in their lives that they barely entertained the thought of pursuing her.

The elevator arrived, and the two friends stepped inside. Ghost pressed the button to the floor that was stamped on his visiting pass. The sliding door slowly closed and the elevator ascended.

"What up, baby bro, you ah-ight? Kinda quiet over there."

"I'm cool, just thinkin' 'bout what you said a little while ago. You always come through for me O.T., you always on time, real talk." Ghost responded.

"Ding!" The metal door opened and they made their way down the bright hallway, in search of the room number.

"Yeah, you know how it go. Jay-z said it best, 'nobody will fall, 'cause everyone will be each other's crutches.' In times of need, we gotta be here for each other. Why is that?" Quron questioned with a smile.

"'Cause you are only as strong as your weakest link." Ghost answered with confidence as if Quron's words were his cue.

"No question, now you see the bigger picture," Quron said, happy that Ghost had absorbed the jewel that he shared earlier in their conversation. "Oh yeah, before I forget. I recall you sayin' somethin' about goin' fishin' for a coke connect. Well, I have a nice proposition for you. If you accept what is on the table for you, then you won't need one." Ghost looked at Quron with an inquisitive stare. Quron read his expression. "Don't worry about it, we'll talk later, ah-ight."

Ghost nodded his head as they continued walking.

Detective Fisher and his partner, DeJesus, exited from one of the many hospital rooms on that floor. Detective DeJesus was plainly dressed. He wore a black leather jacket, blue loose fitting jeans, a Yankee's baseball cap, and a thin dog chain attached to the police badge that dangled from his neck. His partner's attire was more professional. The gray pin stripe Hugo Boss suit made Fisher appear to be dressed for a special occasion. His hard bottom shoes had a floor shine to them. His head had been freshly waxed and his shades looked new.

"Damn." Ghost murmured under his breath upon recognizing the two detectives. Ghost tried to avoid eye contact with the officers, but it was too late. DeJesus had spotted him and Quron as soon as they entered the hallway. Now they were trying to match a name to the two faces that looked so familiar.

In passing, Quron had a brief stare down with the detectives. A solemn silence crept into the air as the tension that existed between the worlds of crime and justice built up. They finally reached the room that they had been searching for. Without knocking, Ghost turned the doorknob and walked into the beautifully decorated room. Two beds were in the large room that the twin brothers shared. A long curtain hung from the ceiling to give privacy if one desired solitude. Upon entering the room, it was clear that the room had a classy woman's touch to it. Flowers of all sort were everywhere. The medicine smell that normally lingered in most hospitals was replaced with a mixture of delightful smelling fragrances. All of the linen that the hospital provided had been folded neatly and placed on top of a chair that sat in the corner. Instead, Polo and Nautica products decorated the twins' living space.

"What's the word, y'all?" Ghost asked enthusiastically. "I'm glad to see y'all makin' it through." This was the first time since Ghost picked him up that Quron had seen a true smile on his face. The love that he had for the twins was genuine, and it showed in his demeanor. The twins were both resting when Ghost burst into their room, shouting. They didn't appreciate the sudden noise, and it showed in their facial expressions as they sat up in their beds. But as soon as they realized that the disturbance came from their brother from another mother, it was all good.

"What up, my nigga? Good to see you." Ja said as he used the remote control to adjust the top half of his bed.

"Yeah, I started to think you forgot about niggas." Dex added with a smirk.

"Whatever, nigga," Ghost laughed. "I know that medication got you twisted now."

"Nah, you know I'm just fuckin' wit' you. These fuckin' police is gettin' on my nerves, though. Ever since the doctor said we are in stable condition, they been on our dick. Constantly comin' through, askin' a thousand dumb ass questions. And they have the nerve to threaten us 'cause we ain't cooperatin'. They act like our story is gon' change. We don't know shit! It's simple. They really got shit twisted. But that's from these lame rat ass niggas they bag that be folding. They must don't know we been schooled by some of the best." Dex stated flatly, then gave Ghost a pound to emphasize his point.

"Word," his brother, Ja, added. "They really tight 'cause they can't do nothin' to us. I don't know how that happened. I know I had my hammer and I was dirty when shit popped, but I ain't complainin', I'm actually glad somebody took it."

"Well, them niggas can eat a dick," Ghost interrupted. "Me and Quron just passed by them on their way out. They was lookin' like they knew us from somewhere. Truth be told though, if they ever holla at me while I'm ridin' dirty and it came down to me or them, you already know how that chapter will end. Fuck them dudes. As long as they stay in their lane, it's cool." Ghost grabbed a chair and sat down.

"So what up, O.G., how you?" Ja asked, directing his question to Quron.

"Takin' it easy, shorty. I'm glad to see that you and your bro' pulled through. My lil man, Ghost, was really affected when this happened to y'all. He has real love for y'all. Y'all got a good thing goin' in ya circle. Make sure y'all keep it tight. Don't let nothin' come between y'all bond. No money, no women, no snake niggas, no nothin', ya dig."

"How couldn't I dig that?" Ja smiled. "At the end of the day, we know all we got is us."

"True story." Ghost confirmed with a glow.

"Quron, my son Ghost speaks highly of you too, so I know you's a stand up dude. It's fucked up that I had to meet you like this, but it is what it is. I wanna ask you a question."

"Go ahead."

"I wanna know if you have anything on the niggas that did this to me and my brother? Dudes ain't just gon' ride on me and mine and think that's it. Somebody gotta be held accountable!" Dex said with obvious malice in his heart.

The room fell silent. Everyone was anticipating Quron's response. Quron looked at the three young men and weighed his options. He felt that explaining the whole story, including the reasons why he was at war with Scar would provide a lot of information that wasn't relevant. He wasn't sure if ill feelings would develop once they realize that their lives had been jeopardized because of him. All of those questions raced through his mind, causing him to act cautiously. But he knew that he had to share some truth, because Ghost was present and he knew what time it was.

In one calm motion, Quron stood from the folding chair that he was seated in and positioned himself so he could face Ghost, Dex, and Ja. "I'm gonna keep it tall wit' y'all," Quron admitted, feeling like being real was his only option. "Son who organized the ambush name is Scar. Y'all probably know him or heard of 'im. He get crazy paper out here and I hear he get busy too. Truth be told, I got drama wit' son. Unfortunately, y'all was at the wrong place at the wrong time. Shit is far from over. I plan to ride, but only when the timing is right. I definitely feel where you comin' from. I feel ya pain, but hear me out. When you ride, you don't just move off of emotions. Y'all gettin' money, so you can't afford any additional heat over no stupid shit. Ghost is my little brother and y'all are his brothers so I guess that makes us one big family with somethin' in common."

Quron paused, lifted his right arm and glanced at his diamond encrusted Rolex. "Damn, I lost track of time. I got a meeting to go to in a minute. Y'all just lay up and get well.

Ghost gon' make sure y'all paper is right when y'all come home. I'ma make sure of that." Quron smiled. "Life is about to get better for your team. Y'all just gotta stay focused and always remember that there is no purpose in puttin' in work and gettin' knocked for it. In that scenario, you still lose. It's purpose and honor in puttin' in work to protect you and yours, and still manage to get away wit' it. Only the wise survive. Be thinkers, not crash dummies, feel me. We gon' kick it some more later tho, salaams." Quron walked up to his young comrades and embraced each of them.

With a smile, he walked out of the room, leaving the younger up and coming soldiers with a lot to think about.

———

While Quron mingled and made preparations to meet with Pedro, Nuri, Steel, and Young-One were investing their time in a task that required total silence and focus. They had been sitting inside an old, stolen, Caravan for hours. Their movement was minimal.

The information had been obtained through a reliable source, according to Young-One. He had used the best bait ever used in a scandal, a woman. Now that he had done his job, the rest was up to his crew to perfect the plan.

The building that they were watching was surprisingly in good condition. Throughout the day, while waiting, Nuri made a mental note that there had not been a lot of traffic going in the building or coming out.

Nuri looked at his G-shock watch then to Young-One. "What up, Young? You think shorty gave you a fake address?"

"Nah, she know better." Young-One answered confidently.

Steel looked at his man, Young-One, and shook his head. *Young bugged out,* he thought then smiled. No sooner than the thought formed in his mind, a beautiful female that he spotted through the tinted window walked up to the building and dug into her handbag, searching for something.

All three comrades watched the young lady's every move, but really thought nothing of her. All except for Steel. He looked past her physical beauty and paid more attention to the slightest detail.

She was gorgeous, with her back toward the caravan. Nuri and Young-One looked on lustfully. Her Fendi printed stretch jeans looked like they were painted on, clinging to her round curves like a much needed hug. The brown boots that she wore matched the waist length fur that complimented her outfit. Her hair was pulled back in a tight ponytail, exposing the elegant earrings that she sported. She definitely was a star.

She hesitated to insert the key into the door and looked back as if someone was calling her name. Her nervous facial expression mixed with Steel's gut feeling influenced his next move.

Not wasting any more time, he swung open the rusted sliding door and hopped out. In three steps, Steel's warm intimidating breath was caressing the nape of the young lady's neck and the barrel of his twelve gauge Mossberg pressed firmly against her spine.

"Don't look back, and, and you bet not scream." Steel stuttered through clenched teeth.

The young girl froze as fear immediately settled in her heart. All she could think of was the words of her sister. When she was a child, her sister used to always tell her that if a stranger ever tried anything, scream for help and run. But if they carried a weapon, then play along because her chance of living would be greater. As the thought continued to revolve in her head, she felt that she was left with no choice. She didn't look back, nor did she scream.

She entered the dimly lit hallway and ascended the staircase with Steel following close behind. They stopped at the first door that they came to. Steel braced himself as he prepared for whatever. The teenage girl's hesitation added to Steel's frustration, and he nudged her hard with the nose of his cannon. The pretty girl knew that this was not the time or place to show any resistance. Obediently, she inserted the key in the apartment's lock.

In one turn, the door was unlocked. The young girl leaned forward and the wooden door slowly opened. Steel shoved her with force and she fell onto the tiled floor. Tears fell from her beautiful eyes. She was noticeably afraid for her life.

Two men who looked like they had a rough life were seated on a plush custom made couch, occupied by the PS3 that they were playing. When Steel rushed in, they both dropped the control pad and reached simultaneously underneath the couch's cushions. A loud explosive sound erupted from Steel's gauge, blowing one of their hands clean off. The nub of his wrist was all that was left. Thick blood squirted from the fresh wound like an air-pressured water gun. Loud screams echoed throughout the lavish apartment.

Nuri and Young-One came speeding through the door right on time. With one hard swing, Young-One's arm sliced through the air. The butt of his Heckler and Koch mp5 created a cracking sound as it connected with the top of the second man's head. Blood poured from his split head like water from a faucet. Young-One followed up with a left cross to the jaw, and the husky man's body fell limp as he suddenly lost consciousness.

"Lock that door, homie!" Nuri demanded with his face screwed up, then walked up to the dude who had gotten his hand blown off. He was curled into a fetal position, rocking back and forth crying out in pain. "Shut the fuck up!" Nuri shouted then kicked him in his mouth.

His big lips split and became swollen instantly. Blood mixed with saliva trickled onto the floor. "Pick both of these clowns up and tie 'em to the chair."

"What about her?" Young-One inquired while pointing to the beautiful girl.

"Sit her on the couch facing these niggas. I want her to see everything 'cause if she don't cooperate, she gonna get it too." Nuri retorted with venom.

Young-One placed what appeared to be a black suede bag on the glass coffee table that sat on the side of him. He unfastened its buckles and rolled it out. The stretched out material had approximately ten separate pockets that carried various tools.

Steel stripped the men of their clothing, grabbed the duct tape, and bound both men to two kitchen chairs, one next to the other. On the floor around the area where they planned to work, Nuri laid two layers of polyethylene plastic on the floor. In his mind, he knew that putting down the thick plastic wasn't necessary, because what he had planned promised not to leave any evidence. But for the sake of normal procedure, he decided to do it anyway.

The beautiful young lady looked on in silence. Her tears dried up and her fear had turned into anger. She still couldn't believe that she was being held hostage. She couldn't believe Scar would allow her, out of all people, to go into such an unsafe environment. She had been using the apartment for the past week to study and prepare for her SAT exam. At the time, she really needed the solitude and she couldn't seem to find it at her own home. Her friend's houses were filled with activity and distractions. Scar's honeycomb hide out was her only alternative.

Nuri felt the presence of someone near. He finished wrapping duct tape around one of the victim's feet and rose from his kneeling position. He peeped through the window and saw nothing. Then he looked around and locked eyes with the young lady whom they had captured. He felt awkward for some reason. He felt like the girl knew who he was, even though it was impossible for her to see through the whole facemask that he and his comrades wore.

Calmly, he walked over to where she sat. Nuri looked into her gray eyes and placed his hand on her shoulder. She cringed. Her anxiety reflected in her stare, and that struck a nerve in Nuri's cold heart. He took hold of her mink and slid the quality material over her shoulders.

"What's ya name, shorty?"

She looked up and contemplated the question. "Kiyah," she answered softly.

"Well, Kiyah, just be calm and answer any questions that you're asked. As long as you cooperate, you'll be ah-ight."

Nuri left his words of truth on her mind for her to think about. He hoped she took heed, because he was dead serious. He really didn't want to torture the girl, but if she rebelled, he would get what he came for by any means.

Nuri turned to face the bound men, pulled a.38 snub from his waist and smashed the blue steel across the victims' faces repeatedly. "Where the fuck is the money"

With what little life he had left, the tall lanky man looked Nuri in his eyes and shook his head, indicating that he didn't know.

"So you wanna play games, huh? Yo, pass me that box." Steel handed Nuri the box that he asked for. Young-One and Steel looked on, admiring Nuri's no nonsense tactics. They knew from experience, that once Nuri let the beast within him out of its cage, there was no stopping him. The beast was definitely loose.

Nuri grabbed four unused gem-star razors from the box that he was handed. He gave two to Young-One and swung aimlessly, slicing the skin of the two men's naked bodies. The razors were so sharp that they could hardly tell that they were being cut.

Steel picked up the aluminum bat that sat in the corner and swung hard and accurately. Each connection from the bat opened their wounds. Blood gushed from their flesh, and agonizing pain was obvious from their screeching outcries. They howled like wolves.

Nuri stood behind them with a gallon of a white crystal like substance in his hand. "Ya'll think this is a game? I'ma show you better than I could tell you!" He shouted harshly then tilted the bottle over their heads and poured the white mineral until the bottle was empty. The salt that covered their bodies sent fire through their wounds. The two helpless men squirmed like worms seeking refuge after a rainstorm. The pain that they felt at that moment was excruciating, and they would rather have been dead than to continue to endure this type of severe torment.

"Let me know, homeboy. Y'all still wanna play fuckin' games, or y'all wanna do it the easy way and tell me what the fuck I wanna know?" Nuri inquired with a cynical smile. "It's up to y'all."

One of the two men gasped for air as he struggled to catch his breath. The other winced in pain as Young-One gripped his face. Nuri's stare fell upon the bound man's eyes. He pleaded and begged for mercy in silence.

Young-One loosened his grip on the man's jaw and whipped him with the butt of his gun. The first blow came with such force, it sent a loud cracking sound throughout the air. Blood ran from both nostrils as the bone protruded through the skin.

The horrifying scene caused Kiyah's skin to crawl. A fearful cry escaped from her mouth every time the chrome handgun connected with his face. All she could think of was her sister and her boyfriend. She loved both of them dearly, and it was terrifying to know that she was awaiting death. Judging by the masked men's actions, she was certain that they would kill her too.

In a tone barely above a whisper, the taller of the two spoke. "Please stop beatin' my man," he pleaded. His chest rose and fell quickly from the short breaths he was taking. "I'll tell you whatever you wanna know. As long as you promise not to kill us, I'll tell you whatever you wanna know." The tall man repeated his plea.

A smile suddenly appeared on Nuri's face. He absorbed the words of the wounded victim. He cleaned the bloody barrel with the victim's shirt, placed his gun in his waistline, then pulled up a third chair and sat down facing him.

"Ah-ight, let's get down to business. We wasted enough of my precious time, don't you think?" He smiled. "So where are the drugs and the money?" Nuri's glare turned cold, as he looked into the man's face and awaited an answer.

The man returned Nuri's stare. Only his gaze was not as intimidating. He was reluctant to volunteer the helpful information that he said he would give, because he was not sure if Nuri would stick to his word. But as he continued his silent treatment, he noticed Nuri's expression change from bad to worse.

"Go into the bathroom and turn the right knob controlling the shower all the way up." Left with the only possible way to keep his life, he gave in. "Then use both hands to place a firm grip on the toilet bowl and yank it twice to ya left and once to ya right. It should click and lift it off the floor."

A look of relief appeared on Nuri's strong features. He extended his arm and patted the man's head as if he was a puppy that had pleased his master.

"See, now that wasn't hard at all, was it?" He turned, looked at Young-One and beckoned with his head for him to go check out the information that he had been told.

Steel grabbed three duffle bags and followed him. Nuri remained lax in the cushioned chair. He crossed his leg and leaned back. His eyes settled on the mangled visual of the badly wounded man that sat motionless. The rise and fall of his chest was the only sign of life. His eyes were swollen, but he was still conscious. His partner was not as strong. The excruciating pain that made him wish for death sent him back into a deep sleep. He sat tied, naked, covered in blood with his head bowed, dangling from his shoulders.

Seconds later, Steel and Young-One came back into the room. The three duffle bags that they carried were filled to the top with cash. An additional three duffle bags had been retrieved from the stash spot.

Nuri acknowledged the items that had been found, but he showed no signs of excitement. Within his mind was a different story. He was pleased, and felt good to say the least. Selling drugs was cool, but nothing could compare to the rush Nuri felt whenever he pulled off a successful robbery. To him, robbery wasn't as risky as the drug trade. And if planned correctly, a stick up could be far more lucrative for a day's work.

"So now that I kept my end of the deal, I expect you to keep yours." Slim weakly expressed with his swollen eye partly open.

Nuri acted as if he didn't hear him, although he clearly had. He twirled his hand above his head in a circular motion and stood from his chair. Young-One and Steel recognized the sign Nuri gave, and immediately started the cleaning process.

While they did their part, Nuri turned to Kiyah as she sat in fear. Tears ran nonstop from her colored eyes. Her beautiful face was red and swollen. Nuri felt bad because he knew Kiyah was innocent, but the rules to the game are dirty. Being that she was at the wrong place at the wrong time, she had to suffer the consequences.

Nuri walked up to Steel and whispered in his ear. Steel continued wiping down the walls, doorknobs, and anything else that he and his crew could have possibly come in contact with. Then all of a sudden, he quickly walked over to Kiyah and grabbed her arms.

"Ahhhhhhhh!! Get the fuck off me," she screamed from the depths of her lungs.

Her puffy red eyes bulged from their socket. Veins appeared through her beautiful skin. She gave all that she had, knowing that her life depended on it. "Please... let... me... go." She continued to plead, panic and fight. The more she resisted, the tighter Steel's grip became. Nuri wrapped her wrist with two layers of duct tape and did the same to her ankles.

Saliva formed in her mouth as her cries turned from that of pain to a whine of defeat. There wasn't anything that she could have done to better her condition. With despair slowly settling in, Kiyah closed her eyes and turned to God through prayer, asking for a miracle.

The cleaning process was finally complete. Steel and Young-One took the money and drug filled duffle bags and made their exit. Nuri was the last to leave the apartment. He picked up the towel that he brought along and unraveled the tin can that it held. He knew from the beginning that he could not leave any witnesses alive. The thought of allowing them to live did not sit comfortably on his conscious. Over the years, he had learned to trust in his gut feeling, if nothing else. His gut always told him the truth.

Nuri removed the top that concealed the toxic fumes and the pleasing aroma filtered throughout the room. Without hesitation, he drenched his captives with gasoline. With the little that was left, he dashed the walls and furniture that was in the surrounding area.

"You fuckin' liar. You gave ya word that if I cooperated, you'll let us live," The slim built man shouted. "Ya word ain't shit!" he continued, as he seemed to be filled with a newfound energy. "You's a coward, and before it's all said and done, you'll die a thousand deaths." Insults continued to rain. Nuri respected that he had the audacity to talk with such venom, but he knew that he only spoke those words so that he could die with a clear conscience.

"You're right," Nuri admitted with a careless smile. "A coward dies a thousand deaths and you's a weak coward for submittin'. Nigga, you knew this room was the last thing that you would see." Nuri cocked his head back like he had gulped down a shot of liquor and let out a psychotic laugh. He then struck a match and tossed it onto his frail, lanky body. "Who's the coward now, bitch?"

The flame engulfed the two hostages quickly. Nuri had never known such a sound. He looked at Kiyah one last time. As bad as he wanted to spare her from his evil wrath, he knew that he couldn't. She had seen too much. Without a second thought, he struck another match and dropped it on the floor. Nuri watched the flames spread, before he fled down the wooden staircase.

"What's wrong, Tay, somethin' botherin' you?" Scar asked.

The new 750 Beamer that he had recently copped sat parked in the lot of an apartment complex. They had only been waiting for a couple of minutes, but Tay had remained quiet during the whole ride. This wasn't like her at all. She wasn't loud or very outspoken, but she definitely was not antisocial, and Scar picked up on her distant vibe immediately. Tay fixed the brim of her fitted cap and opened the passenger door.

"I don't know what it is, but I have this strong feelin' that somethin' ain't right," she admitted with a worried expression. "I'ma go shoot through and make sure everything is good. But I'm tellin' you, Scar, somethin' ain't right."

"Ah-ight," Scar managed to say before pausing. He looked into the rearview mirror, pulled his skully down over his ears and thought about what Tay's womanly instinct told her. "Go wit' ya gut, ya heard me. I'm gon' wait fo' Roc, then I'ma go meet the white kid from up town. Make sho you halla at me lata."

Tay closed the door and hopped into her Range Rover Sport. In less than two minutes, she turned onto a street where one of the stash houses was located. The surprised look that suddenly formed on her face reflected the mixed emotions that surfaced in her heart. The sight of the retreating masked men made her blood boil. Judging by the luggage that they held tightly, she knew that their stash had been hit. Without much thought, she grabbed the.357 Desert Eagle from out of the armrest, cracked the door, and hesitated. It suddenly dawned on her that the robbers were strapped too, and her Desert alone was not capable of holding her down. "Fuck." she murmured.

As she was caught up in her rational thinking, one last body came speeding out of the building. In mid-stride, he snatched the mask from his head and Tay's heart dropped when she saw Nuri's distinct features. Once he reached the van, the driver quickly applied pressure to the pedal and peeled off.

Tay was eager to find out what had been taken. She rushed into the building and hurried up the stairs. Her baggy jeans added to her weight, but did very little to her stride. She raised her cannon and kicked the door as hard as she could. The hinges gave and the door flew open. A black cloud of smoke came rushing toward her. The heat wave behind the black cloud sent instant hazard signs. Off impulse, she jumped back and worked the trigger to her large caliber. Three thumb-sized casings leapt from the chamber.

When no bodies fell, Tay ceased fire. The air that came through the entrance door on the first floor cleared a path through the thick smoke that blinded her vision.

She squinted and realized that there was someone lying motionless on the couch. The intense heat from the growing flames had Tay drenched. She knew that it wouldn't be long before the ceiling and walls gave way. She looked down toward the entrance, then back at the head hanging from the motionless body. Tay contemplated if risking her life for a stranger was really worth it. The better part of her heart encouraged her to sacrifice, and she listened. She ran as fast as she could through the smoke. To the right of where she stood, the two bodies that Nuri torched were fully cooked. Her heart softened at the sight of her two comrades. If they would have only listened and stayed on the low, they would still be alive. Tay thought, as her mind drifted back to the hit that she paid Shawn and Mango to carry out a few months back at the Players Island Strip Club against India.

With all of her strength, she picked Kiyah up off the couch. When she looked into her sister's smoke covered face, her heart became heavy and her knees suddenly weakened. She could not believe that the person who she was about to leave for dead, was in fact, her sister. The thought knotted her stomach.

The imbalance caused her to stumble forward through the apartment's door. The flames had already claimed its territory in the hallway and the wood staircase had started to weaken. Tay knew that she had no time for error. Her toned legs regained life and she descended the stairs with caution, but it was too late. The fire had eaten the pillars of the structure. Tay's next step sent her down forcefully. The wood that she had depended on for support broke in half.

Kiyah's body hurled forward and she landed less than a foot away from the entrance door. Tay cried out in agonizing pain. Her legs were trapped between two burning 2 by 4s and she couldn't get them loose. With all of her strength, she attempted to lift her legs. Veins popped from her head as she strained, but the heavy wood didn't budge. Tears of defeat soiled her face. She felt the fire eating through her jeans and the excruciating pain hurt like nothing she had ever felt before. All she could think of was how she had let her sister down. She looked at Kiyah's wounded body and let out a nerve-wracking scream.

Just when despair started to settle in, the miracle that Kiyah prayed for arrived. The sirens from the fire trucks were loud. Three men wearing whole face respirators came through the door. One of the three immediately grabbed Kiyah and rushed her to safety. The other two went for Tay.

The paramedics were outside of the hazard zone, anxious to be of some assistance. Within minutes, Tay was being carried through the flames. Shortly after, the sisters were attached to oxygen tanks in the back of an ambulance and driven to the nearest local hospital.

Chapter 19

"Kiyah, wake up sweetie. There is a handsome young man here to see you." The elderly nurse whispered into Kiyah's ear then gave a warm smile.

The teenaged boy returned a smile then stood from his seat. He had been sitting in the room for a while, watching Kiyah sleep. So much was going on in his own life; he needed some down time to really gather his thoughts.

The nurse came out of the bathroom and waved Kiyah's guest closer. When he complied, she slowly made her exit from the room.

Kiyah's eyelids fluttered like the wings of a butterfly as she came to. Over two weeks had elapsed since the fatal fire incident, but this was the first time he had visited his girlfriend. His worrying started when he didn't hear from her. Communicating in one form or another was their daily routine. When days passed and Kiyah failed to return his calls, he considered Kiyah's sudden distance to be strange, and that's when he began to investigate. As the young man stood over his wounded queen, a smile formed from the beautiful thoughts that Kiyah's presence naturally produced. It was so delightful, much different from the world he was used to.

Her vision finally became clear and she realized that someone was standing over her. She quickly snatched the white linen sheet that covered her bandaged body over her head. She winced from the sharp pain that her sudden movement caused.

"What's wrong, sweetie? You don't want me to see your gorgeous face?" Lamar smiled as he rubbed her arm reassuringly.

Kiyah placed a face with the masculine voice that caused her insides to tingle. She smiled and slowly lowered the sheet from her face. She was embarrassed because she hadn't taken a shower in days, and her long silky hair that was usually styled, was now tangled in one big puff. She looked terrible. Her embarrassment dwindled with the sight of Lamar. She had no idea how he had found her, and at that point, she really didn't care. She was just happy to have someone like him by her side to care for her during her time of need.

"Hi baby," she said in a feeble tone. "I can't believe you are here. How did you find me?"

Lamar walked around the front end of the bed and stood at the large window. The drapes were pulled back and the calm scenery outside was much easier on his eyes. The more he looked at the woman, who brought light into his life, the angrier he became.

"I became worried when I didn't hear from you. At first, I took your distance as a sign that you wanted space. But then at school, everybody started askin' 'bout you 'cause they haven't seen you. That's when I started goin' crazy." A humorous chuckle lingered. "I guess God sensed my stress 'cause I ran into one of ya friends and she told me about the accident." Lamar suddenly became quiet. He turned from the outside scenery and walked back to Kiyah's bedside.

She placed her palm on his face and rubbed his cheek with her thumb. "Don't be sad, I'm going to be okay." Kiyah said, trying to be strong for her man.

"I know, babe. I just can't believe someone would do some psychotic shit like this to my baby." Lamar shook his head in disbelief. "I don't know who did this to you, but if I ever find out, I'll make 'em pay." The sincerity in Lamar's voice matched the seriousness of his stare. "I swear, I'll make 'em pay."

Kiyah's heart pumped faster as she sat attentively and absorbed how her man felt for her. She was flattered, and she enjoyed how it felt to be genuinely loved by someone other than her sister, Tay.

Kiyah looked at Lamar's slinky arms and his small frame. In her mind, she knew that he meant well, and was even serious about his threat. But she seriously doubted his ability to protect her. He was a schoolboy, for God sake. It was one of the main things that attracted her to him. He was not the loud, rowdy type. He was calm and smooth, with a swagger that made him stand out from others. He never got into arguments or any type of altercations, and everyone had a lot of respect for him. Kiyah didn't understand it. Even the supposed thugs humbled themselves while in his presence.

When Kiyah asked how he gained such popularity, he simply replied, "When you give respect to people, you receive respect back from people." The simple answer was enough to ease her curiosity. She just loved his style. When he asked her out on a date, she was surprised and excited all at once. She didn't hesitate to accept Lamar's offer. From that day on, Kiyah was floating on clouds. The unique emotion found its way into her heart and she was in love.

On their first date, Lamar was the perfect gentleman. He did things that Kiyah didn't know men did. He showed her things that only her imagination could fathom. And to top it off, his mind was well advanced. Lamar was a smart young man, but because of Kiyah's luck, she perceived Lamar to be too good to be true.

His touch broke Kiyah's daydream. She opened her arms and Lamar bent over the bed rail and embraced her. The burnt, smoky smell seeped from her tangled hair and filled his nostrils. He didn't care though. He was just happy to have his wifey in his arms. "Boo, you are blessed. The doctor said you had a few minor burns on your upper body, but nothin' that'll cause you any dysfunctions." A brief silence settled between his words. "Sweetie, they said you were soaked with gasoline when they found you. It's a miracle that you are here talkin' to me." The thought of Kiyah being dead brought a level of pain that surprised him. At that moment, he knew that he couldn't live without her. "I love you, ma, and I promise I won't ever let anything like this happen to you again."

She took his hand and smiled. Kiyah felt that this tragedy had actually brought forth some good. Lamar and she had connected on a higher level, and she knew that it was Lamar's support during her crisis that was responsible for the greater love and respect that had developed.

Kiyah looked into his red eyes and decided it was time for her to stop holding back. It was time for her to re-live the painful truth that composed her life. It was time to let the man who had introduced her to the unique emotion of love, into her dark past. Indeed, it was time. Lamar was not aware that she was a foster child with no parents. Nor did he know that the sister that he had heard so much about, the sister that she often glorified, was probably more masculine than he was. But she wasn't afraid anymore. She no longer wanted to hide behind the facts of her life. At that very moment, she was sure that she did not want any secrets to exist between the two of them.

"Lamar, have a seat, sweetie." Kiyah pulled his hand forward and guided his steps toward the chair that was inches away from her bed. "I want to share something with you."

Lamar sat as he was asked to, and the couple held hands while gazing into the windows of each other's souls. Before Kiyah could begin, the same elderly nurse that had excused herself earlier, entered the room. Both Kiyah and Lamar's focus shifted and the nurse sensed that the young lovebirds wanted to be alone.

"I am sorry to interrupt," the nurse admitted, feeling bad that she had to end their intimate moment. "But darling, getting the proper amount of rest is the key to your recovery." She exhaled then looked at the plants that seem to be dying off. "I'm sorry, young man, but you have to come back a little later. This beautiful young lady has to get her beauty rest." She smiled reassuringly.

With obvious frustration reflecting in Lamar's facial expression, he turned back toward Kiyah. "Well, Ki," he said as he reluctantly stood to his feet. "I guess whatever it was that you wanted to share will have to wait 'til later."

"Yeah, I guess." Kiyah sadly agreed. Lamar leaned over and kissed her moist lips. When he tried to rise up, she pulled him by the neck of his shirt. Their tongues danced to silent music inside each other's mouth. Lamar loved the way Kiyah kissed. Her skill aroused his hormones and reminded him just how much he loved and missed her.

"I'ma come through early tomorrow," Lamar promised and Kiyah smiled. "That's my girl," he continued, referring to the smile that replaced her sad expression.

Kiyah waved goodbye and the elderly nurse smiled, remembering her younger days. Lamar exited the room feeling good, just like old times.

Tay laid in the comfortable confines of Cornwall's Hospital. Her hands were heavily wrapped in white bandages and her legs were layered with a thick antibiotic cream. Her stabilized limbs prevented her movement, leaving her with ample time to entertain the different scenarios that raced through her mind.

The second-degree burns on her legs weren't as bad as they could have been if she hadn't had on thick clothing. Even her sweat served her well. The DNA soiled her jeans, which made the material less cooperative toward the scorching flames.

Tay knew that she was in worse condition than her sister Kiyah, but she was not complaining. Tay wouldn't mind dying, as long as Kiyah was spared. Tay's gratitude went beyond measure and she silently gave thanks to the creator for preserving their lives.

Tay had spoken with Kiyah on numerous occasions since the incident, and her heart twisted in agony every time. Kiyah was not as strong emotionally. Until the visit from Lamar, continuous crying had been the answer to all of her pain. This is why Tay was surprised to hear the renewed strength and confidence in Kiyah's voice when she had spoken to her over the phone that morning. When Kiyah told her about Lamar's surprise visit, a genuine smile spread across Tay's face. Sadness quickly replaced her smile, as Tay's mind envisioned the handsome features of her first and only true love, Trey. It was times like this that she missed him most. The void that his death left in her heart couldn't ever be filled, so there would always be an imbalance within her soul.

Tay's mind had regained focus, and she caught the last bit of detail that Kiyah shared. Lamar's support had earned him a higher level of respect in Tay's eyes, and she really looked forward to meeting the young man who had earned the key to her sister's heart.

Tay's gaze settled on the elevated TV screen, but one could easily see that she was not absorbing anything from it. Nuri's image saturated her mind. The worst mistake that he and his crew could have made was touching her family, and it wasn't a doubt in her mind that she would bring about their demise. Even if she had to pick them off one by one, she was determined to make them suffer severely.

The heavy metal door to Tay's room opened, and a cool breeze that only traveled with a cold soul brushed across her skin. The clear vision of Nuri's dismantled face slowly faded into a foggy mist. She turned her head toward the entrance and a semi-smile formed on her face. It was not hard to see that she was bothered.

Scar, Snake, and Trife walked in, one after the other. They all seemed to be genuinely happy and enthusiastic about Tay's conscious state. Scar noticed how her dull facial expression had not changed, even upon seeing them. Even as Snake and Trife conversed with her, she showed little interest in what they were saying. They didn't pick up on her distant gaze, but Scar, on the other hand, recognized the unusual silence immediately.

Scar placed a dozen roses in a flower decorated vase that sat on a wooden table next to Tay's bed. He took off his Polo leather and hung it on the multiple hook coat rack.

Tay read through Scar's silence and knew that he was on to her. After Snake and Trife finished bringing Tay up to speed on the latest happenings, they both grabbed chairs and sat down. Scar seized the opportunity. He dug into his Polo jeans and retrieved a gift certificate. Not giving his comrades a chance to start another topic, he walked over to Snake and handed him the certificate.

"Do me a favor, baby boy. You and Trife gon' down stairs to the gift shop that's in the lobby an' get' a buncha gifts fo' my partna. Take yo' time, I'ma be up here waitin'." Scar posed his request in the form of a favor, but he was not asking for anything; he was demanding and Snake knew that.

"Ah-ight cuz, I'll do that for you." He and Trife walked out of the room. Once they were gone, Scar turned to face the only person who had earned his wholehearted trust and walked up to her bedside. Tay was indeed his best friend.

"What's up, Tay?" Scar asked, trying to set a less tense tone for their conversation. Tay remained silent, not uttering a word in response. "I see you still haven't found it in yo' heart to fo' give me." Scar shook his head in disbelief. "After all we been through, you really think I would purposely put Kiyah in harm's way? C'mon, Tay, you know me betta than that. I love Ki like she my own blood. Don't play me like that."

The remote control was angled for Tay's comfort. She pushed a button and the TV screen went blank. She turned her head and allowed her eyes to absorb her friend's presence. She beckoned with a nod and Scar brought the cup of clear liquid to her lips. Tay sucked through the plastic straw and quenched her thirst. Scar removed the straw from her mouth and waited.

Tay cleared her throat and spoke for the first time since Scar had entered the room. "It's just hard for me to see my sister's life put in jeopardy like that." A brief silence replaced Tay's words as she gathered her thoughts. "I can't lie, Scar, just me knowin' that you are responsible hurt me to my heart. You are the brother that I never had, but you know Kiyah is my everything. You know how hard I work to protect her from this dangerous game," Tay grew more emotional with each word that she spoke.

Scar looked on attentively, acknowledging that she needed to vent.

"All I keep thinkin' 'bout is, what if I decided not to go back in that house to get the body that laid on that couch? Scar, I didn't know that the girl on the couch was Kiyah. If I wouldna left that house, my baby girl would have burned to death." The terrifying thought brought pain and a tear of hatred rolled from the corner of her eye. Nuri was a dead man walking. "In my heart, I know you meant well when you allowed Ki to utilize the crib to study. But Scar," Tay said with emphasis and their stares locked on each other. "You gotta state ya word that you won't ever under any circumstance, put my baby girl in harm's way again."

Without hesitating or giving it much thought, Scar responded. "You have my word, Tay, never again. I give you my word, not if, but when we find out who pulled this here stunt, they finished." He repeatedly rubbed his hands together as if he was brushing them off. Poisonous venom dripped from his threat. Scar was oblivious to the fact that Tay had seen Nuri's face while he was making his getaway.

Tay's adrenaline started to rush as thoughts of revenge soiled her mind. The mangled features of Nuri reappeared, giving Tay a feeling of contentment. She spoke with a newfound energy, but Scar's mind had drifted to a world of its own. He was bent over, with his head in his hands. He felt terrible, because no matter how he looked at the situation, it all boiled down to him and his careless decisions.

True, Tay had forgiven him, but that alone was not enough to soothe his guilt. He knew that the streets played by rules that differed with each player. And he had known better than to question one's ability to find the location to any one of his stash houses. Indeed, he was a major player in the game, and as long as he carried such a title, he would also carry the mark that made him a target. In the game, no matter how much weight your name held, there was always somebody who just didn't care. Scar acknowledged his blessing to still have Tay and Kiyah alive. He knew next time, he wouldn't be as lucky, so he was determined to assure that there would not be a next time.

Tay's voice traveled through the tunnel in his ear and disrupted his thoughts. Even though he heard her, he remained hunched over, not wanting to look into the eyes that reflected so much pain.

Tay saw that she was not getting a response, but she allowed the truth to flow anyway. "I know who hit our spot."

Scar immediately regained his composure and sat erect. He looked at Tay with an inquisitive stare. His eyes squinted, hoping that he had heard Tay clearly.

"What did you say?" Scar asked just to make sure that he had heard correctly.

"I said... I know who is behind everything." Tay repeated. She didn't entertain another question. She immediately revealed how she knew Nuri and his crew was behind their loss, pain, and suffering.

Scar was enraged. For the next twenty minutes, Tay explained what she witnessed. Scar paced nonstop from one side of the small room to the next.

Moments later, Snake and Trife re-entered. They held two large gift bags that were filled with various items. Scar's deranged expression stood out like a sore thumb. The growing tension was obvious. Trife and Snake looked at each other, wondering what had brought all of this about.

"I'm tired of these fuckin' bustas. I told dude to stay in his fucking lane, but no, he wanna be a fuckin' hero. Ah-ight, we ain't gon' keep goin' back and forth. I'ma show these fuck boys what time it is."

"Hold on—"

"Nah, Tay, fuck that," Scar retorted. He waved his hand at her in a dismissing manner. "I can't wait fo' you on this one. Its gon' take you a while to get betta. Just fall back and heal up, I got this one!" Tay put her index finger to her mouth and told him to quiet down. Scar continued. "They really don't know who they're fuckin' wit'. First they got nerve to hit our spot, then murder two of our soldiers, damn near kill you and my baby girl, Kiyah, and think it ain't gon' be no retaliation fo' what they done did. They got me fucked up! Real bad boys move in silence. They ain't gon' neva heal from the Scar that I'm 'bout to leave."

Scar walked over to the coat rack and snatched his leather jacket. He was so angry he did not realize the muscle that he put in the grab. The coat rack smashed down hard on the shoe shined floor. His lips had chapped from the excessive talking, and not a drop of saliva moistened his tongue.

He reached the entrance door, swung it open, and stormed out of the room. The plastic shades on the heavy door rattled, sending a deep echo through the tranquil hallway.

Snake looked at Trife, and Trife responded with a questioning glare. Neither of them spoke a word. They shrugged and calmly walked out of Tay's room.

"I don't know what just happened, but somethin' tellin' me shit 'bouta get real heated."

"Yeah, I feel the same thang, Trife. I feel the same thang."

Chapter 20

"Hello... Oh hey baby, how are you? I knew you would call me once you woke up and realized that I was no longer in the house... Awww, I know you miss me," Bri blushed. "You make me feel so special... No not at all. I plan to be here with your mom preparing this delicious meal... What do you mean why are we starting so early? You know she always start during the week... Yeah, I know... Yeah, you're right. She's such a sweetheart... Oh, you wanna speak to her? Don't get me in trouble, boy." She smiled and a soft chuckle followed. "Here she is." Bri took the phone from her ear and attempted to hand it to Ms. Johnson.

"Bri, who is that?" Ms. Johnson inquired from across the counter. She wore a disturbed expression that spoke for itself.

"It's Quron." Bri answered in a soft tone.

"That boy knows I don't like to be bothered while I'm cooking. But that's my baby." She giggled.

Bri twisted her wrist, teasing Ms. Johnson with the phone. She cleaned her hands with the checkerboard apron that hugged her body then took the phone.

"Hey baby, how is my boy doing?"

"You know me, Mama. Takin' it one day at a time."

"That's the best way to do it."

"How are you, though?" Quron inquired.

"I'm blessed, just a lil tired." She exhaled upon sharing her truth. "Me and your future wife is over here making these pots sing." Ms. Johnson turned toward Bri and winked her eye.

Bri blushed from the compliment and continued to season the porgy fish.

"Well Mama, I ain't gon' hold you on this phone. I just wanted to check on you and make sure everything is good."

"Well, thanks baby, I appreciate it."

"Not a problem. Oh, before I forget, remember that gift I told you I was plannin' to purchase for you?"

"I remember."

"Well I got it, and you'll get it soon." Quron smirked as he envisioned his mother's facial expression. "I gotta be careful though, cause once you see what it is, you might faint." He giggled.

"Baby, you always spoil me."

"You my mama, that's what I'm supposed to do."

"But umm, I'ma let you go now. Love you, and tell Bri the same."

"Okay."

"Alright, Ma. Love you."

Ms. Johnson disconnected the call, shook her head, and placed the phone on its charger. "That son of mine is something else."

"Who you tellin?" Bri stated with her hands on her hips. They both laughed. "So, Ms. Johnson, how is Amil doing? Quron and Nuri are always talking about her."

"I'm not surprised. Them boys love their sister. She's the purest thing they got. When they went to prison, it was a great strain on her. She's the youngest, but very strong. It was only by the grace of God that she managed to maintain and stay focused despite the internal issues of our family. I'm very proud of them all."

Bri walked around the counter and stood over the pan that was layered with chicken breasts. She took the diced garlic, onions, and bell peppers and placed them onto and alongside the poultry.

"Now that they're back, I know that she is excited to get home and spend some time with them. I can't wait to see her, I heard about her making the dean's list."

"Yes, honey. She is serious about her books. That's going to be my lil lawyer right there. She'll probably be in town during the holidays. Her schedule is so tight. She hardly has any leisure time. That's okay though, it'll pay off in the end."

Ms. Johnson and Bri continued to converse about various things, from fashion, to food, to men, to plain girl talk. Over the years, they had developed a great bond. A bond similar to that of a mother and a daughter. Ms. Johnson respected the way Bri picked up the slack that was left once Malai, Quron's ex, abandoned him while he was in prison. At one point in time, the frequent visits to the prison were more than enough for Bri. Quron's love used to stimulate her heart, and made her view her sacrifice as something that was truly worth it. But over time, Ms. Johnson noticed how Bri's joy had slowly dwindled, and a suffering misery replaced what she once felt.

Bri's demeanor had noticeably changed, for what most people would say, the worse. But Ms. Johnson understood. Being a woman who was once her age that endured the same struggle of trying to maintain her dignity while her man was incarcerated helped her relate. It was not easy for her, and she knew that it was not easy for Bri.

Years prior, Ms. Johnson had made it her business to inform Bri that her secret was no longer a secret. She knew of her dealings with Young-One. Upon learning about Bri's betrayal, Ms. Johnson was heartbroken. She knew how close her son's ties were with both Bri and Young-One, and she could not believe that either of them would stoop so low.

Bri became an emotional wreck when Ms. Johnson confronted her betrayal. She cried and begged for hours, trying to justify her wrongs. Deep within her heart, she knew that her desperate cries had fallen on deaf ears. After all, Quron was her son.

To her surprise, Ms. Johnson never uttered a word to her son. Either that, or they both were handling it very well. The unknown ate at Bri's conscience and compelled her to question Ms. Johnson's reason for keeping what she knew to herself. Upon doing so, Ms. Johnson shared how she didn't believe in getting involved in other people's affairs, including her children. Bri felt relief overcome her when Ms. Johnson shared her logic, but what shortly followed, gave her goose bumps. Ms. Johnson had added that her disloyalty warranted an exception to her rule, and the only way that she would remain quiet about her secret was if she promised to tell Quron herself upon his release from prison. Without hesitation, she agreed.

Lately, this same skeleton that has been hiding in her closet seemed to be anxious to come out. The truth often tugged at her soul, and now at her conscience. Not knowing how Quron would react filled her with anxiety and kept her uneasy. She wanted to do right, but wanting to do something and actually doing it are two totally different things.

Silence filled the kitchen area that the two women occupied. Ms. Johnson hummed a beautiful tune and moved around, catering to the various dishes that they had been preparing throughout the day. Through her peripheral, she noticed Bri was in deep thought. Bri's distant gaze did not appear to be abnormal or anything out of the ordinary. The bothered expression accompanied her gaze is what stood out.

A look of concern covered Ms. Johnson's face and the tune that she hummed suddenly came to a halt. She turned the dial on the stove down, took off her colorful checkered apron and walked steadily over to the stool that Bri was sitting on. She placed her soft hand on Bri's shoulder and gave her a firm motherly squeeze.

"What's wrong, baby? Somethin' on your mind?" Ms. Johnson posed the question with concern tracing her every word.

Bri blinked a few times to regain her focus, then looked into Ms. Johnson's eyes. The barely visible lines that settled in the smooth skin around her pupils revealed the years of struggle that help mold her into the woman she now knew. At that moment, Bri was envious of Ms. Johnson, wishing that she had the same clarity she saw in the elder that stood in front of her.

Bri cleared her throat and spoke softly. "Actually, there is something on my mind, Ms. Johnson."

"Child, I been sitting here all day listening to you call me Ms. Johnson. You know you're like my daughter, so please call me Ma. I don't think I can stand to hear another Ms. Johnson come from your mouth." Her irritated expression changed to a warm smile.

Bri accepted her advice and giggled at Ms. Johnson's frankness. "You're right, I'm sorry." Bri conceded.

Ms. Johnson placed her hand inside of Bri's palm and rubbed up and down gently. "So what's the problem, baby? Talk to me."

Bri exhaled. "Lately, I find myself being unusually stressed behind my secret. Then my mind drifts to you, and I can't help but wonder why would you allow your son to be with me, knowing that I wasn't on my best behavior while he was away? I mean, I am truly thankful that you have upheld your word by not taking it upon yourself to tell Quron, but I just don't get it, and it is eating me up. For God sake, look at me." Bri stood and pulled at her loose fitting jeans. "I'm losing my hips, my butt, my mind, gosh." A soft giggle followed her words, but she couldn't hide her worry.

Ms. Johnson stood to her feet and began to pace through the cluttered kitchen. Bri's question struck a nerve and Ms. Johnson didn't like the awkward feeling that it gave her. But at the same time, she felt the need to provide an answer.

After gathering her thoughts, she stopped pacing and leaned half of her body across the old wooden counter and found contact with Bri's questioning eyes.

"Well baby, honestly, if God blesses you to see my age, you'll understand that some things are better when they are kept a secret. But sweetie," a brief silence settled as Ms. Johnson allowed her words to trail off. "Don't think for a second that I kept quiet to protect you, 'cause I didn't." She shook her head. "I kept quiet because I knew what you was going through as a woman in the struggle. But what you did was lower than low. Cheating altogether is definitely wrong. But if you do it, take it away from home. Never cheat with a friend!"

Ms. Johnson's words struck Bri hard. She was obviously torn by the truth, and what ate at her conscience even more was that she was still caught up in Young-One. She was still indecisive about what to do.

Ms. Johnson noticed Bri's rattled expression, but she felt a responsibility to enlighten the beautiful young lady that she had embraced as a daughter. She continued. "I didn't mean to sound harsh, Bri. But you seek the truth, so I'm giving you what you want to know." Bri shook her head to show that she understood. "I love my kids just like any other mother, and I know Quron loves you unconditionally. I'm sure that your secret would have literally drove him crazy. So to spare my baby from such pain and suffering, I knew it was best to remain neutral. I don't know if you see it, but Quron glows whenever your name is mentioned. That is true happiness, and I would rather see him happy than miserable any day. But Bri," Ms. Johnson said sternly, grabbing Bri's attention. "Like I told you earlier, I love you like you are my daughter, but sweetie, I advise you to keep your word and tell Quron the truth. Clear your conscience, baby, clear your conscience. Your secret won't be a secret forever. What's in the dark will definitely come to light. The truth will set you free." She stood erect, rounded the counter and kissed Bri on her cheek.

Ms. Johnson's kiss seemed to trigger Bri's emotions and a tear rolled down her face.

Ms. Johnson retrieved a napkin from her pocket and dabbed her cheek. "Don't cry, sweetie, everything will be alright. Trust me. Everything will be all right when you make it right. Now pull yourself together, and run to the store and pick up some more sweet potatoes." Ms. Johnson demanded with a smile and a soft chuckle, trying to lift Bri's spirits. "You know my boys love my yams and my pies."

She reached into her small Louis Vuitton purse, pulled out a few small bills and attempted to hand them to Bri.

"I got it, Ma," Bri said, not accepting the money. She picked up her red Coach bag and grabbed her car keys off the glass coffee table. "I'll be back."

A slight smile showed before she walked out of the house, but Ms. Johnson could see that her words were weighing on Bri's mind. Ms. Johnson felt bad, but she had shared what she thought was best. Now, her duty as a mother figure was done, and the rest was up to Bri.

After a few minutes, Ms. Johnson gradually drifted back into her zone. Her hands were busy mixing, and her head was steadily moving to the beautiful sound of the soft melody that she hummed. She was so consumed by what she was doing that she didn't hear the front door open. The sound from it closing caught her ear and she realized that Bri had already returned from the store.

"Bri, is everything alright? You got back quick." Ms. Johnson cleaned her hands with her apron and turned to face her future daughter in law. Her heart dropped to the bottom of her stomach at the sight of the long shining barrel of Scar's .38.

Trife and Snake back peddled with their fully loaded machine guns cocked and ready to fire at anything that came through the front door. Startled, Ms. Johnson jumped back and placed her hand over her heart. Her quick movement knocked the boiling pot of collard greens off balance. The scorching water leapt from the large pot and an agonized scream forced its way out of Ms. Johnson's throat, as the boiling water burned her legs.

"Shut the fuck up, lady!" Scar spat.

"Please stop. Why are you doing this?" Ms. Johnson cried and pleaded as she continued to back up. So many thoughts raced through her head, she couldn't even think clearly. She quivered with fear and it wasn't until the cool air hit her panties that she realized she had urinated on herself.

She took another step back and the room seemed to have closed in on her. Her maneuvering space had run out and her back pressed firmly against the wall. Scar continued to advance forward, and the undeniable fear that he saw in Ms. Johnson's eyes contributed to his massive ego. Standing within arm's reach, Scar cocked the hammer to the gun. The clicking sound that the revolver made stuck in Ms. Johnson's head like an old antique clock that struck midnight. At that moment, despair settled in her heart and she knew that the click from the pistol signified the expiration of her time line on earth. The dark tunnel of the barrel made her envision how it would be in her grave. She made no attempt to fight for her life, this was her fate.

"When you see ya son in the next life, tell 'em it's all his fault."

The hollow point slug smashed with extreme force against Ms. Johnson's forehead killing her instantly. She died with a peaceful expression on her face. Her eyes were open and her body descended slowly down the cream colored wall. Fragments from her brain plastered to the wall and the thick mixture of blood and other lubricants streamed down, trailing her lifeless body.

It was a sad ending for the woman who showed genuine love and concern for everyone that she encountered. Never in her life did she imagine it was possible for her demise to come about like this. She was innocent as an individual, but guilty by association. Quron was the life that she had brought into the world, and was the same life that brought about her demise.

Scar hovered over and looked down at the woman he had murdered. He stared down, as Ms. Johnson lay motionless with her eyes fixed upward, locked on him. A chill crawled up his body as he shook her gaze off. He tucked his revolver and beckoned for Trife and Snake to follow. They uttered not a word. Scar looked down one last time then walked in a calm stride out the back door.

"Ma, I'm back. The traffic was kinda thick today for some reason. Sorry it took me so long," Bri said as she walked through the front door and headed toward the kitchen. It was unusually quiet, but she paid it no mind.

"I bought the sweet potatoes that you wanted." Bri continued as she entered the kitchen, seeming to be in better spirits than before. The paper bag that she held in her arms against her breast was heavy. She placed the items on the counter and allowed her eyes to wander in search of Ms. Johnson. She realized that the door leading to the back yard was left ajar. That stood out in her mind, but the dried up substance plastered to the wall caught her attention. Bri stepped around the wooden counter trying to get a closer look, and her heart felt like it had literally stopped.

"Oh my God, no Ma, no Ma!"

She raced to Ms. Johnson's side, hoping that there was something that she could do. Bri dropped to her knees and embraced the dead corpse. Tears fell from her eyes nonstop. While in her arms, Bri looked closely and it dawned on her that the hole in Ms. Johnson's head was indeed a bullet wound. That truth sent chills through Bri's body and made matters worse. She felt her heart thumping hard and fast against her chest. Her hands were shaking uncontrollably and she sensed a nervous breakdown was near.

Not wasting a second more, she stood to her feet and grabbed the phone. When she pressed the power button, the phone showed no signs of life. Panic settled in and she ran full speed through the front door, almost knocking Nuri over. He was immediately bothered by Bri's distraught state. He hugged her tightly as she buried her face in his muscular chest while crying hysterically.

"Calm down, sis, what's wrong? What happened?"

Bri couldn't find the presence of mind to explain what she had discovered in detail. "It's Mama, Nuri. Mama is gone." was all she managed to say.

Nuri quickly pried himself from Bri's strong hold, drew his .50cal and entered the brownstone with caution. When he reached the woman that had been like a mother to him, he dropped to his knees in disbelief. He felt crushed, hurt, defeated, and responsible all at once. He rocked back and forth. Tears of the deepest pain that a person could feel fell from his eyes. He scooped Ms. Johnson in his arms and held her for what seemed like forever. After minutes of grieving, he pulled himself to his feet and walked outside. The whole neighborhood seemed to be in front of the building mourning. Someone had obviously called 911 because the paramedics had arrived.

Bri stood at the bottom of the staircase staring up at Nuri through saddened eyes while embracing Young-One. They both were an emotional wreck.

Nuri stood on the porch, away from the large crowd. The paramedics sped past him, but it felt as if they weren't even there. Nuri felt alone, in a world of his own. One tear at a time in even measures trickled down his cheeks. In his heart, he knew that the hardest part had yet to come. Even worse, he knew that it was incumbent upon him to be the giver of the heartbreaking news.

Reluctantly, Nuri scrolled through his phone and stopped on his brother's name. Within seconds, there was a voice on the other end of the line.

"Yo, Ron." Nuri spoke with not a trace of enthusiasm.

"What's up, bro?" Quron answered, sensing something was wrong. The sound of Quron's voice triggered Nuri's pain, and tears started trickling more rapidly.

Quron heard the sniffles and immediately knew that whatever Nuri was about to tell him was going to affect him the same. Nuri was not one to let his emotions show through tears. Whenever he cried, it was because the tragedy inflicted that much pain and warranted no other way to mourn.

"N.O., what up? You there?"

"Yeah, I'm here," Nuri stepped down a few steps and sat. "It's Mama, Ron, something bad happened to Ma...to Mama." Nuri could no longer compose himself. His sobs grew louder and their loss hit his heart head on. At that point, it had become obvious.

"Hold it together, Nur, I'll be there in a minute." Quron spoke encouragingly to his brother but he was the one who needed the advice.

From the second he heard Nuri's voice, the emotional imbalance that he sensed revealed that something was terribly wrong. When Nuri confirmed Quron's feeling, his stomach knotted and filled with butterflies. What had happened was already done. Quron just hoped that whatever the problem was could be fixed with money, a doctor, or through prayer.

———

Pedro had his seat slightly reclined on an angle that suited him. One hand gripped the big steering wheel, while the other lay limp across the armrest. He looked over at his friend and noticed how Quron's whole demeanor had suddenly changed. Quron ended the call and looked over at Pedro. Pedro became concerned about what was bothering his friend, but he knew that certain things were personal. He felt the only way he would learn of the problem was through Quron volunteering the information.

As if he could read Pedro's thoughts as they crossed his mind, Quron tapped Pedro's arm and spoke with dismay. "Take me to my mother's house on Lander Street. That was my brother..." Quron paused as the painful words became caught in his throat. "He said somethin' bad happened to my mother. Hurry up, I gotta get back."

Not uttering a word or breaking his focus, Pedro glanced through the rear view mirror in search of state troopers. When none crossed his view, he quickly located a ditch that was usually occupied by the police, and whipped the Mercedes Benz steering wheel. He made an illegal u-turn in the middle of the highway.

When they arrived, Quron knew by the scene that the situation was far more serious than what he had expected. The small one-way street was congested with dozens of people. Everyone was embracing each other. The ambulance was parked in front of the brownstone and there were unmarked police cars across from them. Quron did not want to believe what the pain in his heart was telling him.

Yellow tape set the barrier mark, but not even a steel wall could have prevented Quron from getting to his family. Pedro and he made their way through the thick crowd. The closer they got, the weaker Quron's knees became. He looked around and finally spotted his brother. Nuri was sitting on the concrete curb, bent over with his face buried in his hands. Surrounding him, stood Steel, Ghost, Ja and Dex. All of them were tense. Young-One had accompanied Bri to the hospital after she suffered an anxiety attack.

Quron rushed over to where Nuri sat and that's when he saw the paramedics carrying out a body covered in a white sheet. The worst settled in and he lost it.

"No Mama, oh God, please nooo!" Quron rushed over to the stretcher.

"Please, sir, back up."

He paid little attention to the paramedics that spoke to him. Quron brushed past him and grabbed the metal rail of the stretcher. He then used his free hand to ease the white sheet from over Ms. Johnson's face.

"AAHHH!" A loud outcry tumbled from his throat. "Why, Allah, why?" He screamed while looking toward the sky.

"Somebody grab this man!" Another paramedic instructed as she became startled by Quron's deranged state.

Pedro and Nuri went to his aid. The sight alone brought pain. Quron crumpled to his knees, drained from all feelings of life. He was emotionally crushed. He felt at that moment, there wasn't anything left for him to live for. The murderer had killed two souls with one bullet.

Pedro picked his friend up and embraced him firmly. It was truly a hug of love. Pedro looked on helplessly for the first time, feeling his friend's pain.

Detective Fisher and his partner, DeJesus, walked over to the distraught family after exiting the house and handed Ghost their card.

"Whenever your friend feels up to it, tell him to give us a call. We have some questions pertaining to this homicide. Please pass on our condolences. From what we understand, the victim is his mother."

Ghost took the card and they walked off toward their car.

"Fish," DeJesus turned toward his partner. "Watch how hectic things get around here. After we saw them two at the hospital that day, I did a background check on them. They looked familiar, so I checked photo arrays and our software, and guess what I stumbled across?"

"What's that?"

"I found out that the lighter one, the one that's not handling his mother's death too well was convicted for manslaughter almost nine years ago. But before that, him, his brother, and their crew used to run these streets. When I think about it, their names do ring bells, Nuri and Quron. When you get a chance, check out their file. It's interesting how much information was gathered on the two of them. Now they are back on the street and their mother just got murdered, execution style at that. The pieces of this puzzle just aren't adding up. A sweet lady like that meeting such a brutal death, I'm willing to bet that her death had something to do with something they did."

"Time will tell," Fisher added. "Time will definitely tell."

Fisher put the car in drive and slowly drove off.

Chapter 21

It was eleven o'clock in the morning and everything seemed to be running behind schedule, including the airport. The plane had landed fifteen minutes late, setting Amil back, due to its delay. She found herself rushing through Stewart Airport with her small case of luggage rolling close behind. On a normal day, the delay wouldn't have bothered the pretty young lady. In fact, she loved whatever leisure time that she could get, but today was different.

After about a quarter of a mile jog, she finally reached the small storefront that she had made arrangements with. Bent over with both hands clutching her knees, her chest rose and fell as she struggled to regain control over her breathing.

"May I help you, ma'am?" The store manager asked from behind the desk.

Amil stood erect and walked toward him. Normally, the manager would not have gone out of his way to cater to a store customer. Amil had caused him to make an exception. Even in her old Gucci sweat suit with a scarf covering her hair, Amil's beauty was still prominent and undeniable.

"Yes, my name is Ms. Amil Johnson. I made reservations over the phone to rent the newest Maxima that your company had available."

"Oh yeah, right this way, Ms. Johnson. I've been expecting you." The young manager recalled as he escorted Amil to a separate section of the store.

She followed close behind as she had been asked to do. Not a single word exchanged between the two. The handsome manager found Amil's silence to be awkward, and he sensed that something of importance was weighing heavily on her mind. Out of respect, he changed his game plan, deciding not to pursue her.

Amil accepted the car key that the manager handed her, and a faint smile briefly appeared.

"Alright Ms. Johnson, your luggage is secured in the trunk. If you happen to have any problems, just call and ask for Tom."

"Okay, thank you."

Amil shook Tom's hand and got into the car. In less than five minutes, she had navigated through the chaotic parking lot, and she was headed down Broadway to the house that had captured so many family memories. Driving down the long strip was literally like driving through memory lane. Amil looked around with a mixture of disgust and sympathy as she patiently sat behind the BMW that awaited the changing color of the traffic light.

Many of the people who loitered on the street had been caught up in the addictive lifestyle long before Amil was born. Some of the faces she remembered from back in the day when her brothers ran the street. Others, she recognized from high school and casual encounters. In her mind, the different status and generations of people that she recognized only confirmed that no one was safe from genocide. If you were born in the ghetto, there was a great possibility that you would fall victim. She shook her head in shame.

The traffic light turned green, but the BMW in front of Amil did not move. Frustration settled in, and Amil forced the gear in reverse, and then shifted back down to drive, swerving around the ignorant couple that was still stuck at the light. Amil gave the couple a mouth full through her gaze as she sped by. She could not see much of the driver's face because he was turned on an angle, leaning over the armrest, kissing the beautiful woman that sat in the passenger seat. But she did catch a glimpse of the woman's tear streaked face, and their eyes locked until traffic separated them.

When Amil pulled up in front of her childhood home, the pain that she had been dodging ambushed her without warning. Tears rolled down her face as she accepted the fact that her mother, the woman who molded her to be the person that she had become, would never return. A smile formed when beautiful memories that her mother and she had shared flashed through her mind.

The opening of her car door interrupted her moment. She looked up and knew everything would be okay. Her older brother, Nuri, stood over her. When their eyes met, he smiled. This was her first time seeing him since his release from prison. When he was released, school had just started back and her job wouldn't give her any days off. Her boss stressed how much they needed her around the office. This moment that she shared with her brother was a moment that she had longed for, and it felt so good.

"C'mon Mil, we on a tight schedule. We gotta be at the church in an hour and a half."

Amil stepped out of the car and threw herself into her brother's arms. Nuri held her tightly as they hugged and mourned silently together. Moments later, she rushed into the house and headed straight for the bathroom.

An hour later, two stretch Mercedes limousines parked one behind the other in front of the House of Joy church that was located on Liberty Street. Things were tense. Uniformed, on duty officers patrolled the area and posted every corner within a three-block radius. The Chief of Police feared a violent gun war would break out in retaliation for Ms. Johnson's violent death. So instead of waiting it out to see if his prediction was correct, he beefed up the security to minimize the possibility.

Quron was the first to emerge from the seclusion of the dark tinted limousine. The sidewalk and streets alike were overflowing with people. People of all ages and races had found time to come and pay their last respects. Black Gucci shades with gold trimming shaded Quron's eyes. A black and gold turban wrapped neatly around his fresh waves, and the color coordinated Gucci suit that he sported was tailored to perfection. Women stared with lust in their eyes, almost forgetting the reason why they were there.

Amil held onto her brother's hand as she stepped onto the cold pavement. She was drop dead gorgeous, like an angel that had descended from the heavens. Her silk black Versace dress clung to her shapely body. Her thick, round curves were hereditary, and all her years of running track, swimming, and playing softball while in high school had definitely paid off. Amil's long jet black hair dangled pass her shoulders, forming in layers around her smooth brown skin, noticeably enhancing her Indian features.

Quron eyed the many faces that surrounded him. It pained him to know that any one of the people present could have very well been his mother's killer. In the small of his back, beneath his suit jacket, was a compact holster that concealed the 40 caliber that he carried. He knew that his mother's death was a hit, and it was killing him. He couldn't seem to shake the burden of guilt. It nibbled on his soul like a flock of crows that devoured a corpse. Deep down inside, no matter how bad he wanted to believe otherwise, he knew that what had transpired had everything to do with him. It was the only thing that made sense. He could not believe how naive he was. Back in his time, there was a universal rule that family members who were not in the game would not suffer for the actions of a member that was. That golden rule had obviously become obsolete, and Quron and his family had found out the hard way.

After everyone gathered, the crowd parted and made way for the family. The much-needed support was definitely there. Bri held Quron's hand, and Young-One, Steel, Ghost, Ja and Dex trailed behind. They looked stunning in their suits and custom designed attire. As they reached the door to the small church, a black Rolls Royce with chrome factory rims rolled up and parked behind the two stretch limos. Pedro stepped out of the luxurious car, accompanied by his beautiful sister, India.

Jealousy and envy flowed through Bri's veins at the sight of India. And the brief smile that flashed across Quron's face upon seeing her didn't help. Bri immediately peeped game. *I definitely have to keep my eyes on this bitch.* Bri thought as she gave a warm smile.

Nuri raised his hand and beckoned for them to join, and they all entered the church together. The first three rows had been reserved for Ms. Johnson's immediate family. They sat and listened to the preacher attentively. Quron was Muslim, and didn't believe in the Christian teachings, but the preacher was dropping words of wisdom on this day, that couldn't have come at a better time.

People from all over the tri-state area and even from other states had come to give speeches that reflected the highlights of Ms. Johnson's life. Quron smiled as he realized the beautiful effect that his mother had on people's lives. His gaze shifted toward his sister, Amil. She wept uncontrollably and her gaze locked on the pearl white casket.

Nuri looked over at his brother and the shadows of death reflected through the glossiness in his eyes. Quron lowered his head, knowing that his brother's glare confirmed what was in his heart as well, and that scared him. He reasoned if both of them drove off emotion, and not intellect, a lot of blood would be spilled. At that moment, he didn't care. Many souls would compensate for his loss.

The sermon had concluded and a soft heavenly sound eased into the air. The organist worked the keys of the oak wood instrument with skill, and people starting from the last row of benches made their way toward the front of the church to view Ms. Johnson's body for the last time. Many people wept as if they had lost one of their own. Family members showed Amil lots of love, but turned their lips up at the sight of her brothers. Many of their aunts and uncles felt that the death of their mother was their fault, assuming the exact truth.

Quron and Nuri held their composure, not allowing themselves to feed into the evil stares of their so-called family. Most of them were phony anyway. In Quron's eyes, having the same blood flowing through their veins did not classify a person as family. The unconditional love and loyalty that an individual demonstrated through their deeds, no matter the circumstance, is what made a person family. He looked to his right then left, and accepted the fact that his crew who he broke bread with in the streets was indeed his family.

The funeral attendees had gradually decreased in number as they made their exit after viewing the body. Nuri, and his street family was all that was left. Pedro stood over the casket with his hand gripping India's shoulder. This was the first time Pedro had attended a funeral that really touched his soul. It surprised him, because he hadn't ever met the woman who he learned was Ms. Johnson, but he felt like they had been acquaintances for many years. Pedro absorbed her peaceful expression and his mind drifted to the families, including children, who he had ordered to be killed over the years. He wondered what type of person his past decisions made him. Did the lives of innocent people really free the debts of those who owed? He questioned.

Quron, Nuri, and Amil were the last three to pay their respects. Quron looked on in silence with teary eyes as his brother spoke aloud as if Ms. Johnson could hear him. The funeral home did an excellent job with Ms. Johnson's make-up. It was impossible to tell that she had been shot in the head at point blank range. Nuri's pain was as noticeable as his voice cracked and built up saliva dropped from his mouth. Quickly, he was overwhelmed with emotion and he couldn't hold it together. He crumbled and Steel had to escort him out of the church.

"Mom, I know you are somewhere close, watching over us and listening," Amil continued to cry as she stood over the casket. "I just want you to know that we all love you and we'll...we'll..." she stumbled over her words, her sobs growing louder and her breathing harder. "We'll always remember your soft smile and you will always be alive in our hearts." Amil could not bear the pain any longer. She bent over, kissed her mother's cool skin, and walked off.

Quron was speechless, scarred for life, and heartbroken. His arms were behind his back and tears ran streams from underneath his black Gucci shades. But not a word was uttered. Within his heart and mind, a conversation had already started.

First and foremost, I would like to apologize, Mama. Apologize for complicating your life at times and causin' you a pain that no child could understand. But know that everything I did was done to better our livin' condition. I mean, if I could, I would do anything or give up everything that I have to bring you back. But we know the extent of that claim is impossible. Tellin you the truth just helped me feel better. Oh yeah, that gift that I was tellin' you 'bout is here with me.

Quron dug into his pocket and pulled out a key.

This key is for you, Mama.

He placed the key inside the casket. *I bought you a brand new home in the town of Newburgh. Could you believe it, Mama? You were actually goin' to move out of the hood.*

Quron smiled then bowed his head. *I guess it wasn't meant. But don't worry about it. I plan to give it to Amil. I know, I know, you don't have to worry. We're goin' to take care of our baby sister. And yeah, I almost forgot. Just in case Bri didn't tell you, I went with her to the doctor and she found out that she was pregnant, a few weeks. Funny thing about it is she didn't seem excited when the doctor informed us. I can't call it though, maybe somethin' was on her mind.*

Silence settled in his mind, and Quron's thoughts seem to have discontinued. Then suddenly he began again.

I know you aren't goin' to like what I'm about to say, but I feel like I gotta assure you. I promise that whoever did this to you, I will find them. Mama, they will die a horrible death. A horrible, horrible, death. Nope Ma, don t even try and talk me out of it. I can't let this ride. I'm sorry, Mama, but I just can't.

Quron leaned over and kissed the woman that made it all possible for him. When he rose, the presence of someone behind him was felt. He turned around and eyed the spitting image of himself, just older and worn down. Quron looked at the older man and the love that he had for him quickly overshadowed the negative emotions that he harbored for all his years of absence.

The man's face was sagging, complexion dull, and a hard life was obvious. His age and the continuous drug abuse had caught up to him. His gray hair was combed and his face shaved. His eyes were glossy, reflecting pain and regret. Regret for choosing the heartless streets over his beautiful family. In his calloused hand was an old Polaroid picture. The picture was of a man, woman, and children. Quron remembered the photo as if it was taken yesterday. That photo held one of his best childhood memories as a family.

Quron gave his father a nod and walked out of the church, leaving the old man alone to pay his last respects. A pain filled cry sounded throughout the sanctuary as the man wept from the sight of his lost love.

Chapter 22

More than a month had elapsed since Ms. Johnson's untimely death. The effect of her demise still hovered over Quron's head. He hadn't been himself. Bottles of cognac seem to be his only concern. On a few occasions, Bri had found him sprawled out in the middle of the living room floor, lying in his own vomit. She understood her man's pain, and she had even tried to cope with his inappropriate actions. But as time went on, she became overwhelmed with grief, due to his disrespect. He was a nasty drunk; the type that became a totally different person under the influence. His nasty words cut like razors, and a real dislike formed for Quron's new addiction.

Whenever she tried to seduce him, he showed little to no interest. Bri was hurt by this. He had never denied her sexually in the past. Quron was a horn dog, always inclined to take it to the next level, sexually. While under the influence, everything about Quron went from bad to worse. His moods swung like an amusement park ride. She never took his words lightly, because deep down inside, she truly believed a drunken man spoke with a sober tongue. Life for the two had not been ideal until this point anyway, so the wedge only spread more. While Quron forced her away, Young-One was welcoming her with open arms as he had always done.

Inside Ms. Johnson's home on Lander Street, Ghost and Quron sat across from each other on the soft couches. Old memories bounced off the living room walls, not making things any better. Amil was upstairs packing the remains of her mother's belongings. After discussing what they would do with her possessions, they agreed to donate everything to charity. The donation would serve a better purpose.

Quron felt like shit, and looked just as bad. His beard was thick, mustache hair overlaying his upper lip, and his frizzy hair was adorned with small lint balls. The hangover from the night before had his head thumping. He reeked of cognac and musk. If it wasn't for Amil making sure he was up in the morning, he would still be enjoying the solitude that accompanied deep sleep.

Ghost glared at his mentor and felt bad. Quron looked defeated. Ghost hadn't ever seen him like this. Quron's state really threw him for a loop. Ghost continued to stare, not knowing exactly what to say. At that moment, he really felt blessed, and appreciated the fact that he was a young boy when his father was murdered. Judging by Quron, he knew he would not have been able to bear such pain if he was older. He lowered his gaze, leaned forward and picked up the glass of water that sat before him. After a deep gulp, Ghost cleared his throat and leaned back.

"O.T., what's up wit'chu play boy? This ain't you. I don't know how long its gonna take for you to bounce back, but I hope it's soon." Ghost paused in hopes of getting some feedback. "Since you don't wanna talk about it, what up wit' that otha thing you was talkin' 'bout in the hospital that day? My team is ready, but I ain't got no product. I need a connect, bad!" Ghost stressed.

For the first time since they'd been seated, Quron opened his eyes. Ghost's words were heartfelt, they expressed genuine concern and Quron absorbed every word. Quron's ego was bruised, though. He felt Ghost, nor anyone else was supposed to see him in such a vulnerable state. It wasn't rocket science to him. He knew he had to shake his new addiction while he still could. But it was difficult, because the potent cognac was the only thing that took him away and coated his pain. The intoxicant made everything seem okay, just how he liked it.

Quron focused on Ghost's inquisitive stare and realized that his little man was seriously depending on him. He slowly stood from his seated position and a drum roll pounded in his head. The pain caused him to stumble and Ghost rushed to his side.

"You ah-ight, O.T.?" He asked with concern tracing his words.

"Yeah, I'm ah-ight." Quron assured as he walked down the hallway holding his head. When he returned, his hand clutched the straps of a duffle bag. He tossed the bag on Ghost's lap and flopped back down in the soft couch. Ghost eyed the bag, but hesitated to open it.

"Well, you gon' open it, right?" Quron questioned in a tired drawl.

Ghost didn't respond. He just slid the zipper back. The bag opened and a satisfied smile crept across Ghost's face. The neatly wrapped kilos of cocaine gave him a rush.

"That's six bricks, think you can handle it?" A different type of seriousness dangled from Quron's question and he seemed to be more focused than he had been in months.

Ghost shifted his gaze to the compressed keys again and his heart beat with joy. It was a great feeling. This confirmed that he had earned a level of respect from Quron, and along with that came additional power, and more control in the streets. He had been waiting for this break. He had the soldiers, and the demand was there, but the product until this point was not enough. Now, the game had finally flipped, and the cards had fallen in his favor.

He stood and walked over to Quron. "Good lookin', O.T." He smiled. "Of course I can handle it."

"Good. Bring me back $102,000. That's like eighteen apiece. The rest is you. Only one stipulation…"

"What's that?"

"From this point on, you can't deal with no one else. I'ma take care of you, but understand this is another level. I love you like a brother, but I do business like a stranger. Keep it a hunite wit' me at all times, and I'll do the same." Quron massaged his temples and squinted his eyes in an attempt to ease his headache. "I'm not gonna be around for a while. I'ma take a vacation. I need it, got a lot to think about. I need to find some peace. This ain't me. Don't take a lifetime, hit me when you ready."

Ghost embraced Quron firmly. The love and appreciation flowed through his grip. Quron was more than pleased to be in a position to help someone who he held close to his heart. Ghost gave a head nod and made his way toward the door.

The six kilos was all profit. Scar's stash house had six bricks and $300,000 in cash. Quron kept the coke and allowed his team to split the rest. He had Ghost in mind the whole time.

"Yo, keep your ears to the street. Somebody gotta know somethin' about what happened. It's been months and we still don't know who hit Mama Love. That's crazy!"

"I got'chu." Ghost assured. "Be easy."

Ghost looked back, smiled, and stood in the doorway. "Glad to have you back..." Ghost's words trailed off with the sound of the closing door.

Quron sat in silence. His thoughts seem to subdue the continuous throbbing. He knew that his condition was unacceptable. Thoughts of Bri crossed his mind and softened his heart. She would soon give birth to his first child. He had to get it together, because the way he had been treating her lately had complicated their relationship more than what it already was.

His gaze settled on the bottle of Absolut Vodka that peeped out of his coat pocket. There was no one around, just him and the clear fluid. Quron looked around for assurance, and there was nothing. Just him, the bottle of liquor, and the ruffling sound from the plastic bags that Amil was packing his mother's belongings in. He walked over to the coat rack and gripped the neck of the bottle that held the poison. Before it dawned on him, he was standing over the sink with the bottle tilted. The vodka splashed in the sink and disappeared down the drain. It was time for a new start, a new chapter.

He dialed a number.

"Hello my friend... I'm comin' along... Oh, so you say I sound better? Well, I feel better too. I just wanted to tell you I'm gonna accept your vacation offer. I need it, ya know... Totally understand, it's not a problem... Great, I'll be ready then."

Chapter 23

The days were shorter, due to the season. On this winter day, the gusty wind that usually swept through the streets were calm and settled. Throughout the day, pretty flakes of snow, varying in size, fell from the charcoal colored sky.

The blizzard left the city's habitants with no choice but to use public transportation to commute. The roads were in terrible condition, cluttered with recycled slush and traces of ice. Either you had a garage or your vehicle had a snow barricade formed around it, preventing any movement.

Ghost had unfortunately suffered from the latter. The new Benz Truck that he had recently treated himself to was encircled with snow, extending from the ground, up to the driver side window. He was mad as hell when he first saw his ride. But as his adrenaline settled, the wheels in his head started to turn. The more they turned, the clearer his advantage stood out to him. He was stuck in front of St. Luke's, a public hospital, so to the average eye, no suspicion would arise.

Down the block, the drug trade was heavy. Everybody knew about Fat-Roc and the smooth, lucrative operation he had going on Dubois St. Ghost never occupied his time with clocking how much money the next man was pulling in. He was too focused on coming up himself. Ever since he accepted those keys from Quron, his state of mind, along with his approach to the game had changed. Either you were with him or you were against him, and Fat-Roc certainly was not with him.

The cloudy dark sky added shade to the three comrades slumped in the truck. Ghost, Dex, and Ja sat in silence with high tech binoculars glued to their eyes. They had scoped out

Fat-Roc's operation for the past week. Their observation had opened their eyes to a new world of facts. Facts that made them want in. Either get down or lay down, no in between.

"It's that time, y'all ready?" Dex inquired from the back seat.

Ghost took a quick peek at his watch. "Yeah, we ready."

Dex opened the door and stepped onto the cold sidewalk. He stretched his limbs and a relieving yawn escaped from his depths.

Ja grabbed the brown paper bag from underneath his seat before joining his brother.

Donned in all black, Ghost climbed over the armrest and exited through the passenger door. Once outside, he straightened his look, gave his boys an acknowledging nod and walked across the street.

Dex and Ja's stride was steady and normal, while Ghost's steps seemed staggered and slow. Ghost keyed in on the two soldiers that stood on the same side of the street as he. Judging by their posture and their alert demeanor, he knew that the possibility of them being strapped was great. Even with the high possibility, Ghost wasn't hardly worried. He brushed his hand across the warm steel that was concealed in his Marmot coat, and a devilish smile crept across his face.

Across the street, Ja and Dex reached the rotted, wooden porch that held the small gathering. Life appeared to be treating the young hustlers well. They were obviously seeing a lot of paper. All of them were dipped in the finest urban brands, varying in designer names, style, and colors.

The youngest of the crew squinted, and his humorous laugh ceased upon noticing the two dark shadows slowly ascending the steps. Startled, he reached for his Glock, but hesitated when Ja and Dex removed their hoods. The oldest amongst them recognized the twins and an uncomfortable chill tickled his stomach. Word on the street was, since Ja and Dex had been stabbed and shot, their career in the game was over. Ghost hadn't been seen around town much since the incident, giving credence to the rumor.

"What up, fellas?" Ja calmly asked, interrupting the flow of their conversation.

The small group looked at each other, exchanging thoughts with their expressions.

"Whatever you want to be up!" The young pretty boy stated aggressively. "Who y'all here to see, anyway?"

Ja and Dex exchanged stares. The insolence in the young fella's tone, told them that he didn't know who he was speaking to. But it didn't matter. Dex's level of tolerance had rapidly decreased. He knew exactly how to get results.

Young-Cory and his man, Butta, stood amongst their crew awaiting an answer. Dex looked at the young men that couldn't have been any older than he and his twin. That just ignited his anger more. He tapped his brother and made a head gesture to leave. The cynical smile that crossed Dex's lips stuck in Butta's mind. Something within told him that this wasn't the end of it.

As Dex turned on his heels, he quickly glanced across the street to see if Ghost was in position. He reached the top wooden step and spun around. The quickness of the sudden move startled the four hustlers. The potent angel dust and marijuana that they smoked paralyzed their reflexes and provided the pause that the twins needed.

Ja's identical.357 revolvers spit four hollow point slugs from their barrels in rapid succession. The hot lead chewed through the young boy's chest cavity at the speed of light, killing him before the loud boom echoed through the streets.

Young-Cory tried to dart past Dex, but his man's body fell in front of him and slowed his stride. Dex swung with extreme force, landing a deafening blow. Blood squirted from the split cartilage in his ear and a bitch made scream tailored his pain. Dex aimed his pistol downward and squeezed the trigger. The slug destroyed tissue, ligaments in his knee, and scattered pieces of blood and bone everywhere. Young-Cory screamed and squirmed helplessly.

The gunplay caused the two soldiers from across the street to react. They ran toward the porch with murder on their minds. Shells flipped from their smoking chambers as bullets chipped away the wood porch. The naked bushes along with the built up snow banks provided very little coverage. The closer the two soldiers came, the closer their bullets got to their targets. Ja and Dex sent slugs back at them, but it didn't slow their forward progress. The twins were their focus and little did they know, they were Ghost's focus.

Ghost eased off the porch that he had been chilling on and crept low behind the cars. He peeped over the hood and seized the opportunity. He stood and ran up behind them. Flames extended from the barrel of his Mac-10, sending an ambush of spiraled bullets their way. The soldiers never saw their assassin. The first six bullets tore through their hamstrings, backs and thighs. Before they hit the pavement, six more slugs found their target and ended their misery. Blood seeped from their multiple gunshot wounds, forming puddles in the snow on Newburgh's barren streets.

Butta and his man knew that their time was limited. If they had any hope of living, they had to make moves, and fast. The two scrambled to their feet and hurdled like track stars over the railing. Ja looked back and forth from the fleeing men and Young-Cory. He contemplated what he should do, but before an answer registered, his brother Dex sped past him in pursuit of the two.

Butta landed on his feet and stumbled forward as his momentum pushed him. He put one hand down, then the other, managing to keep his balance. As he rose to stand upright, he realized that his life was over. Visions of his newborn daughter flashed through his mind, and it was the first time in his life that he wished he would have made better life decisions. The loud thunderclap from Ghost's Mac told him it was too late to make any more decisions. The.9mm slug blew Butta's eye out of socket and opened the back of his skull like a lightning bolt that had struck a tree. Thick chunks of brain dropped from the large hole. He laid face down, eyes open with a smile.

John had watched his man, Butta, get gunned down. It hurt to see such a thing, but there wasn't anything he could have done. Down the block, he squatted behind a parked car and mourned for his man while inhaling deeply, trying to regain a normal breathing pattern. He rose and looked around nervously, knowing that he had to get to safety before anything happened. Across the street from where he stood was a pay phone. John hurried over, inserted coins, and dialed a number as fast as his fingers would press the buttons. As he awaited an answer, someone tapped him lightly on his shoulder. John turned with an irritated expression until he recognized the person who sought his attention. Urine streamed down his legs and warm feces dropped from his rectum.

Dex smiled and put two in his face. "Got me runnin' all over the damn place." Drawing up the nastiest mucus, Dex spit in his face and kept it moving.

———————

"These lil niggas dun lost their fuckin' minds." Fat-Roc whispered to himself while looking out the window shades. He ran to the nearest closet and rambled through the cluttered space. He retrieved a pistol grip Mossberg and tucked a.9mm with an extended clip in his waistline, just in case back up was needed.

Neatly stacked bills were wrapped and organized on a nearby glass table. The money machine was still turning bills and counting. A tightly rolled blunt of haze burned slowly in the marble ashtray, and gangster rap banged from the stereo system. Chips of paint were missing from the wall and ceiling, but that was nothing. This was the spot. Everything was all good until these young niggas lost their mind. Roc contemplated his next move and glared at the pile of cash on the table. He instantly moved to secure his money. A loud thud in the hallway made him reconsider. He didn't want to get caught slipping, so he turned off the lights, clicked off the music, and waited.

"Get the fuck up, nigga! Don't cry now!" Ghost spat through clenched teeth as he kicked Young-Cory in his ass. "I said, get up!"

Ghost was furious. He had hoped his plan would flow smoothly, but because of Cory's smart mouth, things had spun out of control. Ghost looked down at Young-Cory's frail body sprawled out on the steps and a greater strand of anger engulfed him. He raised his foot and stomped forcefully on Young-Cory's face. The dull wooden edge cut through his cheek and broke his molar tooth. A high-pitched squeal leapt from Cory and a stream of blood oozed through the deep gash in his face.

Dex came rushing through the hallway door and climbed the stiff staircase. Young-Cory was in noticeable pain, but Ja felt no sympathy. He knew that police would flood the scene real soon, and he did not intend to get knocked. Time was of the essence.

In one motion, Ja clutched a handful of Cory's limp collar and tossed him up the steps. "Argh!" Young-Cory cried out.

"Shut the fuck up, faggot, what door he's in?" Dex questioned aggressively. When Cory didn't answer, Dex cocked his hand back and pistol-whipped him repeatedly. The pain was too excruciating, and finally he gave in. Young-Cory pointed his finger, and that was all Ghost, Ja, and Dex needed.

Ja propped up Young-Cory and clutched his belt and clothing from behind. His head dangled as he became weaker. He had no idea he was being used as a shield.

Ghost and Dex eyed each other and took their position on each side of the apartment's door. Ghost's index finger went up, and his middle and ring finger followed. On the third count, Ja cocked his leg up and thrust forward with all of his might.

The fragile door ripped off of its hinges and Fat-Roc rose from behind the couch in darkness. He pumped his shotgun without hesitation or remorse for whoever received the twelve gauge slugs. Long streams of flame extended from the barrel and lit the room.

All six slugs devoured Young-Cory's body. Chunks of meat and muscle fell from his limbs and his young life had ended before it had really begun.

The clicking from the empty gauge gave Dex the few seconds that he needed.

Ghost heard the sound too, and used his athletic ability to hurdle over Young-Cory's lifeless body. Fat-Roc reached for his 9mm, but wasn't successful. Ghost's lanky frame connected and knocked Roc off balance. He stumbled backwards and the sharp hook that Ja caught him with sent him down hard to the thin carpet.

The bright ceiling light flickered on, and Fat-Roc looked at the young thugs that weren't masked. He knew that this was the end for him. He felt foolish for thinking the wolves wouldn't ever come for him. His gun was known to go off, and he relied on his reputation to keep the wolves at bay. It dawned on Roc that not even he was untouchable. Everyone has their day, and Fat-Roc was sure that this was his.

Death reflected in Ghost's eyes and Roc's heartbeat sped up as he lay helplessly. Ghost grabbed the brown paper bag that Ja held in his hand. He took a quick glance at the lined stacks of money on the table and dismissed the thought of taking them. The money was very tempting, but Ghost knew that it would benefit him more if he stuck to the plan. His focus switched back to Roc, and the loud sirens echoing in the distance told him to hurry.

"Listen Bee," Ghost spoke with sternness while looking directly in Roc's eyes. "I'ma let'chu decide ya own fate. These dumb lil niggas caused this unnecessary blood bath." Ghost pointed to Young-Cory's corpse to emphasize his point. The small couch was turned over and the lamps that sat on the end tables were broken into pieces. "We came to discuss a proposition, and because I'm such a real dude, the deal is still on the table. You accept what I'm bringin' to the table, and I'll forget the fact that you tried to body us. If you don't accept, well..." Ghost shrugged. "You know how it go." A cynical smile crept across his face then faded.

"So you sayin' after all this, you gon' let me live?" Fat-Roc questioned in disbelief.

"That depends on you." Dex answered seriously then cocked the hammer on his gun.

"I see." Roc mumbled, understanding that he really had no choice, not if he wanted to live.

"So, how many bricks you move a week? And how much ya connect give it to you for?"

Fat-Roc lay silent with a contemplative expression on his face. He thought about the question and calculated the prices in his head. "I move 'bout two birds a week, and I get'em for 30 a piece." As he answered, he tried to sit up, but Ja put his blood stained boot on his chest, forcing him back down.

Ghost looked down and smiled. "This what I'ma do for you." Ghost dug into the brown paper bag and pulled out two compressed kilos. "These are yours. Bangin' coke for a much cheaper price, you can't lose. All I want is 22 each. And from now on, whatever you cop, I'll front you the same."

Ghost extended his hand and helped Fat-Roc to his feet.

He stood in the company of Ghost, Ja, and Dex, feeling humiliated. But even with the degraded feeling lingering in his heart, he couldn't overlook the benefits in Ghost's proposition. Scar was charging an eight-thousand-dollar difference for coke that wasn't grade A.

Fat-Roc looked into Ghost's eyes and respected what he found. Ghost was hungry, and determined to eat by any means. Ghost made a gesture toward the stacks of money and Roc separated $44,000 and handed it to him.

Dex secured the cash and backpedaled slowly toward the door. Ghost stepped over Young-Cory's mangled corpse and shook his head. He then stopped and looked back at his new client.

"Don't be stupid, Roc. I know you get busy, but these lil niggas ain't worth a war. They're expendable. Just be easy an' let's get this money. He was a stupid lil nigga anyway."

Ghost didn't expect a response and he didn't receive one. Fat-Roc smiled because Ghost's departing statement was so true. As he stood alone, he looked around. His focus locked on the stacks of money, then shifted to poor Young-Cory's body. Roc heard the sirens getting louder by the second. He quickly swiped the money off of the table into a large duffle bag, grabbed his coke and hammer, and left.

Chapter 24

An urban radio station muffled with static came through the small Koss speakers that sat on a window ledge inside the cozy office. Gray file cabinets cluttered a corner space, and a Victoria Secret aroma seeped through the clothing of the cute receptionist who sat behind the Maplewood desk. She looked so innocent organizing the documents needed for a patient's discharge.

"Is she ready yet, Darlene?" Scar asked while keeping his stride toward the sliding window.

"I assume so," Darlene answered. "I haven't had time to check on her." She smiled as she looked up from the paperwork. Darlene stood from her cushioned rolling chair and glanced up the hallway from the doorway.

Scar looked on lustfully, his expression revealing the effects of Darlene's beauty. The thick cotton blazer did nothing to hide her round bottom. She was blessed.

"Here she comes now." Darlene announced, shaking Scar from his perverted thoughts.

He looked up and smiled at the site of Tay. She was fresh to death like always. A few pounds lost since she had been admitted into the hospital, but that wasn't about nothing. In just a few short weeks, she'll be back, full and curvy. Her supply of food during her stay was plenty. Darlene, Tay's new acquaintance, saw to it. But the additional stress had no medications; she would have to deal with that sickness on her own.

Tay had become cool with Darlene through casual conversation. Sitting in a room all alone, left her with not much to do, no one to entertain, and a head full of thoughts that seem to bring stress. As a way to escape, Darlene, had become Tay's recreation. Over time, Darlene's genuine concern was acknowledged and Tay started to feel her as a person.

"I thought you got lost for a minute," Darlene stated with a slight chuckle. "Are you ready?"

"As ready as I can possibly be," Tay answered while flashing a Colgate smile for the first time.

"Alright, sign right here." Darlene took off her gold framed specs and pointed to the dotted line, indicating where she needed Tay to sign.

Tay signed on the dotted line, grabbed her bag, and walked toward the double doors.

"Tayasia!" Darlene called out before Tay was out of ear reach. "Be good, and keep in touch."

Tay smiled, nodded, and then walked through the double doors.

Scar navigated the triple black Range Rover through the narrow streets like a ghost in the night. The smoke gray interior was equivalent to first class comfort; soft and plush. The dark cloud of haze moved in a slow wave from side to side. Music banged through the factory speakers, setting a mood for dancing, partying, and the like. Despite all the nonsense that was currently a part of Scar's life, having his partner back by his side made him feel whole again. Business was slower than usual, and the loss that he took had caused a huge setback. But Tay's presence gave him the warmth and confidence that everything would be all right in due time.

"Scar, I'm 'bout to take this blindfold off if you don't tell me where we goin'." Tay threatened.

Scar glanced over at his friend and smiled. "Girl, you ain't been out the hospital for an hour, and you already fussin'." He giggled. "Jus' hold on, we almost there."

Tay exhaled, sucked her teeth, and crossed her arms. "We here, sore sport."

Scar parked the Range and held Tay's hand as they ascended the short flight of stairs.

"I don't like this shit, you lucky I trust you." Tay complained.

"Yeah, yeah, yeah. That's whatchu say now."

Scar responded with a smile, knowing Tay would love his surprise.

They walked down a lengthy hallway. Wooden doors with brass numbers attached to them ran along both sides. The floor was covered with a thin layer of brown and tan carpet. Some of its threads were unraveled from years of abuse, but overall maintained good condition. Elegant lamps extended from the cream colored walls, and vending machines carrying a variety of accessories were placed across from the two elevators near the middle of the hallway.

Scar, retrieved a plastic card from his pocket and swiped it through the slot above the doorknob. He patiently waited for the light on the door to turn green. When it turned, the lock on the door clicked and Scar entered. The lights inside the suite were dim. Full body sized mirrors decorated the surrounding walls, and moans derived from sexual pleasure flowed through the elevated flat screen. The male porn star in the hard core DVD was putting on a great performance. Not able to bear any more suspense, Tay snatched the blind fold from her eyes and a pleased smile appeared on her pretty face.

"Welcome home," Scar said in a low tone, then hugged her. "Call me later, ah-ight? And you make sure you treat Tay right." Scar demanded while pointing to the sexy young lady in front of him.

"That goes without sayin'," The beautiful girl admitted then gave a girlish chuckle.

The door shut behind Scar, and Tay was left with a loss for words. The view of the sexy young lady sent lustful thoughts through her mind and her pecan colored nipples stiffened.

Pink, white, and red rose petals were spread across the thick, cotton comforter. The curvaceous girl lay nude with a layer of scented oil spread evenly over her smooth midnight complexion. Her skin beamed like a radiant moon. She moved seductively, inviting Tay into her world of bliss. Every time she rotated her hips, Tay's vagina throbbed and moistened.

"Damn, Chocolate. I ain't know it was like that," Tay admitted, not remembering the stripper's body being so well developed during their first encounter at the strip club.

Chocolate smiled and continued to put on a show. Scar had let her in on Tay's secret of being a woman by gender. Chocolate was surprised, because Tay never portrayed any feminine characteristics. But after thinking about how well Tay treated her when they initially met, her gender didn't matter. Chocolate had always wondered what it was like to be pleased by a woman, and there was not another person that she would rather experience such intimacy with.

Chocolate rolled onto her stomach, kept her face buried in the pillow, and propped her ass in the air. Rose petals stuck to her skin, and soft moans filled the air as she eased the 10-inch dildo in and out of her heated vagina.

Tay dropped the last of her clothing to the floor. Her womanly adornments were no longer mysterious to Chocolate. Tay was just as developed as she was. Her breasts were a mouth full, perky, with erect nipples. Her butt was plump, perfectly round. Her feet, small and not pedicured, but not ugly, and her stomach was flat with light burn marks covered by bandages trailing down her abdomen.

She kneeled after absorbing Chocolate's performance and became level with her round backside. Tay stuck her thumb deep inside her mouth, lubricating it with saliva. She then placed wet, soft kisses on her ass cheeks and eased her thumb inside Chocolate's tight rectum.

"Uww..." An uneasy sound escaped from Chocolate's mouth, but was instantly replaced with a unique, pleasing sensation once Tay started licking her wet pussy from behind.

"Oh, Tay." Chocolate moaned, encouraging Tay to do what she did best. A soft orgasm clutched her insides not too long after, leaving a tingling aftershock.

Tay rose from her knees and climbed onto the bed as Chocolate rolled on her back. She gazed up into Tay's eyes, and was engrossed in their color. In a slow motion, the pair moved closer until their lips met and they kissed passionately for what seemed like forever. Chocolate then descended slowly, while sliding her warm tongue down Tay's stomach and began to please her orally in a manner that she would have liked.

Tay's back arched, and a vigorous quiver grabbed hold of her body as an electrical shock rattled her nerves. Thick cream oozed from the depths of her love tunnel, and a soft tickle crept through Chocolate's loins at the same time. The excitement of bringing Tay to her climax brought her to a relieving orgasm of her own. The moment was special, and one to cherish. The sensation caused exhaustion, and the pair lay heaving, desperately trying to catch their breath.

Minutes had elapsed and Tay regained her composure while they lay face to face, propped on their sides, gazing into each other's eyes. Chocolate's mind drifted as she wondered what would come of her new relationship, but Tay harbored other thoughts. In a smooth motion, Tay slid into the strap on dildo and straddled Chocolate's thickness.

The head of the rubber penis caused Chocolate to wince. But as Tay stroked in and out of her heated womb, she adjusted and worked what her momma gave her. Her hips rotated with skill, meeting Tay's hard thrusts. The more she threw her pussy, the tighter Tay's grip became on her calves, and the deeper her strokes were. Chocolate's pussy swallowed all 10 inches with ease. Her face twisted and wrinkled, expressing the thin line between pain and pleasure. Her wet pussy farted repeatedly, singing a song of its own.

The sensation was too great. Chocolate's interior became sensitive to the long, deep strokes that Tay gave, and the explosive orgasm that danced on her spine, she could no longer hold back. Ahhh... Tay, shit baby... Ahhh, I'm cumin'. Right there, Tay... beat this pussy... Ah, Ah, Ahhh."

The seductive moans came to an abrupt stop while Chocolate's body shook violently. Her juices slid down the 10-inch rod and a circle of cum stained the cotton sheets where she lay. Chocolate's movement was minimal. Her small hands, she placed over her face. But it didn't hide anything. Tay could still see the red flush in her cheeks; she was embarrassed. Never in her life did she imagine sex with a woman being so good. Her large breasts rose and fell from exhaustion, but she still couldn't muster up the courage to look her lover in her eyes. She needed time to get her emotions together.

Propped up, resting her head on the palm of her hand, Tay looked over at Chocolate and smiled. She leaned over, kissed Chocolate's hand, and cuddled next to her new trophy until a peaceful slumber overtook her.

Chapter 25

"Tonya, thanks girl. I really appreciate you coming over here." Bri expressed while hanging up the new picture that she had bought from the art gallery. Tonya wiped the perspiration from her brow and smiled.

"Nah, seriously girl. God knows I couldn't have changed this living room around by myself." A serene cackle penetrated the air. "It almost seems impossible to get my man to do anything around here," Bri continued with her hands on her hips. "You would think since I am pregnant, things would change for the better. Shh, only if you knew how true I wish that was." She rolled her eyes.

"Grab that lamp and bring it over here. It'll look better in the corner over there, wit'cho mean ass." Tonya said, and then giggled. "I personally think it's just a phase that he's going through. We both know Quron is a good man, he has always held you down. That nigga love the ground you walk on and you know it. He's just going through it right now. You know, with his mother being murdered and all... It isn't easy for him. Just be patient, Bri, just be patient." Tonya rubbed Bri's back reassuringly. "You know you're my girl, and I wouldn't be stickin' up for that nigga if I didn't think he was for you."

Bri smiled, but within, she felt terrible. The truth deepened her guilt, and what her friend had shared about Quron was all so true. Quron was a thorough dude with a heart of gold. This was a fact that Bri couldn't deny. It just hurt because of the dangerous game that she was playing with two friends.

While Tonya spoke, it dawned on Bri that the chance that she was so willing to take just weeks ago, was no longer an option. Her truth made her soul feel dirty, slutty, and disloyal for being so weak.

Tonya giggled and rambled on, but Bri was mourning in a world of her own. Her gaze of sorrow slowly descended and settled on her slightly round belly. The child that she had always wanted was slowly developing. Tears started to fall from her eyes while her mind produced reasons why she should not do what she had decided was best. And although her reasons were true, and worth considering, the facts still remained. Bri was uncertain who her child's father was. She had been very irresponsible during her sexual encounters with Young-One, and that left her with no choice in the matter.

"Excuse me, Tonya. Let me get by." Bri stepped around her friend and the loveseat.

"You alright?" Tonya questioned with true concern, upon seeing Bri's glossy eyes.

"Yeah, I'm okay!" Bri lied before closing the room door behind her.

Words could not explain how bad she felt. As she sat down on the soft mattress, she eyed the telephone and contemplated her decision. She placed her hand on her stomach, rubbed in a circular motion, and mumbled, "Sorry," before picking up the phone and dialing the number that she'd found online. The phone rang numerous times with no answer, and Bri took it as a sign.

Just when she reached over to disconnect the call, someone answered. Bri exhaled a hurtful breath and all of her hope faded.

"Good afternoon, I would like to make an appointment... my name is..."

"Yo, Nuri. You heard from Ron since he went on that vacation?" Young-One asked.

"Yeah, we spoke for a second."

"He... he ah-ight?" Steel inquired from the back seat.

"Yeah, he good. Jus' try'na bounce back. Our mother's death really fucked him up."

"That fucked all of us up, word."

Young-One's words were the truth. Ms. Johnson's death touched them all in a different way. The jeep became silent as each of their minds reminisced on their special moments with Ms. Johnson.

The tinted windows were ajar. Smoke from the blunt of weed that Steel puffed on, thickened and created a cloudy veil. The three comrades had been parked in the same spot for the past three hours. The flow of customers had gradually picked back up. The police seem to have fallen back over the past couple of weeks, and the whole hood was thankful for that. Lander Street was in full rotation. The dope boys were doing what they do, so everything was good. The keys of coke that Young-One, Nuri, and Steel bought with their cut from the robbery were moving fast. Pedro had blessed them with that grade A raw. They all maintained and upheld their obligation to their team, but it felt good to have their own product. Everything was profit.

As they sat back and kicked it, observing the functions on the block, a smoke gray XJ Jag with chrome 22-inch rims and a light tint rolled to a halt not too far from them. Young-One leaned forward and squinted. The Jag silenced them all, grabbing their attention.

"Who dat?" Nuri questioned.

Steel focused in on the luxurious whip and wondered the same thing.

"I don't know." Young-One answered while shaking his head.

Nuri focused on the license plate and found the answer to all of their questions. "That's that bitch nigga, Scar."

"What!" Not giving thought to the situation, Steel, gripped the handle to his fully loaded Glock that was on his lap, grabbed his coat, and tossed it over his arm to conceal his pistol.

"Hold up." Nuri said as he reached back and tapped Steel's knee, preventing him from stepping out of the jeep.

A maroon Durango with dark tinted windows rolled up right behind Scar, confirming Nuri's gut feeling.

"Son ain't stupid," Nuri stated. "He knows this is enemy territory, so he ain't gon' come through on some dolo shit like shit sweet." A brief silence left Nuri words lingering. "I betchu them his goons in that Durango."

Steel sat back in his seat and shut the jeep's door. "I... I... I... don't give a... a fuck who he wit' Nur... Nur... Nuri." Steel voiced angrily. "I'm tired of this nig... nigga. He's the reason why I got thi... thi... this in... indictment now. I wish I woulda murdered his bitch... his bitch ass."

Nuri looked at his comrade's screwed up face through the rear view mirror and nodded his head. Steel was obviously venting, and he respected that.

"It might not be so bad, after all." Young-One smiled as he spoke and gestured with his head toward Scar's ride. When the passenger door opened, a female stepped out. Her back was facing them, but Young-One knew exactly who she was from her signature stance. He had acknowledged her beauty for years, and he had to admit that she looked even better since he had last seen her. Her three quarter length mink stopped at the top of her heart shaped bottom. The knee high leather boots that she wore, overlapped her brown stretch pants, and the mink ear muffs that donned her head went well with the brown leather gloves that covered her hands.

"Who... whooo dat? Fee-Fee?" Steel questioned in disbelief as Fee-Fee's face became visible. His words still held traces of anger.

"Yeah, that's shorty." Young-One confirmed while watching the pretty Jag disappear around the corner. Its loud roar echoed throughout Campbell St.

"This bitch dun lost her mind," Nuri flat out stated.

"Nah, she good," Young-One said calmly while looking at Nuri. "She just made things a lot easier for us." A devilish grin etched his lips. "What, y'all forgot? She been on my dick for years. It's time to give her what she want." He grabbed his leather coat, wrapped his scarf around his neck, and gave his man a pound. "Gotta play the game." Young-One smiled.

Nuri and Steel nodded their heads, agreeing with Young-One's vision.

Young-One crossed the street and ascended the porch stairs. After a few hard knocks, the door flew open. Fee-Fee's hard expression softened upon seeing Young-One's face. Her eyes lowered to the ground as her eyelashes fluttered and her cheeks stiffened from the blood that filled them. She blushed like a teenage girl who had just been given her first kiss.

Young-One and Fee-Fee hugging was the last thing Nuri and Steel saw from across the street. Nuri shook his head and smiled. Steel hopped in the front seat and cranked the volume. Jay-Z knocked hard from the back speakers, *"You can't turn a bad girl good, but once a good girls gone, she's gone forever!"*

Nuri and Steel looked at each other and burst out laughing as they pulled away from the curb. Simultaneously, they sang, "I mourn foreva, plus I gotta live wit' the fact I did ju wrong foreva!!"

Chapter 26

The soft, powder blue sky, decorated with fluffy white clouds extended over the Atlantic Ocean. Every so often, the bright, beaming sun would hide, causing a veil of shade to overlap the huge body of water. It was a very beautiful day. Whenever the sun's rays penetrated the tides, layers of sparkling crystals appeared.

Right there in the middle of it all, Quron stood on the deck of Pedro's yacht, bent over the stainless steel railing, taking in the beautiful sights. His cargo short-set, along with the tranquil setting gave him peace. The warm ocean breeze caused his shirt to lift and dance in the wind. Sprinkles of salt water mixed in the air and entered his nostrils as he exhaled deeply.

The past couple of days had been very peaceful. There weren't many distractions out on the ocean. Quron looked as far as his vision would allow. There was not a piece of land in sight. With a pair of binoculars, one could see a part of Miami and a portion of Cuba. But those bodies of land were many miles away.

Pedro's yacht was exclusive. It held ten separate bedrooms below the main deck. A spa, state of the art kitchen, exercise room, theater, nice sized library, and a club that converted into a casino were all included.

A genuine smile crept across Quron's face when Bri's pregnant body popped into his mind. He was glad that he had taken a vacation to clear his head and get his priorities in order. He couldn't imagine being a deadbeat father; the mere thought knotted his stomach. His mind traveled back to when he was a child. He remembered vividly the days when all he wanted to do was please his pops. The feeling was a great inspiration and was the least he could do for his own. He definitely didn't want his seed to turn out like him. Black, with a felony, no work history, kilos of coke, dirty money, and drama that could end in death. But if he didn't get his shit together, the same cycle was a great possibility for his seed. That wasn't an option.

Quron blinked away his negative thoughts and rose from the railing. He stretched his limbs, yawned, and then walked to his room. The comfortable Gucci flip-flops that he was wearing sank into the soft carpet of the spacious suite that he occupied.

A king sized bed with satin sheets sat in the middle of the floor. The 55-inch TV in front of the bed was on an old episode of MTV cribs, and the full-length mirrors behind the brass headboard reflected Bird Man's stunning crib. Off in the corner, a walk-in closet hid behind wooden panels that resembled the oak wood walls throughout the rest of the room.

Quron stepped in front of the bathroom mirror and smiled while spreading toothpaste across the soft bristles of the toothbrush. His reflection told him that he was back. His beard was full, a tad darker than a 5 o'clock shadow, and round like the crescent moon. His line was straighter than a ruler, and his waves were like the ocean. He was feeling himself.

The mint flavored Listerine that swished around in his mouth stung like hell. It was cool though, a brother couldn't be walking around with stank breath. Quron cupped the warm water that overflowed his hands and rinsed his face. While in the mix, a soft knock at the door interrupted his serene state.

"Come in," He said as he clutched the miniature towel on the rack above him and rose. Through the mirror, he noticed India's presence. Surprised, his movement slowed. *This chick done lost her mind.* Streams of water trickled down his forehead, eyelids, nose, and slid off the curve of his chin. His handsome features had been replaced by distorted expressions. He turned around, dabbed his face gently and shook his head.

India closed the door and stood bare foot near the entrance. In her hand, she held a silver platter that carried an aroma that would have made anyone curious. Her long silky hair was pulled up in a claw like clamp, not tight, just holding. Loose strands of hair fell from its hold, and no make-up covered her skin. Her eyebrows were arched, lashes long, curled at the end, and Quron couldn't help but notice India's curves that barely hid under the fluffy white robe that wrapped her body with little effort.

She noticed his demeanor change upon entering his room, but she didn't care. She removed the lid from the platter and she could literally see the combination of the aromas tickling Quron's nose. His stomach growled embarrassingly and India smiled. *Mom always told me the quickest way to a man's heart is through his nuts and his stomach.*

Quron looked at the scrambled eggs, turkey bacon, wheat toast, and freshly squeezed grapefruit juice as India sat the platter down. He licked his lips as India walked toward him. He didn't know if it was the food or her beauty that caused his tongue to trace his lips.

"What's the problem? And why are you treating me like this?" She asked calmly, but held Quron trapped in her unwavering stare. "This is what I have to do to see you? Cancel my plans and come on this trip, just to see you? Is this what it's come to Quron, huh?"

"Well good morning to you too, India." Quron smiled, attempting to hide the uneasy feeling that settled in his veins.

"I'm serious." India continued her beef while stepping closer and unraveling the tie that secured her robe. Her soft breasts eased from under the cloth that fell slightly off her shoulder.

Quron was speechless. India's front view was more than he'd imagined. A glob of saliva forced its way down his throat as he began to back pedal. "India, you buggin'."

"No, I'm not buggin'. This is what turns you on, right? You like hood bitches, right? Ratchet ass hood bitches, right? 'Cause your shorty damn sure ain't classier than me, in fact, it's somethin' about her that ain't right. My intuition tells me so." She continued to close in. "Yeah, I know you lookin' at me all crazy, 'cause you haven't ever seen me act like this, but don't get it twisted, it's a lot that you don't know. This is how you make me act, Quron. I've been try'na contact you for months. You either send me to your voicemail, or you give me a two-sentence conversation. What type of bullshit is that? Why Quron?" India's voice lowered to a submissive whisper as she suddenly transformed back into her innocence. "What have I done to you?" Her words trailed off and she held Quron's gaze when she eased the robe from her shoulder. The heavy cotton collapsed to the floor.

Quron's penis instantly stiffened. India's stride never slowed and the room had closed in on him. The wall held him hostage as India walked right up on him. He was trying like hell to honor Pedro's wishes, but India was making it impossible.

"Look me in my eyes and tell me you don't want this." India teased while rubbing her naked body.

Quron's throbbing dick nudged her in her stomach and she suppressed her smile.

"What, I'm too much of a good girl for you?"

He looked down into her gorgeous eyes and quickly turned away, afraid that he would become hypnotized. Her shaved lips tickled his thigh, and the heat from her juicy pussy almost caused him to erupt.

"Listen Ma, it's not you—"Quron tried to explain, but the soft, moist kisses that India planted on his chest confiscated his thoughts.

India brushed her lips teasingly across his. Their eyes met and the kiss that they shared was full of passion. Quron squatted low, and scooped up India's proportioned frame by her ass cheeks. She wrapped her smooth legs around his waist and covered his face with lustful kisses as he carried her to the bed. His hands gripped her ass, forcefully spreading her cheeks wide. Quron's erect dick protruded through his boxer slit and rubbed across her throbbing clit like a violin string.

"Oh my." India moaned while nibbling gently on Quron's ear lobe.

Quron felt himself ready to explode already, and he hadn't even felt her silky interior yet. He laid India on her back. She wouldn't unlock her legs from around his waist. The moans that caressed his ear made him want it more. He gripped his dick and guided it in the right direction. No condom covered him; his lust had taken over. She winced in pain when his head parted her lips. Her legs shook a little and closed more and more as he applied forward pressure.

"It hurts." India cried out, clenching her bottom lip with her teeth.

Quron eased up a bit, but the feeling was too intoxicating to stop. India started to move, and her pussy slowly swallowed more and more of his big dick. Her muscles loved his stroke, they gripped him like a glove, something that he'd never felt before. He stroked her slow and lovingly. India's eyes closed, her mouth slightly parted, and her breath was warm, carrying a scent sweeter than candy.

Quron ingested her beautiful features as he pumped in and out of her. His rhythmical movement got slower, then suddenly stopped. He calmly removed himself from her womb and crawled from between her legs.

"I can't do this," he murmured. Flashes of Bri's pregnant body made him feel guilty and disloyal. Disloyal not only to Bri, but to Pedro, and to his unborn child as well.

India's innocent stare caused his gaze to drop to the bed.

"Why'd you stop?" She questioned, oblivious to his reasoning, and extremely upset that the heavenly sensation had stopped.

Quron didn't know what to say. It felt strange to him, because he was strong-minded, usually outspoken. But now, when faced with something so simple, he felt clueless and confused to the point where he couldn't honestly give India an answer.

Sitting in silence with a sheet pulled over her breasts, India's eyes started tearing. Quron heard her sniffles and felt like shit. He knew he should've used his physical advantage to avoid India's advances. With a firm, caring grip, he held her shoulders and forced himself to look into her pain filled eyes.

"Listen," he spoke softly in a low tone. "You aren't the issue, India. It's me sweetie, I'm the problem. I'm no good for you." He shook his head.

"But I don't want anyone else, can't you fuckin' see that?" India spat, not trying to hear Quron's logic.

"I understand you're angry, and I am sorry for causing it," Quron admitted honestly. But, love—"

"How dare you call me that!" India shouted and backed away like Quron was a monster. "How dare you, you don't love me!"

"But I do have love for—"

"No you don't, 'cause if you did, you wouldn't be doing this to me. You wouldn't, Quron, you just wouldn't." India's eyes filled again with tears of pain.

He grabbed her foot and shook it gently. "Would you just listen?" He exhaled tiredly. "I really do have somethin' special in my heart for you. You make me feel so good inside. When we're around each other, I'm at ease. I can relax and be the guy I wish I can be every day. I don't have to be a gangsta, constantly schemin' or plottin'. Nah ma, I can just fall back and enjoy ya company. I really appreciate what most people would call the little things. It's just unfortunate for us—"

Quron suddenly became silent and gathered his thoughts. "The easiest way for me to put it is... I made choices when I was younger that I'm still bonded to. My shorty did almost ten long years with me. A sacrifice like that, I can't overlook. This is why you must move on and live ya life."

India was at a loss for words. She felt like she had played herself by doing chicken head shit like giving up her precious pussy, thinking it would earn her a more meaningful position in Quron's life. For her plan not to work made her feel lower than low. Tears started falling nonstop.

"I know, India," Quron said, referring to her tears. "But what do you want me to do? You rather me lie?"

"Stop ask... asking me silly questions," she said between sobs. "I've made it obvious what I want."

"I'm really sorry, India, but I can't grant chu that. Loyalty is everything to me, and if nothing else, whether to you or whoever I bond with, I'm loyal to the end."

Hurt beyond words, India wrapped herself in the satin sheets as if Quron hadn't already seen her goods. As much as it hurt, Quron knew that it was something he had to do. Every tear that dropped from India's eyes cut deeper and deeper in his conscience. *Damn, look at this mess I dun got myself into. Baby girl all fucked up 'cause of me.*

Quron felt things couldn't get any worse until Pedro's voice pierced through the door. And what made it so bad was that he was walking down the hall, shouting India's name. "Fuck." *What a mornin'.*

India looked at Quron one last time, giving him a final glance at what he had turned down. She then stood at the door, hastened to fastened her robe, and grabbed the knob.

"Hold up," Quron told her as he forced the door closed with the palm of his hand. "You can't go out there like that, fuck you try'na get me murdered?" Quron spat angrily and felt even more heated when India gave him a 'you deserve it' look.

But although he deserved it, she didn't really want him dead, so she wiped her face and tightened the straps to her robe.

India opened the door, just as Quron finished sliding on his shorts. She stepped out into the hall and walked right into her brother, Pedro.

"Bueno dias hermana, where were you?" Pedro questioned with a smile.

India pointed toward Quron's room and gave a girlish smile. A toddler could have seen through her mask of happiness, and her brother noted it immediately.

"You all right, sweetie? You look bothered."

"No, I'm fine. Woke up this morning and decided to cook breakfast for our guest." She smirked.

"Okay, you had me worried, but I am happy everything is good." Pedro stated and continued on his way.

Quron stood from the platter of delicious food as they passed. "Mi amigo, how are you?"

Pedro looked back and responded, "I'm fine, my friend, I'm fine."

Quron closed his room door and sat back down. He chewed on some turkey bacon and shook his head. *He gotta know what time it is, I swear he knows.*

Chapter 27

A week had passed since Quron returned from his vacation. It had turned out to be the blessing that he prayed for. On the cruise, he was able to experience different cultures on the various islands that they stopped at. It provided an inner peace, and compelled him to go over his steps toward exiting the game. He'd met other Muslims who were what he would consider poor, but they didn't have the drama surrounding them. They were very humble and serene people.

Through visual testimonies like this, he was afforded different perspectives. He repented for many of his sins, and enjoyed the smaller things that would have been overlooked in the past.

Pedro was a thorough dude, to say the least. Quron really appreciated the extended family treatment that he'd always shown him. But India, India was definitely the barrier between the two. The thought of her gave Quron an uncomfortable feeling. Hurting her feelings was not on his list of things to do. But at the end of the day, his loyalty was to Pedro. Loyalty was his backbone and he would never compromise that at any cost.

When he returned to town, his position in the crew was easily re-established. To his surprise, he had to admit, things were running smoothly. He was pleased to see everyone playing their positions. They were getting major paper, keeping a low profile, and most importantly, being strategic when it came time to put in work.

Quron learned of the territorial hostile takeover that had taken place in his absence at the meeting he held upon his return. The news wasn't surprising. To be honest, Quron knew he and his brother, Nuri, were like night and day when it came to leadership.

Nuri was the type to send one verbal warning or proposition, depending on how one looked at it. If they failed to comply, it's a wrap; he would let his gun convince them that he's far from a game. With Young-One and Steel's psychotic asses riding with him, the end result was always tragic. They were like a three-headed monster that put the fear of God in a lot of people's hearts. Apparently, Nuri's method was working. Their profits had increased over 100%. They took over half the city.

Ghost and his team were bubbling hard too. The streets tried to plant some negative seeds but it didn't work. Rumor had it, Ghost and his team would soon collide with Quron and the crew over territory. But what they didn't know was Ghost and his soldiers were fam, and they were the only team with a green light to hustle on their turf, so it was all love.

Nuri, Steel, Young-One and Quron were all in awe when Ghost, Ja, and Dex told them in detail what had transpired with Fat-Roc. Until this point, no one knew what went down. Ghost felt it was best to leave it up to the streets to figure out what went down, if anything at all. It wasn't his plan to deteriorate Roc's reputation. Ghost knew that wouldn't have been a wise business move; Quron had taught him better than that.

Truth be told, Fat-Roc was a 'G' in his own right, and Ghost knew the only reason he accepted his offer was because he didn't have a choice. Come to think about it, the deal wasn't bad at all. The profit margin was highly in Fat-Roc's favor, so why provoke a war when the chips were still falling for you? Fat-Roc was far from a dummy. It didn't take a genius to know an all-out war just wasn't worth it.

The move Ghost made against Roc definitely raised his status in the eyes of his older comrades. Scar, on the flip side, was a major problem. He was stronger than ever. When Tay recovered, they bounced back hard, showing no mercy to anyone. They ran what was left of the city, and they did it with an iron fist. They sold large quantities of coke, recruited some shooters, and murdered whoever didn't like it. The heat was definitely on.

Chapter 28

The important people in both Quron and Bri's lives were all seated in different sections of Bri's apartment. The classic R&B in full rotation set a laid-back vibe. Everyone in attendance was aware that tonight was a special occasion. Tonya brought along her date, a young college grad that was apparently rocking her world. The way she snickered and blushed whenever he whispered in her ear was sickening. But Bri was genuinely happy to see that her girl had finally gotten her groove back, it had been a while.

Nuri, Steel, Ghost, Ja, and Dex had other motives. They all knew Bri had mad friends. Five, including Tonya, were present. It didn't make sense to bring sand to the beach. And judging by the way that the young women were acting and competing for the hustlers' attention, they were right.

Young-One took the cake, though. He had the nerve to bring a pretty young thing to the gathering. She was bad too, about 5'5", 130 pounds, with a Halle Berry cut. Shorty wore a fitted dress with rhinestones running across the dip in her cleavage area, and down the slit on her back that stopped suddenly at the crack of her curvy bottom.

Bri was on fire, she couldn't even front. The stunt was a blatant disrespect, in her eyes, but it was cool. Bri took the smack in the face with a smile. The last laugh would be hers. The king of the throne had yet to arrive. In fact, Quron didn't have a clue about the get together, which made it even better. Everyone had pitched in and helped. It was Amil's job to occupy his entire day, and what a great job she did.

After patiently waiting for hours, Bri finally spotted a pair of headlights flicker the high beams on then off. It was the signal she had been waiting for. She hopped out of her seat, stepped quickly to the stereo, lowered the music to a whisper, clicked the light switch off, and told everyone to shush.

Quron walked up the few steps in good spirits. He was clad in official designer threads with a black skully pulled nice and tight on his head. The New Year was near and he was just happy to be back. A pair of Louis Vuitton medicated glasses gave him a gentleman's look, and the pair of fresh nubuck Tims that Amil had copped, he rocked with swag.

The lock to the front door clicked, and then opened. Simultaneously, Bri flicked on the lights and everyone yelled in unison, "Surprise!"

Quron jumped back, causing Amil, who was behind him to stumble. He pulled his.44 Bulldog from his waist, aiming to kill. His heart was thumping hard against his chest due to the sudden scare. He stood puzzled for a minute, with his index finger pressed firmly against the trigger. When what actually was going on registered, he shook his head, exhaled a breath of relief and lowered his cannon. He was literally seconds away from blowing Bri's head off.

Nuri walked up to him and hugged his brother tight. "Good to have you back." Nuri whispered while smiling.

"Good to be back." Quron admitted.

Nuri loosened his hold, and Quron held up his hand in an apologetic manner. "Sorry, everyone." They all burst into laughter, and in no time, the smooth music was back on.

R-Kelly's "Step in the Name of Love" bounced through the stereo and the living room quickly converted into a dance floor. Bottles of champagne were being popped, and blunts of exotic weed were lit. They had the best sour diesel grown, and the best purple haze set a sweet aroma. Quron was in his groove, high off of life, and drunk off bottled water.

Bri and he wined and dined like no one else mattered. In their world, only they existed. They tangled rather intimately, failing to control their wandering hands while kissing passionately.

Bri laughed, smiled, and carried on without care while Young-One looked on with jealousy and envy. Partially, he was the reason why she was showing out. She had to admit, it felt good though, and when it was all said and done, Quron was her king.

After a while, everyone was nice and tipsy. The aroma from the food seemed to have a magnetic pull toward the table. Everyone sat, just like a family and the women shared the duty of serving.

Bri and Amil had really outdone themselves with this one. They had spent hours in the kitchen the day before. Bri used the opportunity to get better acquainted with Amil. Certain points in their conversation drew deep emotions. It was like deja' vu, only this time, it wasn't Ms. Johnson that she was confiding in. Instead, it was her beautiful daughter, who resembled her so much. The ending result was marvelous, though. God knows the two young women put nothing but love into the food.

A small soul food feast was prepared. Baked mac and cheese, fried chicken and beef ribs were included. But most of the meal consisted of seafood. Snow crab legs, shrimp, lobster, broiled fish and a special sauce that went great with the linguini.

For the first fifteen minutes, very little conversation flowed at the table. Forks were too busy twirling and everyone's mouths were too filled to utter much of anything. It wasn't long before the food started digesting and things slowly picked back up to where they had left off. The guests joked and became better acquainted. It was a good look, marked a new start, set a pleasing vibe and Bri decided this was the best time for her to slide off and have some alone time with her man.

She stood from the table, grabbed Quron's hand and proceeded toward their bedroom. Their company looked at the couple's attempt to ease away unnoticed and blew them up.

"I hear dat, Bri. Go get sum'a that gangsta lovin'." Tonya blurted out, causing everyone to turn around and laugh. She was drunk as hell.

"Shut up, silly. Don't hate," Bri said humorously as she looked back and stuck out her tongue teasingly.

When Bri walked into the bedroom, she released Quron's hand, retrieved a lighter from the nightstand and lit two scented candles. The bed was made; sheets and comforter were pulled tightly and tucked. The big square shaped pillows were propped up against the headboard neatly. Pieces of clothing lay on the floor, starting from the closet, and ending at the hamper. Beautiful pictures that captured special moments of Quron and Bri's life as a couple decorated four corners of the huge dresser mirror.

The way Quron was all over Bri, it probably wouldn't have mattered if they were standing in the shadows of a rank smelling alleyway. All that mattered to him was that the love of his life stood before him, looking sexy as hell with a cowl neck dress that hugged her round curves just right. He couldn't play it off like he didn't miss her, because he did, a whole lot, and he wanted some pussy bad.

"Hold up babe, calm down," Bri said in a soft unconvincing voice while prying herself out of Quron's arms. "No, seriously sweetie, I need to talk to you." Bri stressed upon realizing that Quron wasn't taking her serious.

Quron sensed the urgency in her voice and reluctantly eased off of her.

"Sit down." Bri insisted.

"Boo, stop pacin' back and forth like you crazy. You're makin' me nervous," Quron stated firmly. "And please stop beatin' around the bush. Say whatchu gotta say. You know I'm feenin' for that crack you got between ya legs."

Bri looked at her man and gave a weak smile. *Maybe this isn't a good time. Maybe I should wait.* She looked at Quron and felt the pressure of her truth waiting to be released from her heart. *I have to.*

"Alright," she exhaled and twirled her hair as she began. "Well, while you was away, I started thinking about... you know.... us. How things have been over the past coupl'a months. Us beefin', you still being in the game, and all those sorta things—"

"Okay, and?" Quron interrupted, urging her to address her point.

"Well, I decided that we aren't ready to have a child, so I went to the abortion clinic and handled that."

"You handled what?" Quron asked, hoping he had heard Bri wrong. His eyebrows drew together, forming an evil expression and his heart started pumping severe pain through his veins.

"I... got... an... abortion." Bri slowly let out in a voice barely above a whisper.

The pain and confusion in Quron's eyes was too much for Bri to handle. She allowed her gaze to wander to the floor, and she extended her hands, hoping to receive a hug of understanding.

"Don't fuckin' touch me right now," Quron said through clenched teeth while stepping out of her reach. "I can't believe you." He looked away and chuckled. "You're full'a shit! You talkin' 'bout me bein' in the game, an' all that otha sucka shit. But while I'm spendin' my bread on you, it ain't a problem then."

Bri's eyes started to tear. She wanted to defend her point so badly, but she knew her reasons were based on bullshit.

"Look at chu, you can't even say nothin'." A tear dropped from his eye. It took every bit of discipline to refrain from wringing Bri's neck. "And you, outta everybody knew how bad I wanted a seed. I still can't believe you went out like that, without even considering what I had to say! Tsss." He hissed. "Matter fact, I'm outta here."

Quron snatched his coat and stepped toward the room's door. In mid-stride, he suddenly turned around. Bri was sitting at the foot of her bed with her head buried in her hands. Quron didn't bite his tongue. Bri couldn't see him, but she could hear him clearly.

"Don't call me, don't text me, don't e-mail me, and don't come lookin' for me. When I'm ready to talk, I know where you at, but until then, I need my space." Quron stared at her for a second longer then turned and walked into the living room.

"Mil, let's go."

Amil started to question her brother, but quickly reconsidered upon seeing the darkness in his eyes. She gathered her things, said her goodbyes and headed for the door.

"Quron, leaving us so soon?" Tonya questioned in a slur. "My girl put that thing on you like dat?" The room chuckled at her sarcasm and her date's cheeks turned red from embarrassment.

Quron shook his head at Tonya's crazy self. *Only if you knew.* "Nah, it ain't like dat. Actually, I'ma lil tired, gotta handle a few things before I crash." He lied then faked a yawn.

"Well, be safe out there."

"Fo' sho, and good lookin' for the get together, 'preciate it."

"Peace!" Young-One shouted and smiled, knowing it was more to the story than what Quron cared to share.

Quron threw up the peace sign and closed the front door behind him.

"Brrr, its freezin' out here." Amil shivered and crossed her arms. "And which one of these ballaz BMW is this?" She continued, the liquor talking for her.

"That's Young-One's Beemer. It's official, right?"

"Yeah, it's real nice. Seem like I seen it before."

"Girl, you drunk." Quron stated, not really in the mood for anything.

"For real, Quron." Amil looked down at the gleaming rims and she remembered exactly where she had seen Young-One's whip. She shook her head in disbelief and pointed toward the BMW as she got into her car. "I ain't trippin', it's all comin' back to me now. I know where I seen that car."

"Be quiet girl, you drunk as a skunk. I'm really not in the mood. I know where you seen his ride at too," Quron responded sarcastically. "In traffic."

"Yep, that's exactly where." Amil's voice stressed.

The seriousness of her words caused her and Quron to share a stare that made her tell what she'd seen. Some things were better kept secret, but this, she just had to tell.

Chapter 29

"Fuck takin' this nigga so long?" Scar said to himself as he pressed on the car horn repeatedly.

He was parked in front of Fat-Roc's new spot with the engine still running, obviously frustrated.

The gunplay between Fat-Roc's soldiers, Ghost, Ja and Dex left Dubois Street on fire. Roc didn't have a choice but to relocate. Not wanting to move too far away from his gold mine, he set up shop a few blocks away. Word spread fast, and things were running like they had never stopped. Fiends were roaming around, scheming, flagging down customers, and hustling whatever they could to earn a dollar toward their next hit.

Knowing the game, Fat-Roc fell back and cruised under the radar. The police couldn't stand that fact that they had bodies on their hands, at a drug spot that they knew he operated, but could not prove it. They still had not a single witness that could connect him to the murders. Roc did the best thing he could do. He scouted a more experienced team of young boys who could hold their own and handle business at the same time.

Scar was growing more impatient by the second. But not impatient enough to leave his bread that he came to collect. Rain, sleet, hail, snow, real hustlers never stopped hustling. He glared up at the rear view mirror, and was disgusted and turned off by what he saw. He swung a wild backhand from the driver's seat and knocked the bill of dope out of Trife's hand. The off-white powder scattered across the butter soft interior and slid into the seams of the seat.

"I told y'all 'bout sniffin' dat shit while 'round me!" Scar spat in a deep southern growl. "I don't pay y'all to get high an' nod off into la-la land. I pay y'all to stay on point, be my eyes, an' bus ya gun when need be. Dat gorilla on ya back beaten y'all niggas asses, betta start tighten back befo' it's too late."

Trife and Snake were mad as hell, but neither of them said a word. They knew what Scar had spoken was real talk. They had been sniffing dope a lot more than usual lately. It was gradually becoming a need. The addiction was gaining a tighter grip daily. Their growing addiction wasn't cool at all, and they knew it.

Just when Scar had lost his last bit of patience, a loud knock came on the passenger window. He unlocked the door, exhaled a breath of frustration and looked at Fat-Roc with an unbelieving look on his face.

Fat-Roc plopped down on the seat, cheesing like everything was all good. "What up, my dude?" Fat-Roc extended his hand.

"You takin' ya sweet ass time is what up." Scar responded, not hiding his frustration.

"Homie, you got the game twisted. I ain't near one of ya soldiers and Roc don't jump when you say jump!" Fat-Roc screwed his grill up and looked at Scar like he couldn't be serious.

"Ohhhh," Scar smiled humorously then reached over the armrest and patted Roc's chest. "Now that chu getting' a lil paypa, you ain't a soulja no mo'. I hear that, boss playa." Scar carried on sarcastically while raising his hands as if to say you got it. "So let's talk dat talk... Boss!"

Fat-Roc glanced over at Scar, but kept his thoughts to himself. Scar's sarcastic ass had him boiling inside, but he decided to hold his head. Their business relationship was worth his silence. The coke Scar hit him with on top of the bricks Ghost hit him with thickened his pockets, and that's all that mattered.

Roc eyed Trife and Snake through the rear view mirror. Immediately, he dismissed talking business around them.

They had a staleness about them that didn't sit right with Roc. They stared without blinking, confirming that they were attentive and eavesdropping.

Scar followed Fat-Roc's eyes, noticed his sudden silence, and caught onto his feeling of discomfort. *I knew you was a bitch, frontin' ass nigga.* Scar turned slightly to address his gunmen.

"Yo Snake, Trife, step out fo' a second, let me get a few minutes wit' my boy hea'." He reached over and squeezed Roc's shoulder.

Snake and Trife sucked their teeth and did what they were asked.

"So what it is partna, whatchu got for me?"

"I got what I always got." Fat-Roc answered arrogantly.

"That's good talk fo' sho'," A brief silence settled between the two. "I'm kinda worried playboy, you ain't movin' dem thangs as fast as you use to. I'm hearin' you fuckin' wit' dat young folk who shot me. If it wasn't fo' my vest, that fo' pound slug might'a ended me." Scar shook his head at the memory.'"I really hope you ain't fuckin' wit' the enemy. I like you," he lied. "Over the years we made a lotta paypa together. Let dat be a reminder to you and where ya loyalty lie."

"Ho, ho', hooold up, my man," Fat-Roc interrupted in disagreement. "First an' foremost, Fat-Roc is only loyal to his paypa," he emphasized. "I respect you on a certain level 'cause you kept it tall wit' me in these streets. But don't ever get it twisted like we a team." He made sure that Scar could see every feature in his face as he looked into his eyes. "'Cause we ain't, nigga."

Roc slid his butt off the seat and wiggled the plastic zip-lock bag that was in his waistline. The corner of the zip-lock got caught, and unraveled a few threads in his long- johns, but he still pulled until the plastic holding the rubber-band-wrapped money became loose.

Scar reached under his seat and retrieved a zip-lock bag as well, only it was much bigger and filled to the top with cocaine. After the transaction, Roc opened the door and put one foot out.

"Oh yeah," he looked back. "Just for the record, I fuck wit' whoeva I wanna fuck wit'. Last time I checked, I was grown. As long as I come clean wit'cha gwap, we good."

Scar smiled like it was all a joke. "Remember you said it, not me."

"Yeah whateva." Roc gripped the seat, pushed himself up and closed the door behind him.

"Snap the picture!" Detective Fisher blurted impatiently.

Scar's jeep cruised by and the concealed camera clicked rapidly. Detective Fisher and his partner, DeJesus, crouched low in an old tinted minivan two blocks away from Fat-Roc's spot. A confidential informant who was an addict spilled everything he knew when the two detectives snatched him up and threatened to pin the latest unsolved murders on him. Fisher and DeJesus knew their threat was as weak as a twig under pressure, but such tactics had reaped useful information over the years.

Until Scar pulled up, Fat-Roc hadn't been on the scene. The waiting game was frustrating. The young soldiers that Roc put together were holding the fort down. But to pursue the small fish held no weight in the eyes of the two veterans. They were determined to build cases on the heads that were in charge, and only them. So when Fat- Roc set foot on the scene, the DTs were euphoric, and their patience had rewarded them with clear shots of their primary suspect and of the men who came to see him. The apple never falls too far from the tree, so the D's concluded that the unfamiliar faces were possibly involved also. The high tech cameras and computerized equipment that they operated made it seem like they were positioned directly across the street.

When Scar drove past, all movement inside the minivan ceased. They didn't want to blow their cover. The day light kind of stole from their hiding, but they stayed low and stuck to the plan.

"So did you get the license plate?" Detective Fisher asked as he rolled up the tarp that they were kneeling on.

"Yes I did, Mr. Anxious." DeJesus answered then tilted his head back and chuckled.

Fisher's facial expression turned from that of seriousness to that of understanding. He couldn't help but to laugh himself.

"We'll get 'em," DeJesus smirked. "You know more than anyone, that this is a waiting game. They'll slip up." He said confidently. "They always do."

DeJesus turned the key in the ignition and the van came alive. It shook violently, rattled loudly, and spit thick black smoke through the exhaust pipe. The two partners looked at each other and burst out laughing before peeling off.

––––––––––

"Well I be damned, Trulinski. Look what the wind blew in." Captain Rogers expressed with a slight chuckle from behind the huge maple wood desk. He leaned back in his worn down rolling chair and propped his dusty, leaning shoes on the desk. The springs squealed a little, asking for an oil treatment, but the chair held.

"Ha, ha, very funny." DeJesus said with traces of sarcasm.

After putting out his Cuban cigar, he gestured for Detective Fisher and his partner, DeJesus, to come closer.

Captain Rogers was an aging white man with thick hairy eyebrows, no mustache, and thin brown hair that he often combed to one side in an attempt to cover the bald spot that seemed to spread each year. His old slacks hung loosely from his waist, because he didn't have much of a butt or hips. One thing for sure, what he missed in the waist area he definitely made up for in the stomach area. His potbelly overlapped his belt, and almost always popped the buttons on the shirts that he wore. He was a mess.

His new office was a different story, though. It seem to be designed for a classier guy. More than enough for him. The room was square shaped. The rear wall was decorated with green wall paper, not quite forest, more so spinach green. A window was part of its structure and was the only outlet that connected him to the outside world. The front of the office was made of fiberglass windows that began at waist level of an average height man, extending twelve feet up into the foam drop ceiling.

From his desk, he could pretty much see the whole precinct and he loved it. The window shades with drawstrings made his colleagues disappear when privacy was needed. He couldn't have requested a better gift with his promotion.

Fisher and DeJesus stepped closer, fanning the thick lingering cigar smoke from their noses. Boxes of files, family portraits, and other miscellaneous items were everywhere. File cabinets were out of place; the office needed some real organizing. It looked like a tornado had come through and only touched the captain's space. Honestly speaking, the two partners in crime couldn't have cared less about how the captain was living, or rather working. They were just curious as to why they were summoned. Their expression didn't reveal their thoughts. DeJesus smiled kindly and looked around admiringly.

"What's up Capt?" Fisher stretched his hand. "Sir." He turned and was just as cordial with the new face that accompanied the captain. "Nice office." DeJesus added mockingly.

"Thanks." Captain Rogers chuckled, then continued. "Find somewhere to sit; we have some very important business to discuss. But before we begin, I'd like you two to meet FBI Agent Trulinski." The trio nodded in acknowledgement, all wanting to get down to business.

"Okay, now that we're all acquainted, let's get to it. Y'all see this?" The captain asked, not wasting a second more. He pointed to the seven faces on the bulletin board and awaited a response.

"Yeah, we're familiar with them." Fisher confirmed while staring at the photos.

Quron, Nuri, Steel, Young-One, Ghost, Ja, and Dex were all posted and labeled in a tree format from top to bottom.

"Fellas," The Captain stressed, knowing the news that he held would bring negative feedback. "I know these men on this board are suspects in your investigation. But unfortunately, I've been informed that your investigation will discontinue because the big boys are taking over."

"That's bullshit!" DeJesus slammed his palm against the metal cabinet. "We've been bussin' our asses for months!"

"Watch your tone." Captain Rogers reminded. "Let's be real here, Garcia. We've put together our best team of officers to assist you two, and what have youse come up with?"

The silence that followed his question confirmed exactly what he already knew.

"Just like I thought, nothing that means anything. We have phone taps, wire taps, photos from the stake outs and confidential informants that tried to penetrate their system. In the end though, even with all that I've mentioned, what do we have?" He raised his voice at the end of his question emphasizing his point. "We have nothing that'll stick in the court of law, and you two know it." He smacked his lips together and shook his head as he stood from his seat. "I must admit, these guys have something solid going. But never despair," he chuckled. "This gentleman here just informed me before you two came in that we have finally stumbled across the break that we needed." The Captain pointed. "Agent Trulinski, why don't you explain?"

"Don't mind if I do, Captain." Agent Trulinski said with a nod then took over the floor so he could fill in the blanks. He wore regular apparel, Champion sweater, running sneakers, fitting jeans, and a tight leather jacket. His complexion was an olive color. No facial hair disturbed his smooth skin and his blonde hair, blue eyes, and pointy nose kept his youthful appeal.

"First off, let me say this guys, I'm not here to bust anyone's balls." He giggled waggishly. "I know how it feels to be working extremely hard on a project, only to hit a bump in the road what you've done seem to be in vain. Believe me, I know." Agent Trulinski accentuated with a slight English accent. "Fortunately, I have good news. I've decided to keep you two as a part of this operation TAKE DOWN. I've learned of your work ethic, and to say I am pleased would be an understatement, so I am honored to have you all on our team." He nodded and stepped in even strides toward the bulletin board.

"Now that the formalities are over, pay close attention. See this man here?" He pointed then continued, knowing that his question was rhetorical. "Well, he turned against his friends and is essentially one of us. Recently, he was arrested, and two kilos of cocaine along with a fully loaded Calico was seized from his vehicle. The Jersey Turnpike Troopers notified us immediately. The trafficking aspect of the situation automatically made it federal. It didn't take much; this individual was easy to break. Once in our custody, we hardly used our interrogation tactics, and he gave in." Trulinski smiled arrogantly. He was very proud of his work.

"After bonding his words by legal documents, we cut him loose with everything we caught on him. We didn't want any suspicion to arise from his crew. Now that we're in, it's just a matter of time. Any questions?"

Detective Fisher and DeJesus just sat motionless, trying to register all that they had heard. They had to admit the sudden news had was as a surprise. Needless to say, they were definitely thankful.

"Nah, I don't have any questions." Fisher responded.

"You?" Agent Trulinski turned and asked DeJesus.

"Nah, I'm clear."

"Very good," Trulinski shook the detectives' hands as they stood. "It was a pleasure meeting you gentlemen. Here's my card, and I'll see ya soon."

Everyone exchanged handshakes and head nods. "Later Captain." DeJesus shut the door behind him.

Chapter 30

"I wonder who this is?" Quron asked himself while looking at the unfamiliar number that flashed across his screen.

One leg hung off of Amil's plush couch and one of Quron's arms was tucked comfortably behind his head. He had just awakened from a peaceful slumber not too long ago. From where he laid, he could see his sister cooking what smelled like a tasty breakfast. He concentrated on the number flashing across his screen again and it still didn't register.

"This better not be this girl, I swear it better not be," Quron mumbled. "Hello!"

No answer came from the other end of the line. Only panicky breathing was heard. Growing more frustrated by the second, Quron exhaled and spoke with hostility.

"Yo, who is this? Don't call playin' kid games on my phone! Matter fact—"

"No baby, please don't hang up." The feminine voice begged.

"Bri, why you playin' games?"

"I just wanna talk to you an—"

"Ain't nothin' to talk about. You violated and I ain't ready to talk. When I'm ready, I'll make sure I call you. Peace."

Quron disconnected the call, and that was the end of that. He didn't feel any kind of way for acting stank toward Bri. Every bone in his body felt she deserved such treatment, so it was cool.

Amil had done a fabulous job with the interior decorating of the new suburban home that her brother had given her once their mother passed away. A huge twenty-gallon fish tank stood tall, on top of a stainless steel stand, and it extended along the living room wall. All kinds of tropical fish roamed through the clear water like it was in fact the place where they were born.

The living room floor was covered with wall to wall carpet, a lavender color that still had its rich, new look, due to no one being allowed to walk on it while wearing shoes. Amil didn't play that, no one was an exception to her rule.

Quron had to smile at his thoughts surrounding Amil. She was something else. He was very grateful that she had decided to move back home and finish school at NYU. While Quron was on vacation, Amil had started the transfer process her senior year. When she shared her plan to finish her business degree and then pursue a dual MBA/JD degree at NYU to become an attorney like their mother wanted, it was music to her brothers' ears. Having their baby sister around provided a level of peace and harmony that was sorely needed.

His phone started buzzing again and he instantly snapped out of his trance and slid his finger toward the power button. He didn't feel like entertaining Bri's crap right now. Just when he was about to press the power button, he peeked at the number and realized it was not the same number that Bri had called from. Curious as to who was now calling from an unlisted number, he answered.

"Hello."

"You have a collect call from, Grimy, an inmate at Green Haven Correctional Facility, a New York State Facility. If you'd like to hear the cost of this call, press nine. If you'd like to accept this call, dial three now, if you wish to—"

Quron hurriedly pressed three.

"Your call has been accepted, thank you for dealing with Global Tel-link." The recorded operator finished.

"As-salaamu-Alaykum, what up bro!" Quron shouted, his eyes beaming with joy.

"Ain't nothin' Ron, maintainin' as usual." Grimy responded, seeming just as elated as his comrade.

"Long time no hear from."

"I be knowin', my boy, shit been rough on my side of the fence. The belly of the beast is the worst. I heard about what happened to Mama Love, I'm really sorry 'ta hear that." Both ends of the phone line stood still as silence brought sad memories. "But um, it sound like you doin' pretty good."

"I could complain, but it won't change anything, so why complain?" Quron stated honestly. The thoughts of his mother that he so badly wanted to forget had resurfaced once again and dampened his peaceful state.

"I can definitely dig it. I've been try'na holla at you for a while now, but bein' in the box stagnated progress. These pigs locked me up for some straight up bullshit."

"Word?"

"Word, it's nothin' though. You know I'ma hold mine down regardless."

"No question." Quron agreed.

"That shit crazy though, Ron," Grimy chuckled as he thought back to his box experience. "They put you in a cell with anotha man first of all, none of ya personal property outside of religious material, a few magazines, and a novel or two for entertaining purposes. It's so borin' in that bitch, all you can do is eat, sleep, and use the bathroom. And of course, that's only if the younger brothas in there let you sleep. That's my word, Ron, ain't nothin' but babies in there, and half of 'em are goin' crazy. They be standin' at their cell gates all day long literally talkin' about nothin'. They stay violatin' these faggot ass police though, throwin' shit an' piss on'em every chance they get. Oh, don't let somethin' go wrong like one of 'em miss the envelope give out time because they weren't on their gate, they'll try an' kick the metal doors off. Kick after kick after kick. Mad chaos, it is insane.

"In the same breath, it's a shame too, 'cause it's a mentality that is being forced on our youth through their livin' conditions. Whatchu expect? Make no mistake about it, it's our people, blacks and Latinos that populate these prisons. These crackers lock 'em in a small ass cell with a metal desk with two stools connected for sitting. Let me not forget this desk is an all-purpose desk. You eat there, write there, read there, and stress out there. A metal sink, a metal toilet, a metal bunk bed, welded to the cinder block wall is all a part of what I call the torture chamber, 'cause that's exactly what it is. And to top it all off, the solitary confinement is twenty-three hour lock down. That type'a environment will drive anybody crazy. It's a shame, fo'real."

"Yeah, it is." were the only words Quron could muster up. He couldn't help but to think about his own prison experience. He wondered if Grimy's reminder was a sign sent from Allah. The timing of his call sure made it seem that way.

"But you know how it go," Grimy smiled. "All news ain't bad news."

"So stop holdin' out." Quron stated jokingly.

"When's the last time you spoke to the lawyer you hired for me?"

"It's been a while, why? I know he ain't slackin', 'cause I make sure he get his cake every month."

"Nah Ron, son official. He came through for the kid."

"Whatchu mean?" Quron questioned, not comprehending what Grimy was actually saying.

"I gotta reversal. It's over, Ron, I'm outta here."

"Stop playin' like that."

"I'm dead serious, my dude. It's over." Grimy's tone humbled as he spoke. He couldn't believe it himself.

"Ahhhhh! Praise is due to Allah! Yeah baby, I knew you'd get your break!" Quron was ecstatic. Jumping up and down like he'd won a billion dollars.

This was just the type of news that he needed to lift his spirits. Everything else around him seemed to be so complicated. The feeling of happiness that ran through him upon hearing the great news was truly genuine. Quron loved his crew wholeheartedly. But there was no bond in the world like that of a group of men while under the harsh and oppressive restrictions of prison. Only an individual that went through it could relate.

"Sit your behind down, boy, jumping around like you crazy. It ain't that serious," Amil said with a trace of a smile while walking out of the kitchen with a plate of food in her hand.

"Yes it is, Mil. My boy that I did most of my time with got his case overturned. The judge ruled in his favor an' he's comin' home soon."

"Oh, that's so good for him. Tell him I said congratulations."

"He said thanks. Mil, you know he heard ya big mouth." They both laughed.

"So when do you touch?" Quron redirected his attention back to his conversation.

"I don't know exactly when yet, the administration s'pose to be straightening out my paperwork now. I think our boy, Ty, conditional release date is around the same time they got in mind."

"That's what it is. You know I'ma set it out when y'all touch. Speakin' of Ty, where is he?"

"In program. He gon' be mad as hell when he find out I called without him."

"He'll get over it."

They shared a laugh, both of them knowing exactly how their boy can be.

"You have sixty seconds remaining on this call." The operator interrupted.

"Ah-ight Ron, I love you, my nigga. You and Nuri stayed true to y'all word, I'll always remember that."

"It's nothin', real dudes do even realer things."

"You have 15 seconds left on this call."

"I salute you, Grimy, send mine to all those who deserve it."

"I will do."

"Peace!"

"Peace, Ron!"

Quron pressed the off button on his phone and stood from the couch. He stretched, yawned, and then smiled. With his arms still extended toward the ceiling and his head tilted backwards, he acknowledged the creators greatness.

"Allahu-Akbar!"

Chapter 31

The clock was ticking and a new chapter of life was near for many people. Everybody seemed to be anticipating the fresh start. The radiance from the beautiful moon gleamed, illuminating the clear sky. The breeze that was normally raging and very much alive was surprisingly calm on this winter night. The weather, minus the intimidating wind had toughened up by taking a dry, cold stance. But none of that mattered. The vibe that people gave showed that they were elated. House gatherings, churches, local bars, and most of the clubs around the hood were packed with people who came together for the annual celebration.

Club Orgasm, in particular, was the place to be this year. Anybody who was somebody was present. All of the players, ballers, and celebrities who happened to have business in the area due to the holidays, had attended. Judging by the parking lot, the party promoters had done their thing. There were well over a million dollars in luxurious cars already parked in the huge lot, and over a million dollars more in value, lined up for about two blocks, still waiting to enter.

In the city of Newburgh, New Years was the time when the major hustlers made a statement. The big boy whips, flashy jewelry, and the best garments money could buy all served as a witness to how they were putting their game down in the streets for the past twelve months.

Nuri and the crew weren't any different. Going all out for the New Year was a ritual. Quron, used to love the spotlight too. Over the years, his views had changed and it no longer appealed to him. Showing off made it too easy for the wolves who were surely lurking, the other hustlers, and the police to guess what he was working with. One of the key rules of survival in the game is fly low under the radar. The mentality of the typical hustler these days made it extremely easy for the police. It didn't take a genius to figure out the occupation of an individual pushing a hundred-thousand dollar car, but still rested his head in the projects with his momma.

Quron's logic made sense, but his crew let it go in one ear and out the other. They weren't trying to hear shit, and it showed, because when they pulled up, everything went into slow motion like a horrific movie scene. They stunted hard.

The bass from their systems banged and rattled the pavement like an earthquake was taking place. Nuri led the pack, swerved around the corner and glided across the blacktop, stopping on the dime. His brand new candy apple red Mercedes S600 with mirror tints and 22-inch deep dish Giovanni rims set the tone. The four whips that trailed rolled up on his side and shut the scene down.

The young ballers' attire was crazy, definitely dressed for the occasion. The lustful stares that they drew in only added to their egos. Each car shared the flawless candy apple red; their shine testified that the V's were straight off the show room floor.

The twins, Ja and Dex, were the first to hop out of their identical 911 Porsches. Dex held a lit blunt of haze between his thumb and index finger, while Ja pulled hard on the blunt he held pinched between his lips. The rims were the only difference on the two coupes. Dex, had laced his with 20-inch five star Milan rims and Ja had the same sized shoes with swerve style by Gianna.

Ghost and Steel shut off their engines and joined their boys. Ghost's S5 Audi was sick too. The cocoa butter seats were piped out. The D'Vinci rims shined hard under the bright streetlight, while the body sat low, thanks to the custom made kit.

No question, those boys hustled hard, and they held no punches when it came to balling. Steel made it obvious that he wanted the world to know that he and his team defined ballin', because he took the cake. His Lamborghini Murcielago had women rubbing their thighs together, trying to stop their pussies from throbbing. It resembled a spacecraft, something futuristic. The candy apple paint made the Lambo appear to have diamond chips embedded, and the chrome and red rims complimented the car perfectly.

Music from inside the club thumped loudly, piercing through the exterior walls. The four comrades were feeling themselves as they joked and danced outside in the cold. Women snickered, blushed, and whispered while watching Ja, Dex, Ghost and Steel act a fool.

Nuri and Quron just sat in Nuri's Benz, laughing at the show. Nuri could tell that his brother was uncomfortable with the whole party thing. He totally understood why. The last time he was in that type of environment, he had caught a slug and damn near died.

Lowering the music, Nuri looked over at his bro and began to speak. "Yo, I already see the uneasiness in ya face..." Nuri reached under his seat and grabbed the hundred shot calico. "But don't worry, shit ain't goin' down like that." He kissed the black gun. "God forbid a nigga act up and let me get to this car." He chuckled. "Shit should be cool, though, it's New Years and niggas ain't tryna act up. Just in case though, here." Nuri placed a small palm size pistol on his lap. "This.45 Dillinger will lay a muthafucka down, you can bet that." He squeezed Quron's shoulder and secured the heavy caliber in his boxer brief.

Quron did the same, gave his brother a pound then stepped out into the refreshing night air to join the others.

"Oh shit, look at the don." Ghost noticed, closing his mouth as if he was about to blow a whistle. He shook his head up and down admiring his mentor's throwback style.

Quron smiled, knowing he was killing it. He had to dig deep in his closet for the occasion. The few garments that he'd kept hadn't been worn in over a decade. Ironically, they still fit because back in the day he had always purchased his gear way too big. Big clothing was the swag at the time. With help from the cleaners, he was good as new, fresh as they come.

A purple, pink, and white Coogi sweater suspended over his upper body, a thick rope chain with a diamond studded fist hung from his neck, and a pair of loose fitting Tru pants partially overlapped the purple, pink and white Prada sneakers on his feet. His all white full-length-chinchilla took breaths away and yelled *money*.

Although he didn't feel that flashy cars were a good investment, he knew that one's outward appearance had everything to do with how people treated you initially. If nothing else, Quron was definitely fly.

"This somethin' light, ya heard." They all laughed at Quron's modesty, waved him off and headed toward the entrance.

"Nobody seen or heard from Young-One"" Nuri inquired as they walked. They all shrugged and shook their heads except Quron.

"Yeah, I talked to'em earlier. He told me to send his love to all the homies and let y'all know he was gon' sit this one out 'cause he got a pretty young thing he plan to bring the New Year in wit'."

"Ol' sucka fo' love ass nigga." Dex joked. They all found humor in his words. "Ghost, do you know the bouncer at the door?" Ja asked.

"Nah."

Steel stepped in front of his partners and headed toward the bouncer. "We... we don't gotta know'em. Everybody know... know Benjamin." He chuckled and waved a knot of hundreds in the air.

"Yo... yo homeboy." Steel called out to the bouncer, interrupting the conversation he was having with a scantily dressed young lady with a heart shaped ass.

The bouncer excused himself and gave Steel an unfriendly stare.

"Don't act like that, homeboy, we just tryna shake out in the party." Nuri cut in, upon seeing the bouncer shifting toward some nonsense. Nuri knew hot-headed Steel would pop the ugly, 6 foot 4 bouncer's head off in the blink of an eye if he tried to front on him. Nuri didn't want that, he just wanted to bring in the New Year with a bang.

"No sweat, my man," Big man said, looking directly at Steel, but talking to Nuri. "You should teach ya boy here some manners." He continued hostilely, making it obvious that he was playing himself for the young lady he was kicking it with. Everybody waiting on line seemed to have shifted their focus toward the scene that was surely getting out of hand.

Steel's nostrils began to flare and Nuri stepped up just in time. "Look B, fuck all that otha shit. It's six of us, an' I got six big faces for you right here, whatchu gon' do?" Nuri extended his hand, waiting for the bouncer to make his decision, because he too was growing impatient with him frontin' like he couldn't get it.

"Ah-ight, son," The bouncer took his bread. "But don't come through like y'all own the spot no more."

"Yeah, whateva duke." Nuri brushed his words off and slid through the entrance.

Steel stopped in mid-stride, eyed the scantily dressed young lady, and out of spite extended his hand toward her. She was pressed to be in the spot; that was the only reason she was giving the security guard any conversation in the first place. With nothing to think about, she gave the bouncer a silly look, batted her eyes at Steel, then clutched his hand and followed suit.

"Fuckin' busta." Steel giggled.

Security was tight, but not tight enough. Neither Nuri nor Quron's gun was detected at the door, which made them wonder how many other gangsters had breezed through with a gun and no hassle.

The inside of Club Orgasm was modern. Upon passing the admittance booth, they were greeted by a thick money-green drape that dangled from the high ceiling, blocking all visual scenery inside the club. Nuri and the crew bobbed their heads to the new club hanger and slid through the slit in the drape. The spot came alive. A long glass bar extended twenty feet down the main walkway. In the center of the dance floor, a smaller, circular bar that only served bottled water and bottles of champagne compelled the shot callers in attendance to ball.

The DJ booth hung high over the crowded dance floor. The vibe was bananas. Lounge chairs and small triangle tables took up the back area of the huge factory space. A stage with speakers inserted and dance poles connected, decorated the front of the club alongside the VIP section.

The team walked through the congested crowd, making their way toward the lounge area. Gold diggers lusted from afar, and the ballers and regular acquaintances exchanged words, shouted compliments, and gave acknowledging head nods.

"It's mad bitches in this muthafucka!" Ja shouted over the music.

"Word!" Ghost admitted, and it was on from there. Everyone settled in and got it popping.

Dex made a quick pit stop in the co-op restroom and returned with a box of flavored cigars.

"That's what it is my dude." Nuri pointed to the box of cigars while bobbing his head to the bass line.

Steel dug in his pocket and pulled out an ounce of loud that had red and lime- green hairs all over it. Everyone except Quron grabbed a blunt and put their skills to use. Quron just sat back and smiled at his fam doing what they do. He clearly remembered the days when he was just like them.

A soft touch on his shoulder broke his trance and surprised him a bit. He slightly turned in his seat and one of the club's waitresses stood behind him looking good enough to eat. She was clad in knee high stockings, a sun visor that read KOMRAD, a lace bra, a pair of four-inch stilettos, and a pair of boy shorts that were painted on her plump ass.

Quron scanned her voluptuous figure from top to bottom before realizing there was a bottle of Dom P on the stainless steel platter that she held in her palm. Noticing there was a tag attached to the champagne with his name on it, he stood and leaned toward the young lady's ear.

"Who is this from?"

The cute waitress pointed to the bar in the middle of the dance floor and a woman dressed in all black stood on a stool and waved.

Quron couldn't believe his eyes. Even more surprising was the hot sensation that zoomed through his heart upon recognizing the woman.

"Thank you." Quron told the waitress as he handed her a twenty-dollar tip then stepped off into the crowd.

"Where you goin'?" Nuri yelled, watching his brother zig-zag around the people who were getting their dance on.

"Over here!" Quron pointed, keeping his stride.

Nuri eyed the female that his brother walked up to and sucked his teeth in disgust, then waved his hand, showing his disagreement.

"Damn, I see your brother still holding grudges." The pretty woman noted as she watched Nuri's reaction.

"You know how that go, Malai. Betrayal in the smallest form isn't somethin' we take lightly, ya know? You left me when I was at my lowest, how's he sposed to feel?" He shrugged.

"Well, you ain't tripping 'bout it."

Quron cocked his head to the side and raised his eyebrows. *No this chic didn't.* He exhaled then said, "I ain't trippin' because it ain't that serious to me anymore. You live and you learn. I'm doin' me and accordin' to what I see..." he fanned Malai up and down. "You still on top of ya game too."

They shared a laugh. Malai had gained a few pounds in all the right places since the last time Quron had seen her. Her long hair was pulled back in a tight ponytail. Her pants stopped above her pumps, drawn by strings, and a halter-top clung to her pushed up breasts. Costume jewelry twinkled under the disco lights and the eye make-up on her lids enhanced their slanted shape.

"Some things never change." Malai chuckled and shook her head. The sparkle in Quron's eyes made her feel like she still held the key to his heart.

She shook her head again, knowing the beautiful life they could have had if she would have weathered the storm. But she also knew that them not being an item wasn't solely her fault. Quron was a whore in every sense of the word before his incarceration, and his blatant disregard back then had a lot to do with how she moved while he was on lock. After thinking about her reason for going astray over and over, she admitted that the way she went about things was wrong. But there was nothing she could do to change what had already happened.

"You're right about that." Quron agreed, knowing some things never changed.

"No hard feelings." Malai opened her arms and smiled.

"Nah, no hard feelings." Quron smiled and hugged her. "It was good seeing you."

"Yeah, you too... don't be a stranger. We can still be friends, ya know." Malai retrieved a card from her bosom and handed it to him. "Call me sometime." She smiled, waved her hand, and left Quron, knowing that she wanted that old thing back. She swayed through the crowd, strutting hard as she got back in her groove.

"Everybody, it's about that time!" The DJ shouted into the microphone as a wall-sized flat screen descended from the ceiling. There was a screen on both sides of the oversized TV, so no matter where you stood in the club, the visual of the ball dropping in Time Square was clear.

"Five..." All the partygoers began as the last few seconds of the year faded.

"Four... three... two... one, HAPPYYY NEW YEAR!!!" The walls shook from the unified cheer and corks from bottles of bubbly shot into the air.

The scene was live. People were definitely enjoying the moment and it was appealing to see folks bonding.

"Happy New Year, bro." Nuri shouted as he climbed onto the bar stool next to Quron.

"Same to you," Quron nodded. "Where everybody go?" He looked around, realizing Nuri was alone.

"Ghost bounced to go with his shorty, and Steel runnin' 'round here fuckin' wit' Ja and Dex."

"Aw man, triple trouble." Quron joked, causing them to share a laugh.

"Oh shit, there go ya shorty. Ya New Year startin' out right." Nuri pointed, then laughed.

Quron followed Nuri's finger, and sure enough, India, Tito, Flaco, and an unfamiliar face were cutting through a wave of people.

"I see you got jokes." Quron mushed Nuri playfully and stood from the stool to greet an approaching Tito. Tito and he hadn't clicked at first, but over time, Quron realized that he was a good dude.

"What's good, y'all? What brings you to the hood?" Quron inquired, giving Tito dap and nodding at the others.

Tito pointed to India and the female who accompanied them. "They wanted to bring in the New Year here, so the boss asked me and Flaco to come along." Tito explained in broken English.

It made sense. Quron understood Pedro's reason for sending security with the women. Like Pedro, he didn't want India to ever be subjected to the terrible treatment that she had suffered in the past.

India stood close by, doing a little two-step, but she didn't engage much in the conversation. Quron ordered both Flaco and Tito drinks, while India and her company declined. A few of his sly remarks earned a smile from India, but overall, she wasn't her normal self. Quron noted her strange behavior, but allowed it to slide. He figured she was still bitter from what went down between them during their vacation.

As he watched her dance alone, Quron's mind drifted back to the day they formally met. At that moment, he realized that after all the time they'd spent together, and everything they had experienced, she remained a mystery. He still had no idea why she was stripping in the club that night, especially after being violated in such a horrible way. *Damn, I've been slippin'.* He had completely forgotten the fact that she was a stripper. *Have I really been that wrapped up in her beauty and my ego?* Quron silently chided himself as he quietly studied India's demeanor.

Nuri, on the other hand, sat quietly like he had lost his tongue. He was so caught up in the pleasant imagery of the woman who accompanied India, that he didn't know what to say. In his eyes, she was by far the baddest chick in the club. That was a hell of a compliment for home girl, because there were definitely some fine women in the building.

Shorty sported a peach casual suit made of rayon. Two hoop earrings dangled from her ear lobes and the eyeliner that traced the edge of her lip-glossed lips gave her crazy sex appeal. Nuri was in love. Her almond shaped eyes, thick arched eyebrows, and deep dimples, made her irresistible and was probably the reason she had an exasperated look. Dudes were trying to holler from the second she stepped her pretty feet through the door. She gave Nuri and the rest of them her back as she turned toward the bar. The DJ must have been playing her jam because she was in a zone of her own.

The back shot view that she gave Nuri unintentionally was the last straw, he could no longer resist. He stood from the stool and passed in front of everyone; no excuse me, or nothing, it was one thing and one thing only on his mind. He didn't know if the young lady was with Tito, Flaco, some other cat in the club. How he was feeling, it didn't matter if she was. Finally reaching her, he climbed onto the stool next to her and beckoned for the waitress to come over.

Casually, she cut her eyes at Nuri and rolled them after a quick assessment. His flooded Rolex along with the two toned diamonds in his ear that matched his attire, helped her write him off as a typical low life drug dealer. Just like the rest who had been spitting their best lines throughout the night.

The waitress put a finger up to the group of men seeking her attention on the other side of the bar and walked up to Nuri.

"Do me a favor and get this beautiful young lady whatever she wants." He pointed toward the girl who was now standing at attention with her hand resting on the dip in her hip.

"No, that's not necessary, I'm fine." Shorty said in a calm but serious manner.

"It's my bread, I worked hard for it, and if I feel it's necessary, then it is." He smiled smoothly, then peeled a big face from the bigger knot inside his pocket. He placed it on top of the glass topped bar and pushed it toward the waitress.

The girl gave Nuri a venomous stare before shifting her gaze back to the waitress. "Since he insists, let me get a bottled water please." She finally submitted, realizing her new pest wouldn't accept no as an answer.

"Well, you're welcome." Nuri chuckled sarcastically.

"If you recall correctly, I didn't ask for this." She grabbed the water bottle and shook it from side-to-side, making her point clear.

"Keep the change," Nuri told the waitress then turned slightly in the stool and clutched the lady's soft hand. She tugged, but not convincingly. Nuri could feel the break' in her defense.

"Look, maybe I came on to you a little too strong, but I didn't mean any harm. And off the bat, you need to know I ain't wit' the games at all. My name is Nuri, and I'm not like no nigga you've ever met before," he boasted arrogantly. "I'm not tryna impress you wit' this material shit or none of that. Whatchu see is who I am, twenty-four-seven, three-sixty-five. And honestly, the only reason I came over here is because I think you're the most gorgeous woman that I ever laid eyes on. I was curious to see if you are the angel that I asked God to send me."

The exotic beauty tried to control her urge, but looking into Nuri's eyes and seeing that he was as serious as a heart attack only tickled her insides more and she broke out laughing.

Not bothered a bit, Nuri too started cracking up. So much so, that India and everyone else turned toward the two and giggled a little themselves, knowing that whatever they were laughing about had to be funny.

"No you didn't try to game me," she mentioned, while holding her stomach, trying to regain her composure. "It was cute though. Goddamn, an angel tho?" She giggled some more. "Boy, whoever you are, you're something else."

"Nah beautiful, I'm somethin' original. I knew I would get chu to smile some way or another, now look..." He pointed to the Colgate smile on her face. "But real talk, everything I said prior to the last sentence was genuine thoughts, and all I want is a shot at gettin' to know you better. For starters, you can tell me your name since I already told you mine."

The pretty young thing stood silently for a minute, gazing into Nuri's eyes, searching for a reason to rebel. She surprised herself when she couldn't find a reason. It didn't help that she had started softening up toward the fly young nigga who had started out like a gnat that she so badly wanted to swat. His persistence was attractive. Not a characteristic of any of the dudes who'd attempted to get at her thus far. That showed her that the man sitting calmly on the stool in front of her, bobbing his head to the music, awaiting her cooperation knew what he wanted. More importantly, he fought until he got it.

She smiled warmly, then straddled the empty stool next to Nuri. "My name is Trinity. India over there is my cousin. I found out about this New Year extravaganza through a local radio station and being that I've attended a few parties thrown by these promoters, I knew it was going to be off the hook, so here we are. Any further questions, sir?" She smiled sarcastically and started laughing.

Nuri chuckled. "You from around here?" Nuri twirled his finger in a circle.

"I lived in Poughkeepsie for a long time, so you can say that."

For the next few hours, the new acquaintances occupied their time getting familiar.

"Sorry to butt-in, but it's getting late and we are ready to leave." Quron interrupted them.

Nuri glared down at his twinkling bezel and shook his head reluctantly in agreement. "I didn't realize how much time passed. Before we leave though, I want you to meet somebody." He stood from the stool and helped Trinity up as well. "Bro, this beautiful young lady who took up all my time tonight is Trinity." Nuri voiced humorously. "And Trinity, this is my big brother, Quron."

She blushed discreetly from Nuri's flattery.

Quron extended his hand and lifted hers to his lips, kissing it like a real gentleman. "Nice to finally meet you, Trinity. India has spoken highly of you."

"Okay, now that we all know each other, can we please leave now?" India rudely disturbed the moment. "I feel sick, like I'm about to throw-up."

No one responded to her insolent outburst, they all just complied and moved toward the exit.

Once in the parking lot, Tito, who was tipsy, shuffled off to get the Lincoln town car that brought them there. Trinity and Nuri stood off to the side and picked up where they left off. Quron figured this was a good time to address the situation with India.

"India, what's up ma? I apologize again for that little incident on vacation, I didn't mean for it to go down like that."

She looked up at him for a split second, then allowed her gaze to roam again.

"I seen how you was actin' in the club, and I'm concerned. You don't look too well, you ah-ight? How much you drink tonight?"

She folded her arms and rubbed up and down as the wind crept under her dress, sending a chill up her body. "I haven't drank anything, actually. I don't know what it is. Lately, I just haven't been feeling well. My stomach hasn't kept down much, it seems like I'm always vomiting."

"Have you considered hollerin' at a doctor?"

"Not really, I figured whatever it is will pass." India answered truthfully.

"I can't call it ma, just take it easy and call me if I can do anything to help. Look at me India, stop actin' like that toward me." She lifted her gaze. "Nothin' changed, I'm still here for you like I've always been. Don't let that little episode that happened ruin somethin' good, ya dig."

India nodded, then moved to Quron's side, startled from the screeching tires of Tito bending the corner. He stopped on a dime in front of the two and hopped out. Something had obviously happened.

"Hurry up, let's go!" Tito yelled. "I just got a call and we gotta go now." His words slurred and carried panic. Tito flopped back inside the driver seat.

India, Flaco, and Trinity shared an alarmed look before they hopped in behind him.

"India, call me!" was all Quron had time to shout before the doors were closed.

Tito had already applied pressure to the gas, leaving Quron and Nuri behind, wondering what could possibly have happened.

Watching the black Lincoln speed out of the parking lot was just what the big, ugly bouncer wanted to see. He turned away from the two cats that were standing with a puzzled look, so that they couldn't hear his conversation. That little conflict they had when they first came in the club had him feeling a certain kind of way, anyway. Bringing his phone up toward his ear, he pressed the chirp button.

"Yo." An annoying squeak dove out of the speaker.

"It's a go. They just pulled off in a hurry too, so be on point. They headed your way."

"Ah-ight. Matter fact, I see 'em right here, good lookin'."

The news that Tito conveyed while in the car had India's stomach twisted with her body slumped and her head buried in her hands. Trinity was touched in the worse way by the tragic news as well. She tried to be strong and console her cousin, but her words were hardly convincing.

"Flaco, what am I going to do? Who's gonna hold our family down now?" India cried and choked on the thick saliva building in her mouth.

"Cono, oh shit, duuuck!!" Tito shrieked, slamming his foot down on the brakes, causing the rear wheels to lift.

"Ahhhhh!" India and Trinity trembled in fear for their lives as they screamed.

A black van with no license plate or windows other than the driver and passenger side, shot out in front of the Lincoln, blocking the street. Snake emerged from the vehicle wearing a black bandana around his face, gripping an AK-47.

Seeing the armed man jogging toward them holding the AK pushed Tito into survival mode. With no other out, he jammed the gear into reverse and floored the gas pedal. The tires spun round and round, kicking up a cloud of stinking smoke before catching the asphalt, and throwing the town car backwards.

Out of nowhere, the green Buick that appeared to be parked and vacant just seconds ago, shot into the street. The collision pierced the neighborhood. Seconds later, thunderous explosions set off car alarms.

Trife sat in the Buick dazed for a minute. The impact was harsh. He quickly regained his senses and hopped out to handle his business. The heroin he snorted had his adrenaline pumping 100 mph, and murder was the only thing on his mind.

The deafening boom shook the hell out Detective Fisher and his partner, DeJesus. They had just come from a gathering celebrating the New Year and were tipsy off of cognac. The explosion seemed to have sobered them up, putting a dent in their smooth groove.

Off impulse, they dropped to the ground next to a nearby gas pump and scanned the area for signs of danger. On their stomach, they looked on in amazement as the crime scene developed right before their eyes.

India and Trinity curled up in the back seat, terrified. They cried hysterically as death crept closer. Tito drew his twin .40 calibers from their holsters and threw his weight against the door, causing it to fly open. Flaco sat helplessly in the passenger seat. The impact from the sudden collision had knocked him out cold.

Tito didn't know who he was up against or why the gunmen had come for their souls. But he refused to lie down without a fight. He struggled to his feet, using the car door as a crutch. Standing erect was his worse mistake.

Snake sized him up, and as soon as his frail frame became visibly erect, Snake pulled the trigger. Finger-sized shells flipped from the AK chamber as the scorching hot lead ate through the car's hood, burst the front tires, and mangled Tito's flesh. Half of his abdomen blew out his back, cracking his chest cavity in half. His lifeless body slid between the crevices of the door and dangled. The fully loaded Glock .40s fell to the pavement. Not a single shot was fired.

Trife crept up from behind, staying low to the ground in a duck stance. He witnessed his boy Snake put in work, and he was starving for that same satisfying feeling that murder brought.

Snake moved in slowly with caution, looking for any signs of life. He beckoned with his hand for Trife to check the passenger side and rear.

Without hesitating, Trife complied.

Flaco was just coming to. He shook his head repeatedly and dabbed the blood that trickled from his face wound as he slowly regained consciousness. Before he could really get a hold of himself, his fate was already decided.

The silhouette of Trife's scrawny frame caused Flaco to turn. The flash from the Mac-11 muzzle was the last thing he saw. The miniature Uzi pumped slugs into his face from point blank range, shattering the window, instantly altering the features of a handsome middle aged man to one big bloody hole.

———

"Police, Freeze! Drop the weapons where you stand or I swear to God, I'll blow ya muthafuckin' brains out!" DeJesus growled.

Detective DeJesus stood directly behind Snake, and his partner was crouched on one knee behind a telephone pole, aiming at Trife.

Both Snake and Trife were glued in their stance. The sudden appearance of the detectives had caught them off guard. Snake heard what DeJesus shouted, loud and clear. So clear, he estimated the detective to be no more than ten feet away, entirely too close to try anything stupid.

A whole minute dragged by and no one so much as blinked. A long silence settled between the two sides of justice. Only screaming sirens echoed from a distance. The four men exchanged deadly stares, begging for someone to bust a move.

"So what's it gonna be? We gon' handle this our way? Or we gonna shoot it out like the Wild Wild West? Y'all call it." Fisher asked from behind the telephone pole.

Slowly, Snake raised his hands. But he contemplated if he should drop the smoking AK that he still gripped.

Before he could get a grip on his thoughts, it got hectic.

In a desperate attempt to save her life, India broke from Trinity's hold and hopped out of the rattled town car.

Barefoot, she sprinted back toward the club. Off impulse, Trife swung his Uzi in her direction and pulled the trigger.

"Nooooo!" Fisher howled and worked his 9mm with skill.

The first slug chewed through Trife's neck, causing him to hurl forward. His face collided head on with the second hollow point bullet that silenced him forever. Brain fragments and other secretions poured through the mothball sized hole above Trife's brow. He was dead before he hit the ground.

"AHHHH!" Snake's pain bellowed from his loins. Seeing his closet friend slayed gave him nothing to live for. In one downward swing of his arm, the long barrel of his AK locked on Fisher. A slew of bullets tore into the thick telephone pole, missing Fisher completely as he stumbled backwards.

Chunks of wood flew in the air. The wooden pole had served its purpose, but nothing was there to save him from the two slugs that missed the pole and smashed into his chest and stomach as he stumbled. The powerful impact from the heavy metal threw the detective to the cold slab of concrete, causing him to squirm in pain.

DeJesus let off one round. Snake never saw it coming. The loud blast from DeJesus' cannon penetrated his ears and ended his misery. The.45 slug left a hole in Snake's face that no mortician could cover. The young thug died on the first day of the New Year.

DeJesus rushed over to his partner and kneeled by his side. Fisher's eyes were closed, his teeth clenched. DeJesus observed his partner's wounds. No blood was anywhere in sight, and it dawned on him that Fisher had worn his vest. A breath of relief eased his anxiety.

Fisher gasped for air and clutched his side. The vest had saved his life, but didn't prevent serious injury.

DeJesus moved to un-strap his partner from his vest, knowing that the lead from the AK was still burning. Fisher winced when DeJesus touched his ribs, making it obvious that they were indeed broken. The paramedics arrived right on time. DeJesus couldn't have been more thankful.

At the other end of the street, India lay sprawled out, unconscious. Her blood gushed from her wounds, seeping into the cracks in the street. Her sprint was fast, but the bullets from Trife's Uzi wouldn't be denied. A bullet ripped violently through her hamstring, as she was falling, three more slugs tore through her slender back.

Quron and Nuri had arrived on the scene moments after India dropped. The gunplay had grabbed their attention. From where they stood in front of the club, they could see a car clearly trapped between two other vehicles. Not once did they think it was India. It had only become apparent as they came closer, and it was too late then.

A sense of urgency settled in Quron's heart. His eyes became watery as he kneeled, scooped India into his arms and cradled her. He looked down the road and saw the paramedics, but none seem to be interested in saving the life of the woman he held in his arms.

"Somebody help us, we need paramedics down here NOW. A woman has been shot!" He yelled as panic started to settle in.

The whole situation felt like déjà vu, only this time, he was playing India's role and she was playing his. India had been the only person there to give him hope when he was shot. Now that the tables flipped, he hoped he could return the favor.

Trinity stood off on the side, wrapped in Nuri's arms. The sight of India stretched out on the ground pushed her over the edge; she couldn't compose herself any longer. She buried her head in Nuri's chest and sobbed loudly. The events of the night seem to rain down on her all at once. It was just too much.

"Oh God, they murdered my cousin. Nuri, they took Pedro, how's my family gonna deal with this?" Trinity's question was soul searing, and the thought of India being dead sent a chill through Nuri.

He didn't know who had taken Pedro, and at that moment, it wasn't important to him. India needed his support. He held Trinity's hand, joined the gathering of people that accumulated on the scene, and whispered a prayer on her behalf, hoping it would give her the strength needed to pull through.

Chapter 32

With the New Year came new problems. The hospital's waiting room was jam-packed. Cries of sorrow reminded the people where they were. Continuous chaos was the norm.

The overhead fluorescent lights throughout the lobby shined extremely bright. Or maybe that was Quron's mind telling him to blink, turn his head, or close his eyes. He was patiently waiting for someone to answer the many questions that ran through his mind. A part of him really wanted to know India's condition, while another part of him knew it was better to remain in the dark.

Daybreak had come and just as quickly gone. Midday had crept around and Quron still hadn't found the peace of mind or comfort to snooze. His racing thoughts played out scenario after scenario, keeping him wide-awake. He couldn't believe how things had gone from sugar to shit in such a short amount of time.

He stared at the couple across from him and sighed. Trinity had cried herself to sleep and Nuri, who was cuddled next to her, had drifted off to a better place as well. Looking at them just brought more headache. He thought back to what Trinity had told him earlier and began to massage his temples.

According to Trinity, Tito was so hasty to leave because he had received a call informing him that the FBI had arrested Pedro. While the world was counting down, welcoming the New Year, so was a special task force with Pedro Martinez as their grand prize.

Everyone that accompanied Pedro during his invitation only party at his new mansion in Long Island had been arrested. DEA Agents poured in from every part of the huge estate. Pedro happened to be in the bathroom getting the blowjob of a lifetime. When the reality finally registered, he made a break for a secret compartment he had built in his master bedroom's fireplace. It was too late though, an agent caught him with one leg in and the other out, literally. He then submitted with no hassle.

Although nothing other than a few thousand was confiscated, the attorney that made the call said Pedro was charged with 'CCE', operating a continually criminal enterprise in violation of 21 U.S.C848. A charge that carried a life sentence, if convicted.

All of this drama was surely enough to cause a nervous breakdown, but instead, Quron stayed focused and remained strong. He found strength where he always did,when all else seemed to fail, in prayer to Allah. No matter how far he strayed away from his Islamic principles, whenever he turned to Allah with sincerity, he was blessed with guidance.

The dilemma was overwhelming at times. He found that there was a big difference between knowing what was best and being disciplined enough to do what was best. Transition just isn't that easy. Anytime he asked himself if the end would justify his means, an answer never surfaced; he couldn't figure out why.

"Excuse me, sir." An African-American doctor addressed Quron, breaking his chain of thought. His white lab coat dangled from his skinny frame. He sort of favored a younger, but taller version of Bill Cosby. His deep voice grabbed Trinity and Nuri from their slumber

They both yawned, stretched, then squinted. Quron stood from his chair and stuffed his hands inside his pockets as he nervously awaited the news.

"Well son, I have both some good news and bad news. I feel it is best to start with the bad and work our way toward the good, if I may," the doctor shared then pushed up his glasses that slid down the bridge of his nose.

Quron nodded his approval and the doctor placed his hands behind his back.

"The bad news is, Ms. Martinez' wounds are serious, she lost a lot of blood. As a result, she slipped into a coma, and we honestly don't know if she'll pull through."

The doctor's words caused Trinity to go into a frenzy. Nuri pulled her closer and gave the other two men an 'I don't know what to do' look.

"Tsss," the doctor hissed while shaking his head. "I really don't like to be the giver of bad news—"

"It's alright doc, what's the good news?" Quron cut in.

"Well, the good news is Ms. Martinez is alive. Fortunately, even with her bullet wounds, we were able to save the baby."

Quron felt like the wind had been knocked out of him. He waited for the doctor to start laughing, but his firm features held, and jealousy surfaced in Quron's heart. He couldn't help but wonder whom India had shared such intimacy with. *And I fell for the innocent act.* Quron shook his head in disbelief.

"I assume from your expression and your loss for words, that you weren't aware of her pregnancy."

"Na-na-no, I wasn't." Quron stuttered.

"Hopefully things will work out for the better," Doc said sincerely. "But, if you'd like, you can see her for a few minutes."

"Thanks, but I'll pass." Quron wrinkled his face. "I'll visit another time. I need to clear my head." He walked away slowly, didn't even say goodbye. Never turned back or even glanced.

Trinity looked at Nuri, hoping for an explanation of some sort. Just a cold stare met her gaze. Through the sliding exit doors, Nuri watched his brother's back fade. Shit just got realer.

Chapter 33

The small motel room looked like it had been turned upside down. Cigar guts were scattered across the wooden dresser. A tilted bottle of Hennessy lay empty on its side. The rug underneath it was stained from the toxic fluid that once lived inside the bottle. Loose pieces of clothing were tossed everywhere. A shirt at the foot of the bed, pants over the lamp, a bra on the floor with a pair of boxers, socks, and a t-shirt next to them. It was wild, and to top it off, a tan emerald print thong dangled from the motionless ceiling fan.

The sun had reached its zenith in the partly cloudy sky. Its rays pierced through the cracked window blind, making thin lines of light across the two naked bodies that rested on the full size bed. The tossing and turning throughout their few hours of sleep had caused the bed spread to ease off most of their bodies.

The young lady that lay asleep next to Ghost was beautiful. Even while sleeping, she looked angelic. Her soft breasts pressed firmly against the springy mattress. Her long hair swerved in different directions, and half of her plump cheeks were exposed and chilled, judging by the layer of goose bumps that were visible.

The speck of sun that kissed Ghost's chiseled back made his brown skin shine like armor. Irritated by the slight feeling of heat on his face, he twitched as his senses gathered then suddenly his eyes fluttered open. He squinted, annoyed until his eyes adjusted and the sunrays highlighted his wifey's gorgeous features. A satisfied grin crept across his face and he thought about how upset he was when the cheap motel was the only place he could find a vacancy. But now, it was a thing of the past. As he continued to stare, it dawned on him that being with her for the first day of the year, regardless of where they were, was all that mattered.

Not wanting to disturb her peaceful slumber, Ghost pulled the cotton spread lightly and disappeared underneath. He crept in the darkness like a lion that anticipated the mistake of his prey. Her unique scent filled his nostrils and caused him to lick his lips greedily. The warmth from her sweet tunnel of love had him open. His tongue slithered like a snake between the split in her cheeks. The wetness awakened the sensitive nerves in the area.

"Shhh." She shivered but remained in a world of her own.

Ghost chuckled lightly then gently parted her legs. With her stomach against the mattress, her arms folded under her chin, and her legs spread gave him the perfect advantage.

The sight of her pretty vagina caused him to stiffen. He ignored his rock and lowered his face. His tongue moved upward like he was licking an ice cream cone. Her tight kitten started dripping with her sweet juices and the pleasing moans that rolled off her tongue confirmed her consciousness. She rose on her palms and knees, forcing more of herself into Ghost's mouth.

"Oh God, baby you feel so good. Eat my pussy, that's right, make me cum, uwww." she whined.

In one motion, Ghost's tongue slid from her pussy and made tiny circles around her butt hole. The sensation caused her insides to tingle. He eased two fingers inside of her and the deep strokes caressed her G-spot. Her hips rotated faster, determined to put out the fire that settled in her kitten.

Not yet a pro, but her skills had definitely improved from when he'd first hit it. Ghost was turning her out; he taught her what his more experienced partners had taught him. Her muscles gripped his tongue, let go, then gripped again. She grabbed two handfuls of the covers and buried her face in the fluffy pillows.

"Ye-ye-yeah boo, I'm cum... I'm..." Her breath shortened and her words muffled.

Her back arched and her soft skin rippled. The thick creamy fluid oozed from her hole and Ghost gladly savored her distinct flavor.

She collapsed and rolled onto her back. Barely able to muster up the energy to speak, she grabbed the nearest pillow and flung it with little force. "I hate you." She giggled humorously.

"Aw, I love you too." Ghost weaved the pillow and smiled.

"Look at this mess, ma. We partied like rock stars last night." He laughed.

"I know, right. I can't believe I drunk five cups of liquor."

"Wow, five cups." Ghost joked while sliding on his pants.

"Shut up punk, not everyone can consume as much as you."

Ghost let out a soft chuckle. "Listen to you, all proper'n shit, talkin' 'bout consume. White girl."

"Whateveeeer." She rolled her eyes while giggling.

Ghost picked up his diamond-link chain and flung it over his head.

"Where you going?" She questioned while watching him walk toward the door.

"Gotta go pay these people for extra time before they come harrassin' us."

"Okay, just hurry up."

"Aw, you gonna miss me?"

"Boy, go head." She blushed.

"Awwww, love you too."

Ghost moved quickly through the crack in the door, barely escaping the second pillow that she tossed.

Outside the room, his whip sat in the first parking space. Ghost shook his head while counting the loose change scattered in his palm. Thoughts of his girl always made him feel good inside. He often wondered what life would be like for them when they completed high school and when he retired from the game. His wifey had definitely become a major part of his inspiration. It got even deeper when he learned that things hadn't always been peaches and cream for her either. He vowed that her future would be more promising, he would personally see to it.

After grabbing two lemon iced teas from the soda machine along the walkway, he stopped at his car to scoop the hygiene products he'd purchased after leaving the club. The new smell from the interior caused him to inhale deeply. Something about its freshness, he'd always liked. He leaned over the armrest and picked up the paper bag from the floor in the passenger side.

The afternoon atmosphere around the motel had been calm and relatively quiet, so the humorous chuckles and lingering voices caught Ghost's ear. He thought nothing of it until he sat upright in the driver's seat. He instantly slumped low off impulse. Inching up in his seat, just enough to see over the dash, his heart dropped as he slumped back down. *I can't believe this SNAKE muthafucka.* He peeped over the dashboard to get another look and rage shot through him at the speed of light.

He slumped lower, checked under the seat, then patted his waist before remembering he had left his gun back in the hood. He dropped it off when thoughts of getting knocked on New Years crossed his mind. "Fuck."

He had to think fast and capitalize off the moment, because he knew that such an opportunity was unlikely to reoccur. Frustrated because time wasn't in his favor, Ghost leaned back across the armrest and clicked open the glove compartment.

"Come on, hurry up." He mumbled as it slowly opened.

Once the opening was wide enough for his hand to slide through, he reached in and snatched his phone from the glove compartment. He fumbled through the pics that he and the team had taken the night before. He prayed that his memory data wasn't full. Just his luck, he had space.

Ghost pulled his fitted low and hurried out of his whip. He walked steadily back toward his room, hoping he didn't blow his cover. He slowed his step then made a quick dip on the side of the soda machine. His head peeked around its edge like a skilled private investigator as he positioned himself to snap shot after shot until the phone froze. Satisfied, he crammed the phone in his pocket then walked into his room.

"Get dressed, we out." He stated dryly.

"Why? What happened? I thought you was getting more time." His girl stood at the door of the bathroom. She had just gotten out of the shower. A towel barely long enough enveloped her curves and a second towel wrapped her hair.

Ghost looked at her and felt no attraction at the time. "I was, but somethin' came up, so we out." He plopped down on the foot of the bed and gave her his back. He had done all the explaining he planned to do.

"Whatever, Mr. Attitude. I don't know who did what to you, but it wasn't me. Make me sick." She sucked her teeth and curled her upper lip. "I'll be ready in a minute." She gathered her clothes, stepped back in the bathroom and slammed the door.

Ghost just shook his head, unfazed by her words. His gaze settled on the pictures that he had just taken. His mind wandered; there were way more important things on his mind.

Most of the ride home was in silence. Ghost zoned out. He felt twisted inside, and his lady felt no pity; she was acting just as stubborn. She knew she hadn't done anything to deserve his bull-headed ways, so if he wanted to be all stank, then that was his problem and not hers.

It was during these times when she wondered just how much of himself was he holding back from her. Most of the time, he was the sweetest, most polite dude that she had ever met, and truthfully she couldn't imagine living life without him. But on the few instances when his whole demeanor changed, it literally seemed like she was dealing with a total stranger. She found it interesting, but at the same time, frightening.

It wasn't personal, just a rule. And this rule was golden to Ghost. The less a person knew, the better off he was. You couldn't tell what you didn't know. Ghost knew when shit hit the fan, the pressure that the law enforcers applied was way too much for most. He had heard of some of the most thorough gangsters folding under pressure. So to give his girl, an innocent civilian, the scoop on what was really good was a no brainer. He could never chance it.

That's why he kept her far away from his corrupt lifestyle. She had proven that she wasn't a dummy. She asked too many questions to be considered naive. To calm her growing curiosity of his mysterious lifestyle, Ghost told her he worked for his uncle and hustled a little marijuana on the side. She didn't dig the illegal aspect of his life, but it was hardly enough to deter her from their love.

Before Ghost dropped her off, he compromised so that they could reach level ground. She had an important event coming up. When he promised to attend, the lingering tension faded and their chemistry was back where it needed to be.

The sight of his boo walking up the steps in front of her house made him hot inside. Her jiggly ass looked so soft. He gripped his dick through his pants and licked his lips, glad all of that was his.

Hours passed, and he appreciated the only thought that brought a smile. Everything else was chaotic. Ghost had switched rides and found himself busting blocks with no particular destination in mind. He rode alone, enjoying the solitude. He received calls from his team throughout the day, which weren't too pleasant either. India was in a coma, Quron's connect got knocked, and the connect's two closest men were murdered.

"This can't be life." he said to himself while looking left then right before turning on to Liberty Street.

His gaze shifted to the passenger seat and there they were. A blue, white, and orange envelope with Kodak printed across the flap. When he turned in the photos through the Kodak app, he really hoped that the pictures had been lost, or at least contradict what he knew he'd seen. Unfortunately, that was merely a thought.

He fingered through the photos repeatedly and his stream of rage intensified. It wasn't supposed to be like this. Official fam' is what they rep' all day, every day. How the fuck did this happen? Quron had told him on many occasions that any type of success arouses envy. His claim was truer now than ever before.

The next track in the mix CD in rotation broke Ghost's deep thought. It suddenly dawned on him that he was sitting still, parked. He looked around with a dumbfounded expression as if he was lost. The scenery started to become familiar and he realized where he was. "Fuck it, I guess it's meant."

Ghost turned the key in the ignition and got out. He slid the envelope into his back pocket and hopped up the stairs. Three hard knocks later, the door flew open and Amil stood with the phone glued to her ear, running her mouth 100 mph.

"Hold on." she said into the receiver then pressed it against her shoulder to muffle any sound.

"Quron here, Amil?"

"Yeah, c'mon." Amil secured the front door and walked down the hallway where there was another door.

Ghost knew he didn't have any business watching Amil's ass sway, but her stretch pants didn't offer him much of a choice. She was a bad sister.

"He's down there." She smiled and opened the door to the basement. Her head rested against the door's edge and her right foot crossed over her left.

Ghost nodded then trampled down the carpet steps. He lowered his head, avoiding the dropped ceiling. A grin surfaced upon seeing his man.

Quron was stretched out on a flat bench, pressing 315 lbs like it was a hundred pounds. After about twelve reps, he racked the weight, hopped to his feet, and flexed in the wall to wall mirror. Sweat poured from his body as if it was the hottest day of the summer, enhancing the thick veins that ran across his swollen muscles.

Ghost's reflection caught Quron's eye through the mirror, causing him to turn around, wearing a warm smile. He grabbed his towel from the couch, picked up his squirt bottle and took two big swallows. After drying himself, he tossed the towel over his bulging shoulder and extended his fist.

"What up?"

"Ain't shit." Ghost simply responded.

Quron's gaze mingled with Ghost's stern eyes and he knew something was up. "Aw man, you got that look in ya eyes, what's wrong? Holla at me."

Ghost let out a deep sigh then took the envelope out of his pocket. There was no need to prolong the situation. He handed Quron the pictures, then sat on the table. An explanation wasn't necessary. The flicks Quron held would tell their own story.

Quron flipped through the photos one at a time. It felt good seeing his team shine; it reminded him of old times. Toward the end of the stack, he paused, squinted, and then brought the photo up to his face. He stared in disbelief for what seem like forever before uttering a word. He cleared his throat and sat down on the couch.

"I can't believe this faggot, snake ass nigga. After all I did for this nigga. After all we been through!" He roared then looked up for the first time. "Where'd you get these?"

"Shit crazy O.T., it seems like the powers that be wanted to bring what was in the dark to light, 'cause the way it went down threw me for a loop," Ghost admitted. "But chu know I gotta keep it tall, so this how it went down. Last night..."

Ghost relived the chain of events that led up to him coming there.

Quron's gaze shifted back to the pictures he held. No one could deny the facts. Right before his eyes, he witnessed the woman who had earned his heart betray their love with his best friend. The deep, dark secret that his very own beloved mother died with on her heart was no longer a mystery. The truth was undeniable. The fire in his eyes reflected the sudden hate in his heart. As he continued to stare, it all started to make sense. It was no longer a mystery how Bri learned about India, who she often referred to as 'ya otha bitch' whenever they argued. Bri's real reason for getting an abortion was perfectly clear too.

A forced cackle came out of nowhere. Ghost looked at his man and immediately knew it came from pain.

"You know what, homie, when me an Amil left that gatherin' y'all put together for me, she told me she had seen Young-One and Bri makin' out at a stoplight when she first came to town. I let it go over my head, 'cause I thought it was her liquor talkin'. Turns out she was right." He held a picture up to the light and hissed. "I still can't believe this nigga, Ghost. You really don't know the half, lil bro. It's funny though. Although I'm not on my deen how I'm sposed to be, I always try to put things in their proper perspective by reflectin' on Allah's words of wisdom. He said, before he destroyed any nation, he would send signs and warnings to the people first. Now that I think about it, the signs were always there. I just didn't wanna see it for what it is 'cause that was my brother, we been thru so much shit together. From the cradle, now look." He giggled, hoping it would suppress the tears of anger forming in his eyes. "It's all good though, Ghost it's—"

"Fuck that! Ain't shit all good! That niggas a fuckin' snake and I'ma pop his top!" Ghost shouted with venom as he stood.

"Be easy," Quron made a gesture with his hand, trying to calm him down. "This is personal my dude, trust me. Son is finished."

Ghost saw the pain that over saturated Quron's soul. Words couldn't quench Ghost's thirst for Young-One's blood. He had heard everything Quron said, and he agreed; it was definitely personal. His mind was already made up. No question about it, if he found Young-One first, he would burn him.

He walked to the back door, looked back one last time then left.

Quron stood in the middle of his personal gym quietly, with his focus locked on the pictures that had changed his life within seconds. Two people who he would have died for had crossed him. His heart sagged from the venom of their immoral deeds, and two tears rolled down his face, splashing onto the pictures.

No form of betrayal shall be forgiven. The thought revolved continuously in his mind. He threw on his shirt, reached under the couch, grabbed his 50Cal and stormed out the back door.

Chapter 34

The brisk weather slid off the new Jeep Grand Cherokee that Fee-Fee navigated through traffic. The jeep was cute, a champagne color with leather interior and a light tint. Perfect for a person that never had much, who had practically lived in poverty for most of their life. Her good sex was finally starting to pay off. She loved the feeling of having money in her pocket on a daily basis; it was something she could grow accustomed to. Chasing behind the neighborhood hustlers to see if they needed their hair braided for the weekend was a long, drawn out process; a process that she could not wait to do away with.

Fee always found herself in compromising positions when dealing with niggas in the hood. It wasn't a secret that her financial stability was twisted and she needed money to provide for her kids. They often played on her vulnerable situation, offering alternatives that always included sexual favors. She was thicker than a snicker with a gold mine between her legs, and everybody wanted a piece. With little choice, she often gave in to their sexual advances. The degrading acts had long-term effects though. Her self-esteem gradually chipped away, leaving her convinced that she wasn't shit and would never be shit. It was obvious that she had never heard the profound words of Patti Labelle, *You aren't what they call you, you are what you answer to.* The bitches and whores that they called her are exactly what she answered to.

Lately, since her new prince charming had come along, things were different. She had been introduced to a whole new lifestyle and she was living it up. But a full 360 doesn't happen overnight. The residue of her past still lingered in her system. She was still a fiend for that ecstatic feeling that only good dick could give her, something Young-One seemed a pro at delivering. She couldn't get enough of that dude.

Young-One himself was surprised at how much he enjoyed her company. The memories that they now created had him wishing he hadn't brushed her off for all those years. Fee-Fee was cool as a fan. It didn't hurt that her pussy was the bomb. Being the neighborhood hoe had its benefits. Her veteran experience placed her in a category by herself. The tricks that she performed in the bedroom, public areas, or wherever she seized the opportunity to get off, had Young-One open like a window. He totally understood why Scar had put her under his wing. She was a good investment, one he himself would have made if his heart wasn't already wrapped up in Bri.

In the back seat, sunk down in the soft interior, Young-One leaned sluggishly against the door with his head pressed against the window. He was on cloud nine, higher than a kite. As soon as he returned from spending his New Year with Bri, Fee-Fee hit him on the hip and shared her plan for the day. Before he knew it, they were on the Taconic heading back to the boroughs.

Fee, had brought along one of her friends. The girl looked familiar, but Young-One couldn't place her until they started conversing. Come to find out, he knew shorty rather well. Chocolate and he used to kick it frequently at the strip club. She just looked a lot different outside of the club where there was light and clothing on her body.

The two women were a handful. They had Young-One going all day. From joking, talking shit, to flirting, it was all entertainment. It seemed like the more haze they smoked, the hornier they became.

Young-One couldn't front though; Fee-Fee fucked his head up when she threw a threesome in the air. She had said what he only had the courage to think. He had fantasized about having both women at once all day. Therefore, to hear Fee-Fee say that, made him a believer in the power of the mind.

"I can't wait to get it in wit' these freaks." Young-One mumbled as he eyed Fee-Fee through the rearview mirror then massaged his penis.

It wasn't long before Fee-Fee beat traffic and rolled to a stop in front of a house on Third Street. Young-One's thirsty ass was the first to hop out, stretch, then grab a handful of shopping bags from the rear of the jeep. He couldn't wait to get it popping. A stripper and a certified freak was a hell of a combination.

The streetlights flickered on and a sudden breeze sent a chill up Young-One's spine. He froze in his stance and looked around. Across the street from where he stood was a community park with a lot of trees, rocky terrain, a pond, and what the hood had called the white house due to the building's pillars. The darkness of night that slowly descended made the park seem spooky. Personally, Young-One wasn't feeling the area. The park didn't sit well with him for reasons he didn't quite know. It was just one of those things that he felt.

Fee, entered the newly renovated building, walked up the stairs and stood in front of the only door on the second floor. Chocolate stood behind Young-One, patiently waiting while Fee-Fee fumbled with the keys. The first two that she tried didn't budge the door.

Growing impatient, and with Remy feeding her raging hormones, Chocolate allowed her soft hands to roam freely up Young-One's back. She stepped closer to him and began to give his shoulders a massage. Her touch helped him relax.

Before Young-One knew it, he had one of his hands on Fee-Fee's wide hips, grinding on her fat ass, and kissing on her scented neck. The fragrance that she wore aroused him more. Fee, snickered then giggled from the tingling sensation that Young- One's lips sent through her body.

The door finally opened and the trio stumbled into the lavish apartment. Outside, the sky was gray, almost dark, but held on to just enough light. From what Young-One could see, the apartment was laced. Nice furniture, pictures of Mother Nature on the walls, and an entertainment center filled with glass sculptures varying in design. *This bitch's pad is laced, she's impressin' me more 'n more every day.*

Fee kept it moving through the cozy set up without flicking on a light switch or stopping to inspect the apartment. Young-One's kisses seemed to have set up a block in her brain, because riding his dick was the only thing on her mind.

They reached the bedroom and Chocolate adjusted the dimmer knob for the light while Young-One and Fee shared a moment of affection. She sucked on his thick tongue, tugging on it like she had done his dick on many occasions. That alone drove him crazy.

Chocolate undressed, piece by piece, and stretched out on the soft queen sized bed. She bent her knees and spread her legs wide. With one hand, she cupped her breasts, and licked her hard nipples teasingly. Her gaze locked on Young-One as she continued to perform. With her other hand, she singled out her index and middle fingers, then inserted them deep in her swollen pussy. She slowly grinded on them like they were Young-One's dick. Soft moans revealed the divine sensation she had succumbed to.

Quickly approaching her climax, she raised her small foot and placed her toes in Young-One's mouth. His tongue slithered between and over each of them while Fee-Fee kneeled at the foot of the bed, released his erect penis from his boxers, and coated the head with warm saliva.

She eased down his shaft, relaxed the muscles in her throat, and allowed his dick head to tickle her tonsils. His eyes rolled to the back of his head, his mouth opened wider, and his legs weakened.

Chocolate fucked herself faster and faster until her toes curled inside of Young-One's mouth. "Ahhh!" While she was cumming, so was he.

Fee-Fee bobbed her head up then down his dick in perfect rhythm. His body tensed, jerked, and a stream of nut followed. Fee dug her nails into his ass cheeks, held him steady and swallowed every drop of his semen.

He braced himself on Fee's shoulders while she continued to blow his dick. Going limp wasn't an option, so she did her until Young-One's dick showed life.

Fee rose to her feet, smiled, then went to assume the position that she knew he loved. She climbed on the edge of the bed and lifted her soft bottom in the air. Her tight butthole sat on top of her meaty lips, clean-shaven and inviting. Her pink interior glistening with juices.

Young-One licked his lips, gripped her hips and slid in from the back. "You want this dick, huh, you want it?" He amped himself as he dug deeper, each stroke strengthening his erection.

Fee just looked back at him and moaned her approval as her head bounced from Young-One's hard thrusts.

Not missing out on the fun, Chocolate positioned herself under Fee's face and draped her legs over Fee-Fee's shoulders. Fee licked, kissed, and sucked Chocolate's clit.

Seeing Fee taste Chocolate only turned Young-One on more. He squeezed Fee's cheeks harder and dug deeper. His aggression introduced Fee to another level of pleasure. Her fat ass rotated in circles, forcing Young-One deeper every time she threw it back. Her pussy muscles contracted forcefully. She quivered and an explosive orgasm clutched her insides.

After creaming all over Young-One's dick, she slowed her groove. He slid out of her womb and joined them both on the bed. Young-One was breathing hard, but refused to let his dream end like this.

He faced Chocolate, who was still on her back,and placed wet kisses on her breast. She moaned louder from the double pleasure. Just when she about to cum, Fee-Fee eased her vicious tongue off Chocolate's clit and pushed Young-One playfully as if she was jealous for not being a part of him and

Chocolate's mix. Chocolate let out a humorous chuckle and Young-One smiled then stroked his own ego.

"Damn, can't we all just get along? It's enough dick for both of you." He rolled on his back and Fee-Fee crawled up the satin sheets, purring seductively.

"So what it's enough dick for both of us, I can't get selfish with mine?" She moved up his chest, making eye contact. Her dripping wetness brushed against his pulsating rod but didn't settle there.

Young-One didn't bother answering her question. She had claimed her territory and he was loving every second of it. He turned his head and looked at the beautiful women through the mirrors that hung from the sliding closet door. The fantasy come true only confirmed what he'd already known. He was the man.

Turned on by her friend's moans, Chocolate wanted in. She eyed Young-One's piece lustfully, turned around, gripped his ankles to balance herself and eased down on his dick reverse cowgirl style. From her duck stance, she commenced her forward and back motion, riding the hell out of Young-One. Her ass jiggled in his hand every time she bounced against his pelvis. She could tell by the swelling of Young-One's penis that he was about to explode. She worked her muscles and threw it more as she too rode the same wave to an indescribable feeling.

"Yes Young, eat it, please don't stop lickin' it, suck my clit, yes babe!" Fee-Fee's expression showed she was sedated. She had stuck to the script and felt proud of herself.

Scar had listened attentively for the past hour, awaiting the agreed upon code. It had finally come, and he eased out from the closet where he had been hiding. His whole demeanor said 'strictly business'. And his attire testified to that. He wore black jeans, black Timbs, a black hoody, with black leather gloves, and a black Mac-11 gripped tight. The death of his cousin Snake, and Snake's partner, Trife, along with him being robbed and all the other shit had Scar vexed.

How was he taking all the losses? He just couldn't understand that. But one thing for sure, the games were over and he was playing for keeps.

He couldn't believe his luck when his newest hoe, Fee-Fee, put him on to game. She ran down Young-One's whole plan to rock him to sleep through her. The shit was unreal to Scar, 'cause he knew shorty grew up with them niggas, but none of that seem to matter. She had a real sour taste in her mouth when it came to Young-One.

Not really wanting to lean on her information alone, in case Fee was trying some underhanded shit, Scar tested her loyalty to him. "Would you do anything fo' me?" he had asked her. When Fee replied, "Anything," Scar damn near laughed in her face at what he thought was a lie. He pushed to see just how far he could go, included her in his plan, and expected her not to follow through, so he could have a reason to end her during the process. To his surprise, now a week later, he watched his jump-off carry out a loyal duty as if she was his wife. Fee-Fee had proven she was his ride-or-die bitch, earning her a special place in Scar's heart.

Chocolate was seconds away from the blissful place that she wanted to be.

Scar didn't ruin the moment. He stood off on an angle and really thought about the power of a woman who combined her brain with her clit. The end result could be deadly.

"Ahh... ahh... uw!" Chocolate's hair dangled in her face as she lost control, practically jumping up and down on Young-One's swollen dick. He released hard. The thick nut that shot up in Chocolate's pussy felt so good and the sweet cream that flow from Fee-Fee's womb tasted like fruit.

The trio climaxed simultaneously, the experience nothing less than heavenly. Their banging escapade left Chocolate crumpled on her knees, Fee-Fee sitting on Young-One's chest, and Young-One with his fist balled, covering his eyes, desperately trying to catch his breath.

"Wuwee, y'all fucked da shit out a nigga." It took a minute, but his breathing resumed its regular pace. A satisfied grin spread across his lips and he opened his eyes.

Seeing Scar standing over him with the Mac, damn near caused his heart to stop. He shoved Fee-Fee hard and jumped up, but the flush hook that Scar caught him with put Young-One back to the mattress.

"Stay the fuck down, faggot!" Scar growled through clenched teeth and raised his gun. "You thought you could send one'a mine at me wit' out me fmdin' out? Nigga you crazy? See this?" Scar smacked Fee's ass hard. "Dat's all me, I own that jus' like da rest of this city, muthafucka."

Young-One lay on his back in a fucked up position. Blood dyed his teeth and trickled from the wide gash above his right eye. An unbearable pain pumped like a pulse in his wound, but nothin' at that moment could compare to the hurt feeling that tugged at his heart from Fee-Fee's betrayal.

His gaze settled on his childhood friend as she hurried to get dressed. Their eyes mingled and the explanation that he so badly sought wasn't there. Only darkness accompanied, with no regret reflected through the windows of her soul.

Young-One's subconscious took over, and flash clips of he and Fee-Fee interacting throughout their upbringing. The school times, the teen parties, the skating ring, the stand ups, then the reel sped up and Fee-Fee's words that she spoken months ago were clear like she was speaking them at that very moment. *Mark my words, I'ma catch you slippin'.* She held true to her word.

Scar grabbed Young-One's pants and rumbled through the pockets until he found his phone. He then scrolled through the memory and pressed send on Quron's name. As the call processed, Scar tossed the phone to Young-One.

Young-One snapped out of his trance, looked at the screen then put the phone to his ear. His dick went limp and shriveled. Dry cum stuck to his pubic hairs and a musky smell lingered under his nose from Fee-Fee's juices.

The phone rang, rang, and rang, but no one answered. While patiently waiting, Scar unscrewed the silencer from the stubby barrel.

———————

Quron stared at his phone as Young-One's name flashed across his screen. He sat alone in Amil's whip under a huge tree next to a graveyard on Southside. His.50cal rested on his lap with the clip ejected.

For over an hour, he had been sitting under the tall tree unloading and reloading the bullets in his clip. With nothing but idle time on his hands, he seemed to have become one with his thoughts and the foul play that haunted him. He had reached a state of no return.

Just when the phone was about to stop ringing, Quron pressed the button. "Hello."

———————

"Yo Ron!... Ahhhhhhh!"

Scar snatched the phone back and put it to his ear. If facial expressions could kill, Young-One and Quron would've been dead. He made sure that his message was perfectly clear.

Young-One grabbed his leg and wiggled back and forth like a pig swimming in mud. The burning sensation was indescribable. Blood gush from the quarter size hole. Young-One looked down at his wound and fainted.

"Listen nigga, I'm not playin'. You got an hour to bring $500,000 to da abandoned buildin' on da corner of Renwick an' Liberty. Y'all niggas robbed me, an' I want mine. Come alone an' don't be a second late. Play games an' you won't eva see this nigga again!"

The line went dead. Quron took the phone away from his ear and looked at it in disbelief. The loud bang from Scar's cannon was deafening. His ears still rang, but Young-One's agonizing scream made Scar's message crystal clear.

Life had a strange way of playing out. Karma had already come back around. The same nigga Young-One crossed was the same friend that his life now depended on. Being a foul-ass dude just doesn't pay.

Quron wiped down the thumb-sized bullets, reloaded the clip, and jammed it back in his Desert. He glanced down at his phone again. A smirk surfaced before he sped off.

Chapter 35

Cedar Hill was a wide, spacious graveyard. For miles around, wherever you looked, there were rows and rows of tombstones. For many beings, the graveyard was a spooky place. A place that compelled people to reflect on cherished memories that had been created with a loved one, and a harsh reminder of their demise.

Kiyah's story was different. Her parents had become a part of the gated community a long time ago when she was just a little girl. Ever since then, it had been a ritual for she and her sibling, Tay, to visit on a regular basis. But as they grew into young adults, Tay's lifestyle consumed most of her time and the trips to her parents' home had become less frequent.

Kiyah, on the other hand, never missed a beat. Her parent's home had been her safe haven for years. Her folks always listened whenever Kiyah needed to vent, and she always felt a lot better after she'd done so.

"Wow," Kiyah inhaled the fresh, cool air and looked around admiringly. "This is one of my most favorite places in the whole world." She smiled gently.

"How would you know when I haven't showed you the whole world... yet?" Lamar chuckled lightly and Kiyah just held her smile. Not even the cool night chill would ruin her moment.

She had been notified that she would be graduating six months earlier than her class. She was elated. So many years of struggle almost put her in a state of despair. Kiyah had been through so many traumas mentally and emotionally at such a young age, her life seemed like it was a script written to break her. But now, the pieces of her life had finally started coming together.

She and Lamar kneeled in front of two tombstones that were next to each other. Excessive dirt, withered leaves, and a few dead flowers made it difficult to decipher the names of the deceased. Kiyah dug in her pocket, retrieved a glove, and dusted off the loose particles until their names were legible. She then moved from her kneeling position and sat Indian style in the cold, hard earth. While awaiting Tay's arrival, she and Lamar talked about some of the unresolved issues in their lives. The content of their talk unleashed a bunch of bottled up pain that Lamar didn't even know he had.

"You alright, babe?" Kiyah snuggled next to her man and rubbed his back. She then kissed his cheek and nudged his side, letting him know she was still waiting.

He let out a deep sigh. "Yeah Ki, I'm ah-ight."

Silence settled between the two as they stared into the darkness. Lamar couldn't remember the last time he'd made a trip to his father's grave. The overwhelming pain he felt wouldn't allow him to do so. He couldn't stomach it. It was a situation he just wasn't ready to face.

Rattling from withered leaves scattered across the ground, whistled with the gusty wind. The skimpy jacket Lamar wore didn't provide much warmth, but he dealt with it. There was nothing like the down time he shared with wifey. The couple was so caught up in their own thoughts that neither of them heard Tay creep up from behind.

Tay smiled from a distance. "Look at my baby girl." She smirked and shook her head. It was odd, but she was happy Kiyah had been afforded the beauty of a relationship. She too remembered those days. Poor Trey.

Tay's rubber sole scraped against the concrete a few feet behind the couple as she crossed the street.

Kiyah turned around and immediately hopped to her feet.

"Hey beautiful." Kiyah smiled while walking toward her sister. "Finally," she was overjoyed. "I want you to meet the man that I've told you soooo much about. Tay, this is Lamar, Lamar this is my sis—"

Lamar stood from his seated position and turned to face his future in law. When their eyes met, the welcoming smile melted from Lamar's lips and Tay's curious expression hardened like concrete.

Lamar stumbled backwards, and Tay yanked Kiyah out of harm's way as she reached for her pistol.

Kiyah never finished her sentence. She fell to the ground, confused, scared, wondering where the fuck did things go wrong. It didn't hit her that this beef had nothing to do with her. Their drama was inherited long before. Streams of tears rolled from her eyes as she stood between the two people that she loved more than anything.

"Kiyah, what the fuck is he doin' here? This nigga's the fuckin' enemy! He don't give a shit about you!" Spittle flew out of Tay's mouth.

"Yes he does, Tay!" Kiyah countered in Lamar's defense. "Why are you trippin'?"

"'Cause you're fallin' head over hills for this punk ass nigga an' he couldn't care less about you!" Every claim Tay made hit Lamar hard. It was obvious she had no clue how real his love was for Kiyah. His heart thumped hard inside his chest as he eyed this bitch.

"Tell 'er Ghost, or should I say, Lamar?" Tay shouted sarcastically. "Tell 'er the truth, nigga! Tell my sista you run wit' the same niggas that tried to burn 'er to death! Tell 'er, you fuckin' scumbag!" The rage mixed with tortuous memories of finding her baby girl left for dead in the blazing fire brought tears.

"I don't know what the fuck you talkin' 'bout! I wouldn't ever let nothin' happen to Ki." Ghost retorted sincerely. He really had no idea. When Nuri, Young-One, and Steel hit

Scar's spot, they didn't seek his permission first. Quron gave the green light and they moved.

His twin.45s held Tay in a bind, but she wasn't the only one in a fucked up position. Her 9mm sized him up as well. Kiyah was the only reason neither had started blazing. Both of them knew of the love she harbored, so slaying each other right there in front of her would affect her forever. Hurting Kiyah was the last thing they wanted to do.

"Bullshit nigga, you try'na tell me when Nuri hit my spot and left Ki for dead, you ain't know 'bout it?" Tay's face balled into a knot.

Kiyah clasped her hands over her mouth and nose while shaking her head in disbelief.

Loud thunder pierced the tense air, and drops of rain fell freely from the sky. "Tell Tay she's lyin' Lamar... tell 'er she's lyin'!" Kiyah cried out. Ghost shook his head no, but Tay didn't allow him to sneak in a single word.

"Ki, you know I wouldn't lie to you. This nigga ain't right! The same crew he run with is the same dudes that tried to murder you. To make shit worse, there's no way he can really love you, 'cause not only did they violate you, they the same muthafuckas that murdered..."

Tay's words drifted off in the rain.

Ghost's body noticeably stiffened as Tay's words chipped away all the love and respect that had accumulated for certain individuals in his heart. It felt like his soul had been snatched from his body and thrown off a steep mountain ledge. All rational thinking had subsided.

He held the twin semi-automatics in silence, almost as if he had left the premises. As he snapped from his daze, Ghost spun around and ran away from the first woman he had ever found love with. Away from the heartbreaking words that could be the truth he'd searched for over the years. He felt played, madder than a mofo, and for his own sanity, he just needed to know.

Don't be naive, the evidence is clear nigga! You could think I'm gamin' you, but the facts prove I ain't. Numbers don't lie. Add nigga! The years don't lie!

Tay's words repeated like a broken record in his head. Ghost clicked open the locked SUV, hopped in and glared in the distance one last time. Kiyah's extended hand could still be seen. He flipped open his trap phone and sped off.

Don't be naive, the years don't lie...

Chapter 36

Quron stood in the dark shadows of an alleyway across the street from the abandoned building he was told to meet Scar at. The rain had grown heavier, dropping faster. Quron was dressed like a bum. His raggedy workout jeans were torn at the left pocket and knee. He wore a long sleeve polo shirt, Gore-Tex boots, a black water-proof Gore-Tex fatigue coat and his fully loaded 50 cal strapped to his hip. Every few minutes, he raised his wrist to eye level and checked the time.

Bri was supposed to have her scandalous ass there five minutes ago. But five minutes had come and gone, and still no signs of her. Quron started to fear he would have to resort to plan B, which wasn't as elaborate. His gaze lowered down to the two gray brief cases that sat at his feet, then back to his watch. *Where the fuck is this broad?* His patience was wearing thin. He glared off in the distance, squinted, then smiled. Bri's Acura was stalled at the corner traffic light. *Sweet.* He rubbed his hands together.

When Quron had called her earlier, she was busy folding clothes, and by the tone of her voice, she was not up for conversation. That is, until she recognized his voice. Before she could get in a word, the joyful feeling that consumed her initially dwindled, replaced with concern and fear. Quron filled her in and stressed how badly he needed her help to get Young-One back. She was hesitant. The sudden silence that settled on the phone told him so, but the desperation in his voice didn't give her many options.

Bri's guilt had surely worked in his favor. She knew her abortion stunt had put her in Quron's dog house, and refusing to assist him with saving someone she knew he loved, would definitely take away any chance of rectifying their relationship. That was something she realized she wanted more than anything. Bri finally agreed to help, as Quron knew she would, and it was on.

As Bri cruised down Liberty Street, a few pedestrians loitered on the strip, but other than that, the street was dead. The raindrops that continued to fall, kept the Acura's windshield wipers swinging back and forth in a wave. *This nigga know damn well it's rainin' cats n dogs out here, an' he got the nerve to have me lookin' for him. Unbelievable.*

She slowed to about five miles per hour and concentrated on anybody with Quron's stocky build. The sky ignited with streaks of lightning, scaring Bri half to death as she slammed down hard on the brakes upon seeing Quron appear out of thin air. She pressed the electrical switch, the window rolled down, and he dropped the two briefcases on the passenger seat.

"Hey ba—" Bri started, but cut her words short when she found herself staring at Quron's back. *Well hi to you too, thanks for makin' me feel like you miss me, damn.*

That was the first time Quron had seen Bri since he had become hip to her betrayal. It took every ounce of discipline in his body to refrain from snatching her through the window and stomping her to a pulp.

If she would've sold her pussy or played herself outside of his hood, it wouldn't have been as bad. But that wasn't the case. His boo, childhood friend, wifey, future baby mother and rider, had not only snaked him in the same hood they had all grown up in, but she did it with a man who was the equivalent of a brother. It gets no worse.

Quron fell back in the shadows the alleyway and watched from a distance. Bri looked around nervously as she climbed the two short flights of stairs in front of the building. Her hoody stopped at her waist and the wet gray sweats she wore did very little to cover her curves.

From across the street, Quron could see her soft, dimpled ass that he thought belonged to him, jiggle with each step she took. *Life is crazy. Still can't believe these muthafuckas, and she got the nerve to act like ain't nothin' happen.*

Flashes of Young-One gutting Bri doggy style was driving him crazy and messing up his focus. The whole ordeal was really messing with his head. No matter how he looked at it, he was reminded of his unconditional love for shorty, and it was eating him alive.

―――――――――

Bri ducked low and slid under the chained door into the darkness of the huge building. The inside was commodious. She didn't know what the factory like structure had been used for back in the day. As far back as she could remember, it had always been an eye sore in the community.

"I don't know 'bout this..." Bri mumbled to herself as she looked around. Thick pieces of plywood sealed most of the windows. The few pieces that had rotted, weakened, and torn off, allowed spurts of light to come in from the outside lamppost. A death related breeze brushed against her cheek, so cold, so noticeable. She shivered and contemplated her decision to help. Each step she took was with more caution.

"Helloooo, anybody herrrre?" Bri's voice echoed.

Mold and mildew scents filled her lungs. Slow, drawn out drops of rain fell from cracks in the ceiling. No other forms of human life seemed to exist. Before Bri realized it, she was a few paces deeper than she wanted to be. She turned around, and the light that slithered through the entrance faded a bit. She turned back around and the hard barrel of Scar's Mac pressed firmly against her temple.

"Shhh, you as much as breathe, an' I'ma blow ya fuckin' brains out."Scar's threat sent chills through her body. Quron hadn't mentioned this part of the plan. She started to sob, and Scar shoved her forcefully. She stumbled then fell to her hands and knees.

"Please don't kill me! I ain't got nothin' to do with this." Bri's self-preservation instincts kicked in as she pleaded for her life. She lifted her gaze, and tears instantly welled up in her eyes then streamed down her cheeks. Right before her, Young-One sat slumped in a wooden chair with no shirt. A pair of wet boxers, and socks were the only clothing on his body. A bloody t-shirt wrapped around his thigh, and dry blood covered his swollen face. He shivered uncontrollably from the winter chill, and life as he knew it was slipping further and further away.

Scar grabbed the handle to one of the briefcases and slammed it on the three legged table he stumbled across.

Bri couldn't get over Young-One's mangled features. The man she had grown to love, who had loved her, and who was always supportive, sat at the gates of death, and there wasn't a thing she could do about it. Her heart cringed in pain as she wondered what type of monster was the man who would decide her fate.

Scar popped both clamps on the briefcase. A smile quickly surfaced at the sight of crisp one hundred dollar bills lying neatly in layers. He picked one of the wrapped stacks up and took a closer look at the content.

"Ahhh!" He growled, then he flipped the table over.

"He still think I'ma fucking game!"

Bri screeched from the pain that shot through her ribs. Scar had kicked her so hard her body lifted off the floor.

"I knew you was a bitch nigga, you like to beat on women, huh!"

Surprised, Scar spun in the direction of the voice. Nuri appeared, walking toward him with his AK locked and loaded, daring him to make a move.

"You's a bitch. Fuck you think you talkin' to?" Scar shot back, unfazed by Nuri's advantage.

"So make my day, nigga, an' we'll see who's who." Nuri wanted to open up in his ass, but Bri would have definitely been hit too, so he couldn't risk it just yet.

"Tuff guy, make our day." Quron said in a sarcastic slur while walking through the shadows of the back entrance. He was mad as hell because he had no intention of showing his face at all. When his brother, Nuri, suddenly rushed into his set up, he had no choice but to come and hold his bro down. Shit had spiraled out of control, just that quickly.

"Nuri, what are you doin'?" Quron moved closer.

Scar's survival instincts turned on and he awaited an opportunity to make moves. He started to grab Bri and bait his way out, but Quron and Nuri were too close. They had his back against the wall, and judging by the size of their cannons, getting hit with one of their slugs wasn't an option.

"Whatchu talkin' 'bout? Bri hit me up and put me on to everything." Nuri's face wrinkled, obviously confused by his brother's question.

"Everything... I bet. Fuck both of them snakes." Spittle fell from Quron's lips. "Since she told you everything, I know she couldn't have left out how she fuckin' our so-called man, our so-called brotha, Young-One!"

Quron's words threw Nuri for a loop.

"You buggin." Nuri knew it wasn't a wise move, but he had to make eye contact, so he turned his head. "You fo'got, we family... loyal family 'til death do us part."

Scar absorbed the word exchange and was blown away by the facts revealed. At that very moment, Quron's whole plot became crystal clear. He had stuffed the briefcase with neatly folded newspaper underneath the real money on purpose. He wanted Scar to find the insufficient funds and murder both Bri and Young-One out of rage, putting an end to his internal strife without spilling their blood himself.

Scar held his game face, but he had to admit that Quron had calculated his emotional response to a tee, and he'd underestimated him. Thanks to his brother, though, it was a new ball game and it was time to play.

"Nuri, I thought the same thang! I thought we was loyal fam til da end!"

"Fuck, I did too... loyal fam, my ass." Ghost shouted then giggled sickly as he slid into the mix, holding his twin.45s cocked and erect. The spurts of light that crossed his face stressed his possessed look.

"Fuck goin' on Ghost, you switchin' sides?" Nuri asked, not believing his lil man had his cannon pointed in his direction.

"Y'all know what's goin' on... y'all been knew. Don't play fuckin' dumb now." Tay added fuel to the fire.

As soon as she left the graveyard, the text message Scar left provided what she needed to know. It had taken some time, but she found the same back entrance that Quron located. Her sudden appearance caught everybody except Scar off guard. She was dressed for the occasion, all black blending perfectly with the overlapping darkness. Two straps crisscrossed over her neck, keeping the twin Mac-12s tucked close by her sides.

"O.T., you played da fuck outta me. Fuck you thought I wasn't gon' eva find out!"

"Find out what?" Quron demanded to know.

"You know what, nigga!" Ghost retorted vulgarly. "Y'all da reason why my life is fucked up! Da reason my moms is fucked up! Da reason why my childhood was fucked up! And y'all da reason why my brothers an' sisters don't know they pops! Lamar fuckin' Strings, Darryl Strings, put it together, nigga!"

Quron and Nuri listened attentively and immediately made sense out of why Ghost was bugging out. Quron wanted to kick himself for overlooking the obvious. He knew from the minute he met Ghost, that the young thug had a striking resemblance to someone he knew. But Darryl Strings, also known as Casper, never crossed his mind. Maybe that was because he had spent the last ten years trying to forget him. Casper haunted him then, and here he was again, a younger version.

Ghost tried to speak, but got choked up on his words. He took a breath then spat it out. "Y'all murdered ma pops... y'all bodied ma fuckin' po—"

The sudden confusion gave Scar the split second that he craved. He peered over at Tay, then made a quick dash behind a nearby wall. His movement caused everyone to react, and the whole building lit up like the fourth of July.

Nuri squeezed the trigger and the heavy metal kicked. Rapid fire leapt from its barrel. A slew of bullets ripped through the rotted material in a desperate attempt to find Scar's flesh.

Tay retaliated with her twin Uzis like a true assassin. But the deafening bark from Quron's 50 cal sent vibrations through her small frame. A loose board on the floor broke her back pedal and saved her life. As soon as she hit the ground, chunks of brick exploded from the wall behind her, in the same place she would have been standing. The thumb-sized slugs devoured the solid compound with no problem. She covered her face from the fallen debris, and scrambled quickly behind a rusted refrigerator.

Quron was breathing hard. His chest rose and fell in short intervals. His back was pressed flush against a thick, wooden pillar. He ejected his clip and checked his ammunition. Only a few bullets remained but he held a fully loaded back up and realized if he wanted to live, he had to be strategic. He slammed the clip back in the handle, took a deep breath, and turned the corner.

"Uwww." Bri jumped back, startled. Quron's sudden appearance frightened her, and he too was thrown off. When she hopped back, Quron lunged forward. He took hold of her slender neck, squeezed with a vice grip, and slammed her through the wall. Old sheet rock crumbled and fell everywhere. Loud gunshots rang out close by.

Bri gasped for air, her eyes teared and bulged, while her dire swings became faint as life slowly slipped away.

The footsteps Quron heard grew louder; the unknown was getting closer. He leaned forward toward Bri's ear and whispered through clenched teeth., "Bitch I was good to you, loved you wholeheartedly, bought you any an' everything you wanted, and you repay me by fuckin' my best friend. My best friend, Bri, c'mon. I promise you if I make it outta here alive, you better be long gone, 'cause if I ever see you again, I'ma murder you. You hear me, you slut? I'ma murder you."

He released his death grip and she sank to her knees. She shook violently, coughed and gasped while holding her throat.

Quron slipped into the shadows of a secluded corner and watched Bri suffer. He felt that she hadn't received one percent of what she really deserved. He calmed down some, and regulated his breathing. He listened closely to the footsteps trampling through puddles of water. Quron had the drop as he watched the stocky silhouette tiptoe past. He raised the Desert from his side and pressed the triangular nose against the back of Scar's dome. Scar spun. His eyes locked on the thick barrel that nudged his forehead, then slid down to Quron's hand, arm, and face until their eyes locked. Scar's serene expression didn't shake. He was a gangster for real.

"Go 'head nigga, you a G. Pull da trigga."

Quron didn't budge. Instead, he continued to stare at the man who had disrupted his life. It seemed like the air they breathed thickened and the five-second stare down was more like five hours.

Scar's lips curled. "Just like I thought, you can't, 'cause you ain't got it in you. Guns don't kill. Its da nigga behind da trigga that kill." A sickly laugh escaped. "Ask ya mama." The

Mac clicked three times and jammed. Not a single bullet spit from the barrel

Boom! Boom! Boom!

The first slug flattened Scar's nose. The second and third blew half his head off.

Quron twitched from the spray of blood that dotted his face. He peered down at Scar's squirming body until he lay motionless.

"Rest in peace, Mama."

When the guns started blazing, Young-One mustered up just enough energy to toss himself to the floor. It took all he had to rise on his feet. Scar had punished his body with hard blows that seem to shift and rupture internal organs every time his fist landed. As much as it pained him, Young-One knew he had to seize any opportunity to escape. His life literally depended on it. The slight feeling of hope that surrounded his heart upon hearing Quron's voice faded when his boy started to vent. Everybody in his vicinity was an enemy. The only way he was getting out, was if he finagled a way himself.

Young-One's steps were short, but steady. He braced himself on protruding beams extending from what used to be a wall. His eyes captured the flash of light, and hope settled in with each step he took toward the entrance.

Out of nowhere, a lanky silhouette overlapped his light of hope like a solar eclipse. Young-One's heart dropped at the sight of the grim reaper coming for his soul. Ghost swung a wild hook, connecting with Young-One's jaw. The cold steel extracted blood from the open cut and shattered Young-One's cheek bone. "Owww!" his loud screech bounced off the wall, echoing in the distance.

Not lying down without a fight, Young-One dug his nails deep into Ghost's face, drawing trickles of blood. The struggle continued. Surprisingly, even in his wounded state, Young-

One was strong enough to combat against Ghost's adolescent strength.

"Let. Me. Go. Muthafucka."

Ghost gave him a hard push, causing their bodies to unravel. At the same time, he pulled the trigger on his twin.45s sending scorching lead through Young-One's abdomen. Young-One dropped to his knees. A loud grunt followed, then clots of blood seeped from the corner of his mouth.

Ghost eased closer as he peered down at his comrade. Young-One gurgled, then reached out, begging for a helping hand. Veins bulged from his forehead. Their good times as brothers flashed through Ghost mind, but his heart didn't move. One thing was clear, the love that he had for Quron was real. Even after he was told that Quron murdered his father, there he stood contemplating whether he should end a life on Quron's behalf. Was he driven by loyalty or was it the principle? Not even he could answer that.

Two hollow points blew through Young-One's head, silencing him forever. Ghost dabbed the tear that rolled down his face. "We was s'ppose to be loyal, fam." He whimpered in a hurt tone barely above a whisper.

Tay sat with her knees pulled close to her chest behind the rusted refrigerator where she had sought refuge. The hail of bullets that flew her way had ceased and she found herself consumed with watching Ghost. She watched him maliciously do Young-One dirty, like he was a total stranger who had committed a grave sin. The thing that had her mind tangled most was the cunning glare in his eyes when they locked on her. Time froze for a second, and the moment had come where it was either him or her, but neither made a move. Tay knew what it was and so did Ghost. No matter their dislike for each other, the mutual love they shared for Kiyah connected them in a very unique way. When Ghost turned his back and walked away, Tay knew a silent code had been established between them.

The chaos behind her snapped her trance, causing her to shift to a kneeling position. She peeped over the refrigerator edge. It was apparent from her angle that Quron had the drop on Scar. Quron's hesitation gave her hope for her boy's life. But her wish was short lived when the thunderous roar leapt from the Desert eagle. When Scar died, so did a part of Tay's soul. He'd taught her so much, the game and the rules that separated a thoroughbred from a lame. It just hurt. Hurt even more, knowing she couldn't do anything about it. Coming to his rescue would have been suicide. With Scar dead, it was less likely she would be able to fulfill her plan to leave the game. She had done too much grimy shit in the street. People just didn't forget sins of the past that easy. Maybe in a fantasy world, but not in reality.

Tay closed her eyes, sighed loudly, then slipped out the same way she came; quietly, unnoticed, only this time she wore a lifetime scar.

Quron scanned the area and gripped his burner tightly as he moved with caution toward the center of the room where it had all started.

The table and chair that Young-One had sat on were both flipped. Loose newspaper and money lay strewn across the floor, but there were no signs of him.

Ghost surfaced from the shadows in front of Quron. On point, Nuri crept from a side angle. Each of them held steady, neither of their presence was a secret to the other. Not a single word was uttered amongst the three. The pouring rain rinsing the earth was the only sound. The tension was uncomfortably thick.

Quron slowed his pace, then stopped. Nuri and Ghost did the same. Quron peered at the young fella in front of him and felt fucked up. The love that he had for Ghost was undeniable. Ghost was more like a lil brother than a soldier of any kind. Quron knew without a shadow of a doubt, that he would ride or die with the kid without second-guessing his decision. He hoped they could get past the situation, but what were the odds of that?

Ghost was engaged in an internal battle where Quron stood between his heart and the obligation to redeem the blood of his father, the man who created him.

The face fighting was getting them nowhere fast, so Quron broke the silence. "What now, Ghost? We should be ashamed of ourselves standing in the middle of a building wit' hammas pointed at each other. I've always looked at you like a lil brother. I never tried to play you. Think about it, I showed you tough love, taught you the game, an' introduced you to anotha level. If I wanted to rock you to sleep, I could've been knocked you off, don't you think? But I didn't, 'cause I see you as one of ma own. I feel fucked up 'bout your pops, I really do. But what you want me to do?" Quron shrugged. "Really though, what do you want me to do? The game is the game."

"So whatchu sayin' Ron?" Ghost shouted with hostility. His stance was still stiff, his focus locked on the brothers, and his grip so tight, his palms got numb. "'Cause he was in the game, he had to get slumped in front of his family? Y'all did 'im in front of his wife an' kids. What da fuck dat got to do wit' the game, Ron? Don't insult ma intelligence, I'm tellin' you!" Ghost's anger grew. The tears rolling down his face wouldn't stop.

"You got it wrong, Ghost. It ain't like—" Quron tried to explain, but was cut off.

"Then how da fuck is it?" His gaze shifted. "Somebody make some fuckin' sense outta this, 'cause I swear to God, if y'all don't, we all leavin' out dis bitch in body bags!"

Ghost was in shambles. Mixed emotions cluttered his heart. He had vowed for years that if he ever found those responsible for his father's death and their family trauma, he would compensate himself with their lives. Now with the facts on the table, he questioned if he could clip the men who had taken him in at a time when he needed love most.

"Gotta try'im." Quron mumbled to himself. "Ghost." Quron kneeled and placed his gun on the ground.

"Ron, fuck you doin'?"

"Nuri, chill!" Quron put a hand up to his brother, telling him to slow his roll. He stood back up and took short steps toward Ghost.

"I ain't strapped, lil bro. I'm try'na show you that I don't wanna hurt you.

"Yo Ron!" Nuri started to squirm. Quron was bugging, and he didn't have a clear shot with Ron in the way.

"Ghost, all I'm sayin' is what happens in these streets ain't personal. Ya pops was a thorough dude, we had mutual respect for each otha, but he forced my hand. I was in a position where it was either him or me." Quron knew he was no longer talking to Ghost. He stood face to face with the little boy that screamed for his father that day on the crime scene. The little boy that haunted him for over a decade through his dreams. The little boy who couldn't understand why his dad never came back home after he had found him sprawled out in his own blood. That same little boy whose pains grew with him as he evolved into a man.

"Ghost, you can't knock me for preservin' me... you would have done the same thing."

Ghost's twin.45s pressed against Quron's stomach. Quron gave him the opportunity that he seemed to so badly crave. If he wanted to spill his blood, the chance had come. Quron gave him the opportunity to even the score.

Ghost's eyes said what his mouth couldn't. He felt like a coward. As bad as he wanted to smoke Quron and Nuri, his heart wouldn't convince his fingers to pull the trigger. There was a genuine love there. He really needed to sort out his emotions. With no clarity within himself, Ghost felt his mind twisting and turning in so many different directions, that insanity was near. He kept his guns up and backed away. He would save his slugs for now, but the feud was far from over.

Quron watched Ghost disappear through the threshold before picking up his gun and facing Nuri.

"You do some real bozo shit sometimes."

Quron smirked at his brother's sly remark. They walked over to Young-One's corpse and stared for a minute. Quron handed Nuri the pictures of betrayal and awaited his thoughts. Nuri avoided over the topic instead. Quron knew what it was without Nuri even saying it; he too was torn by the act. He shook his head and lifted his gaze in disbelief. The woman he thought was amongst the best in the world had turned out to be a slithering snake. And the man he had literally killed for throughout his life had turned out to be an even bigger snake.

Nuri hissed. "This shit is crazy." Turning to his brother, he spoke. "You know we shoulda killed him, right? Trust me when I tell you, he gon' be a problem in da future... watch an' see what I tell you."

Quron peered at his brother's back as he walked away. Nuri's words lingered behind for Quron to digest as his mind drifted to thoughts of Ghost. Deep down inside, it ached, because he knew Nuri was right. Their relationship would never be the same again. He sighed and followed Nuri out of the building.

Chapter 37

FBI agent Trulinski barged into Captain Rogers' office, carrying a stack of photos with Detective DeJesus tailing close behind. He slammed the pictures down on the desk and peered at the bulletin board. Racial slurs saturated his gruesome expression, but tangled in his tongue.

"I'm tellin' you, these godforsaken lowlifes are responsible for this!" Trulinski pointed to the sprawled out photos. "They must've picked up on our contact, because coincidental shit like this just doesn't happen, gentlemen. Our confidential informant, Terrance 'Young-One' Guy was found six o'clock this morning in an abandoned building, decomposed, badly bitten by rats, with a .45 slug in his stomach and two more lodged in his head. Now how in the hell did we allow this to happen?" His voice rose a notch as he walked up to the dartboard, pulled a dart from its center, and twirled it as he continued to rant. "This bunch that we're after are far savvier than I gave them credit for, but no matter the length of their reach," he chuckled cynically, "the final laugh will be ours... It. Will. Be. Ours!"

He spun around and threw the dart with the force and accuracy of a major league pitcher. His upper body leaned forward and his leg lifted off the carpet, opening like scissors. His gaze settled on the bulletin board and a sick grin followed. He gathered the photos taken at the crime scene then calmly walked out of the office as if nothing happened.

DeJesus and Captain Rogers exchanged impressed stares. "Well trained." Captain Rogers admitted.

"And crazy." DeJesus giggled.

They turned their focus toward the bulletin board and smiled. The dart landed exactly where Agent Trulinski wanted, at the top of the food chain, smack dead center of Quron's forehead.

TO BE CONTINUED...

Thank you so much for taking the time to read my first novel. Let's keep in touch!

Connect with me on Facebook: Don Quaheri

Follow me on Twitter: @_Don_Q

Hit me up on Instagram: Don_Q